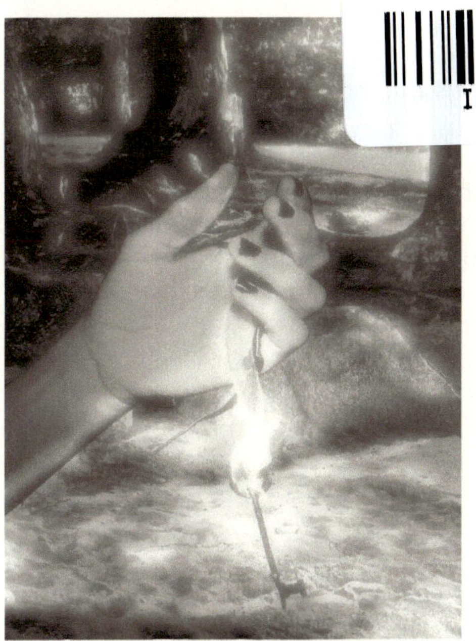

Annie's Odyssey

by K.A. Plouffe

Cover art by: Kristian Michael McKenna, ZERO|END™

Copyrighted 2012
ISBN Number 978-1-932113-55-6

Published by
Lauric Press
1314 W. McDermott
Ste. 106-811
Allen, TX 75013
817-805-3068
www.LauricPress.com

Dedication

This book is dedicated to the Struggle, which, if embraced, becomes the dance of life; but if resisted becomes an unending brawl. My thanks to all those who stood witness to my Struggle and for all those who allowed me to witness their Struggle.

PART ONE

Chapter One

Annie stood immobilized on the sidewalk with slow breath, quivering hands and droopy eyelids shading her vacant stare. People flowed around her oblivious, adjusting to avoid the frumpy girl standing as if frozen in the middle of the walkway. The heat toasted the top of her dirty sandaled feet; sweat soaked through the white muscle shirt she wore under a black hoodie. Beneath the patchwork long-skirt, she had boosted from a bin in a second hand store, her legs wobbled. Lack of oxygen made her dizzy, and the tinny taste of blood filled her mouth as she steadily bit a hole in her inner lip.

Annie? A disembodied voice whispered. *Where are you?*

Annie's paralysis muted her. She could only recoil mentally; trapped by her own body.

I'm waiting for you.

A woman in a white summer dress brushed by Annie with a whispered "excuse me." As arm grazed arm, breaking the social space, the holy disconnection of "me" from "you," Annie's senses buzzed. The sweet scent of Jasminum overwhelmed her senses; the world became a mouth-watering delight of grilled brown sugar peaches. The woman vanished into the jets and eddies of city dwellers, leaving Annie wanting fulfillment of a need so deep, she could not name it. Annie took in a sharp breath. The pain of teeth cutting into her lip made itself known, and Annie winced.

"Yow!" The sound slipped from a pained thought into a muttering that died in a breath full of slobber.

What did I do? she thought. *It happened again; the spells are getting worse. Now I'm zoning out in the middle of the sidewalk. So, this is what it's like at the end.*

Annie moved out of the flood of pedestrian traffic, propping her fatigued body against the wall of a small café and splashing a mouthful of bloody spit onto the concrete. She knew she'd only have a moment to soak up the shade before the owner shooed her away. But a moment was

3

all she needed to gather her thoughts. The teenage girl closed eyes underlined too thickly in black, her ample mascara spiking long lashes; her sweat a relief in the shade. For a split second, she was somewhere else surrounded by the fresh smell of rain.

Did I zone out again? This is how it ends, is it? Quietly slipping away, vanishing in plain sight of everything and everybody?

The day seemed later than it was a moment ago, and the flow of people passing by had slowed to a trickle. No one had come out of the café to move her along and, for that, she was grateful. For the moment, this small piece of dirty wall on a southern California sidewalk provided her with a safe base. Here she had called time out, home base... safe. It worked in tag and hide-in-seek, it could work here, for a few more minutes at least.

It won't last long. The darkness is coming for me, and it is hungry.

The shadows cast by a sun in hasty retreat crept up around her like fears. She felt like a prisoner chained in the dark recesses of a primeval cave, where each dancing shadow might contain the specter of death. What these fears were that haunted her life, she could not shed any light on. Something had happened, something beyond her impoverished upbringing, something that had changed the course of her life. It sat in the darkness of her mind like a hungry jungle beast waiting for the right moment to pounce. Somehow, she managed to keep it at bay, perhaps out of awareness.

She brushed a string of black hair out of her face and thought how hot it made her neck feel. Making the rounds of her face, Annie gave a quick check to her eyebrow, nose and multiple ear piercings. Still there, yet the context of how she got them escaped her. Certainly she had a memory that it was she being pierced, and it was she who collected the piercings one-by-one as she built a persona to hold onto; but specific details of when, where and who did them eluded recall. It was one of many thoughts that led her to the darkness, to the beast of things best left forgotten.

"Well, you need to speak up for yourself," a twenty-something woman advised a friend over her cell as she hurried out of the café with a to-go latte. "Cheryl, you have to be your own person or he won't respect you. Do you want to be someone else's life?"

The woman glanced over at Annie and just as quickly glanced away. It was as if the woman had broken a rule by "seeing" the invisible, the people on the street you weren't supposed to see; the ones left behind.

Annie self-consciously crossed arms over her chest and shrank further back against the wall, looking down in habitual shame. She hide as well as she could in the public space. The thick mascara, the careless eyeliner obscured how she felt, her hoodie hid budding breasts, and her shabby skirt covered an ample rear. Sixteen years of age didn't guarantee her a body that developed with any reasonable coordination.

Annie wished she knew someone she could ask whether or not she looked or acted normal. If she was still in school, she might ask a school counselor, but they always gave her that "yeah, you'll be a waitress for the rest of your life, if you're lucky" kind of look. She had gone back to them several times before giving up in frustration, realizing they were only there to tell her where life had destined her to punch a time card. But what she had really wanted to know was "Am I normal?" Was it normal to cry yourself to sleep every night? To look into the future and see only blackness?

Fall had come, and she hadn't returned to school after the summer break. At the moment, she couldn't recall the reason, another memory ending at the lair of the beast. Something about the past summer had changed everything, although about the only thing she could recall was long stretches of time hiding in her bedroom.

If she had the money, she could go to a doctor. She didn't want to go back to the community health clinic after her experience a few weeks ago. The doctor there had examined her in front of a bored chaperon in a dingy room replete with yellowing posters warning about disease and poor posture. She had gone because what she wanted to know was "Am I normal?" Was it normal to lie staring at the ceiling all day unable or unwilling to move? To cramp so bad and gush so much blood? But, he just washed his hands, gave her some condoms, and muttered that he was tired of seeing girls like her on the maternity ward.

Annie looked up and spied a billboard across the street featuring a clear-faced, full-lipped woman offering the pathway to Nirvana by way of breast enlargements. The sign represented everything Annie knew she could never have and never be.

Where does that leave me? Endless advertisements of her failure to live up to expectations surrounded her; reminders that she was not good enough for anyone to care about. She felt defective and unwanted. It seemed only the music; the angry, painful, lonely music in her head recognized her.

A motion caught her eye, and she saw an employee through the café window making his way toward the front door.

Time for the shove along. Come on feet, let's get moving. I'm in no mood for anyone's crap. Gotta drop by and see Davey.

Night began in typical murky-orange sky fashion, the effect of city light reflecting off a polluted sky. An unassuming breeze floated by, offering an apology for the day's heat. Annie made her way down streets flickering alive with neon lights and a new crowd of bustling people. The hurried business rhythm of the day had, following a brief lull, given way to the edgy energy of the evening.

The sound of a loud metal band pulsated out from a club. Annie smiled, *Sounds like the boys have started their set. I can hear Ogre all the way out here.*

Ogre was the head and lead singer of a band called the "Giant Sloths." He described their music in typical in-your-face posturing language as, "beyond labels, it ain't punk, and it ain't speedmetal. It's just pure hell—electrified Hell!"

Annie had met Ogre after sneaking into the club one night, drawn in by the orchestrated chaos. One look at him, and she knew immediately why he was called Ogre. He had long thin hair; his brow shared the same tendency for thickness as his lips, and his belly protruded without apology over his belt. A monstrous looking figure, he belted out songs with venom, and Annie had fallen in love with him with all the flash like passion of adolescence.

The first time she had wandered into the club, she felt the power Ogre wielded over the room. She wanted so much to be up on stage, to sing her songs, to have people come to hear her stories and see her image the way people came to hear and see him and his band. Of course, never mind that most of the people were in various stages of intoxication, never mind that the band only provided background music in a place where people came for sex or violence or both. But, they did all these things to his music—he became the background sound track to their dark dealings.

Annie's pace slowed. The excitement she felt to get to the club drained as she reached the edge of an alleyway. The sight of the corner of the building that plunged its wall into the dark recess of the alley was enough to send her heart pounding. This some five steps and a skip of sidewalk that stood between her and the next building seemed as large as a ravine. On the other side, a few doors down, stood the club entrance, but in between she must cross the darkness of the alley. Annie swallowed hard and stepped forward.

"Hey, girlie," a voice called to her from inside the darkness. The sinister timbre of the male voice left her cold. "Come here."

She fought to keep her eyes focused on the club entrance as her body urged her to glance down the alley. She did not want to see the man. She had never actually seen him, but he seemed to become more real each time she came here. Her mind conjured images of a dark figure with soulless eyes and razor teeth. Her neck screamed in pain from the conflict to stare ahead and live or to look and be consumed.

Just go away—you're not real, not really, her mind pleaded. Annie again felt trapped in her own body; her engine revving up with the brake still engaged.

"Come here, I want to show you something," the voice leered, sounding closer than before.

A heavy, heady sway overcame Annie, and she felt the man's hot breath closing in on her.

No.

The firm rebuke should have silenced the voice. That's what they say. Say no, say it firm, say it like you mean it, and all's well that ends well. But, it didn't happen like that. And what Annie heard next slowed her heart and senses, shutting her down like a rabbit caught in the jaws of the beast; immobile, hoping for the jaws to slacken in a moment's cockiness and allow her to escape.

The voice sang with the quality of a violin bow across a hand saw:

> *"Scream, scream, oh how she screams;*
> *Down in the cold dark lair.*
> *Scream, scream, oh how she screams;*
> *You ran, you didn't care.*
> *Screaming no more; she hit the floor;*
> *Eyes fixed in a death stare.*
> *Screaming no more; dead as a door;*
> *You ran, you didn't care!"*

"Hey!" Davey called out as he exited the club.

His voice broke the spell, and Annie felt free to move; and move she did, running straight into Davey's arms.

"Whoa, little sister, what's this all about?" he laughed and returned her embrace.

Feeling ashamed of her fear, she regained her composure and stepped back with a shrug. "Nothing, just got a little scared. Boogeyman in the alley, you know, stupid stuff like that."

Davey looked around the street and into the alley. "Gone now."

"Yeah, gone for now."

Davey smiled and said, "You're late, didn't think you'd make it tonight. Still gonna help me at the board?"

Annie gave him an enthusiastic nod, and with his arm around her shoulder, he escorted her into the club.

Davey was older than the rest of the group members, with a scraggly beard and a bandana half covering up his thinning hair. As the technician for the band, Davey took everything in stride. He should have moved on in his career and his life years ago, but he clung on to his dream of the endless summer, even though his aging body made it clear that September was well upon him.

During a break between sets, Annie turned to Davey and said, "Thanks for supper last night; I haven't eaten real food for ages. Your wife's really cool, you know. I like her."

"Yeah, Martha's a good soul," Davey said. "She really liked you, too."

"Really?" Annie had difficulty with the concept.

Davey must have sensed it and said, "Really. What's the surprise? You're a good kid."

From across the room and lost in the din came, "Yo, Davey."

Davey glanced over as a muscular black man with dreadlocks that moved to their own rhythm approached.

Davey signaled to Annie to take a step back, "Shit. Bound to happen sooner or later."

"What's wrong?" Annie asked.

"Five-O. Undercover dude I've known since back in the day."

As the undercover officer approached, wearing dirty jeans and bare chested under a leather vest that looked like it was from some old cowboy and Indian movie, Annie felt a lump growing in her throat and a twist in her stomach. Even the protective stance Davey took by blading his body to shield her from the official did little to qualm her urge to bolt. But stay put she did.

"My man!" Davey greeted as he exchanged a jive shake, clutching hands in a gesture of 1960s style brotherhood.

"What's happening? See you're still working the pits."

Davey shrugged. "On duty?"

"Always, man. The more laws you white folk make, the more chance there are for violations. Keeps me rolling in the bank." The man gave Annie a once over glance and gestured toward her with his head, his locks finding their own freedom of movement. "What's with the kid? She can't be here, are you nuts?"

"Who? Her?" Davey asked in feigned ignorance. "This is Annie, my niece. Annie, this is... what are you going by these days?"

"Rocker. How ya doing, little, Annie?"

"Okay," Annie replied.

Rocker's suspicion still played out on his face. "Your niece, huh?"

"Yeah. Tragic really. Her parents hit head on by a drunk driver and killed." Davey turned to Annie, "I'm sorry to be so blunt, sweetie."

Annie snapped to the cue Davey had given her, and she put on her best expression of grief.

"So," Davey continued, "Martha and I took her in."

"Sorry to hear about your folks, Annie," Rocker addressed her before turning his incredulous attention back to Davey. "That don't explain what she's doing here."

"Oh, that," Davey laughed off. "Well, I'm teaching her the back scene of the music business. Girl's gotta have a job skill these days, right?"

Rocker didn't budge from his scrutinizing stare.

"Hey, it's cool, Rocker, I'm telling ya straight. She's 16, and I got an entertainment permit around here somewhere for her to be working under my supervision."

"Hm," Rocker responded a second before another man at the end of the bar caught his attention. "Gotta jet. Listen, you two stay out of the alley for the next few hours, okay? Shit's going down there. And she shouldn't be here all night, permit or no."

"Of course not, 10 or 11 tops."

Rocker plunged back into the crowd, connected with the man at the bar, and they both pushed their way effortlessly to a side exit.

Davey looked at Annie and smiled with relief.

"I'm sorry if I got you in trouble," Annie said.

"That? That's not trouble. Don't worry about it. One forged permit and never a bother again. These guys have bigger fish to fry." After the band had finished at two in the morning, Annie started rolling up some of the cables to help secure the equipment. Davey stepped out to talk to the club owner, and the band members negotiated with four intoxicated women who had stuck around. A tingle went up Annie's neck; she had a disturbing sense of being watched. Turning, she saw Ogre standing across the stage looking at her with a sweaty intensity; she felt a strange relief—at least it wasn't the dark stranger this time.

"What didja think about the show tonight?" he asked in a gravelly voice.

"It sounded awesome. You guys rocked!" Annie felt an instant hot flash of embarrassment about how worn her response sounded.

Ogre pumped his head slowly as if considering this, then he said, "Come on up and visit for a spell."

"Really?" Annie said, star struck.

"Yeah, finish that shit later. Come on up and hang out."

A spark of electricity arched its way up Annie's spine. *This is so great. This awesome singer is interested in hanging out with me. Me! A nobody, a little rag doll cleaning up after the band. Like Davey would say, far-out.*

Annie looked around the club for Davey, but he had not returned. Not wanting to lose this opportunity, she followed Ogre out a side door and into the alley. She paused in the doorway as Ogre entered the darkness; the night quickly absorbed the ambient light. Ogre turned to her; he appeared only a flicker of an image now mostly shrouded.

"You comin', or what?"

Annie darted toward him as the door closed behind her sealing off all hope of illumination. She grabbed onto his arm just as the door clunked shut.

"What, are you scared of the dark?" Ogre grumbled.

"No, it's just dark."

Ogre snorted. "Give it a second, and you'll get used to it. I like it after all those lights shining in my eyes."

But Annie never wanted to get used to it.

Crossing the alleyway, they climbed upstairs to a small flat. Once inside the naked-bulb lit room, Ogre offered her a drink of Jack Daniels.

"Naw, that's okay," Annie replied.

Ogre shot her an incredulous look, "Don't party?"

"Yeah, lots," she managed to stammer out and then took the glass from his hand.

"Yeah, why not, right? You're gonna die anyway, you know that, don't you?" he growled with a grin.

Annie felt her chest constricting at his sudden intense look; Annie's eyes searched for the quickest way out.

"Oh, I don't mean I'm gonna kill ya. Relax, Amy."

"Annie."

"Right, Annie, nice name. Listen Annie, do you know what the answer to life is?"

Annie could barely force herself to shake her head in the presence of Ogre's menacing smile.

"Death," he hissed, clearly enjoying the feel of the word as it first exploded from his tongue and then escaped with his hot breath. "Do you know what the question of life is?"

"No," she whispered, caught again in a cold paralysis.

"Who is the most powerful among you? You see what I mean? Are you with me, Annie?"

His voice increased in volume and excitement. When he said her name, he drew it out, sending shudders through her body. She felt like a trapped laboratory rat whose examiner had suddenly developed a peculiar hunger. She stood, alone with him, and no one knew it.

"You see, you're cursed with life 'cause all your parents were concerned about was getting it on, and they didn't once, not once, Annie, stop to think about what kind of hell they were putting you into. And, after you're born, all you are to them is a pain in the ass. That's right;

you're just one more obstacle blocking them from what they want. But, life is for the strong, for the ones that can tap into their power and give as good as they get. You know what they say, if life gives you lemons..."

"Make lemonade?" Annie finished the saying with a growing sense of uncertainty and dread.

"Yeah, that's what they *say*," Ogre continued, "but it's crap. When life gives you lemons, squirt the juice into life's eyes; that'll teach it. You might as well get your licks in, 'cause you *are* going to die sooner or later; so, what's the difference? Come on now, sweet sister, live a little or, should I say, die a little." Ogre grinned devilishly as he lifted his glass up toward Annie, drawing from her an automatic response of clinking her glass to his in a toast.

Annie put rim to lips and drank the whiskey down deep, choking on the liquid burning down her throat. She was on fire with no relief at hand.

Ogre bellowed with laughter as he quickly poured more whiskey into her glass. "Where's my stash box, we gotta get on some ghanja up in here!"

Annie winced and nodded as she tried to breathe away the burn.

Ogre retrieved a thick joint from a hand-carved, wooden box that featured a fierce looking dragon with a human skull in its talons.

"Don't mind a little vitamin K, do ya? Chase that rabbit down its hole."

Annie still fought the urge to cough or vomit the whiskey back up. She nodded again and waved off a cough, only half hearing what he said.

The first inhale irritated her throat as much as the whiskey had; the effect of the drug mirrored the experience of her time distorted days, pleasantly at first as a comfortable buzz embraced her. She started talking about her dreams of being a singer, and he seemed to listen, *really* listen to her. He'd help her, he said. Did he say that? She couldn't be sure now as the room wobbled and the floor took a wicked tilt.

Then something started to feel wrong. She had gotten high before, although with whom she could not recall; but intoxication was not new to her. This was turning into something different. Her ability to stay focused began to blur; time was no longer a coherent stream of images, but rather disjointed. A terrifying thought sputtered in and out of awareness with the dying intensity of a Fourth-of-July sparkler surrendering to the darkness.

He slipped me something! Vitamin K? No, no, no. How could I be so stupid?

The thought never stuck around long enough to take root and propel her out the door. As continuity broke down, she became a prisoner of sensory disturbance. Time flipped backward into tomorrow, and she grabbed onto the couch arm to save herself from slipping away into a void. Ogre's maniacal laugh went on and on forever, but in the past tense. "Don't let me vanish!" Annie screamed, or whispered, she could not tell.

"You just hold on, little Annie. We'll ride this bitch together."

Annie lay on the couch; her head bobbled over the side as she hugged the couch arm. Her pounding heart commanded her terrified attention until she noticed the distinct feeling of her panties being tugged at.

She heard Ogre grunting through the haze of her flickering consciousness, "Sing for me, Annie, sing."

The early morning air hummed with possibility, but as Annie wandered down the sidewalk, she felt dead inside: an empty, soiled vessel slumping home on automatic pilot. She thought about how she had come to be on the floor with Ogre snoring on the couch. It was as if nothing out of the ordinary had happened. Was this normal? Did people routinely get raped as casually as shaking hands?

She hurt, sore in places she shouldn't have been sore in. She just wanted to get home, shower, and sleep it all away. Overcome by a searing emptiness, Annie grabbed a fistful of her hair with each hand, clenched her shaking jaw, and sputtered out a guttural protest to the throbbing pain.

So this is what it's like just before you vanish.

Chapter Two

It had been a week since the incident with Ogre. Annie returned to the club during that time to see Davey, who didn't seem to know anything had happened. He did appear to keep a closer eye on her and not let her wander too far from him. Or was that just her imagination? Just wishful thinking that she had a guardian angel looking out for her?

When she saw Ogre again he acted as he usually did: gave her a "what's up," went about his business, and never so much as laid a finger on her. He did, however, approach Davey to make sure he had paid her for helping out.

Maybe that's how it works. Maybe that was an initiation or something.

She was in. That's how she saw it. She had been given her start at the price of her virtue. How normal was all of this?

Apparently, Annie's normal had taken a new twist one afternoon that might never straighten out. Annie often reviewed past events that had changed the course of her life. Although, as of late, it seemed a blind spot in memory obscured something important. It made her nauseous to track down the memory, so she didn't try. Instead, she stuck with what she did know. She knew her dad was not around, she knew the shame when she first learned other kids could see words in the right order without a struggle, and she knew the moment her mom had given up and slipped into the toxic embrace of drugs... and she knew Ogre had taken something from her against her will.

Thinking about her mom made Annie recall going home earlier that day.

"Annie, is that you?" her mother called out from behind the bedroom door as Annie walked into the apartment.

"Yes," Annie answered, rolling up her eyes. She had wanted to get in, get some food, and get out. A risky venture since the probability of any food in the house or credit on the food stamp card was slim.

Her mother floated out of the bedroom in an uneven heroin haze; not bothering to tie off the old tattered robe around her drained naked body.

"Hi, honey," her hoarse voice rattled with a graveyard cough.

Annie's mother fumbled toward the couch, unbalanced by the coughing fit that seized her. She reached for a cigarette on the cluttered coffee table and lit it with a lighter she found among the syringes, baggies and spoons. Inhaling deeply on the burning cigarette, her coughing subsided. "Come sit down beside me, dear, we never get to talk anymore."

"Mom, I really just came in to get some food, I'm kinda in a rush."

"I remember when I used to take you down to the park, and you'd play with your little friends, remember?"

"Is there anything left to eat?" Annie answered as she searched through the cabinets, hoping in vain to keep her mother's thoughts on the need at hand.

"You were so precious. Just a precious little angel. Was it so long ago?"

"Food card, money, anything?"

"Whenever you fell down or hurt yourself, you'd come running to me with your arms stretched out, crying 'Momma, Momma'."

Annie gave up trying to penetrate the years of collected chemical haze that entrapped her mother. She sat locked too deep inside her own personal prison. Exasperated, Annie decided to join her mom on the fourth-hand couch until she could think of something better to do.

"I used to kiss your boo-boos and say 'it's all better, Annie, it's all better'."

Annie really looked at her mother for the first time since walking into the apartment. Her face looked drawn and thin; her body frail and ready to surrender not so much to time, but to mileage. Annie could see the track of bruises that made their steady way up the inside of her mom's forearm and vanished beneath the robe sleeve. The woman smelled sour like old onions and vinegar gone bad. She hadn't bathed in days.

"Annie, Annie. You know where I got that name for you?"

Annie knew. She had heard it a thousand times before and was sure to hear it again a thousand more times. Her mom was of the mind that if she continued to recall the few isolated moments of normality and happiness that lay like rubble in the past, then she could somehow delude herself into believing she hadn't failed as a mother.

"From a song, 'cause you were my precious little song."

As Annie had feared, her mother began to sway and sing:

> *"Annie, come down to the river,*
> *Come down and wash away,*
> *Wash away all you troubles*
> *And find a better day.*
> *Come down, Annie, come down,*

Her mom continued to hum as a pain seared through Annie's eyes. *Was this the same mother from my childhood? she wondered. The same mother who held me in her arms and sang me to sleep with that same song? She's dying right in front of me, and she doesn't seem to care. Is this normal?*

The song trailed off into an absent-minded, guttural hum. Annie's mom lost herself in memory no doubt altered; yet none-the-less painful. Annie watched tears well up in her mom's eyes as her mouth struggled to form words.

In desperation her mom said, "Where's your friend these days?"

Annie tossed her mom an incredulous look, "What? What friend? I don't have any friends."

"Oh, stop it—that girl you hung out with all summer."

"You're crazy, I didn't do anything this summer. You shoot up too much."

Her mom picked up a stained celebrity news magazine and Frisbee threw it at Annie's head. The pages fanned out, flickering in mid-air until it lost momentum and fell short of Annie.

"Don't talk to me like that! I'm your mother," she screeched.

"Chill, Mom, I just wanted something to eat."

"I know what I'm talking about," the woman insisted. "Her name was something like..."

At that point a long, nauseating scream caromed off the walls of the small apartment. Neck veins strained and bulged as Annie bellowed.

Wrapping her robe tight to her body against the outburst, her mom cowered underneath the sheer volume and timber of noise. Something clicked inside her, and she rushed over, grabbed Annie by the upper arms and gave her three firm shakes.

"What is wrong with you?" her mom demanded. "Stop that! Stop it this instant!"

Annie stopped. She stood dumbstruck, scanning the room for a reason for the shaking.

"What? What do you want?" Annie asked.

Annie's mom let loose and stumbled several steps back, shaking her head in exasperation as Annie stretched her neck and rolled her shoulders to recover. Daryl's entrance from the back bedroom halted the logical conversation that might have followed.

"What the hell's going on in here? I'm trying to sleep," Daryl said as he plodded into the living room, pulling at his red eyes.

"Shut up, Daryl," her mom ordered.

Daryl shrugged and made his unbalanced way to the kitchen sink, where he proceeded to dislodge phlegm from his throat. Daryl was just one in a string of men Annie's mom shared needles and sex with, and whose income from shady odd jobs helped keep the parties going. He didn't count, not really, and did as he was told as best he could.

Daryl's scrawny body stopped heaving. He wiped some spittle from his beard and blinked his bulgy eyes several times. "Hey, Annie," he grinned. "Looking good."

Without warning, Annie's mom exploded toward Daryl. Daryl slammed into a wall with a shriek as Annie's mother gave his genitals a wicked twist.

"You piece of trash," she spat, "don't you *ever* even think about touching my daughter, 'cause you can believe I'll kill you. Do you understand?"

"What... what are you doing? I didn't mean nothing by it," he grimaced as her hand twisted a little more.

"Do you understand?" She tightened her grip.

"Yes, yes, for God sakes, let go." He put his hands up in surrender and leaned to one side as if to lessen the pain he felt between his legs.

Annie watched her mom release Daryl's groin and step back. The fire had begun to die down in her eyes, the veil of heroin quickly covering it up once again.

"Didn't mean nothing," her mom snorted at Daryl, "ha, ha, ha."

Daryl covered his groin with shaking hands. "Damn, you really brought me down. I was having a good high, and now I'm totally bummed," he mumbled as he slunk back into the bedroom.

Her mom's gaze still occupied the space Daryl had just retreated from. She spoke to Annie without moving, without wavering, as if a voice from some distant land had passed through her like a transmission wave through a radio. "Go, Annie. Go away from this place. Go away from me. What little I had to offer you is long gone. If you stay any longer, you'll become like me—a filthy, strung out whore. I can only thank God it hasn't happened to you yet, or has it?"

She turned to face Annie, her glassy eyes focusing on her daughter. "Has it already gotten hold of you?" This last question prompted raised eyebrows from her mom, and then, as if forgetting her momentary need for a response, the woman turned and vanished back into the bedroom.

Annie sat in the swelling silence left by her mother's departure. She fought against tearfulness; haunted by the dark realization that in a rare moment of clarity, all her mother had to say was, "Go away. I don't want you to see my death or catch my disease."

It was brave of her, Annie thought, trying hard to find some romantic notion for her exile. But, the weak effort faltered in the face of her abandonment. It's not that her mother had been a good mother; she hadn't even been a functional human being let alone a good mother, or friend.

In reality, Annie knew her mother had been lost to her years ago, but somehow that didn't make this final command to go away any easier to accept. For better or worse, her mother was the only person she had always known; she was the single thread of stability in Annie's troubled life, and now that string had snapped.

Annie stood up, went into her room, threw some clothes and personal items in her old school backpack, and then walked straight out of the apartment before the weight of loneliness could crush her.

Back out in the heat, Annie tried to see her way through the uncertain future.

What the hell am I supposed to do now? I'm homeless! This can't be it. This can't be the way it ends. I want more. So badly.

The only clear path Annie could see was to get Ogre to let her sing one of her songs with the band. It was also the most dangerous path; one that had already produced precarious activities. Annie had grown up in desperate circumstances; surrounded by violence and drugs, she had struggled to keep herself safe. Sometimes she hid in her closet, other times under the bed, but as she grew older she learned to hide in plain sight, an observer of misery. Now she found herself willingly running straight into danger, unable to conceive of any alternative.

What choice do I have? she wondered. *I can't go back home, and I don't want to end up on the street dead and forgotten.*

There were always child protective agencies and foster homes, not ideal but better then surviving on the streets. What she wanted was to be a singer. Hadn't a lot of rock stars come from bad beginnings? Why couldn't she risk it all and live the dream?

Annie retrieved a small spherical object from her backpack. She looked at the ball-shaped rose quartz; the smooth stone felt soothing in the palm of her hand. It was one of the few possessions she had managed to leave home with; a relic Annie's father had left behind. She lifted it up to the sky. A solar ray streamed into the orb and filled an imperfection deep in the center. The quartz glowed with an otherworldly luminescence. Lost in the glow, Annie felt disconnected from the world; unfettered from her pain.

As the sun beat down on her, she found herself daydreaming of someplace cool, where leaves turned magical colors and gray rainy skies cleansed the earth, causing people to huddle together for comfort. She had seen pictures of such places, seen movies, but had never been beyond the city heat, the city smog and grime, never been beyond the decaying world that surrounded her.

Someday, she thought, *someday I'll have money and I'll move to where it's cool and green, where leaves turn colors in the fall, and there's beautiful snow in the winter. So I have to do this; I have to.*

But at what price this time, she wondered, *at what price?*

Chapter Three

The next afternoon, armed only with some songs scratched out on crumpled paper and a back-against-the-wall determination, Annie walked into the club where afternoon rehearsal was already underway. Ogre belted out one of his favorite anarchy songs as Annie saddled up behind the sound and light board. Davey adjusted some settings and gave her a polite nod.

"What's the word for the night, Davey?" she asked as she sat her backpack on the floor.

"Hey, Annie—just jammin', babe, just jammin'." Davey smiled at Annie. She liked the twinkle that lingered in his glance.

Annie smiled back. Davey's kindness made her feel she belonged in this struggling band of musicians.

"What's up with you?" he asked.

Annie shrugged, and then after a pause said, "Kinda need a place to stay for a while. Things are messed up at home, my mom's really crashing, and that guy she's with..." She didn't want to continue.

"Oh, hey, say no more. You can stay with us; we'd love to have you. We ain't got much, but it's a safe place and mostly clean; gotta spare bedroom you can have for as long as you need."

"Are you serious? 'Cause if that wouldn't be a problem—it would be great."

"What problem? Me and Martha love helping people along on their journey. Can never have too much good karma, you know."

"Thanks," she said with a squeeze on his arm. She turned her attention to the band as Ogre vomited out his rage:

> *"And the walls tumbled down,*
> *Down around the President's men.*
> *Hot metal exploding in their head,*
> *'Cause war's begun and the Peace is dead.*
> *War's begun and the Peace is dead...*
> *War's begun and the Peace is dead..."*

Davey stretched out tired muscles, "I hope he doesn't want another run through. Enough is enough, know what I mean? Besides, we have to clear out soon so the DJ can set up."

"Never seen him work this hard," Annie commented.

"Usually doesn't, he's getting ready for tomorrow night. Supposed to be some record reps coming around to scout out new talent. It's just a rumor, but Ogre's taking it damn serious—we've been here all afternoon."

Perfect, Annie squealed inside, *it must be a sign that everything's gonna work out. I have to move quickly, though, and get Ogre to let me do a song tomorrow night. Then, I'll get discovered. Perfect. But first, Ogre.* She winced at that thought.

As the song finally died out a violent death of electric feedback, Annie noticed Ogre seemed completely satisfied with himself.

Act fast, while he's in a good mood.

"Davey, can I borrow your guitar?"

"Sure, hon, it's in the back."

Annie sprinted off to retrieve the acoustic guitar. In the past few weeks, Davey and the band's guitarist, Tye, had taught her how to play, or rather had guided her. She astounded them by how quickly she picked it up; her instinct for rhythm and keen ear made her a natural. She learned enough to put together chords that complimented her lyrics. As her fingers strummed the strings, Annie liked to envision adoring fans mesmerized by her music. She fantasized interviews, videos and movie offers. Fame would certainly right the wrong that was her life.

Returning with guitar in hand, Annie noticed the band dispersing. She waved to Tye and pointed to the guitar. Tye smiled and gave her a thumbs up, then turned to talk to the drummer. Before she could get to Ogre, Davey intercepted her with her backpack in hand.

"Hey, where ya off to? I got to get going; I was supposed to be home two hours ago."

Annie half-heard Davey, but her attention was on Ogre, who walked out the side door, heading for his apartment. "I just have to do one thing first. Can you take my stuff to your place, and I'll come by later?"

Davey looked toward the exit and shifted in his stance. "You sure? I could wait, I mean, how you gonna get there?"

"I know the way—it's only a couple of miles, I've walked further. It'll be totally cool, don't worry. I just want to pitch a song to Ogre, no big deal."

Davey's unease hung on him despite her assurance. Finally he said, "You gotta do what you gotta do I guess, but do me a favor and come by directly; supper will be waiting."

"Yeah, sure, don't worry." She tried to assure him with a smile, and then turned and headed toward the exit.

Annie climbed the metal stairs leading up to Ogre's place and knocked on the door. She swallowed hard; fear trickled in causing her jaw to grind.

Like returning to the scene of a crime, Annie thought.

Annie hadn't been up there since that night—the night she had had her first and only experience with a man.

Ogre opened the door, still singing the final verse in a whisper, "War's begun and the Peace is dead... War's begun and the Peace is dead..." Ogre smiled at her. Unlike Davey's smile, his did not warm her. Ogre's grin set off primitive warning bells in her brain. Her stomach knotted, her heart quickened, and her eyes darted about for an escape route. He yowled out a soft yawn and stretched. His puffy tired eyes made him less intimidating.

"Whatcha need, sister-girl? You look like somethin's on your mind." He scratched his round belly.

"Oh, I don't know. I just heard you talking about wanting new stuff. I was wondering if you're looking for new songs."

"Shit, yeah. I want to have enough for two CD's. Why, did you stumble across something?"

"Well, I wrote some."

Ogre let out a full laugh, "Well, well, little Annie, sister of sadness, looking for the big time in the low down bar scene? These ain't just nursery rhymes you copied, are they?"

"No, Ogre, they're real songs I wrote. I even got the music worked out, sort of."

"No shit? You've been a busy little girl now haven't you? The rock world got to ya good, huh?"

Annie shrugged with a shy smile.

Ogre leaned in so close that Annie felt the heat coming off his protruding brow. "Well," he rasped, "then come on in and play one for me."

Entering Ogre's rundown room was like revisiting a nightmare; the kind people drank heavily to avoid having to come face to face with again. Her body tensed in a sick twist as the shadows cast by the naked ceiling bulb crept around her.

Ogre went over to a table and poured himself a drink. Annie stood lifeless, shoulders slumped, heart sinking fast, with the guitar feeling like a heavy weight. The past intruded on the present, and she experienced an odd sense of reality. Time became disjointed. She swallowed hard, trying to figure out if this was happening now or had already happened.

Like returning to the scene of a crime, returning and reliving it. But there's no other way out. This is my last and only chance at happiness.

To Annie's surprise, Ogre didn't offer her a drink or any drugs. He just hoofed it over to the shabby couch, flopped his weight down on it, and motioned her to a folding chair beside him.

"Well, don't stand there. Let's hear it."

Annie's heart immediately lifted. *Maybe you got to ride all the rides with the price of one admission ticket. Maybe Ogre isn't such a... an Ogre after all. Maybe it had only been the booze and the drugs that had made him do what he did that night. Yeah, that would make sense. That would explain why he acted like nothing happened. That had to be it: he had been embarrassed over the whole terrible mess. He wasn't such a bad guy after all; he had just made a mistake and had been sorry in his own way. Maybe dreams really do come true if you dream hard enough.*

Annie glimpsed at Ogre's eyes as she took her seat and adjusted the guitar, balancing it on one thigh. He looked tired, very tired—almost blank. She worried he wouldn't hear the song at all. Removing a piece of notebook paper she'd stashed in the pocket of her hoodie sweater, Annie smoothed it out, laid the paper on the floor in front of her, and studied the words and chord notations. Not that she had to; she easily memorized all the songs she wrote. She just didn't want nerves to interfere with memory.

"I gotta disease, you know," he stated out of the blue. "Bronchiectasis." The word contorted his lips with the clumsy pronunciation. "Or some shit like that. I don't know why they can't come up with easier names like 'you're-screwed-itis'."

"What is it?"

"My airway," Ogre explained as he waved his hand to indicate his lungs and throat, "is all scarred and flabby. For years. Some days are better than others, and some days I cough up a bunch of snot and blood. Ever cough up blood and snot, Annie?"

"No." *But I bled after you...*

"It hurts like a mother." Ogre stared off into the distance of the small room. His voice and body stiffened, and as if the thought had conjured the disease, Ogre exploded with a coughing fit.

"I'm sorry."

"Uh huh. Everyone's sorry," he said as the cough subsided.

"Shouldn't you take some medicine or something?"

Ogre took a gulp of his whiskey and answered, "This is my medicine. Calms it right down."

"Oh."

"Not too many singing years left for me. Gotta grab all I can get and then—then to hell with 'em all. You know what the bitch of it all is? The type I got is congenital. Do you know what that means?"

Annie shrugged. She felt lost in the situation. She curled her toes up inside her worn sandals, hoping to make herself smaller, or better yet—invisible. She didn't know what her role was in this strange unfolding drama. Was it confidant or dupe?

"It means my momma grew me wrong, and I was born with a ticking time bomb that can end me whenever it wants," he snickered. Ogre took another huge gulp of whiskey, swooshing it around in his mouth before flushing it down his gullet.

"That's terrible," Annie said.

Ogre's trance broke with a resounding belly laugh. "Yeah, no shit, Sherlock. Nothing gets by you." He gestured with his chin toward the guitar Annie fiddled with nervously in her hands. "So, you can play?"

"A little—enough." Annie secretly felt a sigh of relief that the conversation was back on track. "Tye and Davey taught me some stuff to get by on for now."

"Really? Ain't that a kick? Tye practically never talks to anyone. Kinda makes you royalty now, don't it? And good Ol' Davey. Been around, done some shit. Hold on a second," he commanded. He lay down on his back, sinking into the old, stained cushions. He shook and shimmied into a comfortable niche and then pointed to her. "Okay, my mind's open. Play."

Annie took a deep breath, releasing it slowly as her left hand floated up and down the neck of the guitar. She began. It was a measured, methodical beginning, a haunted tune foretelling ghostly vengeance. From a humming deep inside of her slowly rocking body, the lyrics came out with a soft, throaty voice:

> *"Didn't we meet last summer?*
> *Didn't we chase the wind to the sea?*
> *Didn't we gaze at the stars of winter?*
> *Didn't we, didn't we,*
> *Didn't we fall in love?"*

Annie began to pick up the tempo and slowly turned up the intensity; building the song with layers of attitude.

> *"Didn't you touch and heal my wound?*
> *Didn't you stop my bleeding 'til late June?*
> *Didn't you turn and walk away?*
> *When our fruit called out your name?*
> *Didn't you, hey, didn't you slay our love?"*

The song took a vicious, biting turn as Annie began to pound out on the guitar the sound of a woman scorned. The rocking of her body was more marked now; her eyes closed tight against the impending doom of pain and bitterness.

> *"Hey! Didn't you have promises to keep?*
> *Didja, didja like seeing me weep?*
> *Didja hear me scream in my sleep?*
> *Didja even care if I took a leap?*
> *Didja have any intentions?*
> *Oh, baby, any at all?"*

Her voice became hollow and distant, like some far off judge. She threw the words out like hooks, hoping to pierce some growing agony and rip it to shreds.

> *"What was I to you?*
> *What kinda tool?*
> *What kinda fool?*
> *Oh, what was it to you?*
> *Was it making love?*
> *Or was it consented rape?*
> *Didn't we, didn't we,*
> *Almost have something great?"*

The last phrase was almost a plea and transformed the song into a mocking apparition of the first verse, slower now and full of spite.

> *"Didn't we meet last summer?*
> *Didn't we chase the wind to the sea?*
> *Didn't we gaze at the stars of winter?*
> *Didn't we, didn't we,*
> *Didn't we fall in love?*
> *Didn't we? Didn't we?"*

Lost as the song breathed out its last breath, Annie sat staring at a spot on the floor between her and the Ogre laden couch.

"Well, well, Annie, not bad, not bad at all."

Annie returned from her daze with a smile. "Did you like it, I mean, did you really like it?"

"There's some shit happenin' there I think."

Act quickly now, Annie, quickly!

"I was hoping you'd let me sing it one night."

Ogre roared with laughter, "You are an aggressive little thing. I like that, yes I do."

"So, you'll let me try it out, maybe tomorrow night?" As soon as the words came out of her mouth she felt there was no air left in the world to replace her last breath. A change was overtaking Ogre's face.

"Well, I don't know, sweet sister, I guess it depends on how inspired I am to let you go on." He grinned wide like a skull. It looked to Annie that his toothy leer would never end, but would continue expanding until it met at the back of his head. "You know some important people might drop by tomorrow."

"I know," she responded, her boldness rapidly replaced by docility.

"It's not amateur hour. It's a shot at the big show. Awful risky."

"I know."

Ogre reached down and unsnapped the top of his dirty jeans. He unzipped his fly slowly, letting the sound of each parting zipper tooth drill into her spine.

Annie felt her bottom lip begin to tremble. *No, I've paid for my admission, I'm already in; I've paid the price.*

Oh, no, little girl, his eyes seemed to say as they glared wickedly back at her. Ogre's eyes were no longer tired, but were on fire: red, hungry and bullish. *Oh no, you've got to pay for each ride...*

He reached out for her, took hold of her arm, and brought her near him. Annie let the guitar fall to the floor; its hollow thump echoed musical chaos. She advanced toward him choking back her tears. Like a lamb to the slaughter, she went to her knees and he snaked his hand behind her neck.

...and there are no refunds.

Annie thought she could feel the watchful eyes of some distant, objective scientists upon her. She imagined them checking off items from a list on their sterile clipboards.

"Points added for negotiating that turn in the maze."

"Yes, but points subtracted for being too stupid to see the other way out. How does she generate enough brain electricity to keep her heart pumping?"

"It's hopeless; she keeps getting more entangled deeper in the maze. She should have listened to her mother and gotten away from this place."

"Don't be so hard on her; she's just a rodent after all. Perhaps, if we dissect her brain, we'll know why she's so impaired."

"I conclude that the apple does not fall far from the tree. Do you concur?"

"Absolutely. The data supports it—the evidence is overwhelming."

Ogre muttered something pornographic, but his words couldn't reach Annie, for Annie was no longer in that dank room with the naked bulb.

Instead she meandered through a cool wooded place by a stream; glad for the shift in reality becoming commonplace to her. She stood on a rise looking out over a green valley. Suddenly the valley exploded with color as autumn blazed through it, purging the land of summer. Autumn fire cooled, smothered by the white sleep of winter. The frosty chill provided a strange comfort, harboring secrets of glory days just beyond the horizon. As if to reveal the secret, the warm breezes of spring melted winter away, once again laying open the land for the life sustaining heat of summer.

Then the sky darkened blood red, and her heart pounded painfully. A fierce looking dragon swooped down at her from the foreboding sky. It screeched terribly, unleashing a rolling ball of flame straight toward Annie. The blaze permeated her, consuming her being, choking off her air supply...

As quickly as it began, it ended. Ogre released her head, lowered his hips, and huffed and puffed his way to sleep.

Annie sat on her knees, motionless, not knowing what to do. Not knowing whether to leave the room or find something heavy to bash his head in with. Something took control of her, something that shut off all thinking, all feeling, and engaged her in the pure, numb art of just doing. She got up, ran over to the dirty bathroom sink, and spat until her mouth felt dry. She rinsed her mouth out with water, but the bitter taste still lingered.

No thinking, no feeling, just doing.

She spied Ogre's drink, picked it up and filled her mouth with whiskey. She swished the firewater back and forth between her puffed-out cheeks.

I hope you choke to death on your snotty blood, she cursed, wishing she could cast a spell.

The alcohol sanitized her mouth with a fierce tingle. She thought of going back to the sink, considered the condition of the room, spat the whiskey on the floor, and headed out the door.

Chapter Four

That night Annie didn't go straight to Davey's house. She wandered back into the club and sat in a corner, invisible to the world around her. The people streamed in as the hours passed, and the music pulsated through the room. Annie found herself drifting toward the dance floor, guided by the music's invitation to enter the crowd.

The tangled sweaty limbs of the club dancers surrounded her. She lost herself in the moving jungle of flesh. Rhythmic bodies embraced her, covered her, allowing her identity to diffuse into the group. Music pounded and lights flashed, switching unknown connections off and on in her brain until she lost her sense of self.

So this it, she reflected before her mind melted into the group's consciousness. *I'm the filthy little rag doll. It's not so bad, is it? When I make it big, I won't even think about how I got there. It'll just seem like a bad dream. Tonight I just wanna dance, dance it all away—all away into a dream.*

With that, Annie no longer thought. She became the dance. This was her tribe, fellow irredeemable souls surrendering to the night. Together they would rollick away all fear, all doubt, all hurt. Together they would enact through dance the sole objective of the biological: to mingle fluids and reproduce.

The hours slipped away along with Annie's association with her body. The surreal became commonplace. In the snake-like movement of her own writhing muscles, she forgot her anguish. She shimmied back to back with a woman in black leather pants and a white tank-top. A combination of a deep woody scent and tingling spice infused her nostrils until it tickled the back of her throat. Annie and the woman became lost in the music as they dipped down and then up again, balancing against each other. When a drunken man came up and tried to join in by gyrating his crotch between them, the woman shot out her palm. The strike hit the man square on the nose, splattering blood over the unaware crowd. The woman looked at Annie, touched her gently on the cheek, and vanished into the darkness.

The night seemed fragmented, confused, shattered to Annie; like broken glass on the floor—no matter how careful you tread, you're bound to get a shard jammed into your foot. Whispers in darken doorways and alleys amplified in Annie's head. She couldn't shake the nauseating feeling deep in her belly and rising now acidic in her throat that someone intended her harm. This was not *that* someone, not the razor-toothed figure that stalked her from dark corners. This feeling had no connection to her imagination. This felt immediate. Crossing the street through sparse late night traffic, she gained a few moments of thinking time.

I can't focus. I should know where I'm at—I know this area—but everything seems moved around. Nothing is where it's supposed to be.

Annie recalled a story a teacher once told about a blind and deaf girl. The girl's mother would punish her by rearranging all the furniture in the girl's room. All the same pieces, all different. Annie felt an immediate connection to the girl's dilemma. Annie felt like the world was punishing her for what she had done by shuffling reality like a deck of cards and dealing her a losing hand.

But what other choice did I have? People always tell me what's wrong, but never what the right thing to do is or how to fix it.

Looking across the street she had crossed, Annie saw two young males glance her way and then scan the sidewalk and road traffic between them. Annie caught her gasp, realizing they were the ones stalking her. Of course, they could have been going about their own business and not even aware of her, but Annie found her feeling too strong to ignore. Better to be wrong and get away, then ignore the feeling and get jumped.

A woman stood at an apartment building door, talking rapid Spanish into the intercom. Someone inside acquiesced to her insistence and buzzed the door. The woman stormed inside, and Annie bolted up the three steps from the sidewalk to the door. She caught the door before it shut and slipped inside.

The hallway smelled old, thick with years of tobacco smoke and spicy cooking. Realizing her pursuers could use any number of tricks to enter the building, Annie headed for a door at the end of the hall. What she thought lead to a rear exit, however, turned out to be the basement entrance. Hesitating for a moment to go into the basement, Annie heard the front door rattle as random apartments were buzzed.

They're coming for me!

Annie ducked into the basement and closed the door behind her.

The air felt still in the darkness, dead still. It smelled like a tomb Annie imagined, a place time had forgotten. She made her way down the stairs one trembling step at a time, steadying herself on a rickety handrail that separated her from the depths below. The stairway seemed to go on forever as each creak of the timeworn wood issued a warning for her to turn back.

Then it happened. The loud crack of the handrail breaking accompanied Annie's shriek, and she plummeted into the basement, landing with a bounce on a stack of dusty mattresses. She coughed and waved away the musty cloud that had burst out around her. Getting up and wiping her eyes, the darkness of the room swirled around a pinpoint of light that glowed and slowly grew as her jolted head tried to set things right.

"Who's that?" a voice asked.

"Must be the new girl of the century," another voice answered.

A third voice rang out, "She doesn't look like she's doing very well, and you know what that means."

"Yeah," responded the first voice, "we're still being screwed over."

Annie peered hard in the direction of the voices, dust still stinging her eyes. She saw four women in the dim lit basement. The first voice, Annie assumed, belonged to an African woman leaning against a wall. She wore a makeshift dress of burlap, a red kerchief on her head, and a shackle on one ankle. The second woman had a Spanish look from an age long past. She sat backward on a chair furiously fanning herself as the third woman, a California looking beach-blonde, struggled to tighten a corset on the Spanish woman. Curled up in the corner huddled the fourth woman. She looked Oriental and wore a traditional silk robe. Her white painted face appeared sad with a dose of bitterness. They spoke to each other with the ease of familiarity as Annie watched them.

"Can't you get it any tighter?" the second woman begged the blonde. "I don't think my waist is thin enough."

The blonde tossed back her hair with a flip of her head. She wore an erotic red bustier that clung lustfully over her centerfold body, while black garter belts held up a pair of sheer hose. "Hell, you want to breathe, don't you?" "I guess, but I need to look right first, don't I? I mean, what's the use of breathing if I don't look right?"

The blonde glanced over at Annie and said, "Hey, new girl, could you come over and help me strap in Isabel here?"

"Okay," Annie agreed. Cautiously, she crawled down from the pile of mattresses that had broken her fall and approached the four women.

"Come on," the blonde encouraged in a friendly tone. "Don't be afraid, we're all sisters down here. My name is Babes, the sandwich here is Isabel."

"*Hola, Cómo está?*" Isabel smiled, fanning herself wildly.

Babes introduce the black woman, "And this is Kizze."

"What up, girl? Welcome to the hole," she greeted Annie unenthusi-astically.

Babes motioned to the Oriental woman and whispered, "That's Lai." Her gesture indicated Lai should be left alone.

"Hi, I'm Annie. What are you trying to do?" she asked Babes. "That looks painful."

"That's what she wants," Babes shrugged. "Just steady her back, so I can tighten this more."

"Why do you want to wear that thing?" Annie asked, providing the push to Babes pull.

"Well," Isabel answered, breathlessly, "men like it, and that's impor-tant. How else can I get along in the world if I can't get and keep a man? I don't want to waste away in some stinking sweatshop."

"It just seems like a lot of pain to go through for a guy," Annie of-fered softly.

"You right about that," Kizze piped in. "Shit, I slave all day in shame, and do you think my man gives me any respect? Hell, no! He wants to lord it over me, too." Without looking at it, she rubbed her shackled ankle, which looked raw and bloody.

Lai huffed, "You think that's bad? You think you so unlucky?"

"Oh great, here we go," Kizze said, joining the other women in a chorus of sighed annoyance.

"You look; look at what my mother did to me... so I would have to depend on men all my life." She pointed down to her feet, which were bound-up, three-inch stubs.

"Oh, my God," Annie gasped.

"Yeah, that's right," Lai spit, bitterly. "Try being mutilated since childhood so you can be an ornament that won't run away or assert itself. The men of my country dug the Lotus foot for thousands of years, put-ting us right where they wanted us: helpless and weak. The sick part of it is they thought us hobbling around with tiny steps was a turn on! Give me a knife, and I'll show them what it feels like to have parts of their body missing or useless."

"Oh, get over it, already," Isabel said sucking in her tummy.

"You get over it, you're enslaved, too."

"No, I'm not."

Lai raised an eyebrow, "Well, then princess, why don't you walk around with your belly hanging out?"

"Shut up, Lai," Isabel tearfully responded.

"Ladies," Kizze interrupted, "this is not helping."

"She's upset," Babes mentioned to Annie. "Who can blame her?" Babes finished tying Isabel's corset. "There, honey, is that better?"

Isabel sniffed back her crying, "Yes, *muchas gracias*. Lai, I'm sorry."

Lai sighed, "I'm sorry, too. You look great in your cage."

Annie looked Babes up and down, "Well, at least your lingerie looks comfortable."

"It's still a form of oppression," Lai spewed.

"Thank you, Madame Obvious," Kizze retorted to Lai's growing glare.

"True," Babes admitted sadly. "It's a subtle way for men to feel they've conquered me. They unsnap my flimsy restraints and peel away the fabric that separates them from my sex. Makes them feel like they're committing the crime of breaking and entering. They love that. But try and talk about something meaningful, and they look at you like 'what are *you* doing speaking? Shut the hell up, you stupid bitch, and bend over'."

"Yeah, stupid bitch," Lai mocked.

"*Puta estúpida*," Isabel added.

All four of them joined in a chorus of names, "Whore, slut, floozy, dike, cocksucker, bed bunny, slam puppy, ballbuster, cockteaser!"

"Hey," called out Kizze, "what does a woman with amputated legs and a slug have in common?"

"They both leave a slime trail!" Isabel answered with a shout.

They all laughed hysterically, then uncomfortably, and then let it die out.

Isabel turned toward Babes in the surrounding silence, "Should my breasts be separated or pushed up, should I have a high waist or low waist, rounded or flat stomach?"

Babes just shook her head in defeat, "Hell, I don't know. I can't keep up with the fashion rages."

"Well, what am I supposed to do with these tits? I don't know what to do with my tits. Annie, what do you think, dear?"

"Huh?" Annie answered, caught off guard by the invitation to enter the dialogue. "Oh, I don't know. I'm not the best person to ask since I really don't have any."

"And you should count yourself lucky," Kizze insisted.

"Damned lucky," Lai added, still pouting. "Bastards."

"Because," Kizze continued, "once you got them, they become everybody's property or something. Your friends compete with you over them, guys ogle them and go out of their way to try and cop a feel, babies suck on them, and lovers want you to keep them hidden from the world and take them out only for their use. It's a nightmare."

"Damned nightmare," Lai added.

"Hey, Annie," said Isabel, "tell us how things are for you out there."

"Yeah, Annie, tell us something," Kizze insisted.

"Well, I don't know, I guess I can wear a lot of different things."

"Yes, yes, but are things any better?" Babes asked, hopefully.

"I don't know," Annie shrugged with embarrassment. "I had to give head just to get ahead, if that's what you mean."

"I freakin' quit," Lai sneered and rolled over to wail into the wall.

Babes gathered her optimism, "Well, there's always the next century, ladies, we always have the next century."

"Sure, Babes," Isabel weakly offered.

"Sure," Kizze concluded.

It was well after midnight when Annie found herself on the cracked slab of cement in front of Davey's door. It made her stomach feel hollow and sick to realize she had no idea how she had gotten there. The only certainty was the dizziness she felt and the headache that throbbed in time with her heavy heart.

More lost time. Things are getting worse; and if I don't stop having these spells, I'm gonna end up never coming back from Crazyland.

A heavy weight pressed down on her, making the most routine movement seem like a Herculean feat. The twisted feeling in her gut was about more than what she had done for the promise of a shining moment in the spotlight. She felt dirty and ashamed about that, no question about it, but there was something more. Something darker, crawling and clawing its way from the depths of her memory and demanding to see the light of day.

What could be worse than what Ogre's done to me? If there is something worse, I don't want to know what it is—ever. I'd rather slip away into the weirdness forever than find out.

After a time of swaying back and forth trying to connect with the present moment, Annie finally knocked on Davey's door. Martha opened it, her eyes puffy from sleep.

"There you are," Martha smiled. "Thought you might have changed your mind."

Annie could see Davey snoring on the couch and knew they had both fallen asleep waiting for her. She tried to apologize, but no words would come. She felt numb, drained and dead inside.

Martha looked concerned. "Are you all right?" she asked. She took

Annie by the hand and led her into the house. "Come on, let's get you tucked into bed."

Sleep that night for Annie meant black, a nowhere land where she did not exist; where memories were locked away and kept out of sight.

The next morning Annie shuffled into the kitchen, the smell of tea and whole-wheat pancakes caused a grumbling in her stomach.

Davey and Martha looked up from their breakfast and smiled at Annie.

"Hey, sleepy head," Davey greeted.

"Hey, you guys," Annie said. "Sorry about coming in so late, I was hanging out at the club."

Martha got up, gave Annie's shoulders a squeeze, and guided her to a chair at the table. "No problem. Want something to eat?"

"Yeah, thanks."

Annie spent the day practicing her song; she wanted to be ready for Ogre to call her on stage. Martha coached her and helped Annie polish her presentation.

"Did Ogre say he was gonna let you sing?" Davey asked later in the afternoon.

"Yeah, he said if things went well and there was enough time, he'd let me tag on at the end."

"Well, don't get your hopes up, sis, you know folks are supposed to be checkin' him out tonight," Davey said.

"I know, but I wanna be ready."

Martha nodded in agreement with Annie. "Positive thinking, that's the key."

"Yeah, I'm just saying he can be a little flakey, that's all. Well, ladies, we should get going and make sure everything is set up."

"Are you coming tonight, Martha?" Annie asked.

"Of course, sweetie. It's not really my scene but, if you get to perform, I want to see that. You're gonna be great; I just know it."

Martha gave Annie a big hug, which froze-up Annie inside. She didn't know what to make of the gesture or how to respond. She gave a nervous laugh and tried to distance herself without appearing obvious. "Thanks," was all she could muster.

"You know," Martha said, "I got a pretty sundress you can wear tonight. Want to? Come on, let's check out the closet."

Davey groaned, "Oh, *now* the fashion show starts. We gotta get going."

"Just hush, Davey," Martha said and winked at Annie. "It'll only take a second."

Chapter Five

Ogre was in rare form that night. People actually put aside their nocturnal activities to listen. He infected them with a steady stream of destruction, anger and spite. It was easy to tap into the crowd's rage. Almost too easy to contaminate their minds with the virus of his personal mantra—*the world must pay for my pain.* And once he had them, he fed off of their attention, growing into something larger than life: a hot, sweating beast prowling the stage, glaring at his victims.

Annie and Martha hung with Davey at the control board, and had to lean into each other to be heard.

"Things are going good, huh, Davey?" Annie asked. "He's in a good mood, don't you think?"

"Yeah, Annie, you bet," Davey answered.

"I got my fingers cross for you, sweetie," Martha said.

Finally, Ogre finished up the last song. Annie picked up Davey's guitar. "I'm going to wait off stage. I'm sure he's gonna ask me on, I just feel it deep inside. Tonight's my night."

Martha gave Annie a hug and a kiss on the cheek. "Good luck," she said.

Annie nodded in appreciation, and then, working her way around the crowd, headed toward the side of the stage by the exit.

The success of the band's performance excited Annie and filled her with hope. Everything was going perfectly, like never before. Tonight everything would change for her, and she would be on her way out of the dirt and grime. She would be in the spotlight, adored by millions.

"Thank you, minions!" Ogre growled, not seeming to notice a small 16-year-old girl waiting impatiently off stage left in a pretty yellow dress.

Annie clutched the guitar with every ounce of her life. She bounced nervously, hoping to attract his attention. *If only he would see me, then he would remember. He would remember that I paid the price—paid it in full.*

Ogre did indeed look at her with a nod. Annie's spirit soared. She ran the song through her mind a hundred speeding times, along with flashing images of her in a music video and up on the stage of a world tour. She looked over at Tye to express her excitement. But something was wrong. Tye glanced painfully at Annie and then quickly averted his gaze in shame.

Then Ogre looked at her again. All the blood drained from her face and her soul shattered like a frozen autumn leaf. He was grinning at her now, grinning wide like a skull.

"Since you've all been so rockin' awesome, we're gonna play a new song we found scrawled on a bathroom wall. One... two... three..."

Annie took up space blankly, the air suddenly too thick to breath in. She listened in horror as Ogre performed an abortion on the child she had entrusted to him.

> *"Didn't we screw last summer?*
> *Didn't we chase bourbon with beer?*
> *Didn't you suck start my Harley,*
> *'Til I, 'til I, just couldn't hear?*
> *Hey! If you're gonna lay there and weep,*
> *If you're gonna bother my sleep,*
> *You can put your ass back on the street,*
> *Cuz I didn't give any promises to keep."*

Annie's stomach convulsed, she choked on the bitter acid that shot up her throat. Her mind had disconnected from her body and its functions, so she gave little notice to the weakness overtaking her legs. All she could think of was what his eyes had whispered last night, "... and there are no refunds."

> *"Say! Was it something I said?*
> *Was it the strange stains on our bed?*
> *Or was it much, much more,*
> *That sent you out the door,*
> *Out and beggin' me for more!"*

The crowd raged hysterically, not noticing in the least the shell of a girl who quietly slipped out a side door; vanishing from memory like shadows on a moonless night.

> *"Go, go, go,*
> *Go out the door.*
> *Go, go, go,*
> *'Til I, 'til I, just can't hear ya no more.*
> *'Til I can't hear ya no more!"*

The hyped up, edgy energy that pulsated from the city at night could not penetrate her awareness. How long she wandered the streets, Annie had no way of knowing. She wandered mindlessly through darkened side streets and overpasses; her body took over what her mind was too drained to do. She walked past bodies of thrown-away people, past burned out buildings with busted windows from some uprising that was beaten down by the club and the boot, and past highways abuzz with a thousand cars going to a thousand places—places she was not welcomed at.

Her awareness came back to her only when she reached the end of the road. Some subterranean compass had brought her defeated body to a deserted stretch of beach. The soothing roar of the ocean waves gently awoke her, and she smiled at its timelessness. Mother Ocean beckoned to her from under the waxing Sister Moon.

Ah, she thought, gazing out at the glistening waves, *there you are. Have you been waiting for me? Did you know I'd come to you? Seek out your dark embrace?*

Annie walked toward the surf and discarded her sandals, allowing the cooling sand to slide between her toes. The air felt heavy with the scent of rotting seaweed, but the clear starry sky gave a promise of something better, more pure, waiting for her out there.

Promises, promises, Annie sighed, who am I fooling? It's easy for stars to promise something, because they never have to deliver. That's all a promise is anyway, it's just the start of a lie. How many lies have I already been told? Too many to count. It would be easier to count how many truths I've been told. That would be easy, 'cause there has only been one: I'm going to die.

Shifting through a lifetime of lies, the fact of her inescapable death was the only nugget of truth she could find. Her mother had known it and tried to delay it, hoping foolishly that Annie could actually escape the genetic curse of decrepitude. Ogre knew it, had directly told her so, but amused himself by toying with it.

Her frail body shivered as a breeze blew around her. Looking up at the stars, she saw the whole night sky shatter in an instant and fall to the earth like a broken mirror, leaving only a molten red mass burning up the heavens. Fear should have been her reaction to this break with reality, but Annie felt unmoved by the hallucination. She had already accepted the fact her mind was breaking up, and soon it would be silenced. She smiled sadly to herself as the sound of falling glass tinkled musically in her ears.

The cold ocean foam tingled her sore feet and eroded the sand from beneath, the ancient waters pulling her in closer. The sky returned to its sparkling self, the hallucination gone, her insignificance once again contrasted with the night's vast splendor. Silently, Annie let her dress slip off her body, stepping out of it into calf-deep water. Her panties soon joined her dress, both floating away in the black water. She looked into the celestial night with awe. Then she lowered her gaze and became aware of her own naked body.

A horror engulfed her in a firestorm of purity.

And she knew.

For the first time in her life, it all became painfully clear. She had finally seen the birthplace of her fear.

"Oh, God!" Annie burst out loud in tears, her mind no longer able to contain her thoughts. She wailed to the surrounding nothingness with a throaty voice that choked on her tears. "I'm so uglieeee!" Her chest heaved and shuddered in rhythm with her sobs. "Why am I so ugly? Why, why, why, why, whiiiiihihi? I can't stand it anymore. I just wanted to be beautiful, just a little bit. But, I'm not, not at all. I'm just ugly, ugly, ugly."

Annie looked down at her small girlish breasts that mismatched her wide hips. Her sadness exploded into rage as she put fist to body and beat herself. "I hate you!" she screamed. "I hate you, I hate you! You're ugly and you deserve to be beaten. You're ugly, and I hate you. I... *hate*... youuuuuuu!"

Annie turned her face heavenward and let out a shrill cry that echoed back through the passage of time, to when humans first became aware of their imperfections, "AAAHHH! Why did you do this to meeee? Why did you make me so ugly? I can't, I can't get away from this ugliness!" Grinding her knuckles into herself, she tried desperately to scrub the flesh from her face, her chest and her legs.

Her head swum from the revelation and her throat burned from screaming. She sank her bottom down into the surrounding waters and wept into her knees. "I can't, I can't; I can't get away from my ugliness. I can't, I can't; I can't wake up one more day knowing that beauty exists, but not for me."

As sobs convulsed her shivering body, the ocean continued its patient, gentle dragging of Annie's body into its secret depths. She felt the heavy water rush past her, embracing her affection-starved skin. There had been a time long ago when her parents held her, but those memories lingered in the darkness just out of reach. Depravation and yearning along with images of her mom helplessly passed out were her only accessible history.

Soon, she thought quietly now, but still trying to form words with her mouth. *Soon it'll be over.*

She glanced up from her knees, and the world dissolved, her eyes and face prickled as objects around her morphed into globs and then separated out to a new reality.

As if someone had flipped a switch, Annie found herself in a courtroom sitting in an oversized witness chair.

The prosecutor was in the middle of his opening statement to the court. Turning toward Annie, his appearance stunned her. He possessed a strong chiseled face, clear tanned skin, straight white teeth, and a muscular body perfectly adorned by an expensive suit. Annie blinked and rubbed her eyes while looking around the courtroom. The jurors, the judge, the spectators, all of them were gorgeous women and handsome men, and all of them were looking right at the little ugly girl in the witness chair.

"The prosecution," the prosecutor bellowed, "does not need to parade witness after witness to testify, it does not need to bore the jury with endless exhibits of evidence, nor does it need to conjure up some dramatic persuasive argument to prove its case. I mean, for God's sakes, just look at her. She's ugly!"

The courtroom rumbled with murmurs, and the judge hammered down the rumble with his gavel. Every time his gavel came down, Annie could see lightning shoot out.

"Order! I'll have order in my court. And, Mr. Prosecutor, I'll have no more absurd statements made either. Court Reporter, strike the prosecution's statement from the record."

"Which part?" the court reporter asked with a honey dripping voice. She crossed her shapely tanned legs and winked.

"Why, the part about not having a parade of witnesses, of course. Christ, everyone in this court room is a witness to how ugly she is."

"Very well, your Honor."

"Prosecution may proceed."

"Thank you, your Honor. The prosecution intends to prove beyond a shadow of a doubt, and using only the pathetic evidence sitting now before you, that Annie is a mistake of nature. That she is taking up space that could be better used by a real person or a vintage lava lamp." As an aside to the judge, the prosecutor whispered, "Something with the plasma lamp for those awesome lightning effects would be lovely."

"Oh, yes," the judge agreed, stroking his chin. "I like that. Court Reporter, make sure that gets in the record."

"Yes, your Honor," she breathed heavily, running her tongue over her ruby lips.

"Ladies and gentlemen of the jury," the prosecutor continued, "how can you not look at this wretch of a... of a thing, and not immediately conclude that she deserved to be abandoned by her father, ignored and ill-nourished by her mother, discarded by her teachers, beaten by her mother's drug impaired lovers, pawed by the boys at school and scorned by the girls, and finally raped and abused in ways she couldn't even imagine. That's better treatment than something so ugly deserves."

The jury foreman jumped up from his seat, "We the jury find..."

"Wait a minute, hold on!" the judge insisted with a bang and flash of his gavel. "We haven't heard from the defense yet."

"Oh, yeah." The foreman sat down.

"The defense may now present an opening statement," the judge instructed.

Annie looked over at the defense table and saw her attorney. The man was well dressed, but possessed no face, just a blank, solid piece of flesh from forehead to chin. The defense gave a shoulder shrug and went about shuffling papers.

"We the jury..."

"Sit down, for crying-out-loud. The defendant has a right to speak."

"Oh, yeah."

"Now, Annie," the judge addressed her, "what do you have to say on your own behalf? And remember," he warned handing her a mirror, "you're under oath."

Annie gazed into the mirror at a blank reflection. "I'm guilty," she declared solemnly. "Guilty as charged."

The jury foreman wasted no time in announcing, "We the jury find Annie guilty of crimes against humanity, of fraudulently impersonating a human being, and of taking up space in the world that I could have used for a lava lamp with plasma effects. Thanks a-whole-lot, you self-centered waste of life!"

With that proclamation the room erupted in yells, screams, jeers and cheers. Chairs flew; papers rocketed up and rained down, while the crowd pressed forward toward Annie. It seemed at once a celebration and a protest, but one thing was for certain: Annie had been convicted by her own admission.

The chaotic courtroom scene dissolved and morphed, and Annie found herself back on the beach and chest deep in the beckoning ocean. She had run out of tears for her pain. All that was left was a dry mechanical laughter. The sky clouded above her, obscuring the stars and blurring out the crescent moon. Lightning outlined severe cloud shapes in flashes, as thunder announced the coming of a storm.

"Come to me, Annie," the ocean invited through its soft endless roar. *"Come home, let me embrace you with a love you've never known."*

Annie thought of all the hands that had ever touched her and all the arms that had ever encircled her. None of them ever providing warmth or love. They had all sought to suck her dry of life, to drop her out of intoxicated weakness, to slap her, punch her, to pin her down and hold her helpless while she was violated. These hands she knew well. She shook her crouched body violently in an attempt to rid her flesh of the tactile memories. The flow of the tide and the ripples of raindrops quickly erased the splashes her body made in the rushing waters.

She was ready to join the ripples and be forever absorbed into time. She was ready to repent for her sins and accept her punishment. She was ready to surrender to the darkness and let the strong currents suck her to the depths. She was ready, but through the veil of rain danced a rich haunting tune. She turned her attention toward the beach and was greeted by a full aroma.

Is it sandalwood? Maybe jasmine? Maybe both?

Annie stood up, awakened from the spell of the ocean, and waded back to shore. She walked a short distance down the shoreline until she came upon a small circus tent, the kind that might house an exhibit or a fortuneteller. Through the seams of the tent she saw candlelight flickering and heard music, inviting otherworldly music that floated out of the tent on a river of incense. She approached the tent, drifting ghostlike toward it as rain ran in rivulets down her naked body. She didn't know if it was just another trick of her mind, and she didn't care whether it was or not. The scent and the music grew not only in intensity, but also in depth and richness as she neared the tent's entrance.

Standing at the door flaps, Annie felt a chill run through her. The sky rumbled, lightning flashed, and cold thick drops of rain continued to stream over her locks and down her face. She stood reluctant to enter even though the divine smells, the glowing light, and the caressing music begged her to enter. Still, she stood, hesitating.

What waits for me inside this tent? My life? My death? Annie looked back at the ocean. She was tired, and the flowing water offered sleep. *Just a little fight, just a little thrashing toward the end, but then sweet eternal sleep.* She had turned to heed the seductive call of the deep, when a voice called out from inside the tent. Annie faced the tent again and squinted to hear.

"*Einna, ni emoc, ni, ni.*"

Annie snapped awake, shook her head, and peered closer at the flaps, as if closer visual scrutiny would explain what she had heard.

"*Einna, ni emoc.*"

Annie slowly pulled back the flap and stepped into the dancing light.

Chapter Six

The woman wore black. She was an older woman who might fit the definition of a crone, if not for the illusion of softness afforded her by the surrounding candles, hundreds of glowing candles oozing wax and warmth inside the tent. Black adorned the woman: a lacy black dress, black rings on her gnarled fingers, black beads around her fleshy neck, and a black shawl over her black hair. Despite her age, her raven hair had not surrendered to gray. She reposed behind a small mahogany table that supported a large crystal ball. A tarantula made its steady way across the scratched tabletop. The heady aromatic smell inside the tent made Annie woozy in a warm way.

"*Uoy rof gnitiaw neeb ev'I, Einna, olleh.*"

Annie knitted her brow in confusion. "I don't understand what you're saying. Do you speak English?"

Now it was the old woman's turn to look at Annie in dismay and confusion. "*Tahw?*"

"Huh?"

"*Dlihc, ylegnarts kaeps uoy.*"

Annie shook her head in hopes of clearing out the communication barrier. *This is worse than trying to talk to my mom.* Judging the situation as hopeless, she opted to stand self-consciously until something else happened.

With a look of revelation, the woman's eyes grew wide, and she laughed a loud long cackle that the soothing music softened. "*Detsujda daeh ruoy deen uoy ees I, ho.*"

The old woman stood up from her chair behind the table and approached Annie with a knowing smile. She planted herself firmly in front of Annie; her bent and twisted body barely taller than the young girl's. Annie tensed as the woman reached out and placed her hands on Annie's face. She expected the old woman's hands to be icy, but the thick haze of incense gave them warmth. There was a terrible "POP!" and Annie found herself facing the entrance of the tent. That is to say, the front of her body still faced toward the old woman, but the woman had twisted Annie's head around backward. Another "POP!" exploded in her ears, and she faced the mumbling old woman again. Annie stumbled back a few steps, bewilderment sloshing her consciousness, preventing focus.

The woman sized Annie up and nodded in approval. "There now, dearie, is that better? Can you understand me now?"

"Yes," she answered. "How did... what was... who are...?"

"Easy, Annie, steady yourself. Take a moment to regain your bearings." The woman looked at Annie's nakedness. "Cold, dear?"

"Yes, freezing," Annie responded, only now realizing that she stood shivering.

The woman retrieved a black crocheted blanket and draped it over Annie's shoulders. "There, is that better?"

Annie hugged the blanket around her. It felt soft and secure. "Yes, thank you."

"Would you like some hot tea, Annie? I was just about to have some. Please sit down and join me for a cup," the woman offered. She sat down at the table and motioned Annie into the other chair.

Annie sat down quietly and waited. The woman poured tea from an exotic teapot, which had a skull for the container and a snake for the spout. The tea soothed Annie's tired body as she sipped it.

She looked at the smiling woman, the obvious question coming to her mind, "How do you know my name? Do I know you?"

"My name is Esmeralda. You don't know me, but I've been waiting a long time for you."

"Why?"

"Why were you going to kill yourself?"

"I wasn't," Annie blurted out. *Or was I? I can't remember what I was doing, I just wanted to sit there and let the tide do whatever it felt was necessary. It's what the ocean wanted, wasn't it? That's not the same as killing one's self, I don't think.*

"Well, you can certainly call it what you want," Esmeralda said as if reading Annie's mind, "but you were putting yourself in a fatal situation. Why would you want to do that?"

Annie was stopped in mid-breath from answering. She squinted hard against the twinkling candlelight and leaned forward slightly. *That's odd; she looks much younger than she did a moment ago.* "I don't know, I guess I saw no use in going on. It all seems so pointless."

Esmeralda took a sip from her own cup of tea and asked, "So, life isn't giving you what you want, is that it, Annie, dear?"

"No, you don't understand. I'm just saying it's pointless."

"I understand. You want a point, and life isn't giving one to you."

"Yeah, I guess. Either that or it's giving me a lot of what I don't want." She shook her head, it felt sluggish; her breathing became labored. "I don't mean to sound weird or anything, but are you getting younger or is there something in this tea?"

"It's not the tea, Annie, I am getting younger. Don't bother yourself with how or why. After all it's only time, and we're all subject to time one way or the other. But what I'm wondering is if you think the rules apply to you?"

"They don't seem to be applying to *you*, hell, nothing in the past hour has followed any rule I know."

Esmeralda laughed with a gentle fullness. She was now a vigorous woman of thirty with the same long black hair, but sharply defined features and a curvaceous body. "Oh Annie, the point is I can only be one thing at a time. Well, perhaps with some transitions on the fringes waiting for the next moment. The rest, well, the rest is all smoke and mirrors, isn't it?"

Annie felt as if she wanted to cry, "Have I gone completely mental? I don't understand any of this."

"There, there, sweetie," Esmeralda soothed. She rose from her chair and glided over to stand behind Annie. "You're not crazy." Taking a brush from the table, she stroked it through Annie's hair and said, "You're just a little confused right now, and who could blame you? Just relax for a bit. Does this feel all right?"

"Mm-hmm," Annie answered closing her eyes. *It feels great. When was the last time anyone brushed my hair? This is a nice madness; if I ever snap out of this, I'll be caught between the streets and the ocean again. What else is there?*

"You're fretting about something again," Esmeralda said. "What is it?"

"I don't know what I'm supposed to be, or what I'm supposed to do."

"And do you search for something out there to tell you?"

"I used to, I guess, but I didn't find anything. I mean, everywhere I looked someone wanted me to be something different. Am I supposed to be daughter, slut, star, student, junkie? I can't get a straight answer."

"Silly, sister! That's because there isn't anything out there that has the answers. You're a person not a designation, for goodness sakes. It's not like the Cosmos designed something just for you. How grim that would be: Annie the automaton. No, She creates and then, well, moves on about Her business."

Annie perked up, "Exactly, that's exactly right. That's what I'm saying, there is no point to it; no one cares. That's why I was in the ocean."

"No, sweetness, exactly wrong," she rebutted softly. "You know you have wonderful hair, but it looks uncomfortable and a pain to keep up. You ought to shorten it a bit. You want me to cut it for you?" Esmeralda offered, gently touching Annie's cheek and chin.

Annie blushed. She felt fragile inside, but the usual tenseness caused by someone touching her was gone; there was no sense of invasion. "Well, I don't know, I guess. Just not *too* short."

"No, not too short, just enough to afford you some freedom. Convenient on journeys."

"What journey?"

"Whatever journey, I'm not picky," Esmeralda shrugged.

Annie started to ask for clarification, but dismissed the thought.

"So what do you say, Annie?" she asked snipping in the air a pair of scissors that appeared out of nowhere.

"Okay, sure," Annie answered with a shrug.

Esmeralda hummed a dreamy melody as she carefully cut away at Annie's hair. Annie enjoyed the feeling of strong fingers combing through her dark locks.

"You were in the ocean," the beautiful woman began, "because you thought the Cosmos *ought* to attend to you. And if it didn't, you couldn't be happy. Now that's better," she concluded. She wiped Annie's face with a warm cloth that smelled of lavender. "Stand up, please."

Annie obeyed the request and when she stood, she noticed Esmeralda had again regressed in age. She looked like one of the young women Annie saw in the city, bustling with coffee or bottled water in hand to catch a class, pull a shift, or pop in for a workout. They seemed so focused, so taut, so unblemished.

Annie felt a chill as the blanket fell from her shoulders, leaving her once again naked. She rubbed the back of her liberated neck, feeling lighter and cleaner.

Esmeralda stepped back and visually examined Annie from head to foot and front to back. Then the woman felt around Annie's body, sizing up muscle tone and palpating her abdomen. When she finished her odd physical exam of Annie, she cupped her hand around her chin thoughtfully and said, "Now what is so bad about your body that you beat it?"

"Well," she answered as if stating the obvious, "it's ugly."

"I get the feeling you see everything as ugly. Although it's true you don't look properly nourished; you have a girlish slump when you stand and you haven't developed much muscle tone. But all of that is due solely to your lack of body maintenance and poor self-confidence. A sensible low-fat diet, yoga and some meditation will help you out."

"I think it will take a lot more than that. I mean, I'll certainly never be as beautiful as you." She sat back down and tossed the blanket carelessly onto her body.

Esmeralda shook her head sadly and sat down. "Annie, Annie, Annie, whatever am I to do with you? So obsessed with image, so hungry for the love of a clamoring crowd. You don't see your own beauty."

"That's easy for you to say," Annie retorted. "You're so pretty. I bet you have guys fighting over you all the time. And I bet they treat you real nice, too, not like you were some kinda towel to wipe their dirty hands on."

"Oh, I see the problem here," Esmeralda mused as she faded into adolescence. "You think your worth is measured by your desirability to others."

"I don't know about all that. I just know I'd like to be treated nicely by people, like..."

"Like I've treated you?" Esmeralda asked, finishing the sentence for Annie.

"Yeah, I guess," Annie murmured as self-conscious feelings crept in again.

"Let me ask you something. If I were to cover your body with blood and throw you into a tank of hungry sharks, what do you think would happen?"

Annie couldn't let this statement go by without a heartfelt, "What?"

"Come on, what do you think would happen?"

"They'd eat me up."

"That's right. Now, what if I anointed your body with oils and put you afloat on an air mattress in the middle of a cool, blue swimming pool?"

"I guess I would just float around and get a tan. I'm not sure I understand what you're talking about."

"Quite simply, my dear, you go through your life like a bloody victim in a world of sharks. You are oblivious to your divine nature and therefore, *so is the world*."

Annie stared down at her lap in silence. She struggled to keep another tearful outburst at bay.

The woman-turned-teenager motioned to a crystal ball waiting on the table. "Look into this, Annie. Look deep. Look with everything you've got left in you. Let's see what's rattling around in that head of yours."

Filled with trepidation, Annie looked into the crystal, not really wanting to know its secrets. At first, all she could see was a distorted view of the rest of the room. Then, as a flash of lightning exploded somewhere outside the tent, the inside of the crystal blazed with a fireball. Smoke consumed the flame, and then the smoke dispersed. The haze thinned in the orb to reveal an image of Annie in a tattered gray dress, standing on the front yard of a frightful house.

Annie found herself hypnotically drawn into the scene of the crystal. *Where am I now? Am I inside? Did I somehow leave my body? How much more of this can I take before I run screaming into complete madness?*

From outside of her awareness, Esmeralda's voice entered as a welcomed comfort and guide. "Don't be afraid, you'll be okay. Just breathe slowly and watch. Float with the images. Relax. You won't get sucked in if you just relax and don't fight. Relax, let it wash over you."

Annie took a deep breath and adapted to the terrifying image of herself standing in a yard surrounded by a ramshackle wooden fence. A cruel wind screamed around the figure as lightning distorted the jutting shapes of a house, which stood three fierce stories high. Silhouetted against an unforgiving sky, the building teetered on a treeless bluff, where grass struggled in vain to survive. Thunder crashed; Annie took another deep breath to calm herself.

"Good," encouraged Esmeralda's disembodied voice. "You're doing fine. Now I want you to see yourself going into the house."

Annie began to cry and shake inside, "No, I don't want to. I can't."

"Steady... calm... breathe... relax. They're just images, Annie. They can't hurt you. Don't be afraid, I'm here with you. Walk into the house."

Annie became confused as to whether it was her or the image of her that started toward the wicked building.

"Don't get sucked in, Annie, relax... breathe."

Annie took a long slow breath and realized she only willed the image to move, but she wasn't actually the image. She found courage in that realization and continued to will her image up to the house. It opened the door and stepped inside. The entranceway was dark except for flashes of illumination afforded by the frequent lightning. Her image creaked cautiously down a long dusty hallway that seemed to have no end.

Annie stopped at the first door in the hallway. The paint blistered and peeled along the frame. She turned the rusted knob and entered the dark room. The room stood quiet, except for the dull throbbing sound of a dying heart.

"Hello?" Annie called out into the darkness, trying to keep her voice steady.

"Hi, Annie, longtime no see. Remember me?"

Annie peered toward the voice as a soft glow lit the room, revealing a broken bed, and on it naked and smiling sat her friend, Shelly.

"Shelly?" Annie could barely recognize her, because Shelly's body looked like a road map. Long lines of thick black stitches crisscrossed her body, creating a tangled and distorted appearance. Even the girl's face appeared twisted and uneven, as if someone had cut her up and hastily sewn her back together again. Her eyes looked grayer then Annie remembered, with the left pupil dilated and the right one constricted.

"Yeah, you do remember!" she proclaimed.

"Of course I remember you, you were my only friend," Annie said, approaching Shelly.

"I see you still got your piercings. Didn't let them close, huh?" Shelly said.

Annie automatically touched her eyebrow and then her nose, "Of course not—not after all you went through to pierce me."

"Yeah, you cried like a big baby."

"A big titty baby," Annie agreed.

"Hey, Annie, remember, we used to cut school and hang out at the tattoo parlor and hope some metal-head rock star would come by?"

"Yeah, and the time you tried to get me to start smoking," Annie laughed, "and you stole some of your mom's cigarettes, and we hid in her car..."

"...and you puked all over the seats!" Shelly squealed as she finished out the story.

"Oh God, I got so sick. But you stayed by my side until I hurled the last chunk. You always looked out for me."

"Well someone had to, Stinky, you just let people push you around."

"I know," Annie admitted in a small voice, "but what was I sup-posed to do? I didn't know how to be strong like you. You could tell anyone to 'piss off' or 'eat me'." To illustrate, Annie, grabbed her crotch and pulled at it while pumping her hips in and out. Both girls erupted with laughter.

"Hey, Annie, remember that time you almost set your mom's apart-ment on fire?"

"Yeah," Annie said, sprawling out on the floor, "you wanted to get laid by that loser Jared, so we burned your panties as an offering to the sex goddess."

"You freaked me out, you little pyro. You just held the panties and stared at the fire. I kept yelling, 'Drop it in the ash tray, drop it in the ashtray!' but you were like in a trance or something, and you almost burnt your frickin' hand."

"Yeah, that was a dumb thing to do," Annie admitted with a grin.

The girls' shared laughter quieted, and they sat staring into each other's eyes, lost in the calm of a memory storm. The pulsating sound of a heart throbbed slower now.

"Remember the time," Shelly reminisced, breaking the silence, "when we were going to meet behind the gym and hitch our way to my aunt and uncle's house in St. Helena?"

"Shelly, I waited for you all day, and you never came, and I never saw you again."

"And you forgot about me, Annie, you totally forgot about me!" Shelly spat.

Annie was near tears, "What are you talking about?"

"You never thought about me after that day, did you?"

Annie cried into her hands.

"Did you? You erased me from your thoughts, you back-stabbin' bitch!"

"You left me all alone, you deserted me, you stupid whore!"

"I didn't desert you, look at me, damn it. I was tortured, raped and hacked to death!"

"No, no, no," Annie cried out. She frantically gripped the sides of her head to keep from exploding. "I didn't know, I didn't know."

"The hell you didn't, you just didn't *want* to know, so you forgot about me, 'cause it was the easy way out. That's the story of your whole pathetic life, Annie, always taking the easy way out!"

"Stop it, Shelly, please stop it. I loved you, you were my only friend ever, and you went away. Don't you understand how much that hurt me? I had to face everything all alone."

"Well, excuse me; I guess I was just too busy getting a broom handle shoved up me to think about your pain."

Annie bolted up, her breathing rapid and shallow. It was then she noticed there was no comforting voice to guide her and no sense of ob-jectivity to shield her. The observer had become the observed.

"I'm sorry, Shelly, I'm so sorry... I can't... I can't... Oh God, it didn't happen... it didn't happen... no... no...no..."

Suddenly the dull thud of a beating heart stopped. Shelly's eyes grew wide in desperation, her mouth gasped to form words, "Annie, no, please, please don't block me out again."

Annie backed away in horror as blood gushed from Shelly's sutured gashes. "I'm sorry, Shelly. So very, very sorry."

Shelly's brutal scream reverberated as her draining body sucked in-ward, imploding on itself and leaving flesh to cling to bone. "Annie, no! Don't forget about me again! Annie!"

Annie backed out into the hallway and the door slammed shut, muf-fling Shelly's pleas. Terrified, Annie did the only thing she knew how to do—she ran like hell. She ran as fast as she could down the hallway, her footsteps echoing loudly around her; mocking her. The hallway twisted and turned like a maze, threatening to steal her balance. She again encountered the nauseating feeling of being watched and evaluated.

"You're not good enough. You're a piece of shit."

The words of judgment struck her like a judge's gavel.

"You're in the way. You're taking up too much space. Why don't you just disappear?"

The flashing lightning acted like a strobe, causing everything to move toward her in a jerky, deformed dance. A howling wind shook the house with increasing violence, keeping her level of terror at its peak. Annie unleashed a scream as the floorboards rattled, buckled and weakened under her feet.

I got to get out of here, she thought. *Got to run away. Keep running and never stop!*

The floor gave way and, with a shout, Annie crashed through into the depths below. Like waking from a dream about falling, Annie jerked and gasped for air. She found herself back in Esmeralda's tent and in the middle of a raging tempest.

A bone-chilling howl rushed through the tent, whipping the fragile candle flames—some of them to death. She was immediately seized by the intuition that the howling sound was not an act of weather, but came from something or some *things* outside the tent. The wild and hungry chorus grew closer, louder. Rain cut into the tent, slicing its way through the straining seams and billowing flaps. Annie looked around panic stricken, trying to find Esmeralda in the chaos.

"Esmeralda! Esmeralda, help me! Where are you?" Annie tried to shout above the noise.

A calm, clear voice penetrated the bedlam. "I'm here, Annie."

Annie stood up and looked over the table. There sat Esmeralda, she had regressed into a five-year-old child.

"What's happening?" Annie pleaded.

"I'm sorry, Annie, but it's for your own good. Believe me."

Annie experienced new levels of fear. The howling turned savage, crying out with an ancient blood lust.

"What are you talking about, what's going on? Am I going to die? Am I going to hurt? I can't stand this anymore!"

"I know. That's why you have to go. You must save yourself. You need to stop reacting and start acting!"

With that Esmeralda, the tent, the candles, the table, the chair, the incense, the warmth, and the security flew away from her and vanished into the darkness. Annie was left standing alone on the beach, her eyes bulging as she choked on her breath. She had reached the zenith of her fear; a point that seemed out of reach as the evening offered up horror after endless horror. But as Annie stood alone underneath an exploding sky, she knew that this was the final terror. A terror so great she felt she would drop dead on the spot and rot to dust. Her urine gave way and gushed down between her quivering legs as she stood in the sand, encircled by a pack of snarling black wolves.

Annie spun around and around slowly, drunk on her body's own fear-hormone cocktail. She could not cry out, she could not run. She could only stand in her usual self-conscious defeated way and wait for something to happen. She barely flinched as the first wolf lunged at her, catching her throat in his salivating mouth and crashing her to the ground. Annie's back hit the sand brutally, and the wolf bore down on her neck, splintering her spine with his powerful jaws. Other wolves leapt into the dark deed, and she felt a sharp tugging at her shoulders and hips. With a whip of his muzzle, the wolf tore Annie's head from her body.

And then there was a quiet blackness.

Peace, finally, peace. It would have been so much easier to let the ocean take me. Why must I have so much bother in my life? Couldn't I have died without being terrorized? At least it's finally over, at least I have that much. Although, now that I think about it, I was kind of looking forward to giving life another try. I think I could have done better. What had Esmeralda said? That I've been oblivious to my divine nature, that I've been a bloodstained victim reacting instead of acting? I would have liked to find out what that meant, but it's too late now.

Annie opened her eyes. The world bumped and jerked and moved away from her. She was not dead; she realized much to her amazement. What she was, was torn apart. She could make out her body as it receded away from her. Or to be more exact, she receding from it as a wolf dragged her head by the hair into the ocean. She could barely make out the other wolves tearing off the limbs from her torso and loping with them into the direction of the four winds. The westbound wolf passed by on the right, indicating to Annie that her head traveled northwest. Her torso lay in the center of the dispersion, twitching and spurting blood.

As the dark green ocean washed over and finally covered her head, she thought, *This night just keeps getting weirder and weirder.*

PART TWO

Chapter Seven

The Sorcerer Rex hunched on all fours over a small hole in which a white rabbit had taken refuge.

"I'm sorry, all right? The stew joke was clearly out of line, and I apologize," he said into the opening.

Sitting up on his knees, Rex adjusted his flowing purple cotton robes that had bound up under his toes and kneecaps. He tucked his long white hair into the back of his collar and smoothed the length of his white beard. Gently, he inserted both hands into the hole and said to the frightened creature, "There now, my friend, I mean you no harm. I merely require a sample of your hair for my collection. Green-eyed bunnies are a rarity."

With further coaxing, the sorcerer carefully pulled the rabbit out of the hole and cuddled it next to his chest. Waving his hand, he produced a claw-handled brush and glided it over the animal's pristine fur. "Only want what you're losing anyway," he said. Humming a tune whose origin he couldn't put his finger on, he became lost in the melody. "You know," he said failing to edit himself, "there's an order of wizards that would pay highly for a pair of green rabbit eyes."

At that the rabbit thrashed in Rex's clutch and wiggled free, jumping to the ground and bounding away.

"Not that I would!" he called after the rabbit. "I would never do that. Oh, bother, what's wrong with me today? My mind is so muddled; I'm collecting specimens and being rude, when I should be paying attention to any sign that might present itself."

Rex pulled at his beard and looked in the direction of the fleeing rabbit. "Please tell me that wasn't one of the signs, and I just ruined 21 years of work. What a tragedy that would be, after a lifetime of work to get to this point, this moment in time that comes once in a thousand years. How could I explain missing this momentous occasion to the brothers? What would I say? 'Sorry, I missed a chance to redeem the world because I was too busy insulting innocent creatures'?" He shook the

51

unthinkable notion from his thoughts. "No, there wasn't a white rabbit in the plan; it's just an anomaly."

The Sorcerer Rex sat down and, redistributing the layers of his clothing, assumed the lotus position. He consigned the brush to a hidden pocket inside his robe and surveyed the quiet valley that stretched out beneath him. The landscape shimmered unnaturally from an approaching wave of heated air, as the late afternoon sun yawned out the latter part of the day. Rex took in a slow, deep cleansing breath of air and worked to enter a meditative state.

Although the journey was long and hard, I know in my mind that I have come to the place where my destiny will be fulfilled. Patience and vigilance are the strengths I must utilize now. How strange to be here, so close to the end. At times it seems like only yesterday when I began, and at other times, like now, it seems so long ago...

Visions of past occurrences rolled across his mind like an ocean fog. A younger version of himself took focus in the mental haze of remembrance. Time seemed to forget her duties as he relived a day years before sitting in the monastery's garden. The imprecision of memory started the scene in late afternoon, but he knew what he recalled actually occurred later in the evening. He breathed in the surrounding flora, stimulating deep olfactory memories. Although in reality, it was a patch of yellow petal jetfire daffodils behind him that sweetened the air, it was not difficult for his mind to reinterpret the aroma as the scent given off by the four o'clock flowers of the monastery. The flower only blooms in the early evening, yet thoughts about the monastery always involved that smell, no matter what time of the day or season of the year he thought about.

How I loved to sit in the garden when the temperature dropped and smell the rich fragrance released by the opening of the Mirabilis Jalapa. *Such a beautiful flower, such deadly seeds.*

He had been pledged to the monks by his birth parents, who he never knew, in exchange for a miracle the monks had performed to save his parent's village years before. The monks raised him, cared for him, taught him, and ordained him into their order. He was only 21 when he was welcomed into the "Brotherhood of the Sacred Spear"; the youngest person in the Order's history to receive full admittance.

Nine o'clock in the evening was the actual time of the event he recalled, despite his memory's reconstruction using details from various serene afternoons of youth. It was the evening of his 21st birthday, he reminisced with clarity, when the head of the Order, Brother Joseph, had come to him.

"Brother Rex, how are you tonight?"

"I'm well, Brother Joseph, and you?"

"Oh, you know how it is," Brother Joseph sighed. "My bursitis is acting up again." As if to confirm the statement, the balding elder monk hobbled over and sat down next to Rex on the wooden bench with a groan. A smile replaced the expression of discomfort on Brother Joseph's goateed face as he settled into the seat. His forest green robe contrasted with Rex's tan robe, highlighting the difference between student and teacher; untilled earth versus actualized growth.

"Rest, ice, compression and elevation is the answer to that problem," Rex prescribed. "I think Brother Hendrix is still about—he could give you another acupuncture session. That helped last time."

"Yes, that was relaxing and took my mind off the pain. But it's not so bad today. I think I'm in a bit of an emotional state, that's all. Being upset just amplifies the discomfort."

Rex's mind raced to calculate meaning. Brother Joseph upset plus Brother Joseph seeking Rex out equals Rex had done something wrong. A tremor of concern quaked through him, and he ran his hand back over his short bristly hair and across his clean-shaven face, grabbing onto his chin for emotional support. "What's wrong, Brother? What ails you? Have I transgressed?"

"No, Brother, you haven't. Calm yourself; don't lose confidence. You are again thinking you need approval."

Rex inhaled a cleansing breath, released it slowly, and cleared his mind. "Of course, you are right. I meant to ask if there is any way I can be of service."

"Let me ask you, Brother Rex, are you happy here?"

The question perplexed Rex. "Yes, very happy. Are you unhappy with me?"

"Not at all, no. You've given me only joy; you're like a son to me."

"And you're like a father to me. And what better mother than the Order could anyone ask for? Truly, I'm blessed."

"Truly," Brother Joseph replied. He rubbed his knee and gazed about the garden. Finally he looked into the youth's eyes with a painful smile. "You, as you know, were brought to us as a fulfillment of a pledge, but now the obligations of that pledge have been discharged. You've reached the age of 21; you've reached the end of the contract your birth parents made with us. It is time for you to leave."

Rex's heart and face both fell in disbelief. "Leave? How can this be?" He cried out a sorrowful wail and threw himself at Brother Joseph's feet. "I have transgressed against you and the Order. Oh, forgive me, Brother, forgive me! I will perform whatever penance you choose. I will fast the cycle of eight moons, eating only the morsels of knowledge that fall gracefully from your holy lips. I will tear out my teeth and pray 40 days and nights in the freezing rain. I will live out the rest of my days in ash and sackcloth. Anything, I will do anything, but please, Brother, please do not banish me from my beloved home. Please do not banish me from you, my beloved father. I implore you, do not do this thing! *Mea culpa, mea culpa, MEA CULPA!*"

"Stand up, Brother Rex! By the stars, you're carrying on like a fledgling. Have you been spending time around Brother Simon again? Where else could you have learned such groveling and self-abasement? Certainly not from my instruction and, I dare say, not by my example!"

Soberly, Rex stood up. He searched his teacher's eyes and, finding that the sternness was motivated by love, sat down beside him again. "No, Brother," he answered regaining control of himself. "You've only offered wise counsel in the ways of reason, and your example has been nothing more than the realization of that wise counsel. And to be truthful, only a small group of us have been keeping company with Brother Simon. He just seems so interesting."

"He's an agitator given to fits of mania. Although entertaining, his thoughts are compromised by bad biology and infect the minds of others like a virus."

"Yes, Brother," Rex submitted.

"Don't grieve so, Rex," Brother Joseph soothed, switching to a familiar form of address. "I tell you the truth, you have *not* transgressed."

"Then why do you doom me to the worst fate imaginable? To be banished from this place will only find me dead in a week from a broken heart."

Brother Joseph smiled, "So much drama. Well, the hallmark of youth I suppose—hormonal overload. In time it will balance out."

"That may be, but at this moment I am drowning in despair."

"You underestimate yourself. This is not easy for me either, you know. I love you. It is because I love you that you must go. Walk with me, Rex, and I will explain."

Rex steadied his beloved mentor as they walked through the aromatic gardens. With the sun tucked away for another day, the music of the night began. Small things scurried, insects chirped and buzzed, and an evening breeze rustled leaves.

"When you were brought to us," Brother Joseph explained, "it was with the understanding that we raise you in the spirit of the Brotherhood."

Rex nodded his head, thoughtfully, "To pierce through appearances, to seek the eternal which lies underneath, to go beyond form to that which is formless."

"Yes, and you learned well and became ordained. But, tell me, have you noticed any difference between you and the other monks?"

"None other than the obvious, that all are at different levels of understanding, and this must eternally be so, though we judge not one level against the other."

"Forests and trees, Rex, forests and trees. Have you not noticed that you're the youngest person in the monastery? Even though throughout your life many have come and gone, you remain the youngest."

Rex raised his eyebrows and cocked his head in acknowledgment to what was now obvious, but had never occurred to him before. "My goodness, it's true—how odd. I must have grown so used to it that it seemed normal and not strange. Why is this so important, and more directly, does this difference have a connection to the High Council's plan to banish me?"

"Rex, you are *not* being banished. Please contain your hysterical paranoia."

"I apologize," he nodded, respectfully.

The old man swayed his head with clear exasperation. "Brother Simon, again?"

"Undoubtedly," Rex conceded. "But please continue so I can learn the truth."

"You are the youngest, because all others who come here seek solace from a meaningless life. They come here after life has eaten away at them, they come here broken and in need of healing. You, however, came as an innocent and grew up within these walls oblivious to the harshness of life."

"Is this not good?"

"No, my son, it isn't. Knowledge without experience is empty, a useless tool. A holy man alone on the mountain is like a corpse in a tomb; he is always true to himself but, cut off from life, he rots away and is of no use. You have come to a time in your life when you must go into the world and not only utilize all that we have taught you, but also add to your knowledge through participation in the outside world—the real world. Once done, return to us if you wish, you are always welcomed at our table."

Brother Joseph's words deeply troubled Rex. However, the more he thought about them, the more he could see the truth in them, and the more he could see that he had no reasonable choice in the matter. If he did not accept the journey Brother Joseph had offered, then he could no longer be a member of the Brotherhood; for a monk of the Sacred Spear must accept whatever quest was presented to him in order to deepen his wisdom. To refuse a quest was to truly be banished.

As they walked in silence a strange thing began to happen. Rex began to wonder, stronger than he had ever done before, what the outside world was really like. The stories the other monks told about their adventures outside the walls took on a new weight. It was as if a veil lifted from his eyes, and he began to question why he had never asked to go. After all, the outside experiences seemed to help the others achieve a wisdom that Rex once thought out of his reach due to his youth. But now he saw that it was not his youth alone that kept him from a deeper wisdom; it was his limited experience of the world. Too long had he tarried within the sheltering walls of the monastery. Rex soon found himself wanting to go, needing to go, on the verge of demanding to go.

"Oh, Brother, what a fool I've been to be content with life within these walls."

"You are assaulting yourself again, Rex."

"Brother Simon," they sang out in unison.

When their laughter quieted, Brother Joseph continued, "Let's look at this clearly. Leaving too soon may have proven disastrous. We had to prepare you for the time of your departure. We've given you the basic tools for life: compassion, reason, logic, self-reliance and resiliency. These are the tools that will aid you as you meet the challenges ahead. The time to go is now; to stay past this time would be foolish."

"You speak truly as always, Brother Joseph," Rex acknowledged, not noticing he had been led to the monastery gates, "and I accept my path. Tell me, Brother, what must I do?"

"You must complete three tasks before you can return. The first two tasks are preparations for the third. It is the third task that the High Council believes is your best destiny. You know what that means, don't you?"

"Yes, I remember your patient instructions very well. One's best destiny is not a thing etched into eternity, but rather it is a course of high probability. One may deviate from this course and forge other destinies, but disharmony is likely to result."

"Well spoken."

The two monks reached the main gate, where two other monks emerged from the shadows to meet them. One handed Rex a bag to wear on his back, and the other presented him with a staff and a purple robe. Rex knew the significance of the color; it was only given to monks on a quest.

"Speak to me, Brother, the hour grows late, and I must make haste."

The elderly monk smiled with pride at Rex's enthusiasm, the smile contained a wisp of sadness in anticipation of the tribulations that lay ahead for the youth. "Very well, my son, hear me now. The first task of preparation is to master the visible material world, and the second task of preparation is to master the unseen material world."

"And the goal?"

"You will lead a life of service to others until you perform a great healing. Once the great healing has taken place, you shall have fulfilled the task and can return to us, if you wish, and join the High Council."

"It shall be done," Rex swore, solemnly. He knew it was senseless to ask for details, for no quest a monk undertook contained details. The nature of the journey was to always keep the tasks in one's forethoughts and move toward them, creating out of daily circumstances the very fabric of the quest.

The gates opened, and Rex felt the chill of the outside. He turned to Brother Joseph, and they embraced. It was an embrace that would give him strength in the years to come, an embrace that would turn doubt into determination. And the final words of Brother Joseph as the gates closed behind Rex, would provide him amusement during troubled times.

"Someone bring me Brother Simon!"

Images of the past faded, and Rex returned his focus to the valley, yet the memory of the embrace still lingered, filling Rex with sentiment. *All these years. It has been 21 years since my 21st birthday. Twenty-one years since I left the Order and Brother Joseph. Twenty-one years and only one task left to do. I only have to fulfill a destiny in order to return back to the monastery and sit on the High Council.*

I never dreamed it would take 21 years to complete this journey, but that's journeys for you. Ten years to master the visible material world and 10 years to master the unseen world. All that work to prepare for the final and core task—to perform a great healing. Took me a year to calculate when and where that would most likely happen. It's here; it's now. I'm sure of it. The dragon Holdfast will be reborn after a thousand years and bare the sacred key of Fornix. A very powerful key indeed; said to have great healing power.

A troubled look overcame Rex's face as a piece of unfinished business made itself known, challenging his obtainment of a blissful future. *They would never allow me on the High Council unless I forgot all about her. If they ever even knew about her, it would endanger my appointment chances. Of course, I cannot conceal the facts. I must give a full honest accounting, but it has to be seen as just a past indiscretion. No matter, my stupidity and arrogance has taken care of that problem. She doesn't want anything to do with me anymore. It's just as well,* he tried to convince himself, but the churning in his stomach indicated his failing at self-deception.

Okay, I must manage my thoughts and regain my concentration.

Rex reached into his timeworn leather backpack and produced a pencil and writing tablet. Putting pencil tip to paper, he made eight points with 12 connecting lines forming a cube. The cube offered a simple optical illusion. The upper-most square appeared, at first, to be the front. As he stared at the geometric figure, the bottom-most square suddenly emerged as being closest to him. The cube drawing shifted perspective in Rex's mind, and he meditated on the paradox of the material world.

In the large material world, objects follow predictable patterns that can be measured. In the unseen world, material that makes up the larger world collapses in on itself. It pops in and out of existence; the wave is the particle—the particle the wave. There is no predictability. Yet all this anarchy masses together to create the predictable and the probable. To see the truth, one must see the point of a singularity not as a point, but as the top of a string of density with length and volume. One must view the paradox as it transitions from one reference point to the other and back again. Eternally zooming out and then zooming in. Certainty into chaos and back again.

The illusion of the paradoxical cube turned and twisted in his mind. Transcendence overcame him as he contemplated the nature of things, the unseen world beneath all things...

...the curve of her thigh as it slopes gently upward beneath soft linens that cascade over hips and pool around a soft, firm belly. The scent of sandalwood permeating everything around her, drawing me in with an intoxicating allure...

Rex's breathing had deepened, quickened, along with his heart rate. Clenching his jaw, he twisted and crumpled the paper around the pencil, and then broke the pencil in half with a frustrated, "Graahh!" He looked around embarrassed; glad no one was present to see the tantrum.

"Well, that was professional!" he scolded himself, his voice sounding flat in the still air. Coaching himself, he said, "Okay, Rex, you can do this. You are the Sorcerer Rex, for crying out loud. Didn't get this far due to incompetence. Still, to be lost again in those eyes... No! Now, come on, Rex, get it together. You can wallow in your regret all you want later. But for now—everything depends on now."

The Sorcerer Rex shook all preoccupations from his mind and sat in full concentration on the valley below. All his energy focused on preparing for the final task, which he felt certain would happen today and in this place. He became oblivious to everything around him; focused solely on the valley, fully centered, single minded, unshakable, undistractible...

...except for that one curious thing happening outside the corner of his left eye.

At first, he disregarded it as only a test from some tormentor who meant to shatter his focus.

But isn't that a human hand breaking the surface of the ground, followed by another hand? Ridiculous! Be gone tormenting illusion! But isn't that a pair of legs kicking their way out of the dirt? The sorcerer could no longer dismiss the intruding image when the muffled sound of a cry reached his ear.

"By thunder! There's someone coming out of the ground!"

Rex jumped up and rushed over to the flaying appendages. He reached down, grabbed a waving arm, and pulled the person out of the ground.

Annie shook dirt from her hair and face. She blinked her eyes in wide amazement. "Where am I?" she coughed.

Chapter Eight

Creatures that never knew the light of day hid cowering in darkened corners as the ogre king, Gororm, stormed down the stone hallway. His red eyes glowed through the poorly lit passage, tearing through the patches of blackness like a hot coal through flesh. The sound of his heavy feet pounding out a quick stride resounded thickly off the dank oozing walls.

"Zoila!" he bellowed. "Where is that whore daughter of mine?" he asked aloud to no one. He scowled as he continued his search through twisting corridors.

"Damn her, if she's late!" he cursed. Stopping for a moment, he raked a large gnarled hand across his thick lips and meaty face. He flung away the glob of mucus and saliva that had collected on his hand during the gesture.

The low timbre of his voice vibrated against the stones as he growled, "I didn't spend years preparing her for this moment just so she can piss it all away. If I didn't need humans of the same blood, I could have done this myself, instead of relying on Zoila and her worthless and disloyal sister, Arias. Is all this worth the aggravation of taking humans under my care? Curses on them for being the ones born on that fateful day of Gemini!"

King Gororm's fists tightened with his growing rage. He exploded once again through the corridors, making his way out of the drafty stone castle he headed for the courtyard. The thick leather of his battle uniform creaked as connective chains whipped about him, and his broad sword trailed behind, wavering in his wake.

"Zoila!" he roared, entering the fading daylight in the courtyard.

A smile twisted cruelly under his bulbous nose, forcing two tusk-like bottom teeth to protrude a little more. He walked at a measured pace through the green haze of a low-hanging stench in the courtyard. The king proudly approached the 40 horseback mounted ghoul warriors.

They were in perfect formation, patiently awaiting the order to move out. His wife, Queen Dezair, who was an ogre trained in alchemy and necromancy, had concocted them using the darkest of magic. They were a scrawny lot, measuring less than two meters in height. Bubbly sacks of pus spotted their dark olive green skin, where the cauldron had over-heated their forming flesh. Although small in stature, the queen created them to be single-minded in purpose and vicious. Underneath the black leather hoods that draped down past their necks, were frightful faces of bulging insane eyes and lipless mouths crammed with razor sharp teeth. One look at them was certain to immobilize a person with fear. Besides the hood, they wore only a sword belt; the lack of clothing and acces-sories enhancing speed and attack intensity.

"My personal army," he announced to the ranks. He thoughtlessly brushed away the flies that constantly flew around him, and then contin-ued to address the ghoul soldiers, "Destiny has found me fit to smile upon. I was born at a time when I find myself king at the exact point when the dragon Holdfast rises again. Only once a millennium does this opportunity come. And it comes to me!"

King Gororm reached out and stroked the nose of one of the horses; it did not flinch or move. Careful breeding, combined with secret invo-cations, produced deaf horses with no sense of smell and a nervous sys-tem that registered only strong stimuli.

Queen Dezair crossed the courtyard to join her husband. Her weight visibly shifted under her clothing as she walked, and the sunlight played reluctantly on her fleshy, warted face.

"What are you out here shouting about?" she said to Gororm.

"My queen, you have done a magnificent job. These horses are per-fect for battle, steady and undistracted," he praised.

The queen bowed her fat head to acknowledge the compliment. "Thank you, husband."

"Unfortunately," Gororm added, "your magic isn't strong enough to get to Arias."

"Leave it to you to hide a dagger in a gift of roses," she sneered.

"It's no matter; with the dragon freed and its power in my hands, we'll take care of our traitor daughter Arias."

The queen nodded in agreement. "Arias is a fool. She doesn't under-stand what you're trying to do, doesn't understand how it is best for the kingdom to unchain the dragon."

The king walked up to one of the ghouls and turning to Dezair said, "Completely obedient and steadfast, eh?"

"Completely," she assured.

"You!" he called out, pointing to one of the ghouls. "Dismount."

The creature leapt from his mount without hesitation and stood at attention in front of the king.

Gororm's eyes burned red, and he shouted at the unwavering soldier, "Zoila knows how important this is to me, to the family, to the whole kingdom for that matter. She's toying with me, thinks it's funny. I wonder how funny she would find it if I snapped her filthy neck!" With that, the king grabbed the ghoul's chin with one hand, and snaked the other behind its head. In one sharp motion, Gororm broke its neck. The ghoul collapsed to the ground as a lump of green, lifeless flesh.

"What was that for?" Dezair demanded. "They don't grow on trees, you know. It takes a long time to cook up a batch."

"Just a field test, my queen." He eyed the rest of the army of which none had so much as flinched. "Damn impressive."

"What would be impressive," the queen said, her voice full of scorn, "is if you'd shite out a replacement soldier."

Gororm glared at her. "Are you so thick as to not see the grand design? I have masterminded the perfect plan. For years I've carefully put the pieces together; laid them in place."

"Did you hit your head on a low doorway again? Or have you forgotten all the research I put into this campaign?" Dezair spat.

"Of course I have not forgotten. Can't I just have a moment in front of the troops?"

The queen muttered curses under her breath and headed back to the castle. As she walked away she said, "I don't have time to listen to another fit of grandeur. Enjoy your delusion, I'd rather take a mallet to my head then hear it."

Rolling his eyes at her departure, Gororm turned his attention to the ghouls. He spread his arms and boasted, "I will be remembered always as the ogre king who brought ultimate order and peace into the land. It must happen this way! The people long for a strong leader. All it takes is a cause to rally behind, and they will follow. Win the minds and fill the coffers! The time is ripe; I reign as Supreme Commander-In-Chief. The troops stand ready to be led by their unsuspecting human leader who... who is still not here!"

Gororm turned in a circle, searching the courtyard for the princess. "Zoila!"

Zoila sat on the stony ground of the mountaintop, sternly staring straight ahead with tension holding her mouth firm. She had her dark brown hair pulled back tight and tied into a small ponytail with thin straps of turquoise adorned leather. She was dressed for battle. The thick leather shoulder covers connected to a section of padded chain mail, protecting her chest and abdomen. Over sturdy black pants, she wore a codpiece to shield her groin. Her darkly stained boots rose above her knees and provided padding for those joints. At 32 years of age, she was a formidable looking figure. Tall and athletic, with muscles hard and enlarged from years of stressing them to the point of failure, and then allowing them to rest and grow strong.

She sat with her legs crossed in front of her and a broad sword lying across her lap. Beside her, a small, rock-encircled fire glowed out of existence. She might have been thinking of the coming campaign, where she would lead her father's army of ghouls into battle, or she might have been thinking of the lifetime of warrior training she had endured and mastered. But, these were not part of her thoughts as her eyes, one blue and one brown, stared ahead, burning with anger inside her strong face.

In front of Zoila stood the target of her intensity, a large crystal that contained her imprisoned sister, Arias. Arias, her twin with which she shared a womb, but not an egg, sat inside the crystal looking weak and tired. She once had strong features like Zoila, except they had never been chiseled into harshness but, now in her illness, her face and body appeared pale and fragile. Arias shifted a little in her translucent cell, her brown hair bouncing gently on the coarse robe that hung from her shoulders and lost interest above her knees, leaving her legs exposed down to where sandals finished the job of clothing her. Around her waist she had fastened a piece of rope, and on the rope hung small trinkets that she fumbled with and caressed between failing fingers. She too stared straight ahead, but her soft hazel eyes did not harbor anger. They were mournful as she looked back into Zoila's eyes, and then she began to hum a soft wispy tune.

The humming animated Zoila, who sprung up with sword in hand and paced in front of the crystal. "Damn you!" Zoila spat. "Don't start singing again, I'm warning you. How can you go on and on, day after day, trapped inside that crystal and still sing and smile when you can manage it? Why do you not cry out and curse my name?"

Zoila often stole away to secretly check on her sister. It wasn't that she worried her sister might die; she knew the crystal would keep her alive, although weak. It was that she... didn't want to think about why she came to visit. It only intensified her anger.

Arias began singing softy, her gentle voice a breeze from a distant land.

> "In the dawning, in the dawning,
> I hear you calling, calling, ooh calling for me,
> And you're falling, falling, ooh falling away from me,

Zoila sneered at the verse. "Fine, you go ahead and sing—sing your demented brains out for all I care. It's entirely your fault you're in this situation anyway." Zoila stopped pacing and targeted her wrath directly at Arias. "You just didn't want to listen to anyone, did you? Had to go around the villages shooting off your big mouth about equality and justice and all that other verbal fodder you so carelessly spew. Just had to piss off dad, didn't you? You don't know, you just don't know, you have no clue, do you?"

Arias stood silently taking in Zoila's anger. Her words caused Arias to weaken and appear faded, but she never lost her smile or eye contact; she continued to look with admiration on her sister.

Arias's tranquil response only served to fuel Zoila's outburst. "Life was always so easy for you, and do you even know why, do you even care? Oh, I'm sure you care, you care about all things: all creatures weak and strong, burdened men, weeping women, lost children, and the whole bloody universe for that matter. But did you ever stop to care about me? Did you ever know the beatings I took for you?" A lump formed in Zoila's throat, and she fought hard not to lose her composure and break down in front of Arias.

The crystal sparkled as if invaded by a swarm of fireflies, and Arias looked away from her sister, giving Zoila time to recover.

With clenched teeth, Zoila resumed her tirade. "I'm your sister, older by an hour and stronger, I could withstand the force of his large hands, but you, you were not so strong. What else could I do, but protect you? You were all I had in the world after we were taken from our parents and given to the king and queen. So, I took beatings for you, but you didn't care, you continued to do as you pleased, wandering around the countryside like an insane prophet rousing the masses. Why couldn't you just keep your mouth shut? I was going to take care of everything, but you just wouldn't stop! Why did you keep talking, why can't you just, for once, shut up!"

Zoila let loose a war cry and attacked the crystal, slamming into the stone with her sword. "Stupid! Stupid! Stupid!" Zoila stepped back unevenly, her strikes having no effect on the sparkling formation or on her sister. "Do you know anything about pain? Huh? Huh? Anything?"

The furious woman picked up a small hot coal and grasped it tightly in her fist. "This is pain, Arias, this is suffering, this is what you couldn't take if you tried. You're weak, and so I had to constantly protect your ass!" Flicking the coal out of her hand, Zoila pressed her burnt palm against the crystal for her sister to see.

Arias pressed her hand against the clear wall in front of Zoila's wounded palm. Zoila shook her head with an apathetic chuckle as Arias began to sing again.

> *"In the blinding, in the blinding,*
> *I hear you crying, crying, ooh, crying for me,*
> *And you're flying, flying, ooh, flying away from me,*
> *In the blinding, in the blinding.*
>
> *In the sighting, in the sighting,*
> *Will you bleed, bleed, ooh, bleed for me?*
> *Do you have a seed, seed, ooh, seed for me?*
> *In the sighting, in the sighting."*

"You're so hopeless; do you know that, Arias?" Zoila asked without expecting an answer. She pressed her cheek to the cool surface and traced her finger around a keyhole in the crystal. "You just stay in there and sing your little songs; it's better this way. You would have only messed everything up, but once the dragon's power is in my hands... well, I'll take care of everything... "

Zoila smiled wickedly at Arias as her finger found its way into the keyhole, "... everything."

Zoila turned away suddenly. She looked down at her palm and saw that the burn had healed. Her face tightened again. Sheathing her sword, Zoila strode boldly to her waiting horse. She mounted the stead, taking immediate control of the animal and, with a final sneer toward her imprisoned sister, she spurred the horse down a rocky path.

I'm late, Zoila ruminated as she negotiated the hillside. *I'm sure that bastard king-father of mine is pulling his disgusting hair out. Well, let him. He doesn't dare touch me now. He needs me, at least for a time. But the times are changing, you ignorant ogre.*

Arias watched Zoila disappear down the slope of the mountainside. Loneliness enveloped her, weighing heavy like a wet wool winter coat. She welcomed it. Seeing her sister was always bittersweet. She loved her as her own flesh, and yet witnessing Zoila's pain and rage filled her with disconsolation.

They'll be here soon. No doubt about that.

Arias looked around the edge of the small plateau. It would not be long before people rose above the crest of the ground. She knew they were hiding on the mountainside, pressed in fear against the dirt, entangled in the brush. Hiding and waiting for Zoila to leave.

They love to come in the evening, when the sun bleeds out the last of his light. What strange notions they have... that I'm a goddess—the Crystal Princess. They come and press their aching bodies against my wall, hoping for a healing, for some peace. And they think they find it. But it is just a trick, an illusion. The sun warms the crystal and they absorb that warmth. The light of the evening sun splashing into the crystal has a hypnotic effect on them. To them it feels like a divine blessing. I've tried to explain, tried to ward them off, tried to warn them to stop looking to me for answers. They think I'm being modest but, in truth, the only one I can heal is Zoila.

Arias stretched as best she could in her confinement. She was depleted. The populace that came in the evening quickly drained what energy she accumulated during the day's solitude. Each day it became harder and harder to recover; here it was evening and she was already running on empty.

Oh, Zoila, forgive me, forgive me. If I told you my plan, if you knew what was to come, you wouldn't believe it. If I could accomplish this burden quickly, I would. I do so hate to see you suffer. I hope that, once it is over, you will forget the days of pain and revel in the glory.

A twig snapped, earth scuffed under feet and Arias readied herself. The peasants slowly appeared climbing up the steep slopes, looking like zombies arising from the grave. Cautiously, they peered for any sign of Zoila. Seeing the area deserted, they came to the crystal. Hobbling, moaning, they came. With broken bodies and weary minds, they came. Filled with a hope that ignores reason and reality, they came. They came to touch the crystal, to be healed by the Crystal Princess.

Queen Dezair frothed at the mouth, cursing the day as Zoila galloped into the courtyard and pulled her horse to a stop in front of the ghoul army. "Zoila!" Queen Dezair called out, sharply. "Where have you been? Your father has been looking all over for you. You've put him in a foul mood, you ungrateful wench."

"Hello, Mother," Zoila greeted, wryly. She strained on the right rein, turning her mount around toward the queen.

"It's your Highness, when I'm angry, damn you. Now get your fat ass off that filthy beast and come with me."

Zoila obediently dismounted and waited for her mother to propel her large crude body over to her.

"What the hell are you looking at?" the queen asked with a slap to Zoila's face. "You smooth, peach-skinned bitch."

Zoila returned her face forward and averted her eyes as was expected of her.

Her mother shook her large head and wiped the spittle from her mouth. "Now look, you've got me hitting you again. Why do you make me hit you? I don't understand it. Especially on such a glorious day for our family when your father's plans will see life."

"I don't know why I'm wicked and ungrateful, Mother, I am sorry for the pain I've caused you both," Zoila responded with rehearsed lines.

"Come on, your father, the king in case you've forgotten, is waiting for you in the command tent. I'll try to calm him, but I don't doubt he'll just beat the piss out of you anyway," Dezair snarled, narrowing her bulgy eyes.

As they covered the short distance to the tent, the queen ranted at the woman beside her. "Because of your delay, the king has been reduced to flights of fancy thinking he is the great mastermind. Phewt!" She gave Zoila's shoulder a push, and then said, "He didn't know the truth behind the legends; he wasn't mastered in the ancient arts. It was *I* who came upon the knowledge of the dragon's power; it was *I* who divined that the millennium was upon us; it was *I* who knew only a human divided could break the chain that binds the dragon, and only a human divided could receive the dragon's gift. What more divided can a human be, then sisters born of the same belly on the same day?"

Zoila remained stoic as they headed toward Gororm's command tent. She forced her thoughts onto other images, so the queen's vile harangue would not evoke a careless reaction.

As if lost in her own thoughts, the queen mumbled more than spoke to Zoila. "Took you two in after your parent's unfortunate accident and raised you as our own, and all we ask is that you help us do one lousy thing. Once Arias left, all we had was you to help us, but you only show us contempt. But, it only takes one human to receive the gift."

Dezair slid to a stop in her footsteps, her weight not allowing a sudden halt. She grabbed Zoila's arm as if to hold on to a fleeting thought whose importance demanded a second look. Speaking to something in the distance, Dezair muttered, "But it does take you both to complete the final deed."

The queen shook her head clear of the complication, pushed Zoila back into motion and followed behind. "No matter," she announced. "Once we have the gift, we'll turn our efforts toward your sister, Arias. I only wish I knew who put that spell on her. It seems so familiar, yet I can't find it in anywhere in the workshop, and I can't seem to break it. But I will, with help from the gift, I will."

Before entering the tent where King Gororm waited, Dezair turned to Zoila and said, "You know you're going to get your head knocked around, don't you?" She pulled Zoila into the tent and pushed her toward Gororm, who stood waiting among carelessly placed maps and charts.

"Here, husband, I found the *mistake* wandering around like an idiot in the courtyard."

A look of surprise overcame Dezair, as the king smiled and said, "Now, now, dear, is that any way to talk about our daughter? Zoila, are you all right? I was getting worried about you."

Dezair rolled her hideous eyes upward and murmured, "Oh, for the love of the damned."

"I'm fine, Father," Zoila responded. "I was making some last minute preparations for the mission."

"You hear that, my Queen?" Gororm laughed. "She was making last minute preparations. That's our Zoila, always thinking of the mission, always thinking of the family. You do love your family, don't you, Zoila?" the king asked, putting a coarse hairy arm around her.

"Of course, Father, your Highness, the family is everything to me. I only wish I were not so ugly, but beautiful like you and mother."

"Well, don't worry about that, we love you just the way you are, don't we, dear?"

"Yes, we do," the queen sighed with a slow head shake.

"See there? Now, Zoila," he stared into her eyes, "you will severe the chain, yes? That's very important to our cause."

"I have been practicing my archery with diligence."

"Good, good. And the dragon's gift?"

"It is to be returned to you, so that you may usher in a glorious era for our family."

"That's right!" the king giddily exclaimed. "That's right! Oh, what a good girl you are, yes, you are."

Dezair sidled up to her husband. She put one meaty arm around his back and rested her warted face on his shoulder. "Go then, brave daughter, and earn the honor our family so nobly deserves."

Zoila nodded respectfully and backed out of the tent. On her way out the king said, "Just damn proud of her." She knew the comment was an act for her benefit, and that as soon as she was away, they would plot her demise.

Zoila quickly covered the distance between the tent and her war-horse, happy to finally breathe some fresh air. *You can take your honor and your family and shove them up your filthy holes, you decrepit pigs!*

She paused briefly before mounting in order to clear her head. *Okay, Zoila, keep it together. You have a mission to do and you have to stay sharp to avoid the thousand different ways it could all go wrong. One thing I do know, it isn't going to turn out the way mommy and daddy think it will.*

She mounted and reared her horse, and then rode back and forth across the ranks, wishing she had her human soldiers, her comrades, to ride with instead of these ghouls. Her mother had insisted though, probably to limit witnesses who might talk about the mysteries that lay ahead. Zoila was not keen on talking witness either, so having the ghouls worked in her favor, too. *Still, I feel empty, unarmed, without my men by my side.*

"Move out!" she ordered to the troops, and they responded without hesitation. She felt a comfort overcome her as she began doing what she did best—lead solders into battle.

Chapter Nine

Annie fought desperately against the swirling whirlpool of disorientation that threatened to suck her back into the black void she had traveled through. Only moments before she had been set upon by a pack of black wolves. They had dismembered her body and dragged her head into the sea. Now, instead of being emerged in dark, green salty water, she was spitting and coughing out black dirt in front of the strange looking man who had pulled her from the ground. She took a quick, dizzy look around her as she swept the dirt out of her eyes. She was on a green plateau overlooking a river-intersected valley. Off in the distance she could see the beginnings of a great foreboding forest.

Looking down on herself, she noticed her flesh was still exposed all the way down to her feet—*their* feet. Her gaze slowly worked its way up the gentleman's body: his sandaled feet, his purple robes with strange gold symbols woven into it, his long white beard and bushy white hair. She looked into his face. He looked puzzled or maybe he was feeling inconvenienced, but whatever the temporary expression was, she could see a twinkle of kindness deep in his sparkling blue eyes.

"You are naked," Rex observed.

Annie folded her arms and covered her breasts while clamping her thighs together and turning to the side. Still jumbled in her thoughts from the journey, she coughed out some dirt and replied, "Yeah, I know. Do you have any clothes or a blanket or something?"

"Yes, of course, how rude of me." He reached into his bag and produced a pair of walking shorts, a loose light shirt, a pair of underwear, some sandals, and a bra. "Here, these should fit you well enough. Oh, let me give you a towel and some soap. You can go to the river below and bathe the dirt off of you. Follow this little trail on down. It will lead to a small inlet free of any dangerous currents."

"Thank you," she said, taking the items and clutching them to her chest. After Rex had turned his back toward her, she slipped on the sandals and made her way down the winding pathway until she came to the quiet inlet. Finding a flat rock, she laid down the towel and clothes, held onto the soap, and flipped off the sandals. She looked up the hill and saw Rex pacing slowly around his camp area.

I guess he's not going to follow and try to sneak a peek, not that he hasn't seen all there is to see anyway. Well, he seemed nice enough, I didn't feel like he wanted to touch me or hurt me. I wonder why I always assume everyone wants to do something to me? That's stupid; I know exactly why I think that way, 'cause so many people have. Could it be there are some people who will just treat me like a person? Of course, there is the question of why he had girls' clothes in his bag. That's weird—though not any weirder then what's happened in the last... how many hours? Well, we'll see.

She waded knee-deep into the cleansing waters and sat down. The shallow water of the inlet was sun-warm with swirling eddies that flushed in from the river for a visit. They caressed their way around her body before bidding a fond farewell and rejoining the timeless waterway that rushed down into the valley. Splashing water on her upper torso and head, she stood up again. Annie rubbed the soap bar between her hands and breathed in.

Is that strawberry and vanilla? It smells great.

The soap produced a trail of froth swirls, mapping out the travels of her circling hand. She scrubbed herself with her knuckles until her skin tingled with freshness, and she felt reborn. Smelling the soap again, she shrugged and used it to work up lather in her hair, and then washed her face. Hesitating for a moment, she fought back a skipping heartbeat and a lump in her belly.

What if I go underwater and come back up somewhere else? Somewhere bad. Fine time to think about that with a head full of soap! If things are going to change again, then there's not much I can do about it. Just have to go with it—what else can I do?

Annie nodded her head slowly and, with a determined set to her chin, sat back down and dunked her head underwater. The sounds of the world disappeared, replaced by the muffled sounds of bubbles rushing gleefully upward from her mouth and nose. Annie wildly worked her hair with her fingers, releasing the soap. Then she erupted out of the water and shook her short hair free of excess water.

Still holding her breath, she slowly opened one eye and then the other. She looked around her. "Whew!" she exhaled.

Okay, I am in the same place; nothing has changed that I can tell. If I can only stay in the same place for a while, maybe I can get my head together. All this twisting reality has me off balance. I don't get it. Am I crazy? Is this some weird kind of insanity? Maybe I'm really in a nuthouse, in a small padded room. Yeah, and the doctors are looking at me through one of those one-way mirrors shaking their heads and saying, "That is one crazy, bitch." Annie chuckled at the thought. *Or maybe I'm dead and this is... what? Heaven?*

Hell? A bad karma joke? Davey and Martha would understand that.

A temperate breeze happened along, and Annie stood up, allowing it to wrap itself around her body as she headed for shore. She picked up the towel and dried herself off.

"Oh dear, oh dear, oh dear," Rex muttered to himself after the girl departed. He punctuated his words with a short-ranged shaking of his head and puttered about, uncertain of what to do with himself.

Oh bother! Unexpected company is such a mixed surprise. Certainly it is nice to have a visit, but what to serve? And such a visitor! I mean really, who arrives by popping up out of the ground? A most peculiar fashion indeed, a most peculiar fashion. What does one offer such a person? Oh, Rex, get hold of yourself. There you go running off again. She's just a girl after all. I'm sure, like any other girl, she will enjoy a nice tea and some cake. And a warm fire might be pleasant after a dip in the water.

With a concrete goal, Rex set about the task of building a small fire. He pondered on whether to cast a fire or build it from scratch. Wanting to occupy himself and stop his mind from wandering, he decided on the traditional method. He forged around the table and among a thin patch of pitch pine and rhododendron.

Rex rummaged through his bag until he found a wad of lint and some flint. He built a small teepee of kindling over the lint, and then struck the flint together. Sparks sputtered from the collision, but fizzed out before finding a purchase in the wad. After several attempts, Rex scowled with disappointment. He looked around, raised a brow, and then took out a Zippo lighter from the folds of his robe. He quickly lit the starter and replaced the lighter. With soft puffs, he encouraged the growth of the flame until the kindling caught. He beamed with pride as he fed small branches to the fledgling fire.

Once satisfied with the fire's size, he glanced down the incline and saw Annie heading back up. *Okay, Rex, be cordial, be kind, and be helpful, but send her on her way quickly—you've got important work to do!*

Annie made her way up the hillside with a new vigor in her step. She couldn't pinpoint the source of her new sense of elation, but knew it had to be more than just the bath. She glanced around the overlook, at the valley, at the river, and the tree line in the distance. *Something about*

this place—it all seems comforting.

She crested the hill and gave the man a goofy wave from her elbow to her fingertips, "Hey."

"Better?" the sorcerer greeted her as she approached.

"Yes, much. Thanks again."

"Nothing of it. Now, I hope you understand I have about a hundred questions to ask you."

"Yeah, I've got questions too, but can I sit down first?"

"Again, convention escapes me. Please do." He gestured to the spread out blanket on the ground on which his staff and backpack rested. "Now, tell me," he started out, "how is it you came to be buried in the earth?"

"I don't know for sure. I was hoping you might know."

"Me? I assure you, my dear; I had no part in the whole affair. I do not make a habit of burying young girls, or anyone for that matter. Well, no one living at least, you know what I mean."

"I just thought maybe you were sent to meet me. I mean, that would make sense, right? Something must make sense around here." Annie began to feel the familiar sensation of welling tears threatening to eradicate her newfound delight. "I'm so confused. I can't keep up with all the strange things that have been happening to me."

"Oh, dear," Rex said with a startle. He rummaged through the hidden folds of his robe. "You're going to cry, here, I have a hankie somewhere."

"No," Annie insisted, sucking back her tears, "I'm not going to cry. I've given up crying."

"Why, that would be a shame. Sometimes a good cry is just what a body needs."

"That's true, but I'm going to stop crying over the little things. I'm tired of it, it sucks, and it never helps."

"Well spoken, my earthy friend," Rex commended. "Tea?" he offered.

Annie nodded, a little uncertain about the offer. She hoped strange events would not follow drinking this tea, but resigned herself to the fact that strange things were bound to happen no matter what.

The sorcerer produced two cups and a steaming pot out of his bag and poured them both a cup of tea. Annie took the cup with a polite smile, not even bothering to be dumbstruck by the magic of pulling a steaming pot of tea out of a small bag that had earlier yielded clothes and toiletries for her.

"Cake?" he offered.

"Yes, thank you," she responded.

He produced a plate with small yellow cake squares. Annie took one with a thank you and bit into it. A soft, tangy lemon taste greeted her mouth from the spongy moistness of the cake. As her teeth closed together, they encountered a thin layer of a sweet, whipped cream filling.

"Mmmm," Annie announced, sharing her pleasure with her host.

"Lemon cream delights. An old couple in the Ucia district makes these. Very nice people—Mr. and Mrs. Patoochie. You know they have been married for 67 years?" The sorcerer took a thoughtful bite with a puzzled look. "Which I always found strange since they are only 50 years old."

"They're very tasty. And that is a handy bag you have. I can understand carrying around the teapot and cake, but the girls' clothes?"

"Strange isn't? The bag is based on expanding awareness theory. Have you heard of it?"

"No," she admitted. "I sorta left school before I could learn very much."

"Oh, what a shame. Well, information is always there when you want to get it. But back to the theory. I admit that even if you had stayed in school you would have not known it since," he smiled and whispered, "I made it up."

Annie giggled.

Rex, full of himself, continued, "Yes, the Theory of Expanding Awareness. It is based on the idea that we as humans have limited attention, focus and ability to see clearly. You never know where a course of action will take you until you pursue that course. That is why many people quit or never attempt long-term endeavors; they can't see the hows. But, as you start on a course of action, things you never saw, opportunities you never thought existed come into your awareness. As you follow up on those, other opportunities show up and so on and so on." He took a sip of tea and bite of cake before continuing. "Soon you're on your way, and the point at which you started seems like such a primitive state of affairs. And that, my dear, is the Theory of Expanding Awareness. So I never know exactly what is in my bag until I'm in a situation in which… well in which I need something."

"That's cool," Annie said, not certain she understood him at all. "I wish I had one. It would have come in handy a few times," she mused, imagining a huge baseball bat and Ogre's head.

"Again, to be honest, it's really just a living metaphor of what you already have," he pointed a steady finger at her head, "in there." Rex settled back on his forearms. "That's what I love about this land, full of living metaphors."

The two sipped tea and snacked on cake in silence as if they were lifelong friends out on an afternoon picnic. The sun had sunk a little further, but had yet to give up on the day.

"Now," Rex began as he sat up, drained his cup of the last dregs of tea, and brushed crumbs from his beard, "let's begin with your name."

"That's one thing I do know. My name is Annie."

"Very good, Annie. You see, things are coming along admirably and falling into order. I am the Sorcerer Rex, High Counselor to the Lords of the Outer Regions, Bard to the Most Honorable (yet snooty) Dragon of the Western Skies, Professor Emeritus at the University of Cosmology, and Questing Member in Good Standing of the Holy Order of the Brotherhood of the Sacred Spear." He swelled with dignity.

"Huh?" Annie squinted at him.

He began to pull nervously at his ear. "Never mind, Sorcerer Rex will do, or just Sorcerer."

"Couldn't I just call you Rex?"

The sorcerer was taken aback with a huff. "Goodness, no. Oh, it is clear you are not from anywhere near here."

Annie shrugged her left shoulder and wondered what the big deal was.

"Such familiarity must be earned. It is reserved for those who have achieved an understanding of life's richness, and you are but a youngster."

"I'm not a youngster," she shot at him.

Rex gave her a questioning look.

"Well," Annie conceded, "not exactly a youngster. I've been through a lot, more than most people my age."

"Yes, but have you mastered it? Do you understand it?"

"Well... no... not yet."

"There it is then. Raw experience, no matter how intense, does not automatically translate into maturity. You must learn to intersect raw experience with wisdom in order to achieve maturity. Please, Annie, do not take offense. These are just words that indicate the position one occupies in life at a certain time. I was once where you are, and I moved on, as you shall move on. Even I have elders I would never think of being familiar with. So let us not quibble over it, but let's examine your situation."

Annie smiled at his concern and interest in her. Whatever occupied his thoughts when she first saw him, appeared to have vanished, and now he seemed completely focused on her. She found this a warm, comfortable arrangement. She did not know, could not know, that the Sorcerer Rex had forgotten he was waiting for the appearance of the magical dragon Holdfast, an event that only occurred once in a thousand years.

It was the event he believed would produce the opportunity to complete his third and final task.

"Tell me, what do you recall before you found yourself buried?" he inquired.

Annie related to him, as best she could, the peculiar events on the beach. How she sat in the ocean at the shoreline, how she had been beckoned to a small tent by the heady aroma of incense and rich music, and how she had encountered the mystical Esmeralda who had shown her the terrors that were rooted inside her.

At the mention of Esmeralda's name, Annie noticed a pained, startled look unfold across Rex's face, but the expression was so quickly controlled that she wasn't sure if she'd imagined the whole thing. The sorcerer listened to the rest of the story patiently, but a little more distracted it seemed, while stroking his chin. She concluded with the wolf attack, gave an exhausted sigh, and sat silently after she finished.

Sucking his teeth, the sorcerer raised a bushy eyebrow. "It would seem you have been sent forth on a great journey, and I dare say there is no turning back."

"A journey? To where? Why?" she asked on the edge of pleading.

"Hard to say where journeys will lead us or what will be found... or lost." Rex grew thoughtful and distance. "Usually though," he continued, shaking something away from his forethought, "we end up where we started, only much wiser."

"You mean home?"

He tipped his cup, only to discover it empty. "Do you desire to go back home?"

His question invited a welling to occur in her eyes, but she fought back with a sharp intake of air. "Home, that sounds so wonderful, but..."

"But what?"

"But I'm not sure what that is. I mean, what I've known as home is not a place I want to go back to, but somehow I feel there must be a place for me—a place where I belong."

"Perhaps that is your journey. Perhaps you are to find not so much where you belong, but *how* you belong. Do you know what I mean?"

"No, not really."

"Well, look at it this way. What you do is more important than where you are. Sometimes we may not have a lot of control over where we are, but often have control over what we do, and that can become the constant in our lives. Of course, that by no means suggests that we shouldn't improve our situation, it only means that the one thing you'll always have is you, so it's important to know who you are and how you fit into your environment, wherever that might be. Do you understand?"

"I guess, so where am I supposed to go, what am I supposed to do?"

"Questions, questions, too many questions," he answered waving his hand as if to clear the air of her inquisitions. "If you are on a journey, the journey will show you the way if you pay attention. Clear your mind of notions, stay sharp; the home you find will be built by the choices you make."

Home. The word seemed foreign on the surface, yet deep down, in places she had not discovered, it resounded with warmth, love and truth.

"So, tell me, Annie," Rex asked as if it was just an afterthought, "this... er, Esmeralda was her name?"

Annie nodded as she took a gulp of the soothing tea.

"Yes, this Es-mer-alda," he stumbled over the name and chuckled awkwardly. "That's a mouthful, huh? But, um, what did she look like?"

"Would that be important?" Annie asked, hopefully.

"Oh, no, no, no," he huffed, attempting to erase the notion. "Just curious. Always curious." He smiled, nervously.

"Oh." She drank some more tea.

"Well," he asked looking more interested in the cleanliness of his fingernails than the question, "did she look, oh, I don't know, happy or well or something like that?"

"She seemed very sure of herself, very confident, if that's what you mean. She was kind and very pretty."

"Of course," he acknowledged, swallowing hard. "No matter, just curious you know. Now back to this journey thing we were discussing."

A twig snapping caught Annie's attention, and she looked over at the brush. Except for a quick glance, Rex didn't seem to register or bother with the sound.

Something's coming—I feel it.

Through a fog Annie heard the sorcerer outline some points he wanted to make about journeys, home, self-discovery, or something of that nature. She couldn't hear very well as she felt the blood leave her face and her eyes bulge. The something had arrived.

Chapter Ten

"By the heavens, child, what is it? You look as if you are going to pass on to the next world," Rex thundered, grabbing Annie's shoulders. He rapidly searched Annie's eyes for signs of severe shock.

Annie pointed one trembling finger to something behind the sorcerer. "Don't... let... them... get me."

Rex looked over his shoulder and saw the silent approach of a white wolf. He sighed with relief and patted Annie's hand in an attempt to comfort.

"It's all right, Annie, she's a friend of mine."

"The wolves... they... they..."

"I know, I know, the wolves at the beach that brought you here in their grisly manner. This is different though—different wolf, different place. I assure you, she comes in friendship."

"How do you know?" Annie asked, not fully convinced.

"Look, see how slowly she approaches—head down and wagging, ears laid back, tail swinging slowly? Trust me, she and I are friends."

The snowy wolf made her way toward the blanket where the two of them still sat. Rex got on his knees and shuffled over to greet her. The wolf put her forepaws on his shoulders and licked his neck, the back of his ears and his face. The sorcerer let out a gentle roll of laughter.

"Hello, my friend. Where have you been these past few days?"

Annie's fear began to subside. In her mind, she instructed herself over and over again, *This is different, there's no danger here, this is different, there's no danger here...*

As the two friends continued to greet each other, Annie found herself entranced with the beauty of this magnificent animal. She visually took in the splendor of the wolf's long legs, her wispy white fur, the clarity of her blue eyes; the image stirred awe within her. Annie edged closer.

Rex noticed Annie's measured approach. "Annie, meet a friend of mine. This is Shiva. Shiva, this is Annie."

Shiva bowed her head slightly and lightly stepped over to Annie.

"Hello," Annie greeted, hesitantly.

The white wolf sniffed the girl quietly and then afforded her the same wet greeting she had given the sorcerer.

Annie giggled.

"She likes you, you must be a good person," Rex commented.

"Oh, I don't know about that," Annie laughed as she rubbed Shiva's silky fur.

"Wolves know," he stated.

"She's so beautiful. Is she yours?"

Rex gave Annie a confused, disconcerting look.

"What? What's wrong? Did I say something stupid?"

The sorcerer replaced his expression with a smile. "I'm sorry, I keep forgetting that you are new here. I should value your curiosity more. Shiva belongs to no one. She is as free as the wind, as old as time, and as wise as the universe. She helped guide me through this land while I sought my quest."

Shiva found a spot on the blanket, circled it a few times to pat the spot down, and curled up beside Annie. She allowed Annie to scratch her behind the ears.

"So you're not from around here either?"

"No, I come from a far away and distant land, much like you, but I didn't arrive in such a bold fashion as you. I walked. I was not so clever as to travel through the ground." Rex paused, but since no chuckle came to honor his quip he continued, "When I got here, Shiva appeared to me, and I've been following her ever since. Sometimes she would walk by my side and sometimes she was nowhere to be found. But you were al-ways there when the path was unclear, weren't you, my noble friend?"

Shiva tagged on a tiny yelp to the end of a long yawn.

"Yes," the sorcerer continued, "wolves hold within their nature the very secrets of the universe."

"What's that?"

"Life through death, creation through destruction. Did you know, for example, that when they hunt a herd of animals, they prey mainly on the sick, the old and the dying, thus cleansing the herd so it doesn't out grow its food supply? And loyalty, oh, yes, they have that, too."

"Where I come from, they're not liked very much. People say they're dangerous."

"Oh, tosh, the cycles of nature have gone on for millions of years, and humans are but one spoke in the wheel, yet we still see ourselves as something separate from nature and entitled. Humph! Did you ever stop to think that to cows, pigs and chickens you are very dangerous?"

"So, you're saying I should be a vegetarian?"

"Be what you want, that's not the point. You could say that you won't eat meat, because you don't want to take a life, but then you will fall into the extremist's trap. For do not fruit and vegetables contain life? And, are you not ending their life by plucking them from the earth or the vine? You would have to sit around and wait for produce to fall or start to rot before you ate anything. There are stories of misguided monks who did this, and I dare say they did not fare very well."

"So there's no real way around it, sooner or later you will kill something to eat?" Annie quizzed.

"That's exactly right, because life feeds off of life and, from that, new life is created. Sooner or later something will feed off of you whether you get consumed by a predator, get bitten by a mosquito, or die and become food for worms and bacteria."

"Gross," Annie winced, sticking out her tongue.

"Quite right, quite right, it is a most unpleasant thought. But the point is... what was my point to this? I was heading somewhere with this whole thing, I'm sure of that."

"How great wolves are?"

"Yes, yes, something like that," the sorcerer said, pulling at his ear. "Well, anyway, what I mean to say is that it's better not to be so judgmental."

The three new friends sat in a comfortable silence as a scented breeze offered the gifts of its motion to them. The fire glowed brighter, as if trying to make up for the fading sunlight.

"I wrote a song about the wolf, you know," Rex hinted.

"Really? You write songs? That's cool, so do I."

"Yes, as a matter of fact, I spent some time as a troubadour."

"Wow. What's a troubadour?"

"A traveling musician of sorts."

"I always wanted to do stuff like that."

"Really, hmm," he paused. "And I wrote a song about the wolf," he hinted again with an air of disinterest.

"Can I hear it?"

"Oh, I don't know," Rex sighed as if put out.

"Please?"

"Well... all right, since your heart is so set on it."

While the sorcerer stood and produced a mandolin from his bag, Shiva sat up and perked her ears as if knowing she was about to be praised. Annie noticed a strange glowing feeling inside her that drew a smile to her face. Annie realized that she felt happy; it had been a long time since she felt so at ease. All her life she had lived in familiar places and always felt uncomfortable. But, here she was in a very strange place, on a pleasant early evening, with a strange, yet kindly man, and she felt a deep, peaceful familiarity.

Maybe, I did die after all, she thought to herself. *Or maybe, I am dying right now, and this is one of those death experiences I hear people talking about on talk shows. Well, whatever it is, I wish it would last. I could sit here forever; it's so dreamy.*

Rex formally cleared his throat and then announced, "I offer you 'Ballad of the Wolf'. Strike a chord."

With that command, he strummed the instrument, and it produced a tingly, folksy sound. The voice his throat produced was full and raspy, like someone who had been kicked around by life, but had refused to stay down for the count.

> *"Standing at the four corners,*
> *With a bag upon my back.*
> *I left my tribal home,*
> *And crossed the Northern track.*
>
> *Reaching out I could not touch,*
> *Seeking out I could not find.*
> *Where did I leave my heart at, honey?*
> *Tell me, where did I leave my mind?*
>
> *Looked into the universal mirror,*
> *But I could not seem to hear,*
> *The reflection of the night fire,*
> *Or the echo of the cave bear.*
>
> *Oooh, but the wind blows, baby.*
> *Oooh, between heaven and earth.*
> *Oooh, how the wind blows, baby.*
> *Oooh, between sadness and mirth.*
> *Ahhh, and don't you know, dear,*
> *That in the blowing wind…*
> *All opposites disappear?"*

What happen next was beyond anything Annie could have possibly expected or conceived. The sound of the sorcerer's mandolin seemed to electrify the surroundings, and the wind wailed in with a sassy reverberation, as the fiery orange of the sunset exploded in the sky. The whole world awoke, and Shiva's chest puffed out with pride and passion. Even the sparse trees tinkled out a background sound. Rex took to the second half of the song with a fresh vigor:

"Whoa, my baby!
Remember those far away summers;
You picked me up in your daddy's car?
We were on our way to the corner store;
But we never made it that far.
Oh, babe, you drove me down south;
And I swore I'd love you forever.
And with the softness of your mouth;
Oh, honey, you burned me with your fever.

Oooh, we ran all the red lights,
Just to get to our dreams.
Yeah, but in the flickering night,
Nothin's ever what it seems."

The sorcerer burned into a searing solo on the mandolin. His fingers worked their way up and down the neck of the instrument as his face contorted from the overwhelming feeling of pumping out solid music.

"Yeah, baby, the summers have gone by,
But you're still my forever life.
Yeah, between the dark and the light,
You're still my forever life,
My forever life,
Oooh, honey, my forever life,
Oooh, babe, my forever, my forever liiiife!"

Annie nearly drowned in the silence that immediately followed the song's end. She looked about with a swimming sensation in her head and a sense of loss in her heart. The world had settled back into its plodding, quiet existence, leaving only the sunset as a reminder of a moment when the air sprang to life. Shiva sat tall, allowing all of creation to worship her. Rex stood casually investigating the underneath of his fingernails.

"So," he asked with a detached voice, "what did you think?"

"That...that... that was the most amazing thing I've ever seen. How did you do that? That was so cool. You really rocked that song."

"Thank you. I did some time as a troubadour, you know."

Annie sat catching her breath as the memory of the song echoed in her ears. Suddenly, she shook her head and looked bewildered.

"But I have a question."

Rex raised his eyebrow in defense.

"Never mind," she shrugged, "it doesn't matter; it was an awesome song. You know you had that whole classic rock thing going on."

"But? Come on, what is it?" He tried unsuccessfully not to sound wounded.

"It's just that..."

"What? Just what? Out with it, girl, what is your concern?"

"Well, you said it was a song about a wolf."

"So I did and so it is," he remarked, searching for her point.

"But you didn't mention anything about wolves."

The sorcerer became flabbergasted. "What do you mean? The whole song was about the wolf. I should know; it came from me."

"I'm not trying to be rude, please don't get angry at me."

Her words softened the sorcerer, and he visibly calmed himself. "I am sorry. I'm allowing pride to cloud my mind. It is I who is being rude, please continue."

"It's just that I didn't hear anything about a wolf. I heard a cave bear in there, but nothing about a wolf."

Rex smiled. "I think I see the misunderstanding here. It sounds like you're saying that since I didn't actually say *wolf* or describe the physical features of a wolf, then it couldn't be a song about a wolf."

"Well... yeah."

His gentle laughter eased the tension created by his earlier defensiveness. "Oh, my dear, dear Annie. The song is about the spirit of the wolf, the essence, and the indescribable matter that moves within and gives the wolf its being. It's a metaphor."

"Oh, I see," she said, not really seeing.

"You still seem confused. I assure you that it's very simple. The essence of things exists within the material fabric of the universe. For instance, if I throw some clothes on the ground they just lay there—just some clothes on the ground. But, if I put them on, I give the clothes life, they conform to my body, and they create character, motion and actualized concepts. Annie, try and see what lies behind the material world, see what it is that has oozed out of the void and permeated the world of things."

Annie thought about this while biting her lower lip. "I wonder what essence is in me."

"Would you like to find out?"

"I don't know about that; might be too scary. From what I saw in Esmeralda's crystal ball, I don't think it's very good."

"Oh, I don't know, it sounds like what you saw there was a layer of confusion created from a life of distortion. Perhaps, if you discharge some of that confusion, you would stand a better chance of discovering your inner essence."

"Do you think so? What if confusion is my essence? What if I'm just not... normal?" Annie could feel the familiar feeling of desperation haunting her from the old question.

"Somehow, I doubt it," he reassured. "Still, it is up to you. But trust me, it will be okay. Okay?"

Annie nodded slowly.

He handed over his mandolin to her. "Take this, and this time you sing me a song."

Annie took the instrument from the sorcerer. "Well, I can play a little, but I don't know if I can come up with anything right here on the spot."

"You don't have to know how to play at all," he assured her. "And you don't have to make up anything. The mandolin will pull it out of you and bring it through you. All you have to do is think strongly on what you want to sing about and say 'strike a chord,' and then hold on, because you're in for one whirlwind of a ride."

"So, you didn't actually write that song you did? It was the mandolin that did it?"

"Does a pen write anything? No, of course not, it's just a bridge between what is inside you and the outside world. That's what the mandolin is—a bridge. I assure you though; whatever comes out will be a part of you. But I sense you are procrastinating. Are you going to dare it or not?"

"Yeah, yeah, I'm going to do it," she said a little irritated. "Don't rush me."

The sorcerer smiled. "No rush."

Annie held the instrument in her hands, feeling the weight of it, feeling the power and promise of it. She felt queasy inside, and her knees wobbled.

Do I really want to know what will come out of me? I didn't like what I saw in the crystal ball. What if this is worse? God, I'm getting scared again. I'm so tired of being afraid all the time. What am I so afraid of? That I'm not normal and never will be? I can't stand all this pain and confusion; I'm so tired of it all. I just want some peace for once. She started thinking about the ocean, feeling its distant call, and then the dark place ebbed inside her, the place she never wanted to look at. *Gotta hide it—it's not there.*

She closed her eyes, took in a deep breath, floated her quivering fingers up the neck of the mandolin, poised her other hand to down stroke on the strings, and whispered, "Strike a chord."

As soon as the command escaped her lips, she was seized by an

intoxicating energy that exploded from below her navel. Her eyes
sprung open as her body jerked and came to life on its own. Without the
hindrance of consciousness, a wealth of musical knowledge fired
through her nervous system and translated itself into the muscle move-
ments of her fingers, hands, arms, diaphragm, vocal cords and mouth.
Black clouds rumbled into the sky with a relentless backbeat as lightning
clashed above their heads.

"Oh, my," Rex declared with grave concern.

Annie opened her mouth, or something opened her mouth, and the
words that gushed out of her echoed in the gathering storm. She sang
out venomously, the pulsating music acting as a witness to her prose:

> *"Blinded on the road to Damascus,*
> *I ain't your martyr no more.*
> *Don't play your games on me,*
> *I ain't your Frankenstein whore.*
> *You found out what you wanted to know,*
> *Now it's time for you to get out and go,*
> *Before I ..."*

The wind picked up, howling in a distorted feedback wail. Annie
hammered violently on the mandolin as she belted out the chorus with
harshness:

> *"Get ripped — Can you see me shakin'?*
> *Get ripped — There's no mistaken',*
> *Get ripped — That I'm close to breakin',*
> *Get ripped — And that I'll be makin',*
> *Get ripped,*
> *A HELL FOR YOUUUU!*
> *HELL FOR YOUUUU!*
> *HELL FOR YOUUUU!"*

The wind faded back allowing the thunder to pulsate its ruthless
background beat. Annie returned to a sneering buzz saw voice:

> *"And no world can stay the storm,*
> *When broken homes become the norm.*
> *And angry children can't decide*
> *Between TV, murder or suicide.*
> *And blood is shed come rain or shine,*
> *And no apologies can pay the fine,*

Of fathers who up and fly away,
Or mothers too drunk to play,
But I'll damn sure find you one day,
And I'll..."

Again the world shook as a wall of sound came crashing down and Annie spat out the chorus:

"Get ripped — Can you see me shakin'?
Get ripped — There's no mistaken',
Get ripped — That I'm close to breakin',
Get ripped — And that I'll be makin',
Get ripped,
A HELL FOR YOUUU!
HELL FOR YOUUUU!
HELL FOR YOUUUU!"

Crimson speckles appeared dot by dot on the instrument. Annie launched into a solo of her own, as blood and sweat testified to the purity of her revelation. In exhaustion, she took it down a notch. Her eyes were hollow; her tight lips barely contained the power of her voice. She bore witness to the whole world with her final verse:

"Well, I breathe the unforgiving air,
As I walk these empty lands,
With the sins of my past,
Burning like nails in my hands.
And your fading memory,
Can't fade fast enough for me,
Before I..."

The music exploded once more to seal the song's fate.

"Get ripped — Can you see me shakin'?
Get ripped — There's no mistaken',
Get ripped — That I'm close to breakin',
Get ripped — And that I'll be makin',
Get ripped,
A HELL FOR YOUUU!
HELL FOR YOUUUU!
HELL FOR YOUUUU!"

Annie shuddered with a gasp, and the mandolin cooled in her hands. The sky returned to a twilight sunset, the gale settled to a breeze, and the air was once again light and breathable. She looked over to where Rex and Shiva stared at her with large unbelieving eyes.

"Oh my, oh my," Rex kept repeating.

Shame began to flood her body. *He hates me now. He's seen the ugliness inside me, and he hates me now. When will I ever learn to keep things hidden?* She let the mandolin fall as her hands rushed up to her face to stop the tears.

To her surprise, Rex did not turn away from her, or pelt her with stones for her crimes, or do any of the dreadful things she felt deserving of. Instead, he hastened over to her and offered a comforting hug, which she accepted.

"There, there, Annie, let it out," he soothed as he stroked the back of her head.

"No, I'm not... going... to... cry over the little things!" she cried.

"Trust me, Annie, this is no little thing, so wail while you got the chance. Get it out."

"I feel so weak and helpless, crying like a stupid little girl... Oh, God, it hurts!"

"Nonsense, you're not crying because you're weak or because you're a girl. You just had a rather disturbing experience, and you've discharged quite a bit of vile energy. If it had been me, I'd be bawling now, too."

"Sorcerer Rex?" she sobbed with fear.

"Yes, dear one?"

"Please don't hate me because I'm so ugly inside and out, please, I don't want you to hate me," she pleaded as if her life depended on it.

"Hate you? Heavens, why would I hate you? And what's all this talk of ugliness? You're a pretty young lass. And as for what's inside of you, well, I dare say we have not gotten to the root of you yet, but I can tell you this—you are one pissed off girl!"

He held Annie, gently rocking her in his paternal embrace. For some reason, Annie had the overwhelming desire to suck her thumb and without thinking much about it, she did.

Chapter Eleven

Rex tended to the small campfire as the last flicker of day slipped into night, stirring ancient fears that they might not be delivered from darkness come the morn. The campfire glowed brighter as if to compensate for the lost sun; its efforts soon aided by a rising full moon. Annie sat quietly with Shiva's head in her lap and watched the moon. It had come quietly, sneaking into her awareness not like a thief in the night, but like an old friend who slides up to you in a crowd with a friendly squeeze and a soft hello.

A golden-orange moon tonight, she mused. *An autumn moon. It makes me feel cozy for some reason. Spring is so simple-minded, doesn't know what's in store for her. And Summer... please, Summer is too full of herself. Thinks the world is never-ending. But Autumn, she knows the truth. Her world worn wisdom smiles and winks—Winter death is knocking at the door.*

Annie shook herself from her thoughts with bewilderment. *Whoa, where did that come from? Is this me thinking or is someone thinking through me?* She gazed over at Rex, who muttered to himself while writing something out on the ground with his fire-stirring stick. *Did he cast a spell on me? Possession, perhaps? No, I don't think so. If there is one thing I know, it's bad. I haven't done a good job of staying away from it, but I know it when I see it, smell it, taste it—feel it. This guy ain't bad, a little stuck on himself maybe, but not bad. I mean, he held me; he let me cry in his arms like a daddy would. And when I was done, he asked for nothing in return. He just did it freely. Free. Free admission to the show with no strings attached.*

"Sorcerer Rex?" Annie asked bending over to nuzzle into Shiva's fur. She breathed in the richness of the pelt; it smelled of untamed forests and roaring rivers.

Startled from his private contemplation, Rex cleared his throat. "Yes, Annie?"

"That was a pretty cool trick with the mandolin. You must be a great magician."

Rex smiled, "Mathgician."

"Excuse me?"

"It's all mathematics. If you know the right formulas, you can unlock the mysteries of the universe. I once produced, seemingly out of thin air, a wife for Al Nova, who is one of the Lords of the Outer Regions."

Annie rubbed vigorously between Shiva's ears, yielding a low moan of pleasure from the wolf. "How didja do that?"

"Simple, really. I mean once you factor all the areas of interest, you look for the one exceptional person who stands out from the population. Some like to conjure this using 90 percent probability, some 95. But since I was dealing with one of the Lords of the Outer Regions, well I went for 99 percent probability. That old alpha point double ought one," he chuckled. "I started with a simple incantation, standard stuff really, nothing radical or deviant. Just took a root of the Southern Vary tree, which is quadratic oddly enough, and waved it over a listing of available women while saying, 'Diminution, each from the mediocre, twice fold and summa!'"

Rex looked over at Annie. She was blowing razzing sounds on Shiva's belly. "Well, anyway, the point is—you just need to know where to look," he half spoke and half mumbled.

Suddenly, Shiva's drowsy eyes sparked open and her ears alerted. She sprung up and sniffed the air; the fur on her neck bristled as she issued a low growl.

"What?" the sorcerer asked, looking around. "What is it?"

The ground began to tremble below them. Rex's face seemed to wrestle with his emotions in an attempt to keep his expression under control.

"By the stars! Have I forgotten?"

Annie sprung up. "What is it? What's happening?"

"Holdfast the Dragon—she comes!"

Annie looked down the hillside to a moonlit patch of land the sorcerer pointed toward. The ground there gave way with a resounding rumble, leaving a perfectly circular hole. The air around them started to reek of burning sulfur. Out of the dark depths of the hole slithered a large, hungry looking serpent. It was black, malignant and primal, measuring at least 15 meters in length and thick throughout. Its tongue stabbed the air repeatedly, and it emitted an ear splitting hiss.

Annie shuffled over to Rex, clutching him tightly. She looked up at his face. He was pale and clutching her just as tightly. Shiva hunched her head, a snarl curled her lip and scrunched her nose; the scent of the snake appeared to burn her nostrils.

The serpent turned its menacing head and raising it looked toward them. Annie screamed the second her eyes met and locked in on the snake's lidless orbs. She felt as if the breath of life had left her. In one exploding moment, all the pain ever visited upon her in her life rocked through every cell of her quivering body. Her mouth hung wide open, but no sound issued out of her anymore. She had become too petrified to produce any noise as she beheld the ancient, sinister and unforgiving terror.

"Don't look into its eyes!" Rex warned, yelling above the unholy hissing.

Shiva broke Annie's lethal trance with the serpent by jumping up and placing her paws on Annie's shoulders. Annie took in a sharp breath of noxious air, gagging on it as she found a stabilizing element in Shiva's steady blue eyes.

A powerful wind blasted above them. Annie followed Shiva's gaze upward into the sky. There, in the new night, she spied a magnificent golden eagle as large as a cargo plane. It passed over them, the wind from the bird's wing flaps gusted through her hair and forced her eyes shut.

Annie opened her eyes to discover the whole landscape had changed. No longer were they safely on the grassy knoll under a sleepy sky, but instead they were in the middle of a parched primordial wasteland. Hard burnt-orange clay cracked beneath her feet. The desolate land stretched for miles in every direction seemingly without hope or mercy. Annie struggled for breath, fighting the hot dry winds for scant oxygen. She felt the moisture being sucked from her pores, and her eyes burned as she looked into the angry, red apocalyptic sky.

"Hold on, Annie, don't let go!" Rex bellowed in opposition to the intensifying winds that grew stronger with every stroke of the eagle's mighty wings.

The shimmering eagle circled the dusty serpent nine times. Then with a screech, it dove toward the snake, its talons fatally poised to strike. The snake coiled around itself, hissing threats toward the imminent attacker. Its breath released a heavy odor Annie could only image came from some forgotten corner in the bowels of the planet. The bird of prey's claws dug murderously deep into the snake's scaly flesh as it swooped down and snatched the reptile up. It soared into the bloody sky once again, unabated by the protesting convulsions of its trophy. The eagle's arc reached its crest and the bird stopped, hanging motionless in the burning sky and suspending all time along with it.

Annie experienced a sudden flashback in that nonexistent moment. She relived an episode from school, when she had viewed a film in health class. The film had projected images of sperm aggressively competing to penetrate an egg's membrane. The battle waged on for only seconds before one sperm emerged victorious inside the egg, beating out the others in a violent struggle for survival.

When the memory cleared away as quickly as it had come, Annie witnessed the eagle swallow the serpent whole. The bird spread its wings wide and gave a mournful shriek; then it plunged with fierce intention earthward, crashing into the snake's pit with a heart-stopping explosion of dust and feathers.

All was still.

Rex glowed with joyous anticipation. "She comes... she comes... Holdfast comes..." he whispered, his voice seemed reluctant to leave the safety of his throat in exchange for the uncertain world outside.

Annie tried to steel herself and wait for whatever was going to happen next. In the stillness, she noticed Shiva was no longer with them. She tried to remember the last time she had seen the wolf. Had it been just before she shut her eyes and the world had changed?

Whatever is going to happen, I wish it would happen soon and be over with, she fidgeted in her mind.

Annie felt the same oppressing apprehension she'd felt when she paid the price to Ogre in his decrepit room: her stomach discharged too much acid, her heart pounded painfully in her chest, and her neck muscles contracted into knots.

Just let it be over with quickly...

Annie's knees struggled not to fail her.

... and please don't let me be torn apart.

Both of the travelers advanced hypnotically toward the crater, hanging on to each other for dear life. They stopped a stone's throw away and waited, unable to speak. The stillness shattered as the earth once again quaked and buckled. Steam and smoke spewed high into the air from the depths of the pit.

"She comes!"

Indeed, she did come, grand and glorious, Holdfast the Dragon rose from the pit. Her emerald skin glistened, highlighting the glow of her golden underbelly. As soon as her folded wings cleared the hole, Holdfast spread them wide, blocking out the sun and enveloping the two small humans in her shadow. Crimson leather webbed itself between jointed bones and highlighted the ebony skeletal frame of her wings. She exercised her clawed fingers, stretching and contracting them with the pleasure of emancipation.

Fear dissolved into awe as Annie, releasing herself from Rex and stumbling forward several steps, beheld the grandeur of Holdfast. She was beyond splendid. She stood seven stories high, a radiant creation whose very configuration was a living testimonial to the eccentric wonder of probability. Annie knew from hanging around tattoo parlors that

Holdfast's head was Oriental in nature. A red beard of bone-webbed flesh framed her living face and long catfish-like whiskers whipped about from the end of her snout. Her eyes, set deep beneath a formidable brow of protective bone, held a keen intelligence. On top of her head sat a magnificent ivory horn. Past Holdfast's head, she resembled the medieval dragons of the Europeans with a strong reptilian body and large bat-like wings.

Holdfast finished stretching her arms and wings and, with a snap of her mighty tail, she let out a roaring howl.

She is so beautiful, Annie gasped to herself as the howl vibrated wonderfully through her body. *I've never felt this way before. I feel like something inside of me is growing and is fixing to burst out. I can see the past, the present and the future without any boundaries. Oh, that I could embrace her, plug into her beauty and power, climb onto her broad back and ride her to the stars.* Annie stood glowing as the two opposing sensations of being crucially important and ultimately insignificant fluxed through her.

From behind, Annie heard the Sorcerer Rex mutter out loud, "What do I do? Confound it! All these years of preparation, and I don't know what to do. How can I master this situation in order to gain the gifts of the dragon? Perhaps I should speak out boldly and command Holdfast. No, that would not be proper. I know, I must humble myself; appear unworthy and implore her."

She turned her head and saw him on his knees with arms outstretched upward.

"Oh, Great and Glorious Holdfast!" he called. "I beseech you, bestow upon me, a lowly human, your gifts that I might perform the Great Healing and return to the home of my origin!"

Annie felt annoyed by Rex's display of servitude. *Doesn't he know?* she asked herself as a million new connections buzzed and jumped and popped in her brain. The rush of understanding was more than she could focus on, but she could feel fear escaping her porous body. *Can't he see? We are not the servant...* Annie turned her head back around and stretched her arms out to her sides like wings *...we are the master!*

As soon as her last thought fired off through her nervous system, Annie became aware of the dragon looking directly at her. Holdfast lowered her head slowly toward Annie, displaying her prominent teeth in a wide grin. Annie reached out to stroke her enchanting skin as Holdfast sniffed her.

Rex blinked with disbelief at the vision of girl and dragon in silent communion.

Holdfast drew her head back up with a sharp intake of air. She exhaled a soft stream of puffy orange smoke, and Annie swore she heard the dragon say, "Sssweeeet hAnnieeee."

Rex heard the dragon call Annie's name, too. "It is to be her?" he gasped. "This doesn't make sense. Have I not done all that was required of me? What cruelty is this? Some girl shows up out of nowhere, out of the ground for Jupiter's sakes, totally ignorant of you and the legends, and she is chosen over me?"

Annie's heart throbbed painfully in her heaving chest. Sorrow had etched itself in the dragon's face, a grave expression that fathomed the depths of existence: the pain of being, the anguish of growing, and the grim pathway one treads to an inescapable destination. A single tear formed in the corner of Holdfast's left eye; it glistened like a piece of lead crystal, refracting the color spectrum's brilliance in its clarity. The tear rolled over the curve of her face, under her jaw and trickled down her neck. There it burst into a flash of bright blue light. When the flash dissipated, there was a steel collar around Holdfast's neck and on the collar's ring dangled the translucent tear. The tear dropped down toward Annie, and as it did a thick chain trailed behind it. Annie reached out and caught the tear; the chain continued until it hit the ground with a metallic clunk.

She opened her hand to see what weighed so heavy in it. In her palm lay a thin strap of leather threaded through an old fashioned key. The worn key appeared ordinary; a common artifact in this strange land. Annie gazed up at Holdfast with a smile, put on the necklace, and took hold of the dragon's leash.

"Sssweeeet hAnnieeee," the dragon repeated with a toothy grin. Then Holdfast jerked her head abruptly, bobbing Annie up off her feet. Something in the air did not agree with the creature. She snorted as Annie slid down the chain to the ground.

"What's happening?" Annie asked Rex.

The sorcerer sprung up from his knees in response to Holdfast's snort. He searched the horizon with a quick eye. "I don't know. Something's wrong."

A dull thunder rumbled from a cloud of dust in the distance.

"We have to get out of here," Rex commanded. "We have to get Holdfast safely to her cave and secure her."

The cloud of dust advanced on them quicker than could have been calculated. Out of it stampeded a number of hooded creatures on fierce horses. In front of them rode a human female circling a sword above her head and shouting out a battle cry. Primitive horns bellowed out with warning, quickening their blood.

"By thunder!" Rex called out.

"What is it?"

"We're under attack!"

"What are we going to do?" Annie became frightened.

"You must hang on to Holdfast. As long as you hold on to the chain, you will be safe."

"Well, what are you going to do?"

"I'm going to defend our ground. The dragon mustn't fall into any-one else's hands, so whatever you do, don't let go!"

Annie wrapped her fingers, her arms and her legs around the chain so tight her muscles burned.

Rex made a quick motion with his arms, and his staff appeared in his hand. He twirled the staff like a baton, and it produced a spear tip on ei-ther end. Spreading his legs shoulder width apart, he readied for the at-tack.

"Come if you dare, Infidels!"

They came. Unnaturally bypassing time and distance they lunged forward until, within seconds, they were no more than ten meters away. The woman raised her hand, and the formation came to an immediate halt. She sheathed her sword and adjusted the bow she had slung over her shoulder.

"You there," Zoila called out, "surrender the dragon, now!"

"Never!" Rex responded.

"I'm not talking to you, old man. I'm talking to the young wench, so shut your hole."

Rex glared at the insolent woman. He turned toward Annie who held onto the chain for dear life. Rex nodded urgently at Annie, convey-ing with his powerful brow the message to respond in kind.

Annie swallowed hard. She could feel her hands slipping as her sweat lubricated the metal links. With a deep breath, she turned her head to face Zoila.

"Never!" she retorted.

"Then," Zoila announced as she unshouldered her bow, "prepare to be taken by force!"

"Whaaaat?" Annie screamed.

"Hang on, Annie, don't let go!" Rex reminded her as he prepared to meet the attack.

Zoila began snarling orders. "Alpha team, to the chain and steady it. Omega team," she paused long enough to give Rex a malicious glare, "keep the old man busy."

Ten ghouls dismounted and charged toward Annie. She screamed, reflexively kicking out her foot. She caught the first ghoul in the face with her heel, knocking off its hood as it flew backward. It got back up and looked Annie right in the face. Its gaze from bulging, milky eyes burned into her, casting darkness upon her very being. Annie's neck muscles locked shut, and the vessels of her face pulsated as blood pumped through them at fatal pressure levels. The ghoul grinned at her with a lipless smile crammed full of lethal teeth that looked perfect for shredding living flesh.

"Don't let go!" she heard Rex call out again.

She looked over at Rex and saw him set upon by the remaining ghouls. His call to her came as he swung his staff in a half circle in front of him, slicing through the first charging ghoul's throat. Its head flipped backward with a spray of ooze, and hung to the torso by a flap of sinew. As it hopelessly flung its arms about, Rex thrust his staff rearward, skewering a ghoul who made the fatal mistake of sneaking up behind him.

The ghoul in front of Annie replaced its own hood, and Annie felt sure it was going to tear her to shreds. Instead, it let out a blood-curling yelp, motioned to its comrades in arms, and leapt up, catching hold of the chain just above Annie's head. Revulsion overcame her as she felt the ghoul's spindly toes crawl their way up her body. The ghoul pulled itself up, using Annie's head as a platform to lunge upward and scamper the length of the chain.

"They're climbing on me!" Annie screamed to Rex as the other nine creatures followed the first ghoul.

"They can't hurt you as long as you hold on to the chain!" he assured her. He side-kicked a ghoul in its chest and then thrust his staff in the opposite direction as his foot came down.

"Hold that chain steady!" Zoila ordered the ghouls who climbed over Annie and up the chain. She reached down to a quiver on her saddle and drew out an arrow. "Weigh it down so it's taut!"

Annie looked up. The ghouls were hanging on the chain with their hands, allowing the rest of their body to dangle. Holdfast stood helpless as the restricting leash pulled down on her.

Why doesn't she do something? Annie asked herself. *She could wipe them all out if she wanted to.* Annie looked over at the exact moment Zoila drew back her bow and took a high aim. "She's going to shoot Holdfast!"

"Nonsense," Rex called back, "it would take a thousand arrows to scratch her." He finished with a parry, a thrust and a slash, and took a brief instant to appraise the situation. "By the stars!"

"What? What is it?"

"She means to release her!" Rex struck a ghoul on the side of its leg, exploding its kneecap. He rushed like a madman toward Zoila. "Are you insane? Don't do this!"

A wall of ghoul warriors thwarted his charge toward Zoila. She smiled at the bogged-down sorcerer, then took skillful aim and released the arrow. It zinged through the battle-laden air and struck Holdfast's collar ring, bursting the chain from the neckband.

"Oh, my," Rex whispered in horror.

Holdfast let out an ear-splintering screech. She reared up high on her hind legs and shook her head violently. Annie, released suddenly from the tension of the chain, fell to the ground. The ghouls above her plummeted to the earth, crashing upon each other, their cracking bones resounding in the chaos.

Holdfast began to change, and Annie could only stand helplessly by and watch the metamorphosis. The dragon's skin rotted to black and hardened into an impenetrable armor, her golden belly turned crimson, like blood seeping through cloth. A dark scarlet stain tainted her noble horn and continued its way down her back, contaminating the bony plates that protruded down her back and tail. Then her face morphed wickedly, thinning and elongating, becoming more serpentine. Her red beard flared up and framed her darkening face like the facial fins of a sea serpent.

She hissed with malevolence.

"What's happening to her?" Annie called out.

"Annie, run to me!" Rex alerted.

Annie turned toward Rex, who ran headlong toward her, trying to shorten the distance between them. Holdfast turned her face toward the night sky and released a torrent of fire. Annie started toward Rex. She felt blinded by the confusion surrounding her. So much was happening so quickly that her mind strained to capture it all. She began to feel a gagging sense of impending death, and she spurred herself on, trying to escape whatever might be stalking her.

Zoila was upon Annie before she even realized the warrior had charged her. Annie felt a burning tug on her neck as Zoila tore the key necklace from her.

"Got it!" Zoila announced victoriously. Then she gasped as the key sizzled in her hand and vanished. She pulled back the reins and snapped her steed around sharply.

"Damn the legend!" she cursed, as she witnessed the key reappear around Annie's neck. "So that part of the tale is also true: that only the receiver of the gift may possess it. I wonder if it is also true that if I cut off her bloody head the gift will vanish altogether."

Annie stood frozen to the ground; immobilized by fear. The air cracked with savage violence, destabilizing the world around her. She took in a sharp breath; time and events flowed slowly, silently—as if dancing in deep waters. She was able to take it all in now and see all the puzzle pieces forming together. Holdfast had leapt into the air, flying away with powerful strokes of her maroon wings. The ghouls who had not been killed by Rex's hand or the fall retreated to their horses. Rex had stopped running, his eyes strained wide, and he seemed to be yelling a warning as he stretched out one hand to halt something unspeakable from happening. No voice came from his mouth though; nothing penetrated the silence. Nothing, save for the rhythmic beat of hooves, so regular in their pattern that it offered to lull her to sleep. And then, Annie saw Zoila charging toward her with a sword leveled murderously at her throat.

Here I go again, losing my head. No sense in running, she will be on top of me before I take a step. I wonder where I will wake up next time... if I wake up at all. Annie closed her eyes and with dignity awaited the inevitable. She felt a great rush of wind gust by, accompanied by the snorting of a burdened beast and the clanking of riding tackle.

Chapter Twelve

The dark fortress appeared barely a sketchy outline in the night sky as Zoila forged her way toward it. Trailing behind her followed the remnants of her unnatural warriors. She could smell the oppressing presence of her home more than she could see it, and feel the coldness of memories more than the cold breeze that wrapped around her with an unwelcomed embrace.

Perhaps, I could keep riding—past the castle, past the borders, past this unforgiving land, past his anger. And what anger he'll have in store for me when he finds out I've failed him. But I am ready, I can't falter, can't stop now. This is but a small setback. I only have to bare his rage for a little longer; certainly I can do that. Just a little longer; let him think I am serving him, offering plans that sound like they will benefit him and the queen.

She sat up taller in the saddle, gathering her courage. *Come on Zoila, don't let the mask of fear blind you. What is the worst thing he can do to you? Yell? Scream his fat ugly head off? Ha, that is no threat, just a lot of noise and spit. Beat me? Kill me? Haven't I already died a thousand deaths? What is death of the body when one is already dead inside? And yet not completely dead inside, but like the seed that slumbers underneath the frozen ground. So, if there is to be no end to this winter, then better death. But if my plans work, and I can bring on the spring, then perhaps I can live again!*

Zoila's hopeful thoughts faded as reality grated its way back into her awareness. There, waddling at the front gate, the queen peered into the night like an anxious parent fearful of her child's nocturnal wanderings. Zoila held no delusion that her mother's concern was for her, she knew the queen waited to see how her ghouls had performed.

Shifting in her saddle, Zoila gave a backward glance and smiled with wicked delight. Out of the army of 39 ghouls, only 14 remained intact and riding tall. Five attempted to ride tall, but clutched various areas of their body cavity as they bobbed sporadically and fought to remain alive. The remaining 20 lay tied across the back of their mounts. Their lifeless bodies revealed tales of mayhem, as their blackening limbs flopped about with unnatural twists and turns.

Queen Dezair clasped her wart-infested hands to her mouth in horror as she saw her army return less gloriously than it had left. "My children, what have you done to my beautiful children?" she gasped.

"What have *I* done?" Zoila shot back at her. "These incompetent fools almost blew the whole campaign! Perhaps you should throw them back into the cauldron; I don't think they're done yet."

"You insolent slut, how dare you speak to me in that tone." Dezair held up a fist to deliver a blow, but the parade of damaged ghouls passing by distracted her. "Oh, dear, oh, dear me, no, no, no."

The queen motioned desperately to her waiting aids. They rushed out, helping her gather the army and take them back to the depths of her lair.

Zoila rode stoically on. With shoulders squared and chin steadied, she headed for the command tent. She paused at the entrance and stole a glance inside to gauge his current mood. It wasn't good.

King Gororm paced clumsily inside the command tent. Sagging fatty flesh audibly wobbled around him as he journeyed from the entrance to the rear and back again. In exhaustion, he plopped into his chair, the material of his clothing straining to contain him. Gnarled knuckles drummed out impatience; a back beat to his fuming frustration. Impulsively, he cast his hand into a green marble bowl filled with a dark gray liquid. Retracting his closed hand, he shoved something still squealing into his tusk-framed mouth and crunched it into a swallowable size.

Zoila's stomach turned at the sight of his foul gluttony.

"Where is she, where is she?" the king called out. "She better not have double-crossed me, the little imp. Since her sister turned on us, Zoila has been acting strangely. Now that I think about it, Arias began slipping away years ago."

As the ogre king rummaged through charts without reading them, Zoila nodded to herself. She was in no hurry to face Gororm, and so continued to spy on him.

He stopped his paper shuffling as a document caught his eye. Cocking his head, he squinted and read it out loud, "Five hundred pieces of King's Gold to whom-so-ever leads royal protectors to or produces to the court the person of Arias, former princess of the Kingdom of Gororm. This felon is wanted for treason, inciting dissension, blasphemy against the Crown, and encouraging wickedness."

Gororm snorted and threw the paper to the ground, giving it a solid stamping. "Why did you let it come to this, Arias? What got into your head? Stupid question. I know when this all started. I thought it was just youthful impetuousness at first, but you were poisoned against me by enemies unseen in the shadows, striking when my attention was averted to other matters."

Zoila knew when it all started, 19 years ago when they were still children. Zoila had hid in the shadows and spied on her father. She shook her head at the memory. Some thing's never change; here she was spying on him still. As a child she had snuck around the castle quietly seeing what others did, gauging moods in order to know when to avoid the king and queen. Maybe that's why she was a good soldier: all those years of practicing stealth to aid her and her sister's survival. But that one day 19 years ago, when Zoila lay hidden behind a trunk and discarded carpet remnants, she could not protect her sister. That day a haughty Arias had stormed into the king's study, dripping wet and spitting mad.

"My lord," Arias had spoken with head slightly bowed.

"What is it? I'm busy," Gororm rebuked her intrusion.

"I know you are busy with matters of state, but may I have a moment of your time? It's a matter of some urgency to the kingdom."

At this, the king's interest piqued. "What is it? What is so urgent? Are we being put upon?"

"No, my lord, it is an issue of legitimacy."

Gororm grew impatient. "Do you have something to say, or am I to endure your dramatic pauses?"

"I have reason to believe you abducted Zoila and me and had our parents murdered, for what ends I cannot fathom."

The ogre king slammed a meaty fist on his wooden desk. "Ridiculous! Who has set this lie in your head? I will have them quartered!"

"Is it not so?" Arias glared.

Gororm sneered back, murky green spittle oozed from between his teeth and down his chin. "Anything else, or do you want to make haste before I pommel you again?"

The little girl's chin remained poised and defiant. "As a matter of fact, there is. I have serious doubts about your monarchy. Do you really think you are better than everyone else? That you were appointed by divine decree? I think you just killed the right people."

A crystal ink bottle sailed through the air, leaving behind it a dripping trail of indigo as it sparkled and shattered on the wall beside Arias. Her eyes flashed fear, but her body refused to abandon its obstinate stance. She looked from the ink stained wall to the king; there was mayhem in Gororm's dark glare.

"Who," he snarled, "has filled your head with this disease? I will personally ram my fist into his backside and pull his entrails out of his filthy hole!"

A thundering roar jolted Zoila from her reminiscence. Thoughts sloshed back groggily from the swamp of yesteryear to the starkness of the present. The sky above her rumbled again and a tremendous wind shook the tent. Zoila peered back inside the tent. Gororm drooled a smile with his greedy lips; the dragon was on the loose and that clearly delighted him.

Her mouth was dry when she entered the tent in the middle of Gororm's victory jig. He stopped and applauded her, laughing, she imagined, like the first time he pulled wings off a bird. Her stomach turned; she knew his gleeful mood would not last—it never did.

"I heard it, I heard it, I heard the dragon fly overhead!" he shouted, not bothering to wipe off the spittle that shot out and hung from his bloated bottom lip. "Come inside, my child, you must tell me everything!"

Zoila stepped further into the tent, but stopped a safe distance from him. She stood quietly with her feet slightly apart; her gloved hands clasped together and resting on the slope of her lower back. Time was marked with measured breaths, as she waited for the moment to defend herself. *I must be convincing; find his weak points and exploit them. If he becomes too angry, he may impulsively strike out; maybe even kill me before I can remind him that I'm still a valuable part of the plan.*

Gororm's enthusiasm grew as he whipped himself into a frenzy, "When I heard Holdfast roar by and imagined her burning and scorching the land, I felt so proud of you. Zoila, you are magnificent! Soon the people will be begging for my protection. They will swear undying allegiance to my crown, they will offer up the servitude of their unborn generations to be rid of Holdfast's brutal fire. Oh, the glory of my kingdom will be a hundred times that of any kingdom that has ever existed. And one day, it shall all be yours, Zoila, yours and your children's, and your children's children, for generations without end. I swear it."

Zoila shifted in her unassuming stance. She had no doubt that at the very moment he was praising her and promising her the kingdom, he was also plotting to betray her. *Not yet, pig, it's not over yet, and it's not going to end the way you think. I promise you that.*

Gororm, too swept away by his own fantasies of ultimate power, failed to notice Zoila's indifference. He fell into his chair, breathing heavily from his euphoric burst of energy. "Show me the dragon's gift. What a thing of beauty it must be."

"I do not have it, my Lord," she replied.

The king chuckled, but the stillness of Zoila's face evaporated his amusement. "What do you mean, you don't have it?" he asked, his rage poised to strike.

"Another human was there, a female child. The dragon had already given her the gift by the time I arrived."

Gororm exploded. He leapt to his feet, sending the desk sailing through the air as he lunged toward Zoila. "Liar!" he screamed.

Zoila darted to the left, escaping the large fist Gororm wielded like a hammer. The king's momentum temporarily threw him off balance and carried him through the space Zoila had occupied. Instinctually, her body's defenses kicked in. Muscles tightened to prepare for incoming blows, nostrils flared to increase oxygen intake and feed a pounding heart, and eyes indiscriminately scanned the whole environment for danger. Through years of training, Zoila was able to quickly take charge of her body's automatic reactions and turn them to her advantage. She relaxed her muscles to maximize her striking ability, took control of her breathing which, along with confidence in her abilities, brought her heartbeat back to a solid rhythm, and narrowed her focus to the only immediate danger—Gororm. She continued to dodge his attacks as he crashed through the tent, initiating an all too familiar dance.

"You lying whore! No other human could have been there, it's impossible, it wasn't in the plan. It had to be a human born on the day of Gemini! It had to be you or Arias!" Gororm picked up a heavy trunk.

"Well, your plan was short-sighted, because she was there." Zoila dove forward.

"Noooo!" he roared, hurling the trunk toward the area Zoila had already vacated.

"Get a hold of yourself!" she shouted in hopes the shock of her command might stall him. He froze for a second, and Zoila took advantage of the pause. "All is not lost."

Gororm shook his head in disbelief at her statement. "You idiot, what in the hell are you talking about?" He stopped chasing her and grimaced. Through clenched teeth he growled, "Without the gift we cannot control the dragon. It will end up destroying us all!"

"I can get it back. I know what the wench looks like."

The king stammered at her ignorance, "It doesn't matter if you know what she looks like. That's not the point. How stupid can you be? Were you not listening during any of the briefings? Once given, the gift cannot be taken away from the recipient, nor can the recipient give it away."

"You are right, of course, my Lord. I tried to take it, but it magically returned to her. However, what if she could be duped into helping us?"

Gororm took in a deep breath and released it slowly, while stroking his chin.

Yeah, mull that over in your thick head, pig. Zoila smiled inside, not daring to express any outward emotion. *Ready? You're going to love this one.*

"She's not traveling alone. The monk is with her," Zoila related.

"Monk? The monk? Which monk? You don't mean *the* monk? You can't seriously be saying that *he* is with her. Not, not, not..."

"Rex," she filled in for him. "Yes, Rex, and he was dressed up like a wizard. I didn't recognize him at first, but something about his fighting style was familiar. It only occurred to me at the last moment, but it was him."

A fresh quiver of frustration and rage rattled through his body. "Well, that's just great," Gororm sneered. "That's just perfect. He's part of the reason my kingdom's in such a mess. And here he goes interfering again. What did we ever do to him? And now you say he's wizarding?"

"So it appeared."

"That worm infested busybody."

"As I said, we can still turn this to our advantage. People can be separated; lies can be fed sweetened with honey. The human can deliver us the gift and do our work for us."

"Yes, I see," the king answered deep in thought. He righted his chair and quietly sat down. "I don't know why I'm yelling at you, Zoila. It's not your fault that another human has intruded in our business, with the aid of a meddling monk, no less."

Zoila relaxed a little. *Out of danger for the moment. He's too confused to see his next moves. Thank goodness for the slow ogre mind. But now, I've got to make sure Arias is not released by the gift.*

"May I go now, my Lord?"

With an absent-minded wave of his hand, the king dismissed her. He rubbed his head and looked about for something to devour.

Arias woke from an uneasy slumber inside her crystal prison. The sound of a large beast swooping overhead alerted her to the starry sky. In the darkness she could barely make out Holdfast circling in and out of the moonlit clouds. She got up, pressed herself against the transparent wall, and peered into the valley below. The valley glowed with a hundred fires that the dragon had blazed with its inferno breath. Her heart sank as she slid back down to the floor.

So, Father has succeeded in getting you to fulfill his wicked plan. Oh, Zoila, why did you do it? Do you even know what you have done? So long has anger guided you that it has finally led you to the end of its path, which is your own downfall... and more than likely the end of our lives. We are the key to the gift. He has only to find a way to join us, his two human hostages, with the gift to unleash its power for himself. And he will find a way. He will find a way.

What curse befell us that we were torn from our parents and handed over to ogres? What did two little girls do to deserve being raised in fear and tempted into unspeakable alliances? You say that I am the weak one, but it was you, my dear sister, who succumbed to their lies and hate. I tried to stop it.

Her thoughts flowed back to a time when she was very young, when she learned about the lies that formed the foundation of her life. It was a time when she put herself beyond the reach of her parents, beyond their ability to hurt. A time 19 years ago when a 13-year-old girl went out for a ride on a drizzling morning and met a man on the road.

Little Arias had taken advantage of the light morning shower to practice tactical riding. She commanded her stead hotly as it struggled to maintain footing on the slick path.

"EEHA! Come on, boy, trot on, trot on!" She clucked several times, irritated with the horse's hesitation. "Oh fine, just walk then. What good are you? I'll have my daddy turn you into meat for the soldiers, you stupid horse."

Up ahead, she spied a lone, cloaked figure traveling on foot. With a wry smile she informed her mount, "Looks like some fun heading our way."

When she was within 20 meters, she shouted to the traveler, "Step aside or be trampled!"

The person stopped and removed the hood of his purple cloak from his head. He smiled as droplets speckled his once shielded face. "Are you aware," the man responded, "that it is customary to yield to the right and allow pedestrians to pass on the left? Here, I give you plenty of room to continue."

"Are you aware," Arias retorted, "that I can have you executed for speaking to me in such a manner?"

"Yes, but that wouldn't change the facts."

Arias looked at the man. His reply did not fit the usual groveling her station in life demanded. He just stood there smiling, the light rain plastering his brown short-cropped hair and beard to his sun-kissed skin. He seemed at ease in the elements; comfortable with a pack on his back, a walking stick in his hand, the rain in his face, and the wind at his back.

"And what f-f-facts would that be?" she stammered. Instantly she hated him for the burning shame the stammer produced in her.

"The facts regarding why you're out riding on this fine wet morning."

"Well, I see you are crazy as well as stupid. I am riding on this *fine wet morning*, because I'm in warrior training. So running you over will give me an opportunity to excel."

"If that is what you want to believe, what can I do about it?" he shrugged.

"There is nothing to be done, because that is the truth. Now yield the road!"

"Shall I tell you the truth?"

"Arrgh!" Arias growled, directing the sound toward the man like a hurled boulder. In one smooth motion, she dismounted and unsheathed a sword. She stood before him, the weight of the blade causing the tip to rest on the ground. "Shall I cut you down at the knees?"

"The truth is the rain is doing a poor job of masking your tears, the wind is failing to muffle your sobs, and your clothes cannot dull the pain of the fresh bruises on your back."

"Sh-sh-shut up!" she demanded. Her earlobes burned and a tightness seized her chest. "I'm a pr-pr-princess, and you don't talk to me." She struggled to raise the sword.

"Arias." The man's resonating voice halted her actions.

"No, no don't," she begged more the insisted.

"You were once a princess, and perhaps you will be again, but right now you are a prisoner. You know you don't belong where you are— that is why you cry in the rain."

"That's... it's a lie. I know what you're doing, trying to put down my parents. You all hate them because they were chosen by celestial providence, and all you common people are just jealous. They took me and my sister in to give us a better life, and you all are jealous."

"They stole you and your sister, as sure as they stole the wealth of this land from the people. You know it, Arias. You see it all around you no matter how hard you try to avoid it. You see the truth. You see that the only thing separating you from everyone else is merely an accident of time."

"Who are you?"

"Who are you? That is the question." The man pointed to a cluster of dwellings crowding a hillside. "What do you see over there?"

"A peasant village."

"A village of people. People like you. It's only an accident that you are in a palace; it's only an accident that you don't live in squalor. And Arias..."

"What? Leave me alone," she cried.

"It is only an accident that you are a prisoner of cruel tyrants. It's not your fault."

Arias yielded to the power of the man's words, bowing her head in defeat. She let the sword slip from her hand, and it fell into the mud with a dull thud. "It's too late, you are too late. I've been stained, and that's all there is to it."

He reached out and gently stroked the girl's moist cheek. "No, that is not all there is to it. Today, right now, you can have the stain washed away. Look, the world has given you rain to do so. Do not use the rain to hide your tears, use it to wash away your shame. The world misses you. It longs to have you back, but not to spread the hate perpetrated upon you. But rather as an agent who knows personal suffering and therefore wishes to ease it in others."

The man's words echoed through the years and comforted her now inside the crystal. Arias's fingertips retraced his past touch on her cheek. Nearly two decades later and his words and touch still gave her strength to persevere through the hardship of reclaiming her life.

"I wish you were here now, Brother Rex," she whispered. "I sure could use a friend."

Chapter Thirteen

Rex sat with his legs sprawled in front of him on the gentle slope of the hill's crest. Staring into the midnight landscape made lustrous from a lunar embrace, he unceremoniously cut locks from his hair and beard. A passing breeze floated some of the white wisps into the night. He was back at his campsite on the hilltop. Behind him Annie lay curled up in a fetal position beside the fire. He had brought her back with him, but she had failed to regain consciousness.

He stopped the steady metallic grind of his scissors slicing slowly through his thick hair. Glancing backward, he checked that Annie was still safe. In the orange glow of the flickering flames, he could see her eyelids vibrating from the rapid movement beneath. Shiva had curled up next to the girl, providing comfort and security. The wolf looked up and met Rex's gaze with sadness and a whimper, torn between duty to protect the girl and desire to comfort an old friend.

"Quite right, my noble companion. First priority is Annie's safety. I'll be all right."

But he didn't think he would be.

He continued to cut his hair while whiffing in the night air. *That smell, what is it? I'm sure it has been around me since my arrival, but I have been too distracted to notice. Rather careless of me. Or maybe the night brings it out.*

Using his arms to prop his torso up, Rex leaned back. With eyes closed gently and nostrils enlarged, he took in a long breath. *Winter air. That's what it is. Winter has dispatched her scent ahead like a scout reconnoitering the land to see if Autumn has finished her task and readied the world.*

Rex pulled his legs up close to his body, wrapped his arms around his shins and rested his chin between his kneecaps. He took in the region around him with slow eye scans, causing a furrow to form on his forehead. He sniffed in again, and then a warm smile melted onto his face.

Ah, olfaction, the hidden sense that operates for the most part below awareness. We adapt to the odors around us so quickly; we scarcely give them a second thought. But this primitive sense is always working, always guiding us with its unseen hand. We vibrate, we feel, we act and we don't even know why—we just make reasons up to feel in control.

I've been to this land before, several decades ago when I was newly upon my journey. Yes, I wintered here, I...

Rex leapt to his feet, instinctually shooting his hands out in front of him and whirling around to face any oncoming danger. His heart pounded in time with his accelerated respiration. Blood flow diverted deep into his muscles, causing goose bumps to pop up across his skin.

"Not here," he muttered to the darkness. "How did I come to be here? How did I come to be here and not know it? No, no, no, this can't happen. Don't tell me I journeyed so long only to end up at the beginning!"

Quivering knees ceased to support weight, and Rex crumpled to the ground. He lay on the grass and stared into the star speckled space, recalling another fall night perfumed with winter's chill. A night that occurred 19 years ago, only a few kilometers from the very spot he now occupied.

I remember I was celebrating...

The young monk Rex had shuffled within the circle of light afforded by a burning torch on a bridge outside a small hamlet. The dark brown hair of his youth shared a close cropping with his beard. He bunched the collar of his faded, travel-worn purple cloak around his neck to keep in his body heat. Intoxicated on honey mead, he searched the ground while attempting to maintain his balance.

"Where is my confounding pack?" he grumbled.

"Lose something?"

The words startled Rex. He peered down the dark road that stretched out beyond the illumination of the torchlight. The soft, full voice of a woman lingered in the air long after the utterance.

"Who goes there?" he asked as calm as he could. "Is that you, Gayle? Tell the mayor I will be along shortly as soon as I find my pack."

"No, I'm not Gayle the mayor's wife. I'm not from this place, although I know of its inhabitants."

Rex peered toward the bridge, trying to penetrate the darkness by squinting his eyes. He could only make out a vague shape of something standing on the stone bridge that also spanned over a jabbering brook. The shape was rather large and bulky for a person, but the gentle snorting of a horse explained the form.

"My name is Rex. I'm a monk. I've lost my pack."

The shadowy figure released a giggle, "I see. Nice to meet you, Brother Rex. I dare say you have also lost some equilibrium and full control of your limbs."

Rex smiled. Her voice warmed him in the chilly night air. A faint aroma of heather and moss surrounded him as if she had extended a handshake.

"This is true, madam. I've had too much honey mead, I'm afraid. But, when you are a guest of the Mayor of Cornerstone, what can one do? They are very proud of their mead."

"Indeed, they are, and there is none finer that I have sampled."

Rex noticed that the torchlight exposed him, while the stranger remained in darkness. Self-consciousness crept into his body along with a brief spinal shudder.

"May I know your name, madam?"

"Perhaps, if you are the one I seek. Otherwise, I will remain unknown and unseen."

"I see," he said, even though he didn't understand at all.

"Tell me monk, what are you looking for?"

"My pack—as I mentioned."

"Yes, of course. How careless of me, I must be tired from my ride."

"You have a beautiful voice," Rex burst out. He silently cursed the mead that put to sleep his impulse control. To his relief the woman was not offended, but again laughed a giggle that felt like an embrace.

"Why thank you, kind sir. Hmm."

"Well," he stammered, "I left it by the bank of the waterway."

"You mean down there?"

"Yes, I believe so."

The stranger's horse shifted its weight with a soft clop. "Then why do you search for it on the bridge road?"

"Well, because the light is better here of course," he replied.

The woman gave out a full laugh this time. "Oh, my, you are sauced, Brother Rex."

Rex shrugged and joked, "I don't drink as a rule—more as a habit."

The woman liberated another round of laughter. Rex felt pleasure resonate through him that he could make this stranger laugh—a stranger whose voice had spoken to him beyond any words used.

"I'm just kidding," he said with a grin. "Actually, I was celebrating a little—shall we say intervention. A little mentoring, or rather a moving of a few chess pieces that will change the course of the future." He shrugged again, "No big deal."

The laughter stopped, and the night became silent. Even the water running over a rocky bed below the bridge seemed to muffle. Rex searched his foggy mind for a clue to what he may have said in error.

"So it is you," the voice declared in hushed tones. "It is you I saw through the rain. You spoke to the girl on the road."

Rex squinted again against the darkness. "You saw me talk to the princess, the daughter of Gororm?"

"I saw. It was wonderful what you did. I have been trying to open her eyes for some time, but she did not want to see me. She can be quite obstinate."

"I'm certain I only lucked out in the timing," Rex offered humbly, the mead beginning to lose hold of him.

"Perhaps."

The horse stirred and tackle clinked. A slow clip-clop neared Rex until the head of a black stallion broke free of the darkness and carried its rider into the glow of the torchlight.

"My name is Esmeralda."

The woman wore green. A forest-green velvet cloak covered her body, its hood hiding her face. She languidly raised a smooth olive com-plexioned hand to the top of the hood. Emerald rings adorned her long fingers, whose nails were painted an opaque green. Jade bracelets clanked as gravity pulled them down her arm. With a graze of her hand, the hood flowed down green highlighted black hair and revealed her face.

Rex took in a sharp breath, the air hanging in his lungs until he no longer knew which part of the breathing cycle he was on.

Esmeralda smiled. Eyes like a green sea flashed deep wisdom and a slow blink of her lids revealed sparkling mint-lime eye shadow. "I am pleased to meet you."

The young woman's beauty was more than Rex could consume in one sitting. He averted his eyes with a respectful bow, tucking a quiver-ing chin to his chest. "The pleasure is mine, my lady."

"It is late, Brother Rex, and the air chilled. I would like to know more about your encounter and more about you. Will you come visit me on the morrow?"

Rex lifted his head as high as he dared to avoid full eye contact, lest he evaporate in the moment. "I am at your call, madam. Where can I find you?"

The stead's hooves began their percussion on the stone as the horse backed into the darkness. Esmeralda vanished with a whisper, "Ask the mayor."

Rex lay fully clothed on a soft down mattress in the Mayor of Cor-nerstone's guest room. He had scant memory of how he got back from the bridge. He knew he recovered his pack, found his way through winding streets, through the front door, and into the room. But it was all accomplished automatically without the aid of awareness. For his awareness was too full with the vision of her to allot any attention to trivial matters.

I'm in love? Surely not. The mead is dancing in my head and toying with my perceptions. I have no time for love; I'm on a quest.

Bringing the sleeve of his frock to his face, he smelled it. Her scent had penetrated the rough material, infusing the fabric with a creamy floral essence.

"Esmeralda," he whispered. Turning on his side, he hugged a pillow and pulled his legs up to his chest. Rex stared at the wooden shudders that kept the damp air from chilling the room. Beyond the barrier he knew there was a moon well into its first quarter, and he longed to gaze at it. Sleep came to him reluctantly; he slumbered as much as a man could with his insides squirming in joyous anticipation.

In the morning, Rex awoke jittery. He tried to convince himself that his hungover body just wanted more alcohol to quell its withdrawal from the night's inebriation. Or perhaps his body quivered from the cold room that had lost its warmth to the night. But in truth, it was not alcohol he needed or the comfort of a hearth, but a different type of spirit, a different type of fire—it was her.

"Good morning, Brother Rex!" the mayor called out too cheerily for a man lost in thought to take in. Sitting at the table made the mayor's short stature of two meters appear smaller. However, he was of average height for the people of Cornerstone. Years spent working in the sun had toasted his skin, yet the rose of his cheeks still showed through.

Rex managed a smile as he entered the small room where breakfast was well underway. "Good morning, Mayor Dawes."

The mayor's wife bustled into the room with a platter of sizzling meats. She lit up at the sight of Rex, and reached her face out to kiss him on both cheeks. "Good morning, Rex."

"Good morning, Gayle," he responded, feeling warm at the familiarity allowed him by the grand lady of the house.

Rex sat at the table as Gayle returned to the kitchen for some fresh bread. "I see you have been up working already this morning," Rex winked at the mayor.

The mayor looked down at his wool work shirt and coarse pants, scratched his balding head, and chuckled, "Oh, yes, being mayor doesn't mean there are no cows to tend or bees to check."

"Indeed."

Gayle reentered briskly with a basket of bread. She brushed at random blotches of flour on her bright housecoat. "Eat boys, eat. It's not going to nourish you by looking at it."

"It smells wonderful," Rex complimented.

"Helps with the taste, now don't be shy, I've seen your appetite," she joked, moving a stray flock of curly golden hair from her kind face with a puff of air.

"Don't have to deliver me an invitation," the mayor proclaimed with a mouthful of pear, the juice dripping down his chin.

"Ah, me," Rex sighed as he sorted through the meat. "Do you know where I might find a lady named Esmeralda?"

The wicker breadbasket hit the floor with a flat thump. A small chunk of fruit tumbled from the mayor's mouth. The couple stood frozen, breathless.

"Um, hello? What happened?" Rex asked.

"Esmeralda..." Gayle stammered, tears welling up in her eyes.

"She spoke to you... did you see her?" the mayor urged.

"Yes, she spoke, I saw. What's going on? Is she a siren? A wicked deceiver?"

"Oh, no, she is the lady protector of these lands," Gayle explained picking up the basket that, thankfully, had not lost its contents in the drop. Gayle placed the breadbasket on the table. "Have you not heard of the Red Queen?"

"Sounds familiar, but to be honest, my mind's a little fuzzy right now."

"I bet," the mayor said staring three centimeters in front of him. "How did she look? I mean to say, was she a child, an old woman, or..."

"She was beautiful, young, probably my age."

"Oh, blessed be, blessed be," Gayle muttered and then busied herself lighting the scented candles that populated windowsills and small wall shelves. Although the morning sunlight streaming through the windows cancelled out the effect of the burning wicks, she proceeded to light them all just the same.

"So, what did she say to you?" the mayor pressed with a flourish of his hands.

"What?" Rex shrugged. "We just talked briefly, and she asked me to come see her today and said you would know where to find her."

Mayor Dawes shot up, unsettling his chair behind him. "She mentioned me?"

"She spoke of you and your wife, quite favorably I might add."

Gayle rushed to her husband and threw her arms around him in joy. "Oh, blessed be! Blessed be!"

The couple danced together in their embrace, murmuring their love for one another.

"Well," Rex said, clearing his throat. "She's obviously very important, this Red Queen you speak of, but I'm not sure it was the same person. You see, this woman wore green."

Rex had hoped this detail would settle down the current jubilee; however, it only fueled the excitement of his hosts. They turned to him in astonishment and spoke as one.

"She's in *green*?"

The mayor and Gayle rained small kisses on each other's face. Both praised and rejoiced that a good year was in store for them. Rex was not clear on the local customs or myths, and quickly found that he would not have time to inquire about them, since Gayle strove to scoot him out the door.

"Oh, you must go. Go now!" she commanded. The woman licked her hand and used the spittle to mat down Rex's hair. "You can't go like this, go and change."

"Change? Gayle, I'm a wandering monk, what do you think I have that I can change into?"

The mayor intervened in his wife's sprucing attempts. "Now, Gayle, he'll be fine." He turned to Rex while guiding his exhausted spouse to a chair. "But really, Rex, at least splash some water on your face. And take your pack, it can be a long journey at times or sometimes it is very short."

"That is all and well, but where am I supposed to go?" Rex stood up, his frustration showing. He did not like all the commotion and fuss about—well about things he had to admit he knew nothing about.

Who is this person? Is she important? Some powerful enchantress? As Brother Joseph would say, "Fear no person, we are all biological, but be wary of those who beguile with words." Is that it then? Has she convinced these folk that she is mightier than they are? A fine game I'm sure, and there does not appear to be any malevolence. Let them have at it if they wish. For me, I'm just curious what she might know about these lands. I have no time for goddess worship, and wouldn't even if I could spare a moment.

Rex wiped his mouth on his sleeve. And there it was. That smell. Her smell. Her scent. It unlocked some deep code waiting to be deciphered and reveal secret longings lying dormant inside him.

"Take the road north into the woods," the mayor instructed.

Rex waited for him to continue, but the man was busy caressing his wife's glowing face.

"And?" Rex hinted.

"Huh? Oh, that's it. Just keep going until, well, until she reveals herself to you. Again."

Rex found it difficult not to roll his eyes, but he managed out of respect for his two hosts. After gathering his sparse belongings, he bade them farewell and headed north out of Cornerstone.

It neared noon on a crisp, clear fall day, as Rex strolled through the woods. As it had for the last several years, his staff tapped out a beat to keep Rex's pace steady and his mind set on the journey. Rounding an arch in the road, he came upon a small clearing with a modest wood-frame house. It stood on a stone foundation and had a thatched roof. Climbing rose vines covered the outside of the wattle and daub walls. Still holding a bloom late into the year, their pink and red flowers provided a soft fragrant boundary.

On a rope suspended porch swing sat Esmeralda wrapped in a green blanket, sipping something warm, and gently gliding. She beckoned to him with a languorous wave.

Blood flushed Rex's face and his mouth watered. A leaf filled gust blew in from behind, pushing him forward. And, with the wind came clarity of mind. Never in his training, never in his adventures, never in the deepest state of meditation had he experienced such clarity. Timeless mysteries vanished, meaningfulness crystallized. The world he had known fell far away and he found himself standing before her on the porch. In the gaze of her sparkling eyes, he realized the one pure truth he had ever known.

I love her.

"Hello, Rex."

"Hello, Esmeralda."

"Will you sit with me and have some tea?"

"Yes."

The two sat on the swing sipping tea and speaking gently in smiles. When the sun tired, drooping in the dimming sky to give way to a waxing gibbous moon, they went inside.

The main room housed a sitting area, hearth and kitchen. Wooden planks created a cleaner floor then the traditional dirt floors, which were slowly vanishing into history. Candles, hundreds of candles, twinkled and warmed the living space. Spices and herbs filled bottles or dangled suspended on twine around, on, and over a cooking counter. A closed door off center on the rear wall guarded a back bedroom. Esmeralda placed their cups in a washbasin and joined Rex, who had sat in one of two wooden rockers in front of the fireplace.

"I like your home," Rex said. He took in the rich, sweet woody aroma of ginger that hung in the air.

"Thank you, I like coming here this time of the year." She sat in the other rocker and started it creaking to and fro.

"You said you saw me talking to Arias in the rain. What were you doing out?"

"I was on my way to visit the queen."

"Queen Dezair?"

"Yes." Esmeralda reached out and flicked off a small leaf that had settled on Rex's shoulder. "I brought her a gift. I came to her as an old crone bearing a spell book." She twittered. "And can you believe it? She took it."

"A gift? You gave a spell book to a terrible creature like her? Do you know what she and that repugnant king have been doing to the people of the region? Not to mentioned to those two children. Why, did you know they murdered..."

Esmeralda placed a finger softly on his lips and then settled back into her chair. "I know, Rex, I know. Think of it as an infection I gave her. She will scratch at it for a time, then discard it until one day it flares up and eats her alive."

"Oh, my."

"Arias's sister Zoila was there, too. She watched me from the shadows rather closely. A very keen girl."

"Hopelessly dedicated to the crown I hear."

Esmeralda rubbed below her full bottom lip. "Yes, that's what they say. Still, there was something in her eyes. Something waiting." She gazed into the fire for a time. "Well, nothing to do now but see what comes to fruition."

"I suppose you're right," Rex concluded. He caught sight of a mandolin in a corner among some scrolls and a folded painter's easel. Excited, he got up to retrieve it. "Hey, I learned to play something like this at the monastery."

"Do you play well?" Esmeralda asked, energized by his enthusiasm.

"Well, you know, just messing around, mostly," he grinned. Sitting back down, he tuned the instrument. "Shall I?"

"Yes, please do."

With a wink and a nod, he set to strumming the strings. Clearing his throat he sang:

> *"Seven sisters dance, but only one for me,*
> *Seven years of bondage, 'till you set me free.*
> *Seven maidens have gone by the by,*
> *Seven planets hidden in the celestial sky.*
> *Seven chakras vibrate inside you as,*
> *Seven colors blaze the spectrum hue.*
> *On seven seas will I sail my ships,*
> *For seven seconds of your sweet lips."*

"Sorry," Rex said abashed. "Just a song I learned relaxing around the monastery garden. I don't know why that one came to mind. My apologies if it offended or embarrassed you, I had forgotten how it ended."

"Oh, no, no, not at all," Esmeralda assured, rubbing her hand on top of Rex's. "I thought it was a nice song. Not one you would expect to hear at a monastery, though. What an odd philosophy your order must have."

"Truth be told, most converts come there much later in life. I learned that song from an old sailor—Quinn was his name. Nice man, lots of tattoos. Unlike other orders, we don't take the young. The High Council waits for its members to come to the monastery out of need, not forced indoctrination." Rex paused thoughtfully. "Actually, I'm told I was the only child taken in and raised in the order. Stayed until I was 21. Hmm. But I'm babbling now, I uh... "

Her hand had lingered on his long past the moment of friendly consolation. A heavy stillness permeated the room. Rex saw that, for the first time, she was not looking at him, but had lowered her eyes, shyly biting her bottom lip.

"Rex?" she whispered.

Rex struggled to find his voice. "Yes?"

Esmeralda stood up, the green blanket that had warmed her since his arrival slid off marble smooth shoulders, cascading down to pool at her bare feet. Standing in a turquoise-green slip dress, hem swaying above her knees, the young maiden took Rex's hand. She sighed when his hand accepted hers, her radiant eyes drowsy in the moment.

He had never known powerlessness until the moment she led him to her bedroom. Even if he wanted to, he could not have spoken, could not have altered his footsteps that mirrored hers. He had been plunged into an ancient torrent and was helpless to swim against it. He could only allow the currents to take him as his awareness became sedate and his body awoke.

The bedroom was like midnight. Hundreds of twinkling candles restrained the darkness from swallowing everything in a smothering embrace. An amber glow radiated softly from the small bedroom hearth, casting light at low angles. Rose oil aromatized the air—swirling mystically, its hidden properties eased inhibitions.

Leading Rex to a modest bed, she drew back several thick quilts and sat him on fresh cotton bedding. Her trembling fingers fidgeted with the bottom of her dress before pulling it up and over her head, discarding it to the floor.

Rex felt tears begin to well up in his eye as he beheld her beauty. The glow of the candles tempered by the sleepy firelight brought out a golden-brown richness in her supple skin. Slowly he reached out, using his palm to kiss her warm belly. His hand slid over to her round hip, caressing a path down her thigh and then returned home to his lap.

"I've never..." he started.

"Shh, I know, my Rex, I know." She climbed on the bed, embracing him from behind and whispered in his ear, "Neither have I. I chose you."

Her soft hair framed the side of his neck, finding its way inside his collar to graze his skin. *This is crazy; I'm not supposed to be doing this—am I? Who is this woman? Has she cast a spell on me? I just met her, and yet I feel as if we've shared lifetimes together. It's a trick, just a trick of biology; a weakness of the flesh. The order, the quest—these are the important realities. These are the focus, the...*

The small voice inside his head, gallantly battling for stability in the face of confusion, was silenced by the contact of Esmeralda's plump lips on his jaw line. She nibbled and pulled at his beard with playful teeth, until he turned his head and engaged her mouth with his. Her honey flavor slaked his thirst for her, but failed to appease his growing hunger.

Sliding back from him, she all but disappeared under the quilts, leaving visible only her eyes to beckon to him from behind black tousled hair. He answered the call by disrobing and vanishing into the depths of the feathery bed. Time passed unnoticed as the feel of her became his only reality. As Esmeralda shuddered in his arms, he realized once again that he really knew nothing at all. Any confidence he had about his grasp on the world drifted away as they snuggled in passion's after-glow. Their heavy breathing slowly subsided, pulling them both into a deep sleep.

Sometime during the night, she awoke within their embrace and whispered in his ear, "Will you winter with me?"

"Yes," he replied from his blissful slumber.

The winter passed like a moment that never began, never changed, and might never have ended. The couple settled into the cold season concerned only with the simple pleasures of living. Companionship blanketed them as they went about daily maintaining the household, securing sustenance and caring for Esmerelda's horses.

They became known in many of the hamlets and in Cornerstone in particular. They would ride into the villages and fellowship with the local folk at a tavern or in a barn for a festival. Rex worked alongside Esmeralda, who provided midwife care to humans and beasts. Together they sat with families in mourning during times of loss. Often they gathered charitable donations of clothing from wealthier towns, which the pair distributed along with small treats to the children. The lovers sought to do something meaningful each day and make the world a better place for their fellow inhabitants.

During the Winter Solstice, Esmeralda and Rex stayed in Cornerstone as guests of the mayor and his wife. As a gift for the village, they presented two new mead recipes to aid the resident mead makers in expanding their commerce. Rex had created mead by mixing indigenous mulberries with honey. Esmeralda donated the secrets to her rhodomel, which blended honey and attar—a rose petal distillate.

Rex had never known such peace. They lived by accepting what the day had to offer and following the rhythms of life, all the while sharing the experience with each other. But as winter ended, a growing dread grew inside him. He felt the restless pull of unfinished business and, try as he might to ignore it, thoughts of his quest churned deep in his mind. He was certain Esmeralda could sense the conflict that troubled his sleep, but she did not speak of it, as if leaving it to him to take responsibility for his thoughts.

Much to his anguish, he finally did face up to the decision he had secretly made.

Rex sat very still on the porch with pack and staff at hand, waiting for Esmeralda to return from an early morning horseback ride. The first warm breeze of spring flowed around him with the promise of new life. It mocked the dark news he harbored.

"What is it, my love?" Esmeralda asked after returning from brushing down her horse.

"I..." he hesitated.

"Yes?"

Rex released all the air in his lungs as if it were his dying breath. His shoulders sank, and he fixed his gaze on the ground.

"Winter is no more, and I must return to my quest."

"Must you?" She sat beside him and stroked the back of his head. "I'm not so sure. Stay with me—all you require is here."

"Please don't make this harder. You must understand, I have a purpose out there. There are things I must do, things I don't even know about yet, but I'm certain of their importance."

Esmeralda curtly stood up. "Why must I understand your blathering? Are you saying that being with me is a folly? That it has no purpose, no importance? Was my body just an amusement to you, my thoughts mere entertainment, our work just a passing fancy?"

Gulping hard, Rex felt the surroundings closing in on him. He reached for her hand. "No, my love, that's not..."

"Don't call me your love!" she spat and jerked her hand away from his. "I know who your love is. It is the monastery and your little monk friends, and your precious Brother Joseph. These are your loves. They are what you seek a passage back to. There *is* meaningful purpose around here, there is plenty that needs to be done—so don't make excuses."

The sky darkened and thunder rumbled in the distance. Rex stood up weakly and, with his eyes cast down in shame said, "You are my love, there will never be another. I give this vow to you." Looking up at her, he saw she had aged 30 years. "Please don't do that."

A deluge of large raindrops pounded the land. The resounding clatter of the downpour on the roof drowned out his words, causing Rex to raise his voice. "Please, Esmeralda, I do love you!"

"Love?" she retorted, her voice clear and still within the chaos. "Don't speak of things you know not of. Go about your tasks for all it will matter. You are still too young to see what is important, and you never will as long as you live off the teat of the Brotherhood."

"Esmeralda..." he moved toward her.

She shirked back. "Go."

Reluctantly he went, leaving the shelter of the eaves and sloshing through the harsh rain. When he reached the arch in the road from which he first beheld her sitting on the porch that clear autumn day, he glanced back. Esmeralda, having regressed to a five-year-old, stood with hands clasped in front of her, lips trembling. She looked westward beyond the clearing, her eyes no doubt red from the stinging of tears. A horrible tightness seized Rex's chest. He felt the empty cold touch of Death's finger upon his heart—and a piece of him died that day never to be resurrected.

Returning from his remembrances, Rex came back to awareness in the present. He discovered himself biting his fist to prevent an unbearable grief from bursting free of its restraints. Something stirred behind him, and he turned, gulping back his sobs.

Annie lay with eyes wide open and an understanding smile warming her face. Her look comforted him, and he returned the smile. Seemingly satisfied with the exchange, she stretched, snuggled into Shiva's fur, and fell back to sleep.

Rex turned back to the night sky. With a deep, cleansing sigh, he continued to cut his hair and resolved to face up to what his life had become.

Chapter Fourteen

Zoila strode across the courtyard toward the cantina in the soldiers' barracks. She felt a strong desire to be among her peers, to lose herself in the familiar surroundings of the corps of arms. The cantina's smoky warmth embraced her as she stepped inside. Pausing for a moment upon entering, she acknowledged the scattered greetings from the other soldiers. She made her way to the bar, comforted by the low roar of conversations that bursts of laughter occasionally punctuated.

"Some barley and hops for ya tonight, Zoila?" a one-eyed bartender asked.

"A pint of it, Jake," Zoila smiled and nodded.

Jake was the only person in the room that could get away with such familiarity. He had once been under her command, and then he had referred to her as Captain Zoila. But he was no longer in the army. He had lost one eye in battle and was half-blind in the other. Zoila remembered him coming to her in tears, pleading for help. He had told her the corps was all he knew, and he would die if he could not somehow be a part of it. Zoila had taken pity on him and arranged work at the cantina. She had always had a soft spot for her troops; they were her true family.

Them and you, Arias, she thought, taking a long pull on the rich brew. *Why didn't you continue your training? If you hadn't quit and gone off trying to convert and incite the populace, we could have been an unstoppable team. But no, you had your crusade, and I was left alone as usual to think for both of us.*

Despite her seeping stream of painful thoughts, she was beginning to settle into her seat at the bar. The beer massaged her with its friendly tingle, and Zoila breathed more easily. She had fought hard to win the right to feel at ease amongst the other warriors. Most of them were men, but she found that had been the least of her barriers. It was not uncommon for a woman to join the ranks if she proved herself strong and capable; however, to be the daughter of the king—that was a difficulty.

"Barkeep," she asked to confirm her own thoughts, "why is the aristocrat not welcomed in the corps?"

Jake shook his head with a smile. "I've heard it told that they pale at the quickening of their own pulse, fearing it to be a heart attack. It's all that fine rearing that makes them too shy to spill blood lest it spoil their manicure."

"Is that what you believe?"

"What I believe, Zoila, is that people who are raised to think themselves above others, won't cover your back in the thick of it. But that never was you." His last remark was solemn, and he poured her another drink.

"That's right," she confirmed, "that never was me. Arias used to be haughty like that before she began having visions. You remember?"

"A pain in the arse, if you'll forgive my saying so."

"Not at all, that's what she was—so privileged in her thinking. She was only accepted by the other soldiers because of me."

"True, but I must say many were relieved when she quit her training."

"Hmph, I'm sure many wished I would've quit."

"That's not so," Jake consoled. "You were different. You took every difficult duty, no matter how dirty or dangerous. You asked for no privileges, slept on the ground, ate the common gruel, and marched the day into darkness. Everyone respected that. Zoila, you *earned* the right to lead."

With eyelids starting to droop, she shared a smile with Jake. "Thanks, my old friend." No other words were needed.

She allowed the sour drink to tickle its way down her throat as she relived the details of the night's campaign. The beer seemed to awaken tactile memories; ghost sensations revisited lonely skin. Her inner thighs tingled and she felt a phantom pressure of her horse pressing on her groin. The evening's battle had left her body saturated with testosterone; sexual tension gnawed at her like a trapped animal chewing its leg to get free. She squirmed a little in an unsuccessful effort to temporarily relieve her growing need.

"Have you seen Damek?" she asked Jake.

"Naw, not tonight," he shrugged. Then in a low tone he asked, "Are you two, still... you know?"

She shot him a look that clearly drew a line in the sand. "I wanted to tell him how the battle went."

Jake gave an understanding nod, and then waited on some other thirsty soldiers.

Zoila lost herself in a mental reconstruction of the battle. She stared into her brew and blocked out the bustle of the cantina.

The monk fought well, must have studied in some of the hill monasteries. And who was that girl with him? Was she brave or just stupid? Probably a

little of both as is common for a child. She didn't seem to fully grasp the lethal-
ity of the situation; yet she must have sensed some impending doom, but did not
succumb to the instinct to run.

Images coursed through her mind, and her body reacted as if the past were present. Her breathing quickened and became deep, as nostrils flared, muscles tensed, and a pleasurable buzzing vibrated down from her chest to the pit of her stomach.

"You there," Zoila had called out, "surrender the dragon, now!"

"Never!" defied the monk.

"I'm not talking to you, old man. I'm addressing the young wench, so shut your hole."

"Never!" the young girl bellowed so bravely.

"Then," Zoila had announced, unshouldering her bow, "prepare to be taken by force!"

She squirmed on her chair, pressing her knees together tightly to try and dull the ache building urgency deep inside her.

What is it about the fray that feels like being at home — like being in my ele-
ment? Is chaos and violence the stone and timber of my being? Somehow I
don't think it's normal, and yet there it is.

"You look tired," Jake commented, removing her empty cup.

Zoila looked up, distracted from her thoughts. "Yeah, it's been a rough night." She stood and rubbed her fingers vigorously into her scalp. "I'm turning in."

The cold midnight air felt refreshing after the smoked filled cantina. She stopped off at a nearby latrine to alleviate a fullness in her bladder. She had to fumble some with her trouser bindings, since the beer had begun to waltz with her fatigue, but she welcomed the heady sensations.

Zoila made her way to a two-story stone building that billeted the officers. Without ceremony, she unlocked her door and went into her room. Once inside, she walked over to a small hearth and warmed her hands at the fire. She liked the privileges of being an officer, liked having an aide to ensure a fueled fire and...

... oh, yes, the twerp remembered the bath. He might just make it after all.

She did a little shuffle-dance over to the wooden tub and stirred her hand in the water.

"Warm," she said out loud to herself.

The light radiated rich tones from the burning wood, supplying what little illumination she required, so she saw no need to burn a candle. The room was simple, reflecting her tendency toward practicality. She did have a room in the castle, but she hadn't stayed there in years, preferring to reside with her troops and away from her parents.

Undoing her sword belt, she felt the weight of her prized possession slide away from her body. She held the sheathed sword up close to her face, gazing at its strange twisting handle that ended in a dragon's talon. A beloved teacher had bestowed the sword on her after she had first drawn blood in battle. The ceremony that followed officially entered her into the ranks of the royal army. She caressed it gently, and then laid it on a nearby wooden chair.

Returning to the tub, she stripped off the rest of her gear first removing her boots, then her pants. The garments piled quietly on the floor—a lump of external identity worshipping at the feet of its goddess. The cool air felt brisk on her exposed bottom-half and she worked out a small cramp in her upper thigh.

After a stretch, she took off her leather top and rubbed her shoulder through her undergarment. She was about to remove her undershirt, when she suddenly froze.

She was not alone.

The sensation of being watched grew strong inside her. Her warrior training automatically replaced her relaxed mental state. She made herself into a smaller target and prepared her body to spring by hunching down as if to pick up her clothes. Carefully turning toward the chair where her sword lay, she sprung forward and leapt for the weapon. Before she could land and grab her blade, a blur of motion dashed in front of her, and she pounced down upon an empty chair.

My sword!

Stripped of her weapon, she felt exposed and her assessment of the situation turned fearful.

No! I don't need a weapon. I can take this intruder with my bare hands.

She scanned the room, the shadows cast by the fire rippled like water on a breeze blown lake. There were enough dark spots for someone or something to hide in. Again, she caught a flash of movement. Her mind knew where to advance before her wakened self realized it. She launched toward a sound; arms and fingers stretched out like grappling hooks seeking a place to take hold. And take hold they did, as she collided with the intruder and sent them both sprawling. The sword flew out of the stranger's hands and skidded across the stone floor. They both popped up to their feet, eyes locked in combat.

In a flurry, the opponents exchanged rapid blows and counters. Forearms, hardened by years of conditioning battered one another with the dull resonance of wooden clubs colliding. Guttural sounds punctuated the martial dance—grunts of power pushed up from below the navel past suspended vocal cords. Zoila executed an unsuccessful sweep, which the intruder evaded by springing impressively into the air. She spiraled upward as he landed squarely on his feet and immediately threw his fist toward Zoila's rising head. Zoila spun into the punch, grabbing his wrist and slamming her back to his chest. Using the momentum from his missed strike, she easily hurled the man over her shoulder.

The intruder tumbled and rolled across the floor, smashing into the side of the bed. Quickly recovering, he jumped up as Zoila hurled her body toward him like a battering ram. The combatants crashed onto the bed, thumping dully on the feather mattress and causing the bed legs to scrape across the floor. Zoila quickly pinned the man down by sitting on his chest and bringing her weight to bear on his arms as she knelt on them.

Looking down on her captive, she felt the lustiness that had been smoldering in her blood all evening come to a boil.

"So, you've seen fit to steal from me, have you?" Zoila panted as she reached behind her and unfastened the man's pants. "I think I shall take something from you instead."

She plunged her hand inside his loosened pants. "Don't resist," she commanded.

Zoila lifted her bottom off the man's chest, slid back slightly, and set slowly down on him. In the quiet of the room that so recently had echoed the sound of their combat, the two settled into a familiar rhythm. Heavy, deep breaths kept the time and the flicker of the fire transformed the mood. Their embrace tightened and then released.

They lay together in the stillness of the moment; their labored breathing easing into a more even pace. Zoila realized she had buried her teeth softly into the man's chest. She let loose her hold, wiped the spittle from her mouth on his hairy body, and rolled off him into the comfort of her fluffy bed.

The man reached out to her in an effort to reconnect, but Zoila withdrew into herself.

"You're late," Damek sighed and pulled at the patch of beard on his chin. "I've been waiting under the covers for three hours." He stretched out a long yawn, "I think I nodded off."

"What are you complaining about?" Zoila answered, coldly. "You got what you wanted."

"Oh, don't be that way. Hey, how'd it go tonight?" he asked unfazed by her curtness.

"It didn't."

"What happened?"

"Exactly what I told you would happen if the king had his way," she said irritated.

"Oh no, he didn't make you take the ghouls, did he?"

"He did, and they screwed it all up." Zoila got out of bed and pulled one of the blankets from under Damek. Wrapping it around herself, she went over to stare at the fire. "That monk was there."

"What monk?"

"Remember I told you about a monk who came to the villages long ago?"

The man sat up in bed to better engage in the conversation. "You mean the one who turned Arias?"

"Yes. He first spoke with her the same day that old witch brought a gift to the queen—a very odd gesture. I didn't recognize him at first, because he was dressed up like a wizard. Pity, such a waste. And that's not all; there was a young girl with him. She got the gift before I could reach Holdfast."

"What could it mean?" Damek mused, pulling at his jaw line.

Zoila snorted, "It means my life just got harder, that's what it means."

"I'm sorry, love, I wish I could have been there with you."

"Yeah," she answered as she gazed into the flickering light. "I've got to figure out a way to keep that girl away from Arias and get that gift."

"What makes you think she'll head for your sister?"

"I had the gift in my hand for a moment—it was a key. I just know the girl will be drawn to Arias. I feel it as sure as I stand here; it's what the king and queen want." Zoila's voice trailed off, "They'll use her to get to Arias, and then we'll be lost."

Damek fidgeted with his pants and refastened them. He was not a tall man as solders in the corps go, but he had broad shoulders and a strong body. His curly black hair crowned a war scared body, and his playful smile made him easy and welcome company.

They had met in basic training, both of them targets of ridicule—she for her station in life, and he for his size. They bonded against the whispers and jeers, as outcasts are prone to do. Together they grew strong opposing the status quo, and now both of them were leaders in the royal army. But it was his gentleness and persistence that had deepened her feelings for him.

Where does he fit into all this? If Arias and I can overcome and break free, how will he fit into it all? I've never thought much about that. I wish I could just dismiss him as a distraction, but we've stood together on the battlefield and fought common foes. Bonds like that are forged stronger than bonds of blood through kin. Look at him. Ready to serve me at my bidding. Pathetic.

At the moment she saw him as pathetic, a deeper thought betrayed her bravado. She felt the pain of being loved.

"A copper piece for your thoughts," he offered with a casualness that sent an ache to her heart.

"Are they worth so little?" Zoila mused in a far-away voice.

"Of course not. Are you in a difficult mood?"

"If you find me so difficult, why don't you find the door and forget the way to my room?"

Damek made his way over to her by the hearth and touched her shoulder lightly. "Because I love you, even when you're difficult." He brushed his lips against the back of her head.

"Stop," she whispered and fought against the tears that would not obey her command to retreat.

"But I do. I would die for you."

Zoila moved away from him and sat back on the bed. "How easily you men offer up your lives in the name of love. You're so selfish."

He turned toward her in disbelief. "Selfish? I hardly think giving up one's life is selfish."

"Well, it is. What is there to dying? Don't you go into battle facing death all the time?"

"True, but I'm not looking to die then, I'm looking to kill the enemy. But, I would gladly sacrifice my one life for yours. Is that not love? I mean once it's over, it's over."

"Exactly! Once you're dead, your worries are over and the living have to go on facing each tedious day. Dying is nothing, it's living that is frightening, and it's living that takes courage."

"Those are grim thoughts."

"Perhaps, but there it is. I hope you got your money's worth. And here's an extra thought free of charge. Next time you want to wrangle your way into a woman's heart, tell her you'll live for her. Tell her you'll crawl through the pointless years with her and keep her company as the fruit of her youth withers on the vine."

"Okay," he conceded and sat down beside her. "I will live for you."

Zoila sneered, "Sell your lines to the village girls who are content to be your breeding stock."

Damek stretched out on the bed and laughed, "You can be as crass as you want, but I know you love me."

"You don't know anything about me."

"I know more about you than you know about yourself, because I know you love me even though you don't seem to know it yourself."

"Just go, you're giving me a headache."

"I thought maybe I could sleep by your side tonight for once."

"Well, you thought wrong. I want to be alone. Besides, staying would be masochistic—I'm just going to be a bitch anyway."

"It's not such a bad quality," he said.

"I'm not playing around—get out!"

"All right," he shrugged and got up. He gathered the rest of his things in the dim lit room, moving about the tension of the moment with familiarity.

Why do I keep doing this to myself, Zoila thought as conflicting desires and demands battled inside her. *I want so much to... but no, it cannot be. I am not meant for this. I mustn't lose my resolve. I must think of Arias, she is all that matters now. Still I... No still, there is no still. Just maintain control, Zoila. Soon he'll be out the door and you can sleep and forget this wretched world.*

Damek put his hand on the door handle and paused. "You know it's funny, we've faced death together many times. You've watched my back, and I've watched yours. We have put our lives in each other's hands, but you are too afraid to let me share your bed and hold you until dawn."

"Yes," she shot back coldly, "that's so hilarious. Now get out."

"Right," he gritted with exasperation and pushed down the handle.

Somewhere inside Zoila, a voice shouted through her warrior armor, *No!* With a jolt, she stood up. Her voice was small and soft, "Shorty?"

Damek smiled at the sound of her pet name for him escaping her lips. "Yes, Princess?" he responded without turning around.

"See you tomorrow?"

"Yeah, see you tomorrow."

He slipped out of the room like a shadow being sucked into the night.

Zoila sat in the silence of his absence, pulling the blanket closely around her. She looked over at the tub and became aware of the grime the day had left on her body. She got up, removed her undershirt, and walked over to her bath, her feet padding softly on the stone floor.

Golden hued waves of light from the hearth glided gracefully over her well-conditioned body, which now moved unencumbered as she entered the tub. She eased into the tepid water of the vessel, almost able to fully extend her legs. Zoila brought an engorged sponge to her sweaty face and pressed it to her forehead. The cleansing water exploded out and ran down her skin.

A hint of sadness glimmered in her sobering eyes as she looked over her body. The battle scars that slashed across her told silent stories of hardships, victories and defeats. The path down which her life had traveled did not allow her to possess the smooth plump figures of the village girls, who primped and preened themselves to attract a mate and so continue the age-old dance of life.

No, she wore the history of her personal struggles exposed on her flesh, and she wore them proudly. As proudly as she wore the sacred tattoo she had inked following an intense training period at a hidden mountain monastery. There she had learned to externalize her inner powers, to bring about a union of thought and action. She smiled softly and looked down to follow her body art.

On her left thigh a dragon began, its red framed, green head faced furiously toward her inner thigh. Its scaly black-green body snaked its way up her left side, encircled her left breast by coming up through her cleavage and whipping its tail over her left shoulder. Although she could not see it, she knew the tail curled to an end halfway down her spine. The dragon's powerful legs appeared to be caught in motion as it made its way down the front of her body.

Zoila lightly traced the dragon from her breast to her thigh. *And where do you think you're going, my friend? Do you want to get inside me? To possess me? Rule me? I was never told why you were bestowed upon me. I don't know the meaning. Perhaps, it is a sign that I must destroy you, before you destroy me; that we are eternally at odds. But you are so beautiful, too beautiful to destroy and cast out of my life. Is there no way we can live together, my precious one?*

She shook the thoughts away, choosing to concentrate on washing. She did not want to think about destiny or missions, plots or plans. And as her eyes betrayed her by glancing at the empty bed—she knew what she really didn't want to think about. She didn't want to contemplate the thought of another night sleeping alone.

Chapter Fifteen

Annie woke under several layers of blankets. She guessed Rex had draped them over her during the night. The morning air cooled her face as her warm moist breath condensed with each exhale. Sitting up with a yawning stretch, she kept one blanket clutched around her and let the others fall like a petals around her.

Rex sat across from Annie on the other side of the campfire. Gone were the regal robes of a sorcerer. In their place was his travel-worn, faded purple cloak. He smiled at her as he stirred embers around a kettle that sat on the coals.

"Good morning," Annie greeted, still rubbing the sleep from her eyes.

"Good morning, Annie. Would you like some tea to warm yourself? I'm afraid all I have to eat is some biscuits and a drop or two of honey."

"That sounds good, thank you." Annie looked around her, then asked, "Where's Shiva?"

"Oh, she comes and goes as the need occurs to her. I'm sure she'll be back; I think she's taken a liking to you."

Annie smiled. "I like her. I never had a pet—I, uh—okay I know she's nobody's pet, and she is free as the wind and all that."

"Don't fret," Rex assured. "I know what you mean."

He poured them both some tea and divided up the biscuits and honey.

"Eat in good health." Rex raised his cup toward Annie.

Annie returned the salute, and it was then that she became aware of the change. "Your hair and beard are shorter... and darker. Wasn't it white and long yesterday? Now it's brown with some gray, and short."

"Yes, I cut it off last night and, oh, I don't know—it got darker with the change."

"Oh. Well, it looks good. Not like how I would imagine a sorcerer would look, but... "

"Monk," he interrupted.

"Huh?"

"I've given up the wizard-sorcerer vocation. It was mostly a form of vanity anyway—at least for me. So it's just Brother Rex, your humble monk servant from the Brotherhood of the Sacred Spear." He tilted his head as an offering of service.

"Things sure do change quickly around here. So, I should call you, Brother Rex?" she asked not wanting to make the same mistake with informality as before.

"Well, you are the bearer of Holdfast's gift, so call me Rex or whatever you want. Tired old fool will probably do." He sipped from his cup, avoided eye contact with Annie, and then muttered, "I suppose I should lay prostrate in front of you..."

Annie shifted uncomfortably. She was well in tuned with the mood changes of others, especially when it involved aggression. *I don't know what I did, but he's mad at me. Now what am I supposed to do? I don't know where I'm at or what is going on, and the one person who's been nice is angry with me. I gotta do something, maybe if I give him this stupid key around my neck, he'll be nice to me again.*

Annie took a drink of tea and finger-walked her free hand up her body. When her hand came to the key dangling around her neck, she closed her fingers around it in a firm grasp, intending to pull it off.

That's when the vision came to her. Bending lights of color shot toward her as if refracted from a prism. She found herself bathed in hue-saturated brilliance. Emitting from the illumination, or perhaps infused in it, came a voice or voices. She couldn't be certain, only that it was female and reverberated in her head, causing a tingling pressure behind her eyes.

"No, Annie, don't take it off. We need you. Save us, Annie, only you can save us." The words faded behind each other, weaving a tapestry of thought.

With a sharp intake of air, Annie found herself staring at Rex. She shifted her eyes back and forth to satisfy herself that she was still in the same place. Blinking rapidly, she shook her head and looked across the fire.

Rex starred at her with a raised eyebrow, "Are you all right?"

"Yes, sorry." She let go of the key. "I just had a, hmm, well..." Realizing that her stammering was not matching the 'I'm-all-right-don't-worry' look she was going for, she tried a new tactic. "So what happened last night, anyway?"

Rex nodded his head slowly without the look of being convinced she had hoped for.

"Well," he started slowly, "for starters, you almost got your head cut off."

"Yeah," she giggled, nervously feeling her throat. "Guess I'm still alive, though."

"And lucky to be so. Your would-be executioner was Princess Zoila. She is a fierce warrior. I don't know what possessed her to pull up her sword at the last second, but I dare say you did nothing to save your own skin. The dragon's gift you wear around your neck holds enormous powers, but don't think for an instant it will save you from the business end of a blade."

"That's what I don't understand. What is this dragon Holdfast all about? And what is this?" she asked indicating the key. "And what does it have to do with me?"

"The legend of Holdfast," Rex began, sounding as if he were giving a lecture to a class, "is shrouded in mystery. Like all ancient tales, the truth has been altered over the years and even a careful reading of the ancient manuscripts can lead to misinterpretations."

"There are books about this?"

"Oh, yes, scores of them. Much has been written about Holdfast, most of it speculative I'm afraid. The most reliable sources are the most ignored, strangely enough. People tend toward the more sensational accounts, rather than tolerate the careful study needed for true understanding. But, that aside, the reason there is no accurate account is because the last manifestation of Holdfast was a thousand years ago. There wasn't much in the way of books then, and most people couldn't read at all anyway. So, the tale was kept alive through oral history and folklore and those change through time."

"So, what's the real story?"

"Like I said, there is no real story. All that can really be said is that once every thousand years, Holdfast rises from a union of heaven and earth, as we have witnessed, and upon rising bestows upon a deserving human a gift..." he paused to point to Annie's key. "...such as you have around your neck."

"So what's this gift supposed to do? Make me leap tall buildings, fight for truth and justice, or maybe get me a recording contract?"

Rex shook his head and rolled his eyes. "No nothing as prosaic as that. Now, how did that passage go? Oh, yes, 'and the gifts of the dragon are these: to provide a catalyst for growth and new learning, to unlock secrets that separate us from self-knowledge, and to give the power to perform a great healing.' In my research I came across the work of a monk who wrote long ago, 'The great healing spoken of by the Holdfast legends is not, as is commonly believed, the healing of any illness or anything on the physical plane. Rather, it is a healing of the deepest divisions of the soul, a calming of the storm that rages in the human animal's heart—a peace treaty between the world of things and heaven itself.' It was that quote that spurred my desire to seek the gift out."

"That's what you were waiting for when I showed up," Annie said half to herself as she tried to piece everything together.

"Yes. When I first learned of the legend during an intense scholarly period in my life, I felt certain that I would be that human—that I would receive the gift. That it was my destiny. I worked for years trying to track down the exact time and place the dragon would appear. I did all that I could to make myself worthy of the gift, but, alas, it was all in vain."

Annie searched for some place other than Rex's face to set her gaze on. She understood now the reason for his negative attitude toward her.

"I'm sorry," she offered. "You must hate me for ruining everything you had hoped for. I know what it's like to have dreams taken away."

Annie sneaked a peek at Rex and found he too could not look her in the eyes. His silence confirmed the truth of her words.

Rex responded in a quiet voice of shame and regret, "I admit that I passed the night angry at you, blaming you for my mistakes and miscalculations. I lost a lot to get to this point, and I realized last night that I didn't need to lose anything to be here at this time. I know that doesn't make much sense. Let me just say that I am sorry for being angry with you, and that I *never* felt hate toward you. Hate is an ugly thing, and you do not inspire that in me."

Annie felt weak inside. *He said he was sorry. Wow, that's different. Can I trust him? Do I have a choice? He did fight to protect me, I'll give him that, but why did he? It's the why behind what people do that you have to look out for—or else they'll sneak up behind you and take everything you have.*

Feeling a need to move beyond the awkward moment of doubt, Annie tried to steer the conversation off of herself. "So, being a wizard is over? It was just to get ready for... for last night?" *Smooth, Annie, real smooth. Why don't you just throw salt in his eyes? How stupid am I?*

Much to her relief, Rex did not seem offended. He smiled weakly like a man resigned to the decision of the fates.

"Yes, it is over; it was only a means to an end. Certainly, it was fun, while it lasted. You know, watching people's eyes widen like you were special. Like I said, just vanity. I mean magic is just when you don't understand the mathematics behind something, isn't it?"

"I guess," she shrugged. "I didn't do very well in math."

"Hmm, then the world must seem a strange place to you."

"Yeah, very. It's like—have you ever had a dream where you wake up in the dream? And you know something bad is about to happen to you, but you can't move or you go blind and you can't see what's coming."

"I believe I have."

"Well, I feel that way a lot when I'm awake."

Annie glanced up at Rex and confirmed what she was feeling. He was looking at her again, but now the disdain had left his eyes and was replaced by curiosity. He appeared attentive, interested in what she was saying.

Again, Annie felt the need to shift the focus off of herself, and asked, "What are you going to do now?"

"I'm returning to my monastery. There will be an accounting for the last 20-odd years, and I must face the judgment of the High Council. If I'm lucky, I'll be allowed to tend the gardens and gather the waste."

"Jeez, they must be harsh."

"Oh, I don't know," he sighed in exasperation and scrubbed his fingers through his freshly shorn hair. "I suppose I'm just drowning in self-pity at this point and not thinking clearly."

"So, you're going back."

"Yes, but first I'll stop off to see some old friends in Cornerstone, since I'm nearby."

"Oh, that'll be nice," Annie said with a slight bite of her upper lip.

Rex rubbed the short hairs on his jaw line. "I may not be thinking clearly, but I can see you're troubled."

"Well, what's going to happen to me? You're going back to your monastery, and I'm just going to stay here and... and what?" Annie began to tear, but fought to stave off a full-blown cry. "I don't know where I'm at or what is going on. I just pop in, get this thing from a dragon, almost get killed, and now the only person I do know is leaving. I mean—what am I supposed to do?"

"Okay, take it easy, I see your point. I'm sorry; I didn't stop to think about your position. Well, I think I can help, if you are willing to make some concessions."

Concession, huh? Isn't that a clever way to put it? Well, there it is finally—the ugly truth. No free rides for you, Annie girl, but why isn't that a surprise? Behind all the fancy words, he's just another man who sees me as a hole to be filled. This is like some nightmare carousel; no matter what you sit on, it's just the same go around. Maybe that's the way things are, and I'm just too stupid to accept it. I bet paying with your flesh must be the oldest business deal in the world. But what can I do? What choice do I have? I'm a stranger trapped in a strange land.

Annie steadied herself and found she had become adept at keeping her chin from quivering. Without any fanfare, she rose up, unfastened the shorts he had given her yesterday, let them drop to her ankles, and began to lower her panties. "Okay, how do you want it?"

"Great Jasper and the seven moons!" Rex bolted up and stumbled backward, shielding his eyes with his hands. "What ails you, girl? Cover yourself!"

Overcome with embarrassment, Annie scrambled to pull underwear and shorts up, "I thought... you said... concessions..."

Annie crumbled to the ground, tucked chin to chest, hugged her legs close to her, and sobbed into her knees.

Rex remained frozen in place with mouth agape. He shuffled toward her then retreated, as if torn between wanting to comfort and fear his ministrations would prove confusing. From over the rise, Shiva loped toward them.

"Thank goodness, you're here," he called to the wolf in relief. "Please, she needs comfort."

Shiva advanced over to Annie with a slow tail wag and soft whimpers. She worked her nose between the girl's arms and legs, licking away Annie's tears.

It tickled and, even though she didn't want to, she couldn't help but giggle between cries.

"Stop it," she insisted, hoping Shiva wouldn't stop. She buried her face into the animal's soft white fur.

"Are you all right?" Rex asked, slowly sitting back down.

"No," she answered, her words muffled as she spoke into Shiva's neck. She dared not look at him; afraid she would die of shame the moment their eyes met.

"What must have been done to you," Rex's voice was heavy with sorrow.

"I'm sorry, I feel awful. You must think I'm a filthy girl, but I'm not. I just thought you meant... and I'm so desperate."

"It's okay, Annie," Rex assured, his voice warm like a parent's goodnight hug. "Just relax. Take it easy. Everything is all right. It's going to be okay."

Annie's labored breathing evened out, and she ventured a glance at Rex. His patient look of concern calmed her, giving her the courage to loosen her grip on Shiva. She stroked the wolf behind the ears and said, "The last guy who said he'd help me wanted, well, a lot in return. When you said concessions, I thought... "

"Yes, I'm beginning to understand. I'm sorry to have frightened you. I meant that we could go together to the monastery and perhaps Brother Joseph and the High Council will have answers to your dilemma. But what I meant by concession was that we have to stop in Cornerstone. I know you want to get answers without delay, but I have to stop there. Well, that's what I meant."

"Oh, okay, that's a little different than what I thought," she sniffled and managed a small laugh.

Rex smiled, "Just a little? I dare say, this way we can all remain clothed."

The two shared a laugh as the morning chill began to slowly wear off. Shiva went from Annie to Rex and back again, sniffing and offering her head for petting in order to ensure all was well.

"I suppose we should break camp and be on our way—if my plan sounds good to you?" Rex asked.

"Yeah, it sounds good to me."

Annie watched as Rex gathered his things together and performed the impossible feat of fitting blankets, pots, cups and leftover food into his modest backpack.

"Hey, I thought you weren't doing magic anymore?"

"Magic? Oh, no," he winked, "just refraction of light rays, nothing unnatural."

"Uh-huh," she teased.

"I know it's none of my business," Rex began as he spread out the dying embers and looked for his water bucket, "but what happened to you to cause such a perception?"

"Oh, that's a long story."

"Isn't it always," he stated.

"Yeah, I guess it is. But you know, when I was hugging Shiva, I grabbed onto the key, and I remembered something I had forgotten. Or, to be honest, something I've tried to forget, but it never stopped haunting me. It was the day the darkness came and stayed."

Rex ceased dowsing the fire and sat down the bucket to give her his full attention. "What happened?"

"I was five-years-old. It was a Saturday. I remember because on Saturday afternoon at one o'clock *Power Princess* came on. It's a cartoon about this princess with powers who saves people and fights evil, and anyway... Daddy always got up at that time and would come into the living room to watch it with me. He was usually recovering from a hangover. I'm not saying things were perfect, there were problems, but we were all together at least."

"Tell me more about it."

"My Daddy worked as a bartender, and Mommy worked in a nail salon, you know where they do ladies' nails. I think they met one night when mom was getting wasted at the bar where Dad worked. Apparently, after some drunken sex which is totally gross to think about, she got knocked up with me. Nice way to start off a life, huh?"

Rex only nodded empathetically and waited for her to continue.

"So, there were bad times. I call them the darkness. They both drank—a lot. Dad was a frustrated musician. He played great guitar, at least I thought so, but, hey, it was a long time ago. Sometimes there would be terrible fights, but the darkness seemed to go away for a while, and we would just go about our lives. So, I could always wish real hard when the darkness came, and eventually it would go away. I used to think it was my wishing that made it go away, but I think they just sobered up."

A lull came over her story. Shiva laid her head in Annie's lap.

"Like I said, it was a Saturday, and Dad came in. He sat strumming his guitar while we watched TV. I loved it when he hummed and half sung. I could smell the alcohol in his morning sweat. That's how Daddy smelled to me—sour-sweet booze."

Annie now sat in a half trance, staring at the steaming coals as the last of their heat escaped them like a spirit departing a dying body.

"It was Saturday and he asked me, 'Where's Mommy, pumpkin pie?' She was pumpkin, and I was pumpkin pie. 'At work, Daddy, you know that, silly,' I said to him. 'Oh, of course,' he said and then took his guitar to the bedroom. After a few moments, he came out with a bag and his guitar case. 'Daddy loves you, pumpkin pie.'"

Annie reached out her hand into the empty air. "'I love you, Daddy,' I told him. That's the last time I saw him. It was Saturday and the darkness had come again and it had come to stay. There was not enough wishing in the world to make it go away that time."

Annie's eyes adjusted from her recollection, and she saw a pained look on Rex's face.

"I won't leave again," Rex managed to say half holding his breath.

"What?"

Rex shook his head, "Huh?"

"What did you say?"

"I said, I won't leave you. I'll stick with you until we figure this all out."

"But you said *again*. You said you wouldn't leave *again*."

"Did I?"

Annie stood up and walked over to the man. Rex took a small step back at her approach, but then stopped. She touched his sleeve at the elbow.

"Did you have a little girl that you left?" Annie asked, wishing deeply the answer was no.

"Well, she was little when I last saw her, but she was a woman."

"Esmeralda," Annie nodded.

"Well... what... I... how did you know?" Rex stammered.

"It was her, wasn't it? That's why you asked me those questions about her. You two were together."

"She is my love, yes, it's true; there was no other before or since. But I left her to," he looked around the hill, "to do this. If I had stayed, I still could have been here. But I left her and lost her—I lost everything."

"Aren't we a couple of sorry souls," Annie acknowledged.

"Yeah, we are."

Annie slipped her hand into Rex's. "Should we go then?"

"Yes, we must make haste. Can you see out in the distance?" Rex pointed to columns of black smoke far to the east.

"What is it?"

"Holdfast. She is enraged and out of control and burning the countryside. I feel that somehow her fate is tied to yours. We must hurry if we are to save you both."

Chapter Sixteen

The air in the valley felt heavier and more moist then the air on the hilltop, although the descent in elevation seemed manageable enough. Insects buzzed infrequently, as the bloom had left most of the field flowers, and small creatures slithered or scurried through the grass unseen. Gold, red, orange and brown had staged a successful *coup d'état* and replaced green, blue and yellow as the dominant color scheme. The harvest was in, and all living things prepared for the turning of the season.

"It feels funny down here," Annie commented. "Like I'm swimming in the air."

"Well, I guess, you are—we all are for that matter," responded Rex.

Annie stopped walking to give Shiva's neck a vigorous finger rub. "Even the fluffy girl? She's a fluffy girl, yes she is, oh yes she is—a fluffy-wuffy girl."

"You know, she's very ancient and revered throughout the lands. I'm sure she doesn't care for that fluffy-wuffy stuff."

Shiva licked Annie's face gingerly, to which Annie replied, "Well, that just shows what you know, Mister Traveled-the-world-saw-this-and-did-that."

Rex rolled his eyes, "Yes, your hidden wisdom is like a geyser. It spouts off occasionally leaving one all wet."

Annie laughed and gave Rex a quick punch in the arm. She skipped ahead twirling and dancing about. "It's like body surfing!"

"Your mood has improved remarkably since yesterday when you were spitting out dirt."

"Yeah, weird, isn't it?" She waited for him to catch up, and then added, "It's like I feel really connected to everything, you know? For the first time I feel surrounded by life, I feel its vibe."

"An incidental effect of Holdfast's gift, no doubt. Your senses are sharper; your mental processing is faster and smoother."

She grabbed his arm to steady a wave of lightheadedness. "Will it last?"

"Who's to say?" Rex shrugged. "What you are experiencing is the hidden world, hidden to us at least."

"Oh, yeah?"

"Oh, absolutely. The world is like a big haunted house, and we are surrounded by ghosts we can't see, some of who mean to do us harm."

Annie stopped walking again. She spread her legs shoulder width apart, and with a slight squat, she supported her upper body by placing her hands on her thighs and threw up. She felt Rex's fingers comb back and hold her short locks from drifting down to her mouth. His other hand rubbed small circles on her back.

When she had finished emptying her stomach of breakfast, she wiped sweat beads from her forehead and exclaimed, "Did you see that? Whoa! I mean, that was like turning on a facet! Funny, I don't feel sick! In fact I slept great last night! The best sleep ever! Am I shouting? I feel like I'm shouting!"

Rex led her by the arm away from the pool of steamy vomit. "Don't be afraid, you'll be okay. Just breathe slowly and focus. Float with the feelings. Relax. You won't get sucked in if you just relax and don't fight. Your body is adjusting, that's all."

Annie squinted at the familiar words. "Did you and Esmeralda study from the same spell book?"

"Try not to talk right now. Wait until the wave has subsided or you'll go hoarse. And yes, I may have..."

Annie looked at him on the verge of disbelief.

"Okay, *she* may have taught me a few things here and a few things there."

Rex took off a leather water bladder that hung from his pack. "Here, rinse your mouth out and take a cool drink."

Annie obeyed and put the spout to her mouth.

"No back washing now," Rex joked.

She almost spewed what water was in her mouth as she held back her laughter. Waving him off, she swished the liquid around and spat it out. Then after a deep drink, she said in her normal toned voice, "Whoa—it's like someone shot electricity through me."

Annie looked over to where she had been ill. Shiva had gone to the puddle to sniff around.

"Yuck!" she gagged. "Shiva, please get away from there or I'll hurl again."

The wolf cocked her head at Annie's request. She looked at the ground, then at Annie, then at the ground again, as if trying to decide between curiosity and courtesy. Courtesy won out, and she loped over to the two travelers.

"That's disgusting. And you say she's ancient and revered?"

Rex chuckled, "Come on, let's walk, it'll do you good. You know, your stomach contents smell—and dare I say taste—much different to Shiva then to you."

"Please, dare not to say. I don't need that image stuck in my head."

"Ah, but that's what I've been talking about—what gets stuck in your head, as you put it."

Annie tousled her short strands, hoping to accelerate the cooling of her overheated head. "I thought you were talking about ghosts."

"Right, we are surrounded by ghosts. Think about it. At this moment, indeed every moment, we are in the middle of a pool of high pressure sucking air down and spilling into low pressure that spouts air upward. We are showered by sun radiation, and we only see a small fraction of the emitted light. Waves of sound wash past us, but we can only hear the ones at a certain frequency. Electro-magnetic fields attract and repel without our awareness or permission. Chemical particles dance through the air, and yet only a few find connections with our tongue and nose. Then, of course, there are all those microbes, and bacteria, and viruses trying to sneak in and set up residence inside us. The world is alive with the hidden and the secret, but our senses can only tune into small bits and pieces, and then our brain has to make sense of those bits and pieces."

"Sounds like walking around deaf and blind," Annie commented.

"Yes, that's it exactly, but worse since we can never experience exactly what another person experiences. Some people are more sensitive to these ghosts, and others get things jumbled up in their heads. We just grunt and click trying to make our experience match somehow with another's, but it's never a perfect fit."

"Are you saying you don't see this field we are walking through?"

"No, we can both agree this is field. It is an object, and we all have agreed that open land with fauna and flora is known as a field. But, what this field means to me is not what it means to you. We experience it differently. Just like this morning on the hill. What making a concession meant to me was clearly not what it meant to you."

"Oh yeah," Annie responded with some residual embarrassment.

"Annie," Rex soothed, placing a comforting hand on her shoulder. "It's all right; we worked it out, didn't we?"

She nodded and chanced a smile.

Rex continued, "See those bees over there? It means we are nearing Cornerstone. They have a thriving honey industry in Cornerstone: honey, mead, candles, medicinal supplies and so forth. Well, those bees see the world much differently than us. They can see colors that are hidden to us, because they are tuned into some light frequencies lower than we're tuned into, and yet they can't see red—they just don't go that high.

"Well, I don't know about all that, but I hear music."

Rex turned his head from one side to the other, straining to hear. "Nonsense, I don't hear anything."

"Hmm, maybe someone's not tuned in," she taunted. "Wait till we get closer. Cornerstone's that way, right? Sounds like a band playing."

"Aren't we Ms. Tympanic Membrane? As a matter of fact, Cornerstone should be celebrating its fall honey harvest today if memory serves me."

Annie nudged him with her shoulder. "I love it when you talk senses. Get it? Senses, talking sense? It's like a word joke."

With a sideways glance and incredulous grin, Rex said, "You *are* full of yourself. It's nice to see you in a good mood."

"Yeah," she smiled. "I do feel good today."

The two wayfarers continued toward Cornerstone, while Shiva alternated between following along and dashing out to investigate obscured stirrings in the field. Coming upon the town, the sounds of music and human bustle greeted them. In a cleared field outside the community, tents were set up, long tables had been weighted down with food, and children ran about in play, while grown-ups competed in games or sat about conversing.

Annie looked over the festival grounds. The music came from a trio of musicians that played what looked like a small keyboard, an oddly shaped guitar, and a drum that the drummer cradled in his arms and struck with a stubby wooden stick. They played a peppy upbeat song, simple and basic. A game that looked like soccer was under way using an uneven leather ball. Food booths were set up along the edge of the grounds with some games like toss-the-ring and knock-down-the-bottles. It was not a large gathering, probably just the townsfolk and maybe a neighboring village. A man on stilts walked around and threw candy to the delight of the children that gathered around. It was nice, like the modest carnival she had gone to with her parents long ago, before everything fell apart.

"Here we are," Rex gestured grandly toward the festival. "Cornerstone, my favorite little hamlet. Come on."

Annie looked behind her. "Wait, where's Shiva?"

"Oh, she won't come any closer—too many people. Don't worry; she'll be waiting when we leave. Come, come."

As they entered the gathering, Annie noticed an older man in a formal royal blue coat with gold trimming and braided gold epaulets. Like the rest of the adults at the festival, he didn't seem much over two meters tall, although he was normally proportioned for his height. He stood in front of a small group of town folk making a speech. To his right sat a distinguished looking woman, who gazed up at him in admiration. Annie saw him glance up at their arrival, and then execute a double take between the group and Rex and her.

"Brother Rex!" he called out with glee and rushed toward them, the woman following close behind.

"Mayor Dawes and Madam Dawes," Rex returned the greeting.

Annie stood by as the three exchanged salutations, hugs and kisses on the cheeks. Unlike before in her life, she did not stand by self-consciously, painfully waiting in discomfort. This time she stood by enjoying the sight of old friends reuniting. She did not feel left out, rather she felt privileged to be engaged in this strange journey.

"Shame on you, Rex," Gayle chastised. "You have been gone too long with barely a handful of parchments to let us know you were still alive and well." She gave him another tight hug.

"Yes, my good fellow, you have indeed been gone too long. But we are all grateful and have profited greatly from the work you and E..."

His sentence was prematurely terminated by a swift clandestine kick of Gayle's foot to the mayor's shin.

"And who is your friend?" Gayle tactfully redirected.

"My friends," Rex began, "this is my friend, Annie. Annie, may I present the Mayor and Madam Dawes."

"Welcome dear," Gayle said and kissed Annie on her cheeks twice each.

"Yes, welcome, Annie. Welcome to our humble town and our festival. Any friend of Rex's is held in high esteem here." The mayor greeted and embraced her.

Annie returned the hug. "Thank you. Rex has been very helpful since I got here." She noticed some confusion come over their faces as she spoke of Rex informally.

As if feeling a need to put things in perspective, Rex interjected, "Annie is not from these lands, she has journeyed from afar. She has received Holdfast's gift."

A simultaneous gasp issued from the couple's mouth, and they both took a step backward. The mayor bowed, and Gayle curtsied. "My lady," they both offered.

Annie looked to Rex for guidance. She was completely at a loss as to what to do, never having been the focus of reverence.

Again Rex stepped in. "Please my friends, we don't want to attract any attention. I tell you this only in confidence—we don't want to create a throng, do we?"

"Of course not," the mayor concurred. He made a gesture of locking his lips closed and tossing away an imaginary key.

"Call me Gayle," Gayle whispered, cuffing her mouth with one hand.

"Well!" the mayor announced, rubbing his palms together. "Will you join us for our festival? There's plenty of food, fun, music and all the honey mead you can drink."

"Thank you, we would be honored," Rex said, then in a low voice added, "But I'll take it easy on the mead."

The mayor pointed toward Rex with a knowing finger, "Ah-ha, right you are. Come, come with us to our table."

The four walked over to one of the tables. Along the way, village folk came to shake Rex's hand, hug him, greet him, and thank him. Gayle had taken Annie by the arm and escorted her around, speaking with pride about the festival, what it meant, what activities had occurred and what was planned for later. Annie politely nodded, but it was the conversation Rex and the mayor were having that drew her attention.

"Rex, I'm so glad you are here. The town is very nervous about the dragon. She has been burning up the countryside, and we fear she may circle around and also attack us. I heard she ravaged Dinton and lay to waste some of the tribes along the West River. What happened? Was this supposed to happen?"

"I'm not sure," Rex responded, keeping his voice between them. "But Gororm is involved. The Princess Zoila was there and severed the tether."

"Oh my, that can't be good. We've worked so hard to stay out of the grip of his corrupt kingdom, but he has always found ways to creep forward. I can only guess the reason he has not taken over or that the dragon has not hit us, is because we are under the protection of Esmer... um well, the fates are good to us."

The four arrived at the table to greetings from the diners already seated. A variety of foods were passed around, and Annie discovered that she was famished. Annie sipped the honey mead poured for her into a ceramic cup. It was sweet with a slight boozy sting. As the liquid ran down her throat, a warm glow followed behind—a glow that began to spread throughout her chest and blanketed her face with a tingle.

"Easy with that, Annie," Rex said softly to her in between his conversations with the other table members. "That drink will sneak up on you quick and land you on your rear if you didn't grow up with it."

Annie acknowledged him wholeheartedly. Images of her parents accompanied her return of the cup to the table. She located a pitcher of sun tea and poured herself some.

Then she felt it—someone was watching her. She looked around, but everyone was busy eating or visiting with his or her neighbor. No one in particular seemed to focus on her, yet she could not shake the feeling. She looked down at her plate of roast duck, yams and greens and, with a quick head movement, she directed a glance sideways and she saw him.

He was a young man at the other end of the table. Annie surmised he was no more than a few years older than she, and he was secretly looking at her. She had been quick enough to catch him just before he could redirect his gaze. Now, it was Annie who looked, while the young man uncomfortably darted his eyes to see if the coast was once again clear.

Her admirer had black hair with curly tufts that waved easily in a breeze. His face was free of beard, and his cheeks were beginning to bloom in abashment. The full flush made his deep green eyes stand out, even though Annie could only catch a glimpse of them. She looked back at her plate allowing him a turn to sneak a peek. The two exchanged glances until some other boys came and carted the young man off, thus ending their secret cat and mouse game.

She watched as the boy's comrades escorted him to the field in order to resume the soccer game. The contest started robustly with shouts and bustle. The boy played aggressively, gaining control of the ball by breaking free of the players on the opposing team. Taking advantage of the opening, he plowed ahead toward the makeshift goal box. Overconfidence must have taken a hold of him, because he looked over toward Annie and smiled with a half nod. The momentary glance cost him dearly as he ran smack into another player, whom he had failed to see rushing up to him.

Annie laughed into her hands and then turned back toward the table, where the sound of a fussing infant caught her attention. A young mother tried to situate her newborn and adjust its swaddling. The baby started a cry that shook its tiny body as its back arched upward to protest feelings of discomfort.

Annie experienced a sickness inside her as the mother's clumsy attempts to comfort increased the wailing. Horrifying flashes of the woman slapping, shaking or even throwing the child on the ground burned through her mind. With little awareness of her actions, Annie's hand sought out a knife on the table and embraced it with ill intent. Her vision zeroed in on the young woman; muscles tensed, heart pounded, nostrils flared—she was ready to lunge and strike.

But the crying stopped. Her veil of rage cleared, and Annie saw that the mother had tugged the top of one sleeve off her shoulder, taken her breast out, and was feeding the baby. Mother and child were content as the woman began to hum and rock gently.

A rush of relief overcame Annie followed by a deep sense of awe, and she let loose the knife. She felt like floating as she got up and made her way toward them. The sight of the union stirred longings inside her. She wondered if her mother ever held her this close.

"Hi," Annie said as she approached the mother.

The young woman smiled pleasantly, "Hello."

"I'm Annie."

"Nice to meet you, Annie. I'm Sharon, and this is Kaleb."

Annie did not know what to do next. She wanted badly to reach out and touch Kaleb's downy hair and feel his baby skin, even wanted to breathe in and smell his newness.

As if sensing this, Sharon said, "Would you like to come over and meet him?"

Annie nodded and went up to them. "Oh, he's so beautiful," she cooed.

His skin was soft to her touch, fresh and not yet worn by the world. She caressed the baby, finding solace in Kaleb's contentment as he suckled on Sharon's nipple. Sharon continued to hum and softly sing.

> *"Sweet little baby, hush little baby,*
> *Hush little baby mine.*
> *Momma's gonna love you,*
> *She's gonna love you,*
> *Love you to the end of time.*
> *Sweet little baby, hush little baby,*
> *Hush little baby mine."*

Annie felt the pressure of gravity pulling at her being, weighing her down. She could not tell if a great sadness or a profound joy had seized her. She only knew she wanted to curl up and feel protected. Feel safe from all the ghosts. The ghosts in her own haunted house, the ghosts that Rex said surrounded her, even the ghost of this mystery she wore around her neck. The anguish of living uncared for in a precarious world had damaged her, she knew that; and she longed for rest.

Thankfully, the mayor stood up and banged his spoon on the table rescuing Annie from slipping into despair.

"Attention, attention, attention, please! Attention all!" He ceased banging and held up his cup. "A toast to the return of Brother Rex. May his presence be a sign of good tidings and safe passage in these days of the dragon."

"Hear, hears" followed the salute as the group at the table drank to Rex. And then from the edge of the field came a booming voice.

"Rest easy, good people! We have come to deliver you from the scourge of the dragon and save your homes and lands."

Annie joined everyone as they collectively turned toward the voice. Standing at the border, where wild fields met the groomed festival grounds, was a tall bearded man in a richly ordained purple robe. His arms were outstretched, and in one hand, he held a staff with intricate runic symbols etched into the wood. A breeze dramatically billowed his robe and his long white hair and whiskers to one side. Two steps behind him stood another man a head shorter than the first. His rich honey-brown skin stood out from everyone else at the gathering, as did his leather moccasins and colorful hand-woven wool poncho. The man did not speak, and his shoulder-length black hair, kept still by a red bandana, did not billow.

The man who had spoken approached the mayor's table with an air of self-importance and condescending benevolence. The man's companion walked limping on his left leg and, as both men neared, Annie heard Rex mutter under his breath.

"Aphrodite on a half shell. This is the last person I need to show up now—blasted Brother Simon."

Chapter Seventeen

"Mayor Dawes of Cornerstone," Simon addressed the bewildered official. "I am Grand Sorcerer Simon, and this is my apprentice Diné." He gestured to the man with dark, dancing eyes that still remained several steps behind.

"Yes, I have heard of you," the mayor greeted, rising up to shake the man's hand. "What brings you to Cornerstone?"

Instead of accepting the mayor's outstretched hand, Simon stepped slightly to the side allowing Diné to reach out and shake the mayor's hand. "My pardons, Mayor Dawes, but I have been in deep meditation gathering energy, and I cannot have direct contact with people."

"Oh, I see," the mayor said with a nervous twitter. "Well, this is my wife, Lady Dawes, and this is our honored guest…"

"The Sorcerer Rex, yes I know, we were members of the Brotherhood of the Sacred Spear, monks at a monastery under the command of fools." And then to Rex, Simon said, "Here to save the town, hmm? Are you sure you're up to it? I heard you didn't make Grand Sorcerer."

Rex chuckled under his breath. "No, just here for the festival and to visit with old friends. I'm on my way back to the monastery, escorting young Annie here to Brother Joseph."

"Really?" Brother Simon said with a raised brow. "Going back to seek approval from our old master?"

"No, going for a consultation. And for the record, I *chose* not to test for Grand Sorcerer, and besides, I've laid down my wizard robes and walk now only as a monk of the Brotherhood."

"A charming narrative, I'm sure."

Visibly uncomfortable with the growing tension, the mayor interrupted with a cheery, "Goodness, where are my manners? Will you both sit and feast as my guests at our humble Honey Festival?"

Brother Simon turned to the mayor with an accommodating smile. "We would be honored to sit at your table. Although I am fasting, I would like to inform you of my quest."

Annie had sat back down in her seat and watched the whole exchange with interest. She wasn't getting a warm feeling from this

Brother Simon. But, Diné, he was another story. Throughout the introductions and the rivalry, Diné had set his glistening dark eyes on her along with a knowing smile. After asking everyone to move an arm's length away from his seat, Simon took a place on the side of the mayor not occupied by Rex. With a lack of fanfare, Diné hobbled over unnoticed and sat next to Annie.

"*Yá'át'ééh*, Annie," the man greeted in a low soft voice, as if he wanted to keep the conversation to themselves. His face had a timeless quality. Not young, but not worn down with age. The few lines that graced his face appeared carved by wisdom.

In response to his quiet manner, the chatter around them, including the ensuing discussion between Simon, Rex and Dawes, drifted into a distant rumble. The moment between Annie and Diné was cordoned off from the rest of the world.

"Hi, er, Diné was it? You don't look like you're from around here."

"Neither do you."

"I'm not, I'm from... well it's a long story and not very believable."

"Did your animal spirit bring you to this place?"

"Well, I was torn apart by wolves and woke up here if that's what you mean."

Diné nodded slowly and grinned, "And your animal guide, she is nearby?"

"My *animal guide*? I don't understand—do you mean Shiva the wolf?"

"Ah, a *ma'iitsoh*, they are good guides. You are fortunate; your guide and spirit are one."

Annie found it easy to talk with the man and decided to make the conversation more personal. "So, excuse me for asking, but you look like an Indian."

Diné cocked his head to the side as if trying to place the word. "I don't know what an Indian is, I am Navajo. A vision quest brought me to these lands and, during my journey, I was injured." He pointed to his bad leg.

"Oh, I'm sorry to hear that."

"*Ahe'ee*," he thanked her with a nod. "Simon invited me to travel with him as his apprentice while I healed."

"That was nice of him to help you out."

"It was the least he could do, since it was he who injured me."

Annie gave Diné a sideways glance and wagged a finger in the air. "There's a story here you're not telling."

The Navajo man's feathery soft laughter was infectious. He leaned closer toward Annie. "Truth is, I was sitting by the banks of a river

beside a waterfall a few months ago. I heard a loud squawking and saw
Simon tumbling over the falls into the strong currents below."

"Now that's gotta hurt," she said as she imagined the scene.

"He was trying to act out the old parable of a wise man who falls off
a waterfall. In the story the wise man comes out of the water without in-
jury. His students are amazed and ask how he had survived. He tells
them, 'When the current went down, I went down. When it went up, I
went up. I did not fight the current.' But poor Simon, he could not let go
and flow with the current, so he was drowning."

"What did you do?" Annie asked, enthralled by the story.

Diné gestured with his hand, showing his palms, "What could I do?
I went in and pulled him out. He was wiggling like a fish trapped on
land, and I got shoved into a rock. His body hit me and twisted my
knee. Out of guilt or embarrassment he offered to make me his apprentice. I accepted even though where I'm from, a man of his limited skill
would have been my student."

"So why did you do it? Why are you acting like his servant?"

"It seemed like part of my journey. When something like that happens, you go with it. You never know where things will lead."

"Yeah," Annie responded with a faraway gaze, "I've *gone with it* before, but it never turned out very well. I always ended up getting hurt."

"Hard to see what path to take when you don't know where you are
headed. Where are you headed, Annie?"

"Rex is taking me to his monastery to meet his old teacher. I hope
this Brother Joseph can tell me about this." She showed Diné the
dragon's gift.

Diné looked at it and shook his head. "That is just a step in the journey; it is not what I meant. I mean where, Annie, are *you* going? Do you
see? What is your life about, what do you want?"

Annie started feeling the old emptiness welling up inside her, threatening to consume her and wipe her very existence away. She caught a
gasp before it grew into a sob and said, "I don't know. I want to be a
singer I guess, you know stand on a stage while everyone cheers for you
and loves you and digs your music."

"Yes, I see the problem."

"You do? What is it? Please tell me and don't play the find-your-
path game with me," she half pleaded.

"Oh, Annie," he smiled, "I will tell you. You want two different
things, and you must decide which is the most important. Even though
you may end up with both, you cannot seek both equally."

"Okay, so what are the two different things?"

"Simple—do you want to be a player of music or a stony idol for others to worship?"

"Well, when you put it like that, what choice do I have? I mean, does wanting to be loved make me an evil idol?"

"No, not at all, but is your vision of the clamoring crowds really *love*?"

Annie felt the sudden urge to end the conversation before someone got hurt—namely her. But, whatever kept the outside world muffled about them while they spoke, also kept her engaged with the Navajo man. She wanted to make a joke, or excuse herself to run away, or do anything other than answer that question. She found a stillness inside, which bought her a moment to figure things out. She did have something to say and nothing to lose by saying it, nothing, that is, but the weight that had been crushing her for years.

"I don't know what love is," she answered.

"Don't you?" he asked putting his hand on hers. "Or when it was at your front door, were you going out the back?"

That was that. Tears began to trickle down her face. She had fought so hard to avoid crying, but he kept leading her to places that hurt too much. "No one's ever loved me."

"Little *k'aalógii*—butterfly, I think that is not true. I know the love your mother and father had for you did not quench your thirst. They were like a dry riverbed to a withered traveler: a promise broken. But, there was one who loved you. Loved you with all their heart. Loved you with their life."

Annie pulled her trembling hand away from his and laid it in her lap. "I can't," she said hoarsely. "I can't right now. I'm not ready."

"I know, do not worry, I'm only here to help you take one step. I go soon to prepare the way for you. Look for me when the time seems the darkest. When you see me again, you will know what to do. You will know how to fill the riverbed, and drink deeply from it."

"Can you believe the dung he's spreading around?" Rex said as an aside to Annie.

"What?" she responded, coming out of a daze she hadn't known she was in.

"Haven't you been listening to him prattle on and on? So full of himself, he could fast for a month and not feel hungry."

In a flash of light the conversation that had occurred between Simon, Rex and Dawes came rushing into her awareness. It hit her so fast and hard she struggled to regain her breath. The three men's statements shot through her in a continuous stream of words, making it difficult, at times, to separate the speakers.

" What brings you here, Sorcerer Simon? I've come to

offer deliverance from the dragon to your people and the people of these lands. It draws nigh and soon your villages will burn. But what can you do? I have developed the art of reason and diplomacy in these delicate matters. My apprentice and I will seek the dragon out in its lair and offer the peace. Are you crazy? Eat something, I think your low blood sugar has rendered you insane. I would expect that from you, Rex. You've quit everything you started, isn't that so? And now, when the land needs you most, what are you doing? Taking some little girl to daddy in hope of gaining his approval. Been hit in the head lately, Simon? I would be glad to refresh your memory on how that feels. Now, now, that's not how two distinguished gentlemen should conduct themselves. We in Cornerstone are open to any assistance to save our people, and we appreciate that we do not know how that might be accomplished. I'm sure you both have our best welfare in mind. Thank you, Mayor Dawes, now as I was saying, the dragon has needs, and we must ascertain these needs and..."

Annie shook off the dizziness caused by the instantaneous update in her head. She looked at Diné, who just smiled at her and ate some bread. Had her whole conversation with Diné taken place as a single thought—in the space of a glance?

"... and then the beast will come to appreciate that it is in its best interest to cease this destruction," Simon concluded.

"That won't work, she'll kill you," Annie announced in a clear, confident voice. The whole table fell silent, and all eyes turned to Annie. She clutched something at her chest, and what the group couldn't see was the glowing key in her clenched hand.

"The protégé speaks! How fascinating," Simon said, smugly. "Do tell little girl, what do you know about these matters?"

"I know I've looked into Holdfast's eyes. Have you?"

Simon snorted, incredulously. He looked over at Rex who gave a nod to confirm her statement. Simon seemed to pale a shade. "Really, what is the relevance of that?"

"I looked into her eyes when she was first born and full of promise. Then when the chain was broken, her eyes burned with pain. It is a pain that does not know reason or diplomacy. It is hurt plain and simple and nothing you say, no words you have, will change that. She needs something else."

"Something only an underling like you can provide, I suppose? You're breaking my heart. Where did you find this waif, Rex?"

A spark lit in Rex's eyes and he rose up. "Hey, no need to get nasty with her. She was given the gift; respect her for that at least."

"Really? The gift, huh? What a waste."

Rex started toward Simon, but Annie's hand guided him back down to his seat.

"Don't bother, Rex, let it go," she said. "Let him go, you can't reason with him anymore then he can reason with Holdfast."

"I beg your pardon," Simon ruffled. "Are you saying I'm unreasonable?"

"I'm saying you are enslaved by your reason, and you can't see what is best for you because of it. Your reason should be a servant to a deeper mystery. It should be a guide to your unfolding, like the bit and bridle. But you pull too tight on the reins, causing magnificent life to toss her head and buck and rear."

Rex relaxed in his seat with a grin. A look formed on Simon's face as if he'd gotten a whiff of something foul.

Turning to Rex, Annie explained, "So you see, Rex, your brother here is who he is and part of that is a blind faith in his reason that will get him killed. Nothing you say will change that."

Simon glared at her. Rex failed to repress a growing smile of approval.

Annie got up and stretched. "You boys go on though if it'll make you feel better. I'm gonna check out the band." She looked at Diné with a wink. *You—I'll see later.*

As she walked away, she overheard Simon comment, "Did you teach her to be so insolent?"

To which Rex responded, "No, I think you just bring it out in her."

Annie walked down a grassy slope toward the small three-piece band. She was a little wobbly at first, feeling the heady effects the rush of time and the rush of ideas had caused.

Where did all that come from? I never had thoughts like that before. Had I? Well, whatever it was, it was inside of me, and it felt good to get it out. Usually, I say the wrong thing at the wrong time or don't say what I should when I should. But this time I think I was right on. I don't know why, but listening to Simon talk was like watching a car speed toward a brick wall. You know how it's gonna turn out, and you know it isn't gonna be pretty. I only wish I could use that sight in my own life. I wish I could see when I'm headed toward a brick wall. Maybe it's like Diné said—I need to decide what I want and stick to it. These dreams of stardom have only got me kicked around like a beaten dog doing anything to get petted. Damn, that sucks! I gotta stop being such a doormat.

Annie approached the band as they sat enjoying a break and each other's company. They looked at her with friendliness and nods of acknowledgement.

"Hi," she greeted, "I'm Annie."

The guitar player stood up, "Hi back attcha, kitty cat. Hand me that skin." He took her hand and brought it to his lips. He made a kissing sound, but stopped short of actually making contact. "I'm Hawke, lead guitar and head goof of this crew."

It seemed to Annie an odd way for him to speak, given the time period she was in. Even odder still was hearing the slang come from a guy who, along with his band, wore a feathered hat, a colorful tunic, baggy Bermuda-like shorts, and thick purple stockings that desperately tried to blend in with a pair of brown leather boots. But she was getting used to these inconsistencies in reality and decided to let it pass without much thought.

The guitar player introduced the other musicians. "These hep cats over here are Sly tickling the ivories..."

"Hey, Sugar. My, aren't you easy on the eyes."

Annie giggled.

"... and our hide hitter there is the heavy weight champ, Tubs, a real cake-eater."

"Hey, Little Sheba," Tubs greeted in a deep voice. "You lame, or do you blow?"

"Huh?"

They all laughed, but it didn't feel vicious.

"He means," Hawke explained, "do you swing, you know play?"

"Oh," she said joining in the chuckling. "I can play guitar and do some singing."

"The chick's got pipes too, bonus round," Sly interjected.

Hawke smiled, "Hey, Tubs, trip on over to the mule and get my other axe, would-ja?"

"Right on, brother."

The guitarist pulled up a small wooden stool that had held some sheet music. "Have a seat, sister. If you can strum out some rhythm, you can jam with us."

"Cool, I'd like that," Annie said with excitement. She sat down and accepted a guitar from an out-of-breath Tubs. The instrument had a rounded bottom, long neck and eight steel strings. "This is nice."

"Yeah," Hawke shrugged, "it's my slut."

"Your what?" Annie thought she misheard.

"My slattern guitar, my slut—everyone's playing this type these days."

"Every Tom and Dick," Sly added.

Tubs pounded out a quick beat and said, "Yeah, but it was the Hawke man who first brought the new sound up from Chica land."

"Oh, stop busting my chops, I just groove when and where ever," Hawke said, tossing off the compliment.

"Righteous, man, righteous," singsonged Sly with his eyes closed and his head swaying.

Hawke tuned up his guitar. "Annie you take it, and we'll just make believe behind you. If you get the callin', just sing out, baby."

Annie nodded and turned her attention to the guitar. She wasn't used to so many strings, but she got the feeling it didn't matter. In this place something would guide her hands. She only needed to dig deep inside and let the music flow through and out of her. She hoped it would not be the dark, vile tunes she had exposed Rex to yesterday. Annie strummed a folksy rhythm, and Sly joined in with some chords a few octaves below her, laying down a bass line for her on his clavichord. Tubs joined next with a steady beat, from which Hawke started fingering out a soulful melody.

"I gotta verse," Annie announced.

"Wail it," Hawke instructed, his face emoting with the music. "Gimmie something besides this nursery-rhyme jazz we gotta play here. Send me some manna, baby, daddy needs to eat."

She began.

> *"Alone in her room she dreams,*
> *Of love and other imaginary things.*
> *Shadows and ghosts come out at night,*
> *And I know, I know, I know,*
> *She hides her fear in plain sight.*
>
> *Hold her, but then let her go—*
> *She's the reaper of what others sow.*
> *And you can never know her winding way.*
> *Hold her, ooh, hold her as she walks away.*
> *(whispered) Maybe she'll stay—one day..."*

"Sweet, baby, sweet," Sly chimed. "Got a bridge for ya. Can I take it, Candy Girl?"

"Sing it, Sly," Annie invited. She found herself lost in the sound. It felt like rolling around in warm pudding.

Sly belted the bridge out.

> *"Oooh, I got some puddles in front of me.*
> *Oooh, I got some rivers I'm bound to cross.*
> *I see myself drowning in the floodwaters,*
> *I see the girl being swept away.*
> *But hold on baby, baby, baby hold on,*

The moon has got you in her sights tonight.
And it won't be long, no it won't be long now,
Before all you ever wanted comes to you."

"Oh, yeah, that was a real gas daddy-o," Tubs said, a tear wetting his cheek.

Hawke jumped into a guitar solo, and then said, "Break it down for us again, Annie."

Annie sang another verse.

"Aching for arms that don't feel like chains.
Aching for a kiss, but can't take the pain.
She's a burn, yeah, she's an open wound,
And I know, I know, I know,
She dances under the waning moon.

Hold her, but then let her go—
She's the reaper of what others sow.
And you can never know her winding way.
Hold her, ooh, hold her as she walks away.
(whispered) Maybe she'll stay—another day..."

The quartet played unaware of the small crowd that had gathered around them. The audience swayed to the music; couples clutched at each other, while others looked wistfully at the horizon.

Tubs' rich baritone voice washed into the song like a wave creeping up the tide line. "Gotta a different bridge, listen up, cats."

"I saw her eyes, they seemed so sad,
The better to play the cards she had.
I saw her mouth, it didn't smile,
The better to bear the endless miles.
I saw her hands, the scars on her wrists,
The better to sink into Avalon's mist.
Tumble on by, tumble on by, tumble on down the way,
Don't leave me, baby, don't leave me missing you today."

All four players harmonized together for the final chorus.

"Hold her, but then let her go—
She's the reaper of what others sow.
And you can never know her winding way.

The crowd of listeners broke out in applause that for the first time signaled their existence to Annie. She had been so focused on the music she hadn't noticed them. She scanned the faces hoping to find the one face she needed to see. The one face that could tell her all was well. And then she saw him. She saw Rex standing at the edge of the group, standing and beaming with pride. He bowed slightly, smiled, and then walked back to the table and the on-going discussion.

Someone, somewhere, announced the start of a pie eating contest, and the crowd murmured with delight and then slowly dispersed. Annie was left with her new jam mates and a surrounding emptiness.

"Sister," Hawke crooned, "you kill me. That was outta this world!"

Annie blushed. "Thanks; you guys rock."

Suddenly she realized she was mistaken. There was no surrounding emptiness. The crowd had gone certainly, but they were only secondary to what was really going on. She had bonded deeply for a moment with three other beings. They had been united by the mystery of music, by the strange effect vibrations had on the mind when sounds came together in just the right way. She had been part of a creation, and that feeling was nothing short of miraculous.

"Hi," a voice offered behind her.

Annie turned around and there stood the boy she had played peek-a-boo with at the table. The same boy who had so wanted to impress her, he had gotten a mouth full of elbow making sure she was watching his prowess on the field.

"Hi," Annie returned the greeting.

"Groupie time," Sly mumbled out the side of his mouth.

"Uh-huh," Tubs agreed, "It never fails, except where's ours?"

Hawke gave Annie's shoulder a squeeze, and then said to his troupe, "Come on you freaky hipsters, let's walk around the grounds and play some ditties."

Oblivious to the band's patter, the boy said, "My name is Kellem, or just Kell."

"I'm Annie, or just, well, just Annie," she stammered out, suddenly feeling like a complete idiot.

He laughed, and the sound of his laughter, light and real, sent her heart soaring. She feared if she looked too deep and too long in those rich green eyes of his, she would be lost beyond all hope. She lowered her gaze shyly to the ground and drew the outline of a circle in the grass with the tip of her sandal.

"So," she said with a small shrug.

"So, yeah, that was..." his sweet voice responded.

"Did you...?"

"Oh, yeah, completely. You were so great."

They stood awkwardly as a cool breeze drifted by. Clouds that had gathered in the west moved toward them. After much milling around and shuffling of feet, Kell cleared his throat and offered his hand.

"Do you want to take a walk or something? It'll rain soon, and the festival will be over, and I'm afraid you will be gone without me having... I mean without giving me the chance, er, the chance to..., um, without having..."

A boy stuttering nervously as he talked to her felt delicious to Annie. *He wants me to like him. He wants to come off as smooth in front of me. He cares what I think of him. This is too good. If I could freeze the past 20 minutes and live in those moments over and over again, I would be happy forever. This is what happiness must be all about; this is what they mean by it.*

"Yeah," Annie finally said, rescuing Kell from his clumsy attempts at speech. "I'd love to take a walk with you and talk."

"Okay, great, that's great," he said, edging his hand closer to hers.

Annie wondered why they weren't going anywhere, and then it dawned on her that Kell was waiting for her to take his hand. She smiled at him feeling ditzy for not knowing what to do. Taking his hand, she first grabbed his knuckles, and laughed nervously as she adjusted with a turn of the wrist so they were palm to palm.

"Sorry," she apologized.

"No, it's my fault—sorry. Shall we?"

Annie nodded.

After all the things she had done, or rather had been done to her, the feeling of her hand in his was liberating. She had been touched in so many ways, but none of the touches in the past had created the sense of euphoria she now experienced. Her face flushed with a rush of blood, heating up her cheeks. She tried to steady a slight tremble that vibrated through her arm, radiating up from his touch to her fluttering heart.

Hand in hand they strolled through the field, skirting the tree line as the storm moved in behind them.

Chapter Eighteen

The drops of lazy rain plopped with growing frequency on the ground, on the abandoned festival tents and stands, on the empty benches and tables, and on the three men standing at the crest of the high road leading out of town. Oblivious to the precipitation and the darkness caused by thick thunderstorm clouds, they stood talking as men accustomed to the elements and austere living do.

"Come with us, Rex," Simon urged. "Give up this... this whatever you think you are doing and rejoin me. When you stopped coming around at the monastery I knew Brother Joseph had gotten to you. You know he sent you away to separate us. He did everything he could to break up our little group. Couldn't stand the competition."

Rex shifted uneasily in his stance. "I don't think that's what actually happened."

"Of course you don't, you were held too strongly under his spell, under the sway of the Brotherhood—and you still are."

Simon's words stung Rex, not because they were delivered from his old colleague, but because they echoed the sentiments of another. She had, in so many words, said the same thing to him years ago when he left on that stormy spring morning. Rex was tired and did not care to quarrel anymore with Simon. And, besides, he had a deep-seated feeling that Annie was right, and Simon would certainly die in his attempt to reason with Holdfast.

But, Simon seemed of another mind and continued his proposal. "After you left, I too was sent away on a 'quest.' What a bunch of pig's swill. If they can't control you, it's divide-and-conquer time. Oh, your precious Brother Joseph is no fool, I'll give you that, but he is no saint either. We were good together you and I, we attracted followers, we saw the truth."

"The truth?" Rex responded, no longer able to resist getting sucked into what was initially a one sided debate. "I may have still been a neophyte when I left the sacred grounds, but I have learned a thing or two in my travels."

"Of course you have, I didn't mean to imply..."

"And to say we or you or I or anyone clearly sees the truth is asinine. As long as flesh and blood stands between the reality and understanding, the truth will always be victim to gross distortion."

"Words from the grave, the ramblings of dead men too frightened to live, but content to rot behind walls under the guise of higher spiritual attainment. Come on, Rex; wake up. You grew up around people who could not handle the real world. They all came to the monastery broken and failed. Are those the people you want to follow?"

Rex crossed his arms as he delivered a small touché, "Well, don't *those people* include you? After all, I'm the only person raised in the monastery from infancy. You came from the outside world to escape something."

Simon attempted to mask his bristling at the remark. With a terse mouth, he wiped rainwater from his brow and conceded, "True, I had a rough patch of it and thought the way of the Brotherhood was the answer. But, over time, I learned the truth."

"Really, and what was that truth? I don't think I was ever clear on that. All I remember were ramblings about how the hierarchical system of the monastery stifled our true development, and to truly attain enlightenment we had to revolutionize the order of things; making the teacher the student and the student the teacher."

"So you *were* listening. I always knew we were of a kind." Simon gave a wry smile.

"Maybe then we were, but not now. Then your words were the perfect spark and tinder for firing up a young man's imagination. But I'm not a young man anymore, and I have no inclination for shaking the pillars of earth."

"Men like us have a responsibility to set things right and bring justice to the people," Simon demanded.

Taking a deep breath, Rex allowed the sound of the rain shower to calm him. He hated that Simon had the ability to get him riled. His desire not to argue returned; he felt he would rather part on amiable terms. Or as amiable as one could be when one did not fully support or agree with Brother Simon.

In a measured voice, Rex said, "Men like us have a responsibility to make our talents available to those whose needs do not cause harm. We are not responsible for setting things right or impinging on the lives of others just because we think we know better. Reluctance and caution should be our guiding principles, not arrogance and outright meddling."

"Your narrow mindedness is your limitation," Simon snorted.

Rex paused. "I do not agree with what you are going to do, but you are my brother, and I love you. Farewell, Simon."

Rex's soft-spoken peace offering visibly caught Simon off guard and changed his tone. "I love you, too, Brother Rex. I shall not be displeased if our paths cross again."

Rex started toward Simon to hug him, but the elder man balked.

Simon smiled as Diné circled around from behind him, stepped in front of Rex and offered himself as a surrogate.

"Of course," Rex said, realizing what was happening.

"You understand, I mustn't be touched at this critical time," Simon explained.

"I know. Embrace by proxy, an interesting concept. Goodbye, Simon," Rex said to Simon, and giving Diné a hug said, "And goodbye, Diné."

"*Hágoónee*," the Navajo man said in return.

As Rex released Diné from his hold, the Navajo grabbed the monk tighter and stared deep into Rex's eyes. Diné's rain spattered face held urgency as he brought it within millimeters of Rex's.

Rex felt a swimming sensation wash through him and Diné's voice permeated his mind.

Annie, the Navajo's thoughts implored.

Lightning flashed, superheating the air around it and creating a re-sounding crack and boom. In Rex's mind an image burned. He saw Annie's face paralyzed in a hellish snarl. Her eyes were black and blood poured from multiple wounds, as if someone had sliced her face up with a razor.

The two men exploded apart, leaving Rex weak in his knees and breathing heavily. He felt as if he were moving like cold honey; time slowed and blurred.

Simon said something about the emotionalism of Diné's kind and turned to go as Rex looked over his shoulder to the field below him. The figure of a young man running frantically up the slope toward him flickered in his awareness. The boy seemed to call Rex's name, but the hum of electricity that still crackled in the monk's ears distorted the sound.

Rex turned back toward Simon and Diné, and found they were gone. He turned back again to the field as Kell rushed up to him; fear pulsated in the boy's eyes.

Kell collapsed onto Rex, and Rex struggled for a moment to support the boy's weight and regain his own balance.

"I didn't do anything wrong... I don't know what happened... I... I... I..." the boy stammered in between shallow gulps of air.

Visions of mayhem perpetrated against Annie raced through Rex's thoughts, and he felt a strong impulse to throttle the truth out of Kell. He had seen Annie walk off with the youngster without feeling grave concern, and he made only the most cursory of inquiries. Now he questioned his initial assessment on the matter, and the weight of his miscalculation burdened him severely. But his training took over; he quelled the automatic thoughts and guided the boy to the ground, sitting him on the wet grass. After all, this was Cornerstone, which was not known to have a nefarious reputation among its inhabitants.

Squatting down in the rain, Rex said in a calm voice, "Take it easy, young man, slow down. Let's take this one step at a time."

Kell nodded, wiping tears and rain from his red eyes.

"You must be Kellem, right? The cobbler's son? You have your father's strong chin."

"Yes, sir," he shivered.

"You were not yet born when I last saw your parents. Good people. You must be what, 18?"

"Seventeen next month," Kell answered, his shuddering stabilizing.

"That's better now, just take it easy so we can sort this out," Rex consoled. "Does this have anything to do with the young lady, Annie?"

Kell nodded his head frantically and a new panic seared across his face. "Yes, but I didn't..."

"Okay, okay, don't get ahead of yourself. Pull it together—take a breath."

The boy complied. When he had regained himself, he started, "We went for a walk, and it began to rain. So we went into the woods to get out of the rain. We were laughing and talking about everything. She looked so pretty, her wet hair in her face, and you know, you know the sound of the rain in the woods. It's a sound and the sound gets in you and..."

"Okay, pull back, you're starting up again, and I won't be able to understand you."

Kell swallowed hard and continued, "She looked so pretty standing there surrounded by the sound of the rain, and she was shivering. I held her to warm her up, that's all, and she held me, too. Then I..."

"Go on, son, go on."

"I... I... kissed her. I didn't mean to, but she was right there, and so pretty, and the rain in the woods," Kell confessed with trembling lips.

Rex tried to relax his tensing jaw. "And then did something happen? Something bad?"

"No, not then. I kissed her, and when I pulled away she was smiling. I touched her face and whispered, 'Sing for me, Annie, sing.'"

"And then?" Rex spurred.

Lightning and thunder flashed and crashed simultaneously; the heart of the storm was upon them. Kell's face paled, and his eyes dulled.

His voice sounded far away, disconnected, causing Rex's stomach to churn as if he had been free falling.

"And then she—lost it."

"Lost it? What do you mean?"

The boy shook his head and squinched his eyes, "I mean she went wild, pushing me away and screaming. She fell to her knees and started shouting about murder and rape and all sorts of foul deeds."

Rex's thighs began to quiver from squatting. He lowered his head and took Kell's hand to steady himself.

"I tried to help her. I knelt in front of her and begged her to stop, but... but..."

Rex looked up at the youth's face frozen in horror, his mouth struggled to form words, and his respiration had all but stopped.

With a stern shake of the boy's hand, Rex blurted out, "But what? What?"

Electricity burned the atmosphere again. The resulting boom quickened both of their hearts as a fresh torrent of rain soaked them to the bone.

Pushing past the vacuum created by his depleted lungs, Kell shouted, "The blood! Her face started bleeding all over. Cuts just opening up and bleeding all over! Her eyes and, and her voice..."

Kell burst away from Rex, splashing backward in the puddles behind him. He scrambled to his feet against the slick grass. Grabbing his temples he screamed down to Rex, "She growled like a beast! She said, 'You've got to pay the price, Kell, you've got to pay the price!' And then I ran, I just ran."

Rex rose to his feet as the rain lapsed into a softer, steadier pace. He went to Kell and held the sobbing boy in his arms.

"You have to believe me, Brother Rex, I didn't do anything wrong. I didn't hurt her."

"I know, son, I know. It'll be okay."

Annie sat huddled, half hidden by spindly bush branches that had lost most of their foliage. She hugged her folded legs close to her with one arm as she gently rocked. Her other hand raked rhythmically through Shiva's snowy fur, like a cat kneading a favorite blanket. Staring into the gloom, Annie heard a whimper and felt Shiva shift her weight in order to reposition Annie's hand to another spot on her body.

Sorry, girl, Annie apologized without speaking. She looked at her hand and saw she had raked up a fair amount of fur. Returning her hand to Shiva's comforting pelt, Annie changed to long strokes from neck to tail.

Now what? What happens from here? I can't keep getting thrashed about by things I can't even see. When will it be over? This life of mine is killing me, but I don't want to go. I should be able to do something to get myself under control. And you, she held the key around her neck, *you're no help. You just made everything worse, and now I'm alone in this dark place. How can it be that new friends surrounded me, but I still ended up alone in the dark?*

Annie reached down and held Shiva close to her, *Well, at least I still have you.*

With that, Shiva got up and slunk out of Annie's embrace with a low growl. The wolf moved carefully into the small clearing in front of the bush. Her ears were erect and pushed to the side like wings, and she held her tail stiffly in a position of alert. She maintained a wide-eyed stare in the direction of the sound of snapping twigs.

Annie backed away further on all fours into the forest growth. *What the hell is coming to get me now?*

Annie guessed Shiva's sniffing must have gathered some new information as she watched the wolf's body posture change. Her tail began to wag and her head lowered, waving side to side. Annie saw the wolf plod forward to meet Rex as he came into the clearing.

The thicket obscured some of Annie's line of vision, but it was the darkness that made clear sight impossible. Although the sky was nearly clear of the thunderstorm clouds, night had fallen. What little moonlight managed to penetrate through the trees allowed Annie to see shapes and movement. She could make out the two of them greet each other as Rex bent down, and Shiva licked his face.

Rex's moonbeam-highlighted figure straightened up and appeared to look around.

"Annie?" he called out clearly without shouting.

Annie did not respond; could not respond. Something had taken hold of her, and she could not will herself to speak.

"Annie, Annie, all free. Come out, come out, wherever you are," he chuckled. "Okay, not humorous. Aw, come on, Annie, come out and talk to me.

I can't. Don't you know that? You must know that, it should be so very, very clear to you.

"I talked to Kell. He was pretty scared, but he told me what happened. I respect that you might want to be alone, however I'm concerned that you might be injured and in need of some assistance."

Whatever's wrong with me, mister, you can't fix.

The instant she thought that, Rex halted and looked right in her direction. He said softly, "You're wrong, Annie, I can help. But you have to want me to."

He heard me? No, he must have sensed me, figured it out. After all why would I be hiding unless I was feeling hopeless? Damn it! I let the despair take me again. This is crazy, why would I want to hide from the one person who has never let me down? Here he is in the dark of night, in the woods, looking for me. Get your head out of your butt, Annie, how much more proof do you need that he cares?

As if to give her growing resolve added strength, Rex sat down on the wet ground and announced, "Well, Shiva, my friend, might as well get cozy, because we aren't leaving without our companion. Agreed?"

To which the wolf responded with a yowl.

Annie forced a guttural grunt to escape her lips.

"Just wait here all night if need be."

She pulled herself forward, ignoring the small branches that tore at her, that tried to keep her deep inside their lair.

"Not a bad piece of property. Good thing too, we may have to build a house, because we aren't leaving without our Annie."

Slowly emerging from the bush, Annie crawled into the clearing. She stood up in the glow of the celestial light; her body scratched, her clothes dirty.

Even though she stood in plain view of Rex, he still said, "I wonder if she went out to get some scones. Oh, Shiva, wouldn't that be nice on a night like this? Storm gone and here we would sit with fresh warm scones and..."

Annie shuffled toward the monk, like a zombie with an unknown animating force willing an unwilling body forward.

"... and some fresh strawberry jam."

The cool night air lost its bite the closer she came to him. Her body began to tremble, and she welcomed the sensation. She had not been lost to herself, but was alive. Alive and trembling, and now standing in front of a person who cared. Cared about her.

"Hello, sweetie, been waiting for you. Didn't by chance bring any scones, did you?"

She smiled and bent down to give him a hug.

"It was so terrible," she uttered finally, her voice hoarse but steady.

"I know, Kell told me about it. I mean, he didn't hurt you, did he? He said he didn't, but if you say different, I will believe you."

Annie stroked her face and looked at the blood smeared on her hand from the motion. "No, he didn't hurt me. He was sweet. This just came from nowhere. I'm not even cut, at least not anymore. It was just too weird." Annie sat down in front of Rex and Shiva instantly licked her bloodied face. Annie gave Shiva a rub on the head, and the wolf lay down beside her.

"So what happened? I mean if you want to talk about it."

"He probably thinks I'm a freak or something," Annie said looking at her fingers that twirled nervously with each other in an anxious dance. She glanced up at Rex, hoping for a comforting response.

"He thinks you are very pretty, and interesting, and talented, and he is so worried that he did something to you."

Annie brushed her short bangs to one side. "Yeah?"

"Yeah. I had to give him a mild tonic to calm him down and ease the memory of the night, so he wouldn't be frightened recalling it for the rest of his life."

"Hey, I'll take a swig of that tonic," Annie laughed.

"Sorry, only works on the witnesses, not the key player."

She nodded, "Yeah, I guess I need to work it out."

"So did kissing make you feel uncomfortable?"

"No, that was nice. It wasn't anything he did. It was something he said. He said, 'Sing for me, Annie, sing.'"

"He wanted a personal encore performance?" Rex offered.

"I'm sure that's what he meant, but as soon as he said it, I wasn't with him anymore. I wasn't in Cornerstone; I wasn't in today. I was back in a dirty little room and..." she gathered up some courage to finish, "and a dirty little man was doing dirty things to me."

"Oh, Annie, I'm so sorry."

"But that wasn't it. I've had flashbacks before, not quite that strong, but I could have dealt with it if not for..." her voice trailed off, and she looked up through the trees at a patch of clearing sky. "The stars are bright tonight. In the city where I'm from, you don't get to see bright stars like that. The sky is always covered in grime."

"Some say we are the stars," Rex said, joining her in looking above. "Meaning we are made from the same elements, cooked in the same galactic brew."

"And that's the problem, the problem I had when he said what he said and I had the flashback."

"I don't understand."

Annie took the dragon's gift in her hand and held it up. "This little sucker is a trouble maker; I'm here to tell you. It focuses everything, making things more intense—like I really need that."

"No, I suppose you don't."

"When I was still in school," Annie began, resuming her stargazing, "they told us we could be anything we wanted to be. That we were per-fect, and if we just worked hard enough, we could achieve anything.

'Aim for the stars,' they said. 'Shoot for the moon, aim for the stars.'"
She leaned her head on Rex's shoulder without breaking her fix on the
cosmos peeking through the trees. "What a load of shit."

"I'm sure they were only trying to be encouraging. Many people sell
themselves short and, with a little encouragement, they can achieve more
then they dreamt possible."

"Yeah, maybe, but it was a cruel thing to say to us—to us that knew."

"Us? Us who knew what?"

"That we were damaged. The damaged kids, the kids that weren't as
bright, as self-controlled, as cooperative—the kids who were different. I
used to wonder if I was normal—until now. After I saw what the gift
showed me, I know I'm not."

Rex put his arm around Annie and shifted his attention from the
stars to her. "What did it show you?"

"Me. The core me. Me, me, me. Back through time, back through
generations of me all the way back into a past where words and ideas
didn't form in our minds. Oh, the way I looked changed but, at the core,
it was me over and over again. And no matter what, I could never think
as clear as others, or as fast, or pay attention very well. I was always
restless, always waiting for something to happen, something that would
take away the emptiness. But it never came."

Rex gently guided Annie's chin until she was looking at him. "You
saw what you saw, and there is no arguing that. Perhaps though, there is
another interpretation."

"I suppose you have a parable to cover this situation."

"Well, I could tell you the one about the monk who was expecting an
important visitor. He raked up the leaves in his garden and cleaned out
the weeds, making everything very neat. He asked another monk if
there was something he had missed. The second monk said there was
and went to the tree at the center of the garden. He shook the tree vigorously until many leaves fell all over the garden. 'There,' said the second
monk, 'that looks better.' I could tell you that story, but I won't."

"You're such a sneak," Annie laughed while giving him a punch in
the arm.

"Oh, so sorry," he grinned. Then, with a doting voice, he said,
"Look, Annie, life is messy and hard, there's just no getting around it.
And you're right, people have different limitations. Things that happen
in life can make the limitations worse or hardly noticeable, but they will
always be there."

"Yeah, it's hopeless."

"No, my friend, not hopeless. I'll give you that you have had it
harder then some, but not as hard as others. But, regardless of how well

your head does or doesn't work, there remains one fact."

"What's that?"

"You are valuable just because you are alive. And no one, not even you, can predict what the future will bring. You have to empty yourself of these notions of what you are supposed to be and just live the best you can wherever you find yourself. Only an empty cup can be filled."

"Even a cracked cup?"

Rex got up chuckling. "Use some potter's clay if need be. Hey, let's get out of here. What do you say?"

"Oh, I don't know," Annie hesitated. She stood up and brushed herself off. "I know they're your friends and all, but I'd rather not go back to town."

"No, no, I didn't mean go back to town. That's behind us. I meant traveling onward," he said pointing into the woods.

"Er, it's kinda dark."

"We won't go far tonight. There's a nice place by a stream near here. We can set up a little fire to keep us warm, and we can wash off those scrapes and the dried blood on your face."

Annie put her hand to her cheek, "Oh yeah, I almost forgot about that."

"I bet Kell hasn't," Rex joked.

"You're terrible," Annie said trying to hold back a laugh. She gave him another swipe to the arm with her hand.

"Ow! What? What did I say?" he grinned.

Annie buried her face into her hand and found herself laughing at her embarrassment. "Can you imagine? Poor, Kell. Some date I am. I know girls who were mortified because they belched in front of their boyfriends. They should try having blood burst out from their face in front of a cute guy sometime."

"There you go, that's the spirit. We'll get you warm and cleaned up, and get some rest and tomorrow travel on."

"Travel on and what?"

"Travel on and shake out some leaves to decorate your garden."

"You're such a fortune cookie," Annie quipped.

With the open field behind them, the two travelers plunged into the dark forest. Shiva led the way, her white coat acting as a beacon as she guided them through the night.

Chapter Nineteen

A golden glow pulsated in the night sky from the blazing hamlets that surrounded the castle grounds proper. The dragon had struck again, swooping down from on high and searing the land with the combustible liquid that spewed from a gland in her throat and out of her mouth. After issuing an incinerating spray of flames, Holdfast would pull up sharply, her powerful wings lifting her back to the dizzying heights from which her attack began. In her ascent she screeched out a mournful cry as if it was her own flesh that burned.

The attacks of the past two nights followed a spiraling pattern, circling ever closer to the castle. Tonight's attack targeted the villages and farmlands twenty kilometers from the hub of the fiery whorl.

Zoila had dispatched three regiments in an effort to protect the citizens. She held no delusion that her troops would be able to stop the dragon's wrath fueled attacks. The purpose of the troops was more practical. It was an effort to allay the panic that ignited in times of chaos. Experience had taught her that confused and frightened people could coalesce into a single-minded madness, blindly orchestrating their own demise. The soldiers would create a sense of order for the common folk to focus on. They would lead the survivors from the burning villages to safety and provide relief.

The king will spit bile when he hears that I've taken his warriors away from guarding the castle and placed them out in the field to help the people. Well, let him spit, let him choke. Zoila chuckled to herself as she crawled through a dank passageway within the castle's walls.

The passageway was part of a forgotten series of connective tunnels that snaked their way throughout the castle. She had discovered them many years ago as a little girl and, as a little girl, she could navigate through them much easier than her full-grown body could now. Still, there was enough room for her to slide over the cool smooth stone to get to any part of the castle unseen.

It was the old crone, Zoila recalled. *She was the one who showed me these tunnels without ever muttering a word. But when she presented the queen with an ancient book, she looked right at me as if she was giving it to me. Then that finger gesture, slow, deliberate, pointing to a bench built into the wall. Later I found the bench, when moved, hid an opening.*

Reaching her destination, she was able to sit up, albeit not as comfortably as when she was younger. The tunnel opened up to a hollowed out space in what looked like a dead end. She removed a small chunk of stone that had been carefully chiseled out over time to form a peephole. Zoila peered into a room, her line of vision only half a meter above the ground. She could see the interior door of the king's war room and study, a place with which she was all too well acquainted. A place where she had been beaten and berated many times for not performing as expected. She sat in the place where she had hidden and spied many times to learn of the king and queen's treacherous plots.

They'll be here soon, witless and baffled as usual. Just need to be patient and wait; wait for them to create their own downfall.

Zoila shifted her body around to find the most comfortable position to sit and hunch in the small space without moving her eyes from the hole. She worked her right hand down her torso to a pouch that hung from her belt. With fingers that deftly manipulated, as if possessing a will of their own, she undid the strip of leather that tied off the pouch opening and removed a stone. Her gaze never left the opening in the wall to supervise what she was doing. She was well trained in independent motion and could carry out seemingly unrelated tasks while remaining keenly focused.

Besides, she did not need to look at the spherical, apple-green Chrysoprase stone that now settled in a familiar spot of her hand. The gem easily rotated in her loose grasp as her fingers passed the worn round surface back and forth to each other. Maneuvering the stone helped her relax and pass the time while she waited. It had been given to her by a teacher long ago to aid her in working through some now forgotten quandary.

The chest center where all emotional paradoxes meet, she recalled, her memories revisiting her in clusters of images as they often did. Random thoughts drifted in and out of awareness as she waited stoically. *My weakness, my source of greatest strength. Always the riddle, that's how they talk. Ask for a straightforward answer, and you just get riddles, stories and contradictions. Say you are troubled and confused, and they give you a rock and tell you it will calm your emotions; strengthen your insight and higher consciousness. A bald tattooed man in a bad robe said, "Remedy for the Gemini, the rational and restless twins" and that's supposed to make sense? That's supposed to help? I just need to get through this; it is becoming too much for me to endure. I feel torn apart inside.*

Her eyelids begged to close in obedience to her thoughts. She was more than tired; she was weary. *Come on, you two wretched creatures, get in here and have your say; I know you're up to something; I don't have time to just sit here. I have to meet Damek at dawn to figure out...*

The heavy wooden door exploded open, slamming hard against the wall and, as if summoned by Zoila's thoughts, King Gororm stomped into the room with a uniformed scout trailing behind.

Zoila finished the breath she had held following the abrupt entrance of the king. The low vantage point of the peephole, combined with the geometry of the room and a sloping floor, created the strange illusionary effect of making the king and the soldier grow as they entered the room and shrink as they paced back to the door. Zoila tried to focus less on their shifting dimensions and more on their conversation.

"What in blasted brimstone is going on, anyway?" the king shouted with a spray of spittle. "Corporal Ames, status report!"

"The attack seems to have ended," the scout stammered. "The dragon has withdrawn for the night we presume. It will probably continue its campaign tomorrow until..."

"Until it reaches its targeted center, which is us," the king finished the man's sentence. "This is not how it was supposed to turn out."

"I'm sorry?"

"Nothing, never mind. Why did the courtyard and ramparts seem so empty? Where is the rest of my army?"

Ames shifted his weight and cleared his throat. "Three regiments were dispatched to aid the attacked towns."

Gororm loomed large as he stepped further into the room near the peephole. "What? On whose orders?"

"Captain Zoila's, sire."

Zoila could hear the king's teeth grind from the pressure exerted from his clenched jaw. A sly smile crept over her lips.

Under the labored breath of a heaving chest the king ordered, "Bring her to me."

The scout looked about with nervous darting eyes. From Zoila's perspective, Ames shrunk as he edged his way to the doorway.

"Her whereabouts are unknown, sire," he reported.

"Unknown? What is that supposed to mean?"

"She is most likely out with her men aiding the villagers, but that could be any number of places. It will be difficult to find her in such a wide area with all the chaos going on."

Zoila's stomach turned a queasy summersault. It took her by surprise until she realized what had caused her nausea. It was the nausea produced by fear; from the hidden chemicals rushing through her blood screaming for her to run, run for her life and hide. Not that she was in any immediate danger, but the look in Gororm's eyes as he glared at the scout and the tension torquing his body told her danger was afoot. A violent danger she was all too familiar with and which always started with that look and that body posture.

"Come here," the king growled to the scout.

Corporal Ames moved toward the ogre with reluctant steps. "Yes, sire?" His voice was shaky.

"Hold out your hands and show me your fingers."

"Sire?"

Gororm's wart infested face softened as much as it could. "Palms facing me, fingers up. I want to show you how to search efficiently."

With visible trepidation the scout complied.

"Good," Gororm smiled. "Now let's say there are 10 places to look. Oh, there may be more in reality, but for the sake of this lesson we'll say 10, okay?"

The scout nodded; droplets of perspiration beaded his forehead and slowly trickled down his trembling face.

Zoila found herself unable to exhale, and a growing dizziness invaded her head. Her hand ached from the enormous pressure she brought to bear on the stone, gripping the gem as if her life depended on it. She knew the scout. A new recruit eagerly working his way up the ranks, but he had just made the mistake of telling the king that a task might prove difficult or unwise. A sense of helplessness crushed in on her and, despite her strong urge to rescue the underling, all she could do was watch.

"Now," the king continued, "to find what you are looking for..."

Barely missing a beat, the king reached across his body, cross-drew his small sword, and neatly severed the scout's fingers from his hands with one swipe.

"... you eliminate all other possibilities," Gororm finished.

Left with only two thumbs jerking under a fountain flow of blood, Ames howled, shock overcoming him. He clutched the two bloody stumps close to his chest and bent over as his knees began to buckle.

Fighting back rage, Zoila began deliberate deep breathing to ease her panting. *The day you choke to death on the blade of my sword cannot come soon enough; you spawn of the muck and mire.*

"Guards!" the king shouted. And then to the two men who responded to the call, he ordered, "Get this mess out of my sight."

The two guards carried their moaning comrade out of the room.

"And bring Damek to me!" he called after them. Mumbling to himself he added, "We'll take care of this once and for all."

The mention of her lover's name chilled Zoila to the marrow. *What does he want with Damek? If he tries to harm him in the least, I'll bust through this wall, and I will take care of this once and for all!*

Zoila closed her eyes for a moment and tried to relax her body, which was cramping now from the small space and the emotional turmoil boiling inside her like a poisonous brew. *Get a hold of yourself, Zoila. Don't make more of it then it is. It makes sense to call Damek. After all, he is Captain of the Guard, and that's who you call when you need someone found or some deed done that requires discretion. He's just following protocol, the fact that it's Damek is just a coincidence.*

When she opened her eyes the king had once again moved toward the peephole causing him to appear larger than life. The queen frantically entered the room looking small at first, but then rocketing in size as she rushed toward Gororm with a book clasped closely to her waddling body.

"Traitor!" the queen declared. She stopped suddenly and looked about her feet. A quizzical sneer made her flabby face even more grotesque as she sidestepped the dismembered fingers and the puddle of blood that trickled down the floor's incline toward the door.

"Blast it all, Gororm!" she said with disapproval. "Can't you conduct your business somewhere else? There better not be blood spatter on my tapestries."

As Dezair scanned the walls for speckles, Zoila froze. A sinking feeling rippled through her as the queen looked over the wall that contained the peephole. She sighed with relief when the queen passed quickly over the bare wall and focused more attention on the walls with hangings.

"What can I say?" the king shrugged. He wiped his blade on his sleeve and sheathed his sword. "It was an impromptu lesson in tactics."

"Humph," the queen responded.

"Besides, you're trained." He pointed to the book she held in her clutches. "I'm sure you can cast a spell that will get blood out of cloth. Now what's this about a traitor?"

The queen blinked at Gororm and mouthed the word "traitor" as if accessing some distant memory. Then with a sudden animating spark she looked down at the book and thrust it toward the king.

"Yes! Traitor!" she exclaimed. "Look what I found in Zoila's room."

"Zoila's room?"

"I went there to find her and spied this book on her bed, only half covered by a blanket. It was practically in front of my face, can you believe it? She has become more and more brazen."

From behind the wall, Zoila could not be heard silently pounding a fist on her forehead. *Sloppy, sloppy, sloppy,* she scolded herself. *How could I be so careless? I was in such a hurry, too much was going on, my thoughts were too scattered. Still, so what; so they know I stole the book. Doesn't change a thing. Bugger them, bugger them both.*

"Okay," the king said sounding confused. "What book is it?"

With a frustrated grunt, Dezair shook the book at Gororm. "The book, *the* book, you know — *the book*."

"I don't know what in tar pits you're talking about."

The queen shook her head slowly and then, through clenched teeth, she hissed, "The book the old sorceress gave me long ago on the day of my confirmation."

"Oh, *that* book. I thought you lost that one."

Dezair stood stunned and looked at Gororm in disbelief. She rammed the book at him, hitting him squarely in the chest. She shouted, "That's what I'm saying, you dolt! I didn't lose it; Zoila stole it. She's been in possession of it all these years."

"So what? I don't have time for this drivel. So she was young, she took it and was too afraid to return it to you. What does it have to do with the predicament we're in now?"

"Unbelievable," the queen said and pulled on her jowl. "You're a bright one, someone ought to make you king."

"Now, look here..."

"No, *you* look. Come look and see."

The queen went over to the king's desk, and Gororm followed. Since the desk was by an adjacent wall, it looked to Zoila as if they faded a little into the distance. Instead of feeling anxious about being found out, she felt a burden had been lifted. It was one less complication to deal with and, with its removal, her intentions crystallized into a single-minded vision.

The queen slammed the spine of the book down on the desktop. She slowly loosened her hold on the book cover and let the pages naturally unfold.

"Watch," she instructed. The unfolding pages favored a section two-thirds into the manuscript where several pages had been torn out. "See! See what has been torn out? It's an incantation for imprisoning someone in a crystal and warding off those with harmful intent."

The king looked down at the book in front of him. Intense disbelief replaced the look of boredom on his reddening face as his eyes grew wide and his mouth hung open.

"It was Zoila," she continued. "Zoila cast the spell on Arias and made sure we couldn't get close to her. You thought you had Zoila on your side, but she has been against you and protecting Arias all this time."

The king began to mummer out loud, "Somehow she must have found out I ordered Arias assassinated, because that's when Arias was encased in that infernal crystal. How could she have known? My door was closed, I told only the lone assassin... Come to think of it, I never heard from him again."

That's because I gutted him and fed his corpse to a singular of wild boars, Zoila scoffed. She felt gleeful. Her body seemed to conform more easily to the confines of her hiding place.

Gororm snatched up the book and shook it at Dezair, commanding, "Well, break the spell."

Dezair glared at the king's thickness of thought. "I can't, you dolt. All the pages are missing!"

"Whore!" the ogre bellowed as he hurled the book across the room. "I'm going to get her. Oh, yes, I'm going to get her good, and then I'll take care of that conniving sister of hers. Why did we even bother with those two hideous children? Should have just killed them along with their parents."

That remark birthed a new tautness in Zoila. She had long since discovered that her real parents were killed by Gororm's order. But she never got used to knowledge, and hearing the truth from his lips reawakened old pains and hatreds.

"We did it because the prophecy said only a human divided could be granted Holdfast's gift and their reunion would unleash the power," the queen reminded him.

"Well, that didn't exactly work out. Now I got a dragon burning everything up and heading my way!"

Dezair was thoughtfully thumbing through the book. "This all seems connected somehow. It has to be, fate connects things in her spider web."

"What are you going on about?"

Yeah, Zoila thought, *what are you going on about?*

"When I was researching the Holdfast legend," the queen began in a thoughtful, far away voice, "I remember reading about a scholar from the Wundt province. He figured out a connection between what the gift was, the person who got it, and some special event in the land."

"Relevance for the present situation, please," the king said with impatience.

Ignoring him, she continued her recall. "During the last manifestation of Holdfast a thousand years ago, a merchant was given a container with a piece of coal in it. The merchant roasted the coal inside the container where no air entered and made coke. It allowed him to smelt superior iron, and his providence prospered. We even import from them. Once the gift was used, Holdfast vanished."

"Okay, so what do we have? Some unknown girl wondering around with a key, a daughter trapped in a crystal, a..."

"Wait—a daughter trapped in a crystal with a keyhole."

Zoila blinked hard in amazement. *Huh, all those years of study did penetrate your thick head. Too bad you're still playing catch up.*

"Ah-ha," the king mused. "That's what Zoila meant by we could get the girl to help us. She's had plans within plans. Well, we just jumped ahead of her. We'll get the girl to open the crystal, the dragon goes away, we kill Arias, the people are grateful, and with Arias out of the way there is no rebel leader."

Dezair snarled, "The girl has the key, she is the one connected to Arias and to the power. Baffling. But one thing seems clear: we don't need Zoila anymore."

"Don't worry about Zoila. I'm taking care of that right now. Damek, get in here. I see you lurking outside the door."

The small figure of Damek in the background of the two large appearing ogres stood in the doorway. He seemed to dwell in the shadows and would not fully enter the room.

Well, this could be a complication.

"You summoned me, my lord?" Damek offered, his voice steady and calm.

"Yes, Captain, I need you to perform a service for your king."

"You have but to command, and I will carry out your wishes," he responded.

"Good, I'm glad someone has a can-do attitude around here," the king said as he glanced over at the gore that still soiled the floor. "First, there is a young girl headed this way from the east. She will not be hard to find; she will keep to the main road." Then, as an aside to the queen, he mentioned, "Fate is so predictable."

"Shall I dispatch her for you, sire?" Damek inquired.

"No! For goodness sake, no. She is a welcomed guest. I want you to escort her to the castle so we might meet with her." He smiled as he spoke in an over-friendly tone. Then with his arm around Damek, he lowered his voice and ordered, "Don't delegate this to anyone, I want you to take care of it, personally."

"As you wish, my lord. Any other way I might be of service to you?"

"Yes, one more thing. Give orders to your men that if they see Captain Zoila, they are commanded to kill her on sight and bring me her head—she has betrayed the kingdom. A hundred gold pieces to the soldier who does so. You may dispatch her yourself if you like, but don't let it delay you from bringing that girl to us. Understood? You'll be rewarded for bringing the girl, so don't worry."

"I understand," he said without a single change in tone or pitch. He bowed slightly and backed his way into the darkened hall.

"Well, my queen, we may just come out of this on top after all. We'll need a masquerade spell to present a more familiar appearance to the girl. Something human and grandparent-like should do nicely."

"Follow me to my haunt, and I'll whip one up," she said giddily as the two walked out of the room, diminishing in size.

Returning the stone to the pouch at her waist, Zoila also replaced the piece of wall to plug up the peephole. She worked her body around the hollowed out area and started the careful crawl down the tunnel.

So that's how it goes. What will you do, Damek? Where will your loyalty take you, to the oath sworn to the king or the oath sworn in my bed? It's time to be a man, time to choose. And I'll know, before you utter a sound, I'll know your choice; it'll be etched in your eyes, and you'll wear it on your face like a stain. You've died a thousand times inside me, and each time diminished your ability to hide your true self from me.

Whether for or against me, Damek will honor our morning rendezvous at the crystal. If he tries to harm me, I will strike him down swiftly. If he can't bear to shed my blood, I still cannot allow him to bring that girl to the king, for Arias will most certainly be killed.

A pain shot through her heart, threatening to disintegrate what frail composure her fatigued body had left. *But please, oh please, Damek—choose me.*

Turning a corner, Zoila worked her way toward an exit near the outer wall of the main castle. Once there she need only transverse the courtyard and make her way to the back of the stables, where her steed stood waiting.

In the dark tunnel, she came to a dead end. She pulled on a small ledge of a wooden door painted to look like stone blocks. The panel slid easily open, and she entered a hallway from behind a large wall hanging. Turning to the left she headed for a door at the end of the hall that lead to the outside. As she reached for the door handle something did not feel right. Her trained mind and body alerted on danger seconds before conscious awareness caught up. The few seconds saved her life.

Without knowing immediately why, her head dodged to the right, following the lead of her shoulder. She spun around as a spear lodged into the door, centimeters from where her head had just been. The spear made a twanging noise as it vibrated from its sudden stop in the wood.

"Whoa!" she huffed, instantly aware that years of dedicated training had once again paid off.

"Sorry, princess," a gruff voice called out. "I'll try not to miss next time."

Her tunnel vision on the immediate threat of the spear waned, and she saw two castle guards headed her way. She knew the mismatched pair, the large burly man was Guz and the wiry one was a jittery man that went by the name of Lizard, for what reason she never did understand.

"Well, doesn't news travel fast," Zoila quipped. She was fully alert now and ready for action, the fatigue of only a moment ago had completely vanished. She felt back in her element, out front instead of crawling behind walls like a rat.

"*Good* news does, that's for sure," Guz grinned exposing his rotten teeth.

Lizard just bobbed his head and didn't speak. He nervously fumbled with a drawn sword.

Zoila noted the fear. *He's smart to be afraid. He knows he doesn't stand a chance, but greed will make men do stupid things.*

Zoila casually grabbed the end of the spear and said, "Guz, haven't seen you since I drummed you out of my unit."

"You're too kind to yourself, Zoila, you had me court-martialed. Spent a year in a stinking dungeon and not one visit from you."

"Well, you know how it is, social calendars fill up so fast," Zoila answered as she struck the middle of the spear's shaft with the heel of her palm, breaking the weapon in two. She rotated the lodged spear until it came out of the door, all the while noting Lizard's eyes growing wide and twitchy.

Zoila stood feeling the weight of the two equal length sticks, one of which ended in a spearhead. She sized up Guz and said squinting, "Say, didn't I get rid of you for attempting to rape some virgin priestess or something on that order? I say attempt, because what I do recall is that your little dangler was so small, it couldn't poke through her maidenhead."

Guz's face turned red, and he began to quiver with rage. With a frantic hand he struggled to unsheathe his sword. Her barbs had produced their intended effect. She wanted him mad—mad, clouded and mentally off balance.

"Oh, I'm going to enjoy killing you. And while you're choking on your own blood..."

Zoila started a steady approach toward the two men, her weapons out front and ready. Guz and Lizard stumbled back surprised by her advance.

"... I'll be shoving my dangler in your slit throat," Guz finished unevenly.

She did not break stride as Guz, looking rattled, shouldered Lizard out in front of him.

"Do her in, Lizard," he ordered.

Forced to respond by Guz's shove and the pressure caused by Zoila's bold approach, Lizard clumsily thrust his sword forward. Zoila sidestepped to the inside of his weapon and crashed down hard with both sticks. Her left stick hit the sword, pushing it down and out, while her right stick cracked the small bones in the back of Lizard's sword hand with the flat side of the spear blade. The impact popped open Lizard's grip, causing him to drop his sword.

He sucked in air to form a yell of pain, but before he could issue a cry, Zoila continued her unbroken attack motion. Her right spearhead-stick flashed upward and across, effectively gashing open Lizard's throat. Blood spewed out, showering Zoila with crimson droplets. Lizard's mouth gaped wider than it had as Zoila halted her arching slash to the right. She harpooned the spearhead directly into Lizard's mouth until it severed the spinal cord in the back of his neck. Lizard dropped straight down dead.

The fight started and finished with such quick, brutal intensity, it left Guz stunned and paling.

"Oh, I'm sorry," Zoila said, turning her attention to the shocked guard. "Was your plan to have him wear me down so you wouldn't have to work hard? Hate to tell you, but your plan failed. I feel nice and warmed up now."

Zoila reached down with her empty right hand and pulled out her boot knife. She toyed with the stick and knife, slashing and making random stabbing motions in the air to loosen up.

"How about a little *Espada Y Daga* fighting?" she taunted. "Oh, that's right you didn't stay around long enough to learn cane and blade fighting. Pity."

In a panic, Guz turned to run, but misjudged his whereabouts and smacked face first into the wall. Staggering back in recoil, his face hit the wall again as Zoila bludgeoned him with a backhanded club swing to his head.

Zoila wondered how much he felt as she rammed into his back, pinning him to the wall, and jabbed her knife into the rear of his neck and up into his skull. He shuddered grotesquely as she rotated the knife to scramble his brains. Then as suddenly as the jerking had started, it stopped. Zoila backed off and let Guz's lifeless body crumple to a heap on the floor. She reached down and twisted her knife out of him, wiping the blood on the dead man's shirt before returning the blade to her boot.

Breathing heavily from an adrenaline rush, Zoila looked at the door leading to the outside and thought, *How many of these poor goons am I going to have to get through tonight?*

Chapter Twenty

Annie opened her puffy eyelids and wiped away the crusty yellow gunk that had formed on her lashes. The indigo tint in the sky told her dawn was just around the corner. Pulling the blanket closer around her, she wished the dying embers in the fire pit would radiate their heat a little further. As it was, the warmth they had to offer lingered out of reach. Looking around she noticed Rex's blanket laid spread out and empty. She was alone save for Shiva, who snored lightly, curled up behind Annie's back. From the cover of the brush and surrounding trees, she heard a grumble, a groan, and then the sound of streaming liquid hitting the ground followed by a sigh of relief.

The more things change, the more they stay the same, she thought smiling. *As strange as this place is, body functions still rule. Gotta put stuff in, gotta get stuff out, and then there's all that business in the middle.*

"Everything come out all right?" she called toward the direction of the sounds.

"Huh? Er, what? Oh," Rex chuckled. "You startled me. I thought you were still asleep." He emerged from the stand of forest growth smiling and gave her a wink. "Do you want to go back to sleep, or are you rested enough?"

Annie stretched, and Shiva protested against the disturbance to her slumber with a tongue-protruding yowl.

"No, I'm good. I don't think I can sleep anymore. I'm too excited about getting on the road and seeing your monastery."

"Now that's the up-and-at-em attitude I like to hear in a traveling companion." Rex sat down and reached for some wood from a small stack. He fed the fuel to the coals while blowing gently. Soon, little flames appeared as if out of nowhere, adding to their number until an inviting fire sprang into existence.

Rubbing her eyes, Annie asked, "So, are you going to zap us up some breakfast? I'm kinda hungry."

"No more zapping for me, I'm just a simple monk now. We'll have to make do the old fashion way; we'll have to forage."

Annie plopped back down onto Shiva, who wriggled out from under the girl and headed into the woods. "Oh, man, couldn't you have waited until after breakfast?"

"Chin up, Annie. I spotted a berry bush less than half a kilometer down the path. Oddly enough, it still looked to have plenty of berries for this time of year. Also, the baker in town gave me some biscuit mix while you were basking in your celebrity."

"Biscuits and jam, eh?" she asked, liking the idea.

"Well, biscuits and rendered berry topping at least. And tea, don't forget we still have tea."

"Sounds good to me. When do we eat?"

Rex handed her a patch of leather. "As soon as you gather us some berries. Pinch all four corners together, and you'll have a nice pouch. Bring it back full."

Annie took the material like he had handed her a mucous filled handkerchief. "Are you serious? It's still dark out, how am I supposed to see what I'm doing?"

"Well, you can wait until the sun comes up further, but the sound your belly is making tells me that is not the option of choice. Or," he said while wiggling his fingers, "you can feel your way around the berry bushes. Don't worry, your eyes will adjust."

Annie stood up and nodded with the acceptance of the inevitable. "Just tell me you didn't water the berry bushes like you did the ones behind you."

"*No*," Rex said, leaning into the word. "Keep your waste in one area, I always say."

"How about two areas?" Annie suggested as she headed toward the right of where Rex had been. "You boys have a tendency to splash all over the place."

Rex chortled, "Two it is, my dear. Now the quicker you get those berries, the quicker we eat. It won't take me long to slap some batter in a pan and over the coals."

Annie found a concealed bush to hide behind, even though she had lost her clothes often in the past few days, being exposed still brought uneasiness. After relieving herself, she strolled down the pathway until she came upon Shiva sitting in the middle of the trail.

"Hey, girl, you here to protect me?" Annie squinted over at the growth to her left and made out what looked like large raspberries. "And, apparently, to show me the mother lode. Thanks, girl." Annie gave Shiva's head a vigorous rub.

Annie reached into the raspberry patch, clumsily grasping berries, some of which disintegrated to a juicy mush in her hands.

"This is a mess. I can barely see, and I don't know what I'm doing," she muttered to herself. Taking out the key that hung around her neck,

Annie held the gift toward the bushes.

"Fly into the cloth, berries, fly!" she commanded with disappointing results. "What I could really go for is a breakfast burrito. But I don't see any burrito bushes around here, do you girl?"

Shiva gave a full body shake, and then sat down to paw at an itch on the back of her head.

"Didn't think so. Well, one berry at a time I guess."

Annie picked raspberries as she kept herself company by speaking to Shiva.

"Rex says wolves are social animals, so why are you wandering around alone? Don't have any family or did they just not want you? That would be hard to believe, you're so beautiful."

Shiva gave a short bark.

"Oh, me, too? Thank you so much. Let me ask you something. Ever feel like you did something cosmic that you couldn't be forgiven for, you know, like being born? I feel that way sometimes—well a lot of times. And, I'm getting to the point that I just don't care. I mean, why should I beg? Sure I screw up sometimes, but does that mean I deserve to be dumped on?"

Annie looked over at Shiva, who busied herself by licking between her hind legs. "Yeah, I see your point. Nice talking to ya, Shiva."

The sound of giggling and a flickering light gave Annie a startle. She spun around with arms poised to defend and dropped what few berries she had managed to gather onto the ground.

"Who's there?" she called out while shooing some fireflies away from her head.

"Hey, watch where you're waving those hands!" a tiny voice objected.

"Don't worry, blondie, you ain't mussed up," a second voice responded.

A third voice chimed in, "She may not be, but do you know how long it takes to braid my hair? *Ay carumba!*"

Then Annie swore she heard an "Hrumph" come from a fourth source. The fireflies swirled around her, enlarging their orbit with each pass. As they zipped about, they grew brighter and larger, taking the shape of four 60-centimeter tall sparkling fairies.

"Kizze, Babes, Isabel, Lai?" Annie greeted, uncertain of what she saw materialize in front of her.

"That's us, girl," Kizze said. Her black skin glowed through a sheer, yellow short dress with matching knee-high leggings that left feet exposed.

"It's nice to see you again, Annie," Babes greeted. She shared the same attire as Kizze and the other two fairies, only her translucent dress was red.

Annie waved toward Lai, who hovered shyly over the raspberry patch in her jade colored dress and leggings. "Hello," Annie mouthed to which Lai smiled.

Isabel flitted in front of Annie, her wings batting and whirring like a hummingbird's. "*Buenos dias*, Annie, do you like?" she asked feeling her sheer, blue short dress. "It's so much more liberating then that corset. Although..."

"Oh, look!" Babes squealed. "It's Shiva. Look girls, it's Shiva!" Babes swooped down and hugged the wolf. "Oh, for sweet."

The other three took turns petting and flying around Shiva, who clearly enjoyed the attention.

Isabel zoomed through the air back to Annie. "Although," she continued, thoughtfully pulling up a legging that had worked its way below her knee. "I don't know if these stockings leave too much to the imagination, you know? How much skin is too little or too much? I want to give the right message not the wrong one, right?"

Babes rolled her eyes. "Here we go again."

"Damn, Isabel," Kizze scolded as she circled around her, "can't you please stop obsessing about your appearance? It don't matter if you hide it or flaunt it; men will find a way to make it mean what they want."

"I'm just saying," Isabel rebutted.

Babes darted between them and then executed a loop-to-loop. "Kizze's right, Isabel. You're just going in circles, sweetie, just try to respect yourself."

"Can we get to the point of this excursion?" Lai announced irritated.

"See how alone you are for not giving at least a hint of interest by showing some skin," Isabel retorted without seeming to hear Lai.

"Just for that, I'm gonna wrap myself in a burqa and still get hounded," Kizze vowed.

"Please, ladies, focus!" shouted Lai.

The three fairies turned toward Lai as if noticing her for the first time.

"Sorry," Babes offered and buzzed toward Lai. "Why are we here again?"

"To help Annie gather berries, of course," Isabel chimed and flew to join Babes and Lai.

Lai shook her head, "No, that's just the cover story she wanted us to use."

Kizze fluttered over to the other three mumbling under her breath, "I'll be in sack cloth and still get more attention than your fickle ass."

Annie's head spun and tingled from the rapid-fire exchange of the four fairies, who now floated all in a row above the berry patch and gazed at her. She felt her heart skip lightly at the sight of the four women. The last time she had encountered them was in that basement the night she had lost track of so many things. These women were a link from her home to this place, wherever or whatever this place was.

"She who?" Annie inquired as Lai's last statement came into focus. "Esmeralda?"

"Of course, silly, who else do you think we work for?" Babes giggled.

"But that's later, first the berry picking," Isabel declared and began harvesting fruit.

Lai flew to Annie and said, "Here, Annie, let me show you how it's done."

Kizze whizzed to the other side of Annie. "Step aside, Lai, what the hell do you know about picking?"

"We had berries in our garden; I picked them every year," she answered indignantly. Then to Annie she instructed, "Look for the deep red ones, I'll light the patch for you. The deep colored ones are ripe and will slide off—no pulling."

"Hey, Lai, you do know your stuff," Kizze complimented. "Let's get to pickin' then."

Once the makeshift leather bag was full, the fairies escorted Annie and Shiva back down the path to the little campsite.

Upon their approach, Rex stood up from nestling a pan into the coals and called out, "Well, bless my weary eyes! Ladies, where have you been? I've been wandering in this region without so much as a fly by from one of you."

"Hello, Rex," they all responded, coyly. They sped over to him and took turns stroking his hair and hugging his neck.

"You know them?" Annie asked in disbelief.

"Of course. And if they're here, Esmeralda must be nearby. Isn't that right, ladies? Okay, out with it. Where is she?"

"You always spoil everything, *papi*," Isabel pouted as she tugged on Rex's lower lip.

"Yeah, Rex, can't you spare some time for us?" Babes implored, her vibrating wings blowing softly by his ear like a purring cat.

"Come on, sit down and take a load off," Kizze offered. She pushed down on his shoulders until he sat. "We can eat some breakfast first, can't we? We haven't gotten you alone since that one winter solstice party."

"Oof, I was sore for a week after that," Lai said absently.

Silence blanketed the campsite, as all eyes turned from Lai to Rex and then back to Lai.

"What?" she said, gesturing in confusion. "We went ice climbing on that frozen waterfall, remember? My arms aren't that strong and I..." she stopped and a look of slow understanding came over her face. "Oh, you thought I meant... that he and I... oh, there is something *seriously* wrong with you people."

The other fairies laughed, but Lai just muttered, "I'm not talking to any of you for a fortnight at least. Rex, do you have a pot? I'll start boiling these berries."

"Bet she'd like to boil something else," Kizze said aside to Isabel and Babes.

Lai responded with a grimace and a snort, and then set about preparing the berries.

"You ladies are too much," Rex smiled. He handed Lai a pot and sat back to stir the fire with a stick. "Been a long time," he mused.

"Yes it has," said Babes, wistfully.

"Sure 'nough has," Kizze added.

"We missed you, *papi*," Isabel concluded.

Annie began to sit down, but Babes soared over to her and took Annie's arm.

"Uh, Annie, I wonder if you would be a dear and come over here for a moment," she said guiding Annie over to a stand of young oaks.

"Okay," Annie responded with some uncertainty. She noticed Rex was too distracted by Isabel and Kizze's cooing and face caressing to detect the maneuvering.

"I didn't want to say this out loud as it might upset Rex," Babes began in hushed tones. "But it is very thrilling. You'll get to see her at her peak of potency."

"Who?" Annie whispered back. "Esmeralda?"

Babes fluttered with excitement. "Yes, the Red Queen."

Annie considered the title for a moment and then said, "She has more titles than ways of looking."

"Yeah," Babes giggled. "But the Red Queen, now that's her supreme title. Do you know about the Red Queen?"

"No, not really," she said, not knowing at all. "I only saw her in black."

"Most, like Rex over there, only see her in green. It is rare to ever see her in red. The Red Queen, yes, just when you thought you've got it all figured out, she puts another obstacle in your path."

Shaking her head, Annie said, "That doesn't sound right."

"It's the way it is; keeps you growing, but sometimes it's like running just to stand still, you know?"

"Yeah," Annie agreed. "Boy, do I know."

"Berries are done," Lai declared suddenly and loudly.

Kizze did an aerial back summersault, grabbed a chunk of bark, dipped it in the berry ooze, and ended up in front of Rex. "Here, sweetie, give it a taste, and make sure it's done."

"Well, I do have a culinary sense about me."

Annie thought if Rex got anymore full of himself off the flattery of these fairies, he would either explode, or she would vomit.

He let Kizze feed him several bark-dipped helpings of the berry sauce, before turning to Annie and saying, "Come over here, Annie, and try this. It's good."

Annie's mouth watered at the invitation to eat, but as she tried to move, Babes tugged at her shoulder.

"Wait," the blonde fairy instructed.

"Oh, she doesn't want any, *papi*," Isabel said stroking Rex's hand.

"Of course she does, she's..." Rex's eyes bulged and his mouth hung open. "Raspberries, this time of year, here, in this providence; I completely forgot."

Kizze let the bark fall and laid her head on Rex's other hand, caressing it softly, "Hush, sweetie, rest now."

Tears welled in the monk's eyes as he struggled to speak against the paralysis setting into his face. "Not sleepy-tyme berries, no, doe-ont dude dis. I hap do tee er, fleas."

Babes darted to Rex and cradled his head in her arms. She guided his slumping body gently to the ground. "Hush, baby, hush now, you lovely man."

Annie took in a breath to voice her protest, but never got the chance to say a word. The last images she had was of Lai silently and sadly waving goodbye to her, Shiva cocking her head, and Rex slurring, "Bith-kit burnie." Then the vines shot out, grabbed Annie, and pulled her swiftly into the forest depths.

Chapter Twenty-One

Leaves and twigs zipped past her with a loud flutter as she accelerated backward in the clutches of the vines. The speed at which she traveled took her breath away. Worse still was the feeling of her stomach in her throat when the vines decelerated suddenly and came to a halt. The vines let loose and disappeared into the background, leaving her stumbling in an effort to regain some balance.

She found herself inside a dome structure made of intertwined branches, vines and grasses. The morning sun peeked through the foliage, causing the room to sparkle with dancing light. A stream of fresh clear water sang its way past her feet as small birds chirped and fluttered in and out of the walls. The spinning sensation in her head slowed, leaving her with a headache and a growling stomach.

"Hello, Annie," a familiar voice greeted her from behind.

Annie turned, slowly.

The woman wore red. Locks of soft red hair bounced lightly down past her shoulders, framing her face as lovingly as her red lips framed her smile. Rubies, garnets, rubellites and other red precious stones adorned her neck, fingers and the toes of her bare feet. She wore a sleeveless blouse of red silk-chiffon and a layered skirt that ended at her knees. Esmeralda lay stretched out on her side on a red chaise lounge sofa beside a table full of fruits and breads.

"Esmeralda?" Annie blinked, her senses overwhelmed by the rich colors.

"Yes, it's me. Search no further, you have found the Red Queen." Esmeralda smiled and gave a wave of her hand. Even appearing 40, she looked stunning and voluptuous. "Come here, precious," she beckoned as she sat up and opened her arms to welcome Annie.

The sight of Esmeralda propelled Annie into the woman's arms. A flood of relief washed over her as she embraced the woman, burying her face into the space between Esmeralda's neck and shoulder. Annie breathed in deeply. The woman's scent was rich and comforting. It was a smell Annie could not consciously pin down, but somewhere deep inside, a part of her knew it well. It was the smell an infant craves as it suckles to the soft humming of a mother.

Tears flowed down her cheeks as Annie pushed away from the embrace. "What happened to Rex?" she demanded. "Is he dead? Were those berries poisoned?"

"Oh, no," Esmeralda assured. "He'll be fine. The berries just put him to sleep, so we can talk privately."

"Talk? Talk about what—how you deserted me? Why did you do this to me?"

"Whatever do you mean, dear?"

"What do I mean?" Annie could feel rage boil up inside and fuel her hurt. "Did you see what those wolves did to me? You practically threw me to them, and then I ended up here, completely lost and alone!"

Esmeralda looked pained as she reached up and stroked Annie's tear stained cheek. "I'm so sorry, Annie. I know it was frightening, but there was no other way; I promise you."

Annie resisted Esmeralda's attempts to comfort, standing stiffly with her arms crossed and her lips pouted.

The Red Queen motioned with her fingers for Annie to come forward, her green eyes acting like a salve on a blistering burn. "Please, sweetie, come sit by me. Have some food; you must be half starved."

Annie's resolve buckled under the combined weight of hunger and emotional strain. She nodded and sat beside the woman, eagerly accepting a bunch of grapes.

"There you are; that's better now," Esmeralda soothed. "I did leave you in Rex's hands, though. Hasn't he taken good care of you?"

"Yeah, he has," Annie managed to say as she chewed, then stuffed more grapes into her mouth. After swallowing, Annie saw an opportunity to help Rex out. "He loves you, you know; and he's sorry about what happened."

Esmeralda handed Annie a muffin. "I know. I love him, too, and I hold no ill feelings toward him."

"I bet he'd like to know that," Annie said through a mouthful of the muffin.

"I'll go tend to him shortly, but right now I want to focus on you."

Annie swallowed hard, the muffin sticking in her throat, "Me?"

"Have a drink, dear," the woman said passing a glass of cool water.

After guzzling the contents of the glass, Annie let out a long baritone belch. "Sorry," she laughed.

Esmeralda joined in the laugh. "That was a healthy one."

Annie felt a comfort envelop her. The anger she had felt dissipated in the warm loving presence of Esmeralda. She couldn't figure out what it was about the mysterious woman that made her feel so at ease. She only knew that sitting next to her felt safe.

Annie handed back the glass with a "thank you," and brushed the muffin crumbs from the front of her shirt.

Tousling Annie's hair, Esmeralda said, "Look at you; you're blooming right before my eyes." She grabbed Annie's hips and gave them a little shake. "So grown up."

Annie giggled and pushed the woman's hands away. "Stop, that tickles."

"Oh, Annie," Esmeralda said beaming with pride. "What wondrous things life has in store for you."

Annie's face went sour, "If it's anything like what I've been getting, then forget it."

"It's been hard for you, I know," the Red Queen consoled. "But you have to hold on and keep trying."

"Why?" she shrugged. "There's nothing I can really do. It's like everything is against me, has been from the start. My parents weren't worth a shit, I'm no good at school, and I keep making the wrong decisions."

"Poor, dear," Esmeralda empathized.

In the midst of her apathy, the burning question that had plagued Annie emerged. She thought she had come to terms with it after her talk last night with Rex about her vision. But now, she realized she had only understood it at a superficial level. Deep inside she needed confirmation, and although Rex had understood and provided support; it wasn't enough to bring the truth home to her. She needed Esmeralda to say it, to tell her one way or the other. Stoically she asked, "Am I normal?"

Leaning back into the seat, the woman stretched out her arms, rested them on top of the sofa and said simply, "No, sweetie, you're not."

Annie thought she should feel disappointment or outrage at the answer, but she didn't. She felt relief. "I didn't think so."

"Normal is what is common, and you are not that. You're right, Annie, things haven't gone well for you and, even if they had, you still would've struggled more than most people." Esmeralda pointed to Annie's head. "You have to work with what you've got, and if what you've got doesn't work very well—you just have to work harder."

"Great," Annie said throwing her hands up in defeat. "That leaves me with a bright future as a crack whore."

Laughing, Esmeralda stood up and pulled Annie off the sofa as she did. She gave the girl a long hug and said, "Oh, Annie, you have no idea what you might overcome; no idea how far your limits stretch. You just have to go out there and keep trying; keep finding a way."

The maternal aroma of Esmeralda embedded itself deep into Annie as she held tightly to the woman. "I'm so scared and alone. I don't know what I'm supposed to do."

"I don't know either. You just have to keep finding a way, and never give up; like you were about to in the ocean."

Annie pulled away remembering her brush with suicide. She searched Esmeralda's green eyes for answers, but only found the love the woman felt for her, and maybe that was enough. "Can't you help me at all?"

Esmeralda kissed Annie on the forehead, "Of course. I have helped you and will continue to do so. You have the dragon's gift? The key?"

"Yes."

"Good. I'm going to place you on a path; don't let any obstacle stop you. Face the challenges you encounter, and then keep moving," Esmeralda instructed, straightening Annie's shirt. "You have to find a princess trapped in a crystal. Your key will open it."

Annie crinkled her nose and forehead. "What the heck are you talking about?"

"It's all I can say. It's not fair I know, but I can only see the big picture, the details are a blur. I do know that chances to reclaim our lives are limited. The more we pass up, the less chance we have to live fully."

"Will Rex be with me?"

"No," the Red Queen answered. "But you'll see him again at the end."

"The end?" Annie asked, hoping she had misheard. "I don't like the sound of *the end*," Annie told the woman. "What happens to me when I free this princess?"

Esmeralda brushed her fingers through Annie's hair and looked Annie in the eyes with a mischievous grin. "You'll just have to go discover what's waiting for you out there."

"Why? What's waiting for me? Is it my death?"

Esmeralda kissed her on the forehead and whispered, "Oh, most certainly."

With that, the vines shot out, grabbed Annie and pulled her through the wall and into the forest.

Chapter Twenty-Two

From the concealment of the scattered boulders that bordered the line between where the woods ended and the land began its steep ascent to the plateau, Zoila waited. Like a sleek predator she patiently crouched with knife in hand, only her eyes moved as she skimmed the surrounding area. The dirt and dried blood on her skin and clothes told the tale of a night spent fighting.

Lucky me. I sent all my loyal troops out to help the villagers, leaving the disgruntled soldiers to receive the assassination order. Talk about being born under a bad sign.

Her keen senses picked up the signs of a person approaching. There was a snapping of random twigs, a crunch of dead leaves under foot, and the chirping flight of small birds. Her taut muscles readied as Damek emerged from the woods right past her position and took a step on the incline.

Taking advantage of the shift in his center of gravity, Zoila sprang out with a war cry and crashed her body solidly into his. Damek tumbled backward over Zoila as she plowed under and lifted, sending him to the ground. Barely missing a boulder, which would have cracked his skull had he hit it, Damek fell like the well-trained soldier he was: chin tucked and rolling after impact. He didn't get far before Zoila pounced on him, holding a knife to his throat with one hand, while her other hand grabbed the side of his head, her thumb hovering over his eye socket, ready to gouge.

"Hello, lover," she greeted with a sneer.

"Have you lost your mind? What do you think you're doing?" he demanded.

"Waiting for a cowardly pig to show up and, look, you did."

Damek closed his eyes, his face tightened. When he opened them, he said in a controlled voice, "Zoila, what's going on? You told me to meet you at the crystal, and that's what I'm doing."

The thought of how easily the blade would slice through his carotid artery played in her mind. *But only if he betrayed me. If he did, I will not hesitate, but I have to be sure. The truth will be in his eyes.*

She pressed the blade further into his flesh, causing an indentation as skin yielded to the metal. "Came to meet me or kill me?"

"What?" he reacted with a look of true surprise.

"Needed some extra whoring money, did you? Your companions thought they'd collect, but all they received was an early death." Zoila touched her thumb to his eyebrow.

"They were not my companions," he insisted.

"But you left them to me. Did you lose your own taste for blood? Let me rekindle it." She pushed the blade carefully, making a superficial cut that produced a trace of blood.

Breathing in sharply, he stretched his neck away from the knife's edge. "Oh, for the love of the gods, Zoila! Do you think I would put you in peril?"

"I don't know. Would you?" She eased up a centimeter, but kept her blade steady.

Damek exhaled as the knife left his throat. "I had to tell some of the guards, or the king would know I betrayed him. I didn't doubt you could handle the strays left at the castle; all the good soldiers were in the field by *your* order."

Zoila removed her thumb from over his eye and pushed her hand forward, entangling her fingers in his hair. "Oh, so now you don't think I can hold my own with the *skilled* troops."

"Damn you, Zoila!" he shouted in frustration. "You think I betrayed you? Well, bugger you and your suspicions. Kill me if you must; death would be a relief from all this rot you've put me through!"

Zoila sniggered and, placing her hands on his chest, pushed off him to get to her feet. "Don't get so dramatic, Damek. I had a rough night." She sheathed her knife and leaned her back against a boulder.

After rubbing his throat, Damek inspected the blood smear on his palm. "By all means, we don't want any dramatics. Zoila, what's going on? I just betrayed the king for you and, as I walked here, I realized I have no idea why."

"I thought it was because you love me," she said, the fatigue showing in her voice.

Damek got up and walked over to her. Caressing her face he said, "I do love you and, despite your bravado, I know you love me, too. I just want to know what's going on."

Zoila shuddered and tried to justify the reaction as a result of the chilly morning air. The rationalization didn't hold, however. Years of growing up in a home filled with fear and violence wore on her. Each ugly incident was like a wave crashing against a rocky coastline until, over time, the rock wears away. And she had worn away; she could tell by the growing urge to disclose her thoughts to Damek. An urge that took advantage of her fatigue and broke through the bulwark of her inner defenses, forcing her to speak.

"It was me, I did it," she confessed, lowering Damek's hand from her face and moving forward to stand without aid of the boulder.

Damek took a step back to give her space. "Did what, Zoila? You can tell me."

She swallowed hard with eyes closed tight. Taking a deep breath, she opened her eyes, looked directly at Damek and said, "I cast the spell that trapped Arias in the crystal. It was me. I stole a book from the queen and spent years learning the spell."

Instead of the look of shock or disgust Zoila had expected to find on Damek's face, she saw only a deep empathy. She found it difficult to bear; difficult to feel the hurt that comes when someone loves you, but you despise yourself.

A brighter affect came over Damek and he said, "There's good news in that, do you see? You can break the spell, and we can all slip away; find somewhere else to live, somewhere safe."

"No, Damek," she said with a slow shake of her head. "There is no safe place for Arias and me. He'll come; he'll find us, and then he'll kill us. Gororm is waiting for a way to unleash the dragon's gift, and then he'll kill her, just as he's set out to kill me."

"I won't allow it," Damek vowed. "I will kill the king myself and the queen, if need be."

"Don't you think I've tried?" She was near tears now and cursed the fatigue that exposed her. "They're too powerful. I can barely hold my-self together in their presence."

Damek tried to touch her again, but she balked. He backed off say-ing, "They're just flesh and blood like all of us, no different."

"To you, it's no different," she disputed, her tears no longer waiting for permission to flow. "You don't know what it was like; the hell I en-dured. I know in my head they're flesh and blood, and I have the ability to destroy them but, when I draw near, I'm reduced to a little girl beaten down by their cruelty."

"Let me help," Damek said softly. "You see, it will not be the same for me. I can do it."

Zoila rubbed her eyes and cheeks hard. Sucking back the remaining mutinous tears, she said, "No, if you want to help—really help—then help me protect Arias; that is all that matters. The king and queen must not get to her."

"Obviously, your spell is a powerful one, since the queen has not succeeded in breaking it," he offered.

"Yes, but a way has presented itself. Do you remember what Gororm told you to do besides have me killed?" she asked knowing full well Damek never forgot an order.

"Of course," he responded. "He told me to bring some girl to him."

"Not just *any* girl," Zoila corrected. "The girl who has Holdfast's gift. Remember, I told you?"

"Yeah, I remember. The girl who was with the monk or wizard or whatever he was. What was his name?"

"Rex," she said. "But the point is, the gift is a key, and I'm certain it will open the crystal and that will be the end of us all."

"No problem," he shrugged. "I won't take her to the king that seems simple enough."

Zoila's eyes narrowed, and her voice became stern. "Simple enough, yes, but not good enough. You have to meet the girl and then kill her. Bring her head to me as proof."

Uncertainty twisted Damek's face. "This doesn't sound right."

"Lost your nerve for killing?" Zoila taunted.

"No, but I'm a soldier, not a murderer of innocent children," he protested.

"She's not innocent. Whether or not she knows what she is doing, it doesn't matter. Don't you see? Once the king gets hold of her, he will use her against Arias and me. Think of her as a weapon your enemy is wielding. What do you do if your enemy sticks their sword out at you?"

"I hack off their sword hand."

"Exactly," Zoila underscored, coldly.

A shadow accompanied by a howling whoosh passed over them, momentarily blocking out the morning sun. The two warriors instinctually searched the sky, and then Damek sprung forward, sandwiching Zoila between him and the boulder.

"The dragon," Damek informed her in a hushed tone.

Zoila made no attempt to push him off. She knew he had made the right move to protect them both. Her eyes continued to scan across the sky, and she said, "Her lair must be nearby. I wonder why she hasn't bedded down for the day?"

"I don't know," Damek said looking upward.

She became aware of his closeness and, flushed in the face, breathed him in. The sensation of his flesh pressed against her caused a tingling to spread throughout her body.

"Something's wrong. I have a bad feeling about today," she said trying to ignore a restlessness building inside her.

"It'll be okay," he assured.

He was cheek to cheek with her now; she felt his warm breath stimulating the skin on her neck. "No, I don't think so. I don't think I'm going to make it through the day."

He moved his head to face her and said, "Hey, don't talk like that."

The sky darkened again as the dragon made another screeching overhead pass.

Zoila leaned her face forward suddenly, kissing him long and hard.

"Damek," she trembled.

"I know, my love, I know."

Arias sat contemplating inside the crystal, marveling at the early morning light playing off the crystal's angles and casting luminescent flashes and rainbows around her. Although she hadn't figured out the particulars of her captivity, she felt certain there was a beneficial reason for it. Whoever did this to her couldn't have had malicious intent. The crystal took care of her in a sense, providing shelter and somehow suspending the need to eat, drink and evacuate. Although she longed to rejoin the outside world, there must have been a hidden property in the rock that kept her urges tranquil.

How long has this strange captivity lasted? Six months? Maybe more; maybe less; hard to say; the days start to flow into each other. I can hardly remember when it happened, although I can remember the coming of the multitude.

It had only been a curious few at first that came to confirm with their own eyes the rumors of a crystal-encased princess. Then one day a woman touched the stone and despair left her body. After that more came, day by day growing in numbers, hoping to steal away a little comfort and ease their mortal struggles. Sometimes the crystal soothed, sometimes it didn't, and sometimes Arias sang songs to inspire; the crowd would depart with a new inner optimism that they could overcome their tribulations.

The princess tucked her legs to one side and rotated her body in the opposite direction, while her neck rotated to face the same angle as her feet. *Bharadvajasana, the sage's pose,* she whispered inside her head as she continued the Vinyasa she'd begun prior to the interrupting memories. *Without beginning or end; eternal time; I evoke the wisdom of the sacred feminine.*

Breathing in deeply by accentuating her abdomen, she held her pose. *They used to camp out below and climb the slope at sunset when the light made the warm crystal glow like a beacon. But since the dragon's rampage, they've stopped coming.*

The dragon's lair was near, hidden deep in a cave among the rocky cliffs. Holdfast ended each night of destruction by circling above the crystal at first morning's light, before slipping away to slumber for the day. Arias always sang a song for her as the dragon circled, but Holdfast was late this morning. The sun had crested over the horizon, and there was no winged serpent in sight.

The height of the crystal allowed her to stand and extend her arms upward with palms joined together. The heel of her left foot slowly rose up her inner thigh and came to rest against her groin. *Vrksasana, the tree; our great teacher; linking the unknown to the known to the hoped for.*

A familiar screeching howl rippled through the quiet cool of the morning. Arias smiled, holding the pose and maintaining her breathing cycle. *There you are.*

An unusually close passing of Holdfast overhead startled Arias out of her meditation. The creature swooped down a hundred meters from the ground; her screaming dive and pull-up-loop reverberated in the crystal and caused Arias to fall. Recovering from her spill, Arias pressed against the transparent wall to get a better look.

Holdfast's ascent came to a momentary stand still at its apex, followed by another deadly rush to the ground. This time when she pulled up, she dropped an object on the ground in front of Arias. The dark chunk of mass hit the earth with a thud, exploding a cloud of dust around it.

The young woman peered at the smoldering thing on the ground, turning her head one way then the other in an effort to make sense of it. As if sucking hard on a lime, her face screwed up in disgust and she shuffled to the rear of the crystal, trying to control her retching stomach. The dragon's deposit was the charred remains of some person unfortunate enough to cross paths with an enraged Holdfast.

Arias redirected her horror to the dragon's new plunge. This time Holdfast came closer to the earth, pulling up only at the last moment and again releasing something from her vicious claws. Afraid to look at the object, Arias focused on the magical being's expanding talons and crimson belly. Not until Holdfast's mighty tail had passed, did Arias see what the dragon had released. Like a rolled ball, a body tumbled over itself, coming to its feet as the dragon disappeared into the sky. She stared in disbelief at the figure walking toward her.

"Diné!" Arias called out. "Is it really you?"

"*Yá'át'ééh,* Princess Arias. It has been too long; you have grown tall," he greeted, brushing and patting dirt from his clothing.

"Much too long, my friend. I'm so glad you're here, everything's gone wrong it seems." Arias surprised herself with how quickly her inner doubts came rushing to the surface in the face of the Navajo man.

"No, it is all going as it should," he assured. Diné approached the charred body, looking over it with a sad shake of his head.

"Who was that poor fellow?" Arias asked.

"A nice but troubled man I traveled a time with. He suffered from the sickness of conceit." Diné removed a small bag from his belt and sprinkled the contents over the remains of Brother Simon. The red powder scattered over the corpse. "To help with the smell," he told Arias. Then to the remains he said, "Rest my friend, I am honored to have walked with you on the final steps of your journey."

"How did you two end up in the clutches of the dragon?"

"Simon called out to the beast from a clearing. He wanted to convert her to reason. I think he really wanted a battle in his own heart to be still." Diné walked to the edge of the plateau in search of a stick.

"It appears the dragon did not care for that. But you were not harmed."

"No," he said checking the sturdiness of a switch he picked up from the ground. "I stood and accepted what was, until what will be, can be."

Arias smiled with a glance from the corner of her eyes, "Oh, Diné, you're always so enigmatic."

The man nodded in simple agreement. He took the stick and started drawing figures and symbols in the dirt between the body and the crystal.

"That looks interesting," Arias commented. "Will it release me?"

"I come to prepare the path for she who will embrace you."

"Come on, Diné, what does that mean? It's just the two of us here, you can tell me without the mystery."

He stopped his scrawling and shrugged, "How am I supposed to know? I just go where the spirits send me and do what they show me." Diné gestured toward Simon with a flick of his head. "Not good to anger the spirits."

Arias pouted her lips and fluttered her eyelids. "Please? Just a little clue?"

"Now, is that the manner of an enlightened woman? You are acting like the little girl I instructed many years ago," he smiled, warmly.

The pout did not abate.

Diné winked, "All I can say is what I know. A healing is to occur here. A woman is wounded, and I see three paths joining at this place."

"Who? Me?"

"You, Zoila, and a third not of these lands. She is on her way, but will not arrive until after her *Kinaalda*."

"You know I don't speak your language. What's a *Kin-aal-da*," she asked, sounding out the word.

"The changing of girl to woman. She has the gift of the dragon and is becoming very powerful."

Arias accepted the information as all she would receive. She watched Diné finish the two-square-meter sized ground drawing. After outlining with a stick, he removed his poncho and took off a leather pouch. From the bag he removed four small sacks.

Sitting down with crossed legs, she looked on as he gently shook out a mixture of crushed stone and flower petals from the sack into his hand. Each bag contained a separate color: white, blue, yellow and black. He used the different colors like paint, holding his hand in a fist and dropping the fine sandy mixture to fill in the outlined picture.

"That's beautiful, Diné. What does it mean?"

"This figure is Mother Earth; inside her are the sacred plants of corn, bean, squash and tobacco. And this figure is Father Sky; inside him are the star patterns of the night sky, the moon and sun." He moved his hand over the outlined border of the sand painting. "Protecting them on three sides will be the Rainbow God, and to guard the opening on top—a medicine bag and rug. I will give the Blessing Way to restore balance, the *hózhó*."

"I know I feel out of balance, maybe it is meant to help me."

"This I do not know. Many things are out of balance in this place."

Arias continued to watch while Diné completed the sand painting. And once completed, he sat down and chanted the Navajo Blessing Way:

"In beauty, may I walk.
All day long, may I walk.
Through the returning seasons, may I walk.
On the trail marked with pollen, may I walk.
With grasshoppers about my feet, may I walk.
With dew about my feet, may I walk.
With beauty may, I walk.
With beauty before me, may I walk.
With beauty behind me, may I walk.
With beauty above me, may I walk.
With beauty below me, may I walk.
With beauty all around me, may I walk.
In old age wandering on a trail of beauty, lively, may I walk.
In old age wandering on a trail of beauty, living again, may I walk.
It is finished in beauty.
It is finished in beauty."

Zoila heard the chanting as she neared the top of the plateau, and the sound spurred her to finish the climb quickly. "Oh, no you don't," she huffed. She reached the flattop and half stumbled from the force of her ascent.

The scene that greeted her was that of an old chanting man, her sister staring wide eyed at Zoila's sudden emergence, and a charred body.

"Hold it right there, Diné," she called to the Navajo. "Stop whatever you think you're doing right now."

"*Yá'át'ééh*, Princess Zoila. It has been too long, you have grown tall," he greeted as he rose and turned to face her.

"If you're here to open the crystal and free Arias; don't bother—leave it alone."

"I am only giving a blessing; I have no intentions at all," Diné shrugged.

"Yeah, right," Zoila glared. "Your kind never does, but somehow you mystics seem to cause a lot of trouble."

Diné responded with a nod and pleasant smile.

Zoila picked up her foot and began to swing it down into the sand painting. She stopped millimeters from the ground. "Hmm, beautiful. You do nice work, Diné. I'll let it stand, for all the good it'll do you. But start that chanting rubbish again, and I'll cut your throat. As much as I like you and the agreeable memories I have of you, I am determined, understand?"

Again the nod and pleasant smile.

Zoila turned her attention to a disheartened Arias. "As for you, little sister, you're going to stay put where it's safe." Then addressing them both with a commanding jab of her finger in the air, she said, "No one's going to do a thing until Damek returns and we can sort out where things stand."

"Princess Zoila?" Diné said, calmly.

"What?" came her sharp reply.

The Navajo stood silently with a look of concern.

Zoila took a second to regroup and get herself under control. "I'm sorry, Diné," she said sincerely. "A lot's happened since I last saw you all those years ago. I know you mean well, but you don't know what's going on, and you're liable to make things worse."

"I have no argument with that," he assured and then pointing to the body he asked, "I just want to know: would you help me bury my friend?"

Zoila looked at the body and then at Diné. "Oh, that's who that is,"

she said empathetically; the painful memories of losing comrades in battle surged through her. "Of course I will help you honor your friend."

Chapter Twenty-Three

The dreamer awakes to find herself still in the dream, Annie mused as she discovered herself deposited on a forest pathway. Her mind still felt a little unsettled by Esmeralda's words, and the rush through the foliage provided by the grabbing vines felt like she had stepped off a merry-go-round before her senses could stop spinning. It was a heady feeling, but not unpleasant. A stronger sense of herself had developed in the past hour, or more accurately in the past several days in this unfamiliar land. She knew intuitively what had to be done, even if she had no idea of how to go about doing it.

Making her way down the path, she rubbed the goose bumps that the surrounding shade-cooled air caused on her skin. A rich scent of pine streamed into her nostrils, stimulating long ago memories of a family camping trip or a Christmas evening's happiness. Neither recollection came as an intact picture, more of a feeling of being loved while surrounded by that pine smell. With a sad head shake, Annie acknowledge that she could just as well have been recalling hopes and dreams instead of actual past occurrences.

She continued down the dirt path, enjoying the burst of sunlight that broke through the forest growth to fulfill its destiny of dancing on her face. The scattered warmth made her feel the grime and oil buildup on her skin. She'd like to bathe, if she could, and rinse out her dirty and blood speckled clothes. The quick splash of water at the small stream the night before had done little to clean her properly. Although she was used to unclean clothes, often having to implore a neighbor to let her toss some laundry in with their load at the coin-op in the basement, this was different; she didn't usually roll around on the ground or bleed from the face.

The twitter of birds excited by the morning joined in with the rustling of undergrowth and discarded leaves as small creatures scurried about the forest floor. The world around her was alive with its own music, and she hummed in tune with the sounds of the deep woods in autumn, *"Oooooh, hey, hey, hmmm—wooooo."*

"That's how it is around here," she commented out loud to no one.

"One moment can turn everything inside out and upside down on you."

With one hand, she took comfort by clasping, through her shirt, the key that hung around her neck, while the other hand swayed freely by her side. She found herself missing Rex and Shiva and longed for their company. But Esmeralda said she had to face some challenges on her own, and Annie felt her life depended on trusting Esmeralda. It gladdened her to know she would see Rex again at the end, until the words "the end" flashed in her mind, and then apprehension peppered her pleasant feelings.

She had been close to death before, had walked right up to the edge and longed to step over the rim, longed for the waves to cover her up and wash her away. Then she had been overcome with hopelessness along with the thought that her pain was drawing to an end. Today was different, however. Today the thought that death lay down the road was not frightening, nor was it comforting; it did not offer escape from pain or a romantic resolution from her struggles. Today she faced death as it confronts all life: a moment-to-moment probability and ultimately an inevitable fact.

She never mentioned Shiva. I wonder why? Probably because, like Rex said, Shiva is a free spirit. She comes and goes whenever she wants. I sure wish she'd come now.

The woods crackled alive as a wind blew through and shook dead oak leaves from their desperate last grasp on the branch. The leaves fell noisily, colliding into boughs before crashing on top of their fallen comrades lying scattered on the forest floor.

What was that poem they made us learn last year? Something about leaves falling silently at winter's door. Whoever wrote that either was lying or never experienced autumn in the woods. These leaves are not silently falling, they are not accepting fate. These leaves are going out screaming in protest. They're not going along with the program; nope, death sucks, and they're letting everyone know that. That's cool, that's how it should be: don't be lead away quietly, don't shuffle into line. Hell, no, make a mother of a noise. Even if you can't stop something from happening, make a mother of a noise.

"Ahhhhhhhhhhhhh!" she screamed, pulling at her eyebrow three times and plucking out tiny hairs in the motion. "Why was I so willing to slip away? Why was I so willing to believe I didn't have a right to be alive? Screw you all for telling me that, and screw you all for treating me that way. I ain't going away, do you hear? You'll have to drag me away kicking and screaming!"

Annie laughed, whooped and hollered as she felt a burden lift from her and a sense of power infuse her. Her gait became lighter while her breathing became easier. She knew this was only a first step, there were difficulties ahead to be certain, but it was an important step. It was a course correction that she hoped would send her off on a new trajectory; away from victim and toward a wholeness never experienced by her before.

To celebrate her new verve, she sang as she allowed the path to flow toward her and lead her where it may.

> *"Ooooooh, hey, hey, hmmm — wooooo,*
> *Go to the setting sun and see what's new,*
> *See the night coming and the morning dew,*
> *See all the visions that you've found, uh-huh...*
> *A star fell down... and she went un-noticed.*
>
> *Oooooh, hey, hey, hmmm — wooooo,*
> *When you hold me I can't see beyond you,*
> *I can't see if I'm just playing along on cue,*
> *I can't see if I'm just your clown, uh-huh...*
> *A star hit the ground... and she was one of us.*
>
> *Oooooh, hey, hey, hmmm — wooooo,*
> *Do you remember what I told you?*
> *What I told you, baby, it wasn't true,*
> *When I told you nothing's profound, uh-huh...*
> *A star made a sound... and she vanished in dust."*

"That's pretty good, did you just make that up?" a voice called to her.

Annie turned to the left and there, on a moss covered boulder, sat Shelly. She hadn't been there a moment ago when Annie had walked past the stone, but she was there now and not looking well. Aside from a deeper skin discoloration, Shelly's manifestation was much the same as it had been in the haunted house. Thick black stitches still gave her naked body the look of a railway map as they attempted to keep her mutilated flesh in one piece.

These sudden appearances of unnatural beings and unpredictable shifts in perception had begun to lose their jarring effect on Annie. Her heart spiked for only an instant; then her body lost interest and stopped releasing adrenaline.

"Hello, Shelly, I'm glad you're here," Annie greeted.

A smile warmed Shelly's gray-blue face, crinkling her grossly stitched facial wounds. "You are? You're not going to run or shrink away?"

Annie walked over to Shelly and took the girl's cold moist hands into her own warm ones. She gazed deeply into her dead friend's pale-clouded eyes and said, "No, I'm not going anywhere. We need to talk. I need to tell you how I feel about you; I need to explain."

Shelly raked back her stringy, blood soaked hair and then returned her hand to Annie's. "Really? That would be great—really great. You don't know how lonely it's been rotting away forgotten and betrayed."

Annie started trembling, her throat went dry and tears welled up in her eyes. This was going to be harder then she imagined. The resolve that bolstered her and ushered her over to Shelly faltered.

"Shelly, I... I...," Annie stuttered, withdrawing her hands from Shelly's frigid grip.

"No!" Shelly commanded suddenly and grabbed Annie's hands tightly. "Don't run away—don't block me out again, Annie. Please I can't stand it anymore."

"I thought I knew what to say, but I can't, I... everything is lost to me." Annie looked down at her feet in shame. "I've done something terrible, and I can't remember what it was. I just know I did it to you, and I have to make things right. I loved you Shelly, I still do. Can't I be sorry and done with it?"

"You know you can't, Annie. Come on now, what do you think is going on here? Don't you get it yet? Do you think it's an accident that I keep appearing to you? That I've been haunting you? I've been voices and whispers and shadows. You have to face this, you have to remember before it eats you up alive from the inside out." This time it was Annie's hair that Shelly raked through, and then she rested her stiff hand on Annie's shoulder, pressing her palm to Annie's neck.

Annie took in a deep breath with gulps of air. "Help me remember, Shelly, please help me remember."

"It's not so hard," Shelly began. "It wasn't so long ago, was it?"

A vision of Annie's old school filled her mind. After the past few days spent in an austere environment, the sight of the run down city high school was a bit like having a light turned on in a dark room; it took some adjusting. Annie struggled to calm herself and just let the images come to her. She almost had to look twice when she saw her own image: the image of a girl with straight mousey brown hair, non-descript clothes, and no piercings, walking around with a slunk.

The first half of her freshman year had contained all the difficulties and humiliations that tended to define her school experience. The poverty brought about by her addict mother increased normal day-to-day struggles to a crushing magnitude.

That Annie had difficulty paying attention or processing classroom information was no secret to her or her frustrated underpaid teachers.

What was a secret was what had caused her to not connect the way most other students did. Was it that she never got a decent meal at home, the horrible, dangerous neighborhood she had to walk through to get to school, or the pervasive hopelessness for a future life that sat on her chest like a fat harbinger of doom? Maybe all of it, maybe none of it, maybe she just didn't function normally; and maybe she never would.

It was after the winter break that Annie met Shelly, who had transferred in from some other rundown school. Annie liked her from the start, seeing her as a sister in the struggle of the dissimilar against a system that continued on with little recognition of the difficulties endured by people like Annie. Or if someone in the system did acknowledge her circumstances, it was in a patronizing manner, or worse, a "just get with the program" attitude.

"Hey, new girl," Annie called out after school to Shelly, who wore baggy black pants that rattled from the attached chains and d-rings. The black t-shirt the girl wore with a large anarchy symbol on it spoke volumes to Annie.

Shelly turned around with a snarled ring-pierced lip, but the aggressive glare softened and her pierced eyebrow lowered when she looked at Annie. Annie shrunk away without moving; having just mustered all the energy she had to approach the girl. All she had left was painful self-consciousness. Shelly reversed direction and strutted over to Annie.

Shelly's thickly lined eyes danced with life, and her dark hair barely peeked out beneath a black kerchief dotted with white skulls and cross bones. "Shelly, not new girl, okay?"

"Okay," Annie mumbled. "I'm Annie."

Shelly let out a laugh, "Damn, ain't you that girl in gym class that kept getting pounded in dodge-ball?"

Annie prepared for the humiliation she had earnestly hoped would not come from this person. "Yeah."

"You got your ass kicked. Why'd ya let them do that to you?" Shelly reached out and touched Annie's head softly. "You must have a hellava headache. How many fingers am I holding up?" Shelly asked randomly waving her hand around.

"Huh? I don't..." Annie stammered, not knowing what to make of this boisterous girl's actions.

"Hey, I'm just messin' with ya. Seriously though, don't play games where balls fly at your head. That's my motto, and by what I saw of your piss poor coordination—I suggest you make it your motto, too." With that Shelly turned and headed back on her original course.

"That's what I wanted to talk to you about," Annie started, skipping a few steps to catch up with Shelly. "I wanted to know how much trouble you got in for not changing for gym class and saying you weren't gonna play."

"You mean how much trouble I got in at the office?" Shelly asked as she scanned the area around them.

"Yeah."

Shelly stopped scanning and looked into Annie's face. "Why, do you want to give it a try? Wanna tell them no?"

"Yeah."

"Then just tell them no, what do you care how much trouble you get in? How much trouble is your brain worth? Shit, man, I thought they knocked you out at one point."

"No," Annie replied with an embarrassed smirk. "Sometimes I just lie there and hope they'll leave me alone."

"Well, that didn't work, did it? They just pounded you even more. And that fat coach didn't do shit. Too busy trying to boss me around and get a peek at my tits."

A laugh escaped Annie as Shelly propped her breasts up with her hands. She was glad that Shelly laughed, too.

Shelly gave Annie a friendly tap on the arm. "Hey, you wanna come over? My mom's at work, so we can crank up some tunes and hang out."

"Okay," Annie agreed.

"You know, you'd look cool with an eyebrow spike. I could do it myself if you want," Shelly offered as they left the schoolyard.

Throughout the rest of the school year their friendship blossomed and the summer break strengthened it. They continued hanging out with each other, reveling in their oddness and finding other outcasts to relate to. It was the first time Annie could recall summer going by so fast, now that she had someone to be with instead of pining the hours and days away in her room.

The two girls had plotted an end-of-summer road trip. As Annie packed some clothes and personal items into the tattered backpack she had used for the past three school years, she felt her heart flutter. In a few hours, she would meet Shelly behind the school gym, and together they would sneak away and head up north. That would piss her mom off, having her fetch-me-this girl gone for a week or more. But, Annie didn't care; the trip would be worth whatever bitching her mom would do before getting over it. She just wanted to be, needed to be, with Shelly.

Catching a quick glance of herself in the mirror, Annie admired her multiple piercings. She was a sight different than when she first met Shelly, and she liked what she saw. Annie zipped up her pack and, after mulling it over, jotted a note to her mom.

Mom,

Went with Shelly to her aunt and uncle's. Be back in a week. Don't forget to feed yourself.

Love, Annie

With that, she marched out the door without a second thought. She stepped out of the apartment building onto the early morning sidewalk. It was a quiet time of day when people had either gone to work, were still snoozing off a drug, or were wrestling with hungry crying babies.

She picked up her pace in order to meet Shelly on time so they could head toward the bus station together Shelly had an aunt and uncle up north in Mount Helena, and sometimes she snuck away to visit them, especially when Shelly and her mom got into knock-down-drag-out fights.

Like Annie, Shelly's father had taken that never-ending trip to the corner store, leaving behind a broken home and broken lives. Shelly's mom had adjusted better than Annie's mom. Her mom worked a steady job, and there was definitely a better food selection at their house. But, the pressure often produced rages in her mom, and sometimes they just needed a break from each other. Her mom seemed to understand, since she never made a big deal about Shelly sneaking away to go up north, and her aunt and uncle always took her in and paid for her to return.

That was the plan today as the summer break neared an end, the two girls would use the money Shelly had "acquired" to buy one-way discount bus tickets to Mount Helena and visit Shelly's aunt and uncle. Shelly assured Annie that, once there, her uncle would pick up the tab for their return trip.

As Annie entered the schoolyard, passing through the gate of the chain-linked fence, a sinking feeling weighed heavily on her stomach. Sounds of a scuffle and struggle whispered in the air, growing as she approached the gym. Cautiously, she turned the corner of the gym building and saw.

There he was, weasel-like and greasy, with an ill formed mouth and beady eyes that burned contempt for life behind his thick glasses. There he was with a firm hold on Shelly from behind, with one arm across her chest, his ugly face next to her ear, and a large glinting knife to her throat.

"Shelly!" Annie called out.

"Friend of yours, huh?" he snarled into Shelly's ear. Then with a cold reptilian stare, he spoke to Annie, "Hey, friend, if you don't want to see your girlie chopped up, you better come over here. It'll be okay, we're just going have a party, and then you two can go."

"Run, Annie, he'll kill us both," Shelly managed to gargle out between angry sobs.

Like a boa constrictor securing its prey, the man snaked his arm tighter across her chest, brought his face closer to hers, and made an indentation on her throat with the knife. "No, no, no," he hissed. "No need for killing if you just have some fun with me. Come on, what's a little sucking? You sluts do it all the time, anyway. Do it for me, and you can go, I promise."

Annie's mind froze along with her body. She couldn't think, couldn't plan, couldn't do anything but feel a sudden urgency without a direction to take it in. Her focus darted from the man's sadistic grin to Shelly's wide-eyed horror. If she stayed, would Shelly be spared death in exchange for acts of degradation? Or would they both be killed? If she left, he would certainly kill Shelly.

"Come here," the man growled lowly.

Annie placed one foot in front of her.

"No!" Shelly shrieked as she tilted her head forward and then slammed the back of her head into his face. In the brief moment when predator and prey appeared disoriented from the collusion, Shelly bellowed out a guttural, "Ruuuuuuuuun!"

The sudden violence shocked Annie into action, and she turned and ran with only one backward glance. She could stomach no more than the one look that revealed the knife handle crashing down on top of Shelly's head; her eyes rolled up and her tongue protruded out. As Annie turned away from the scene, she saw Shelly's body slump to the ground and convulse. Then came the darkness.

She heard her own breathing in the pit of memory; felt her body running blind and headlong into an unknown. The surreal sensations of the flashback slowly eased; the spinning in her head stopped and she felt certain she was standing still. Annie opened her eyes, bringing into focus the surrounding forest of the present moment. Now in this strange new world, in front of her dead friend on a beautiful fall day, Annie wept.

"I was there?" Annie asked in disbelief. And then, as if the self-deception had become an unwelcome barrier, she said firmly, "I *was* there."

"Yeah, sweetie, you were," Shelly confirmed, her hand vigorously rubbing Annie's arm as if to jump-start her circulation.

Annie tried to wipe dry her tear-moistened face, but fresh streams kept pouring down her cheeks. "I'm so sorry, Shelly. I'm so sorry. I should have stayed; I should have never left you there."

"Come on, Annie, don't you remember anything else? Why have you forgotten what you *did* do?"

Annie strained her memory to catch a glimpse of things she had for too long avoided. "I did something," she began, the statement sounding more like a question.

"Yeah, you did."

"I told your mom, and she called the cops..."

"That's right," Shelly said.

"But that was like a day later. I wasted a whole day hiding away. After I talked to your mom, I remember talking to the cops, then sitting in my room for days and days, and then—it was like nothing had ever happened. I never talked to your mom again or even thought about it."

Shelly looked down and played with Annie's fingers. "Yeah, that's right. That's what happened."

Annie felt drained. "I'm sorry, Shelly. I'm sorry I left you there, I'm sorry I put you out of my mind. Please forgive me. Forgive me for not saying something sooner. I was so scared."

Shelly's gaze rose up from their hands to bore into Annie with a fiery intensity. "Is that what you think the problem is? Is that why you think I'm haunting you, because you left me and forgot about me? Annie, I was as good as dead—no one would have found me in time. There was nothing you could have done; and if you had stayed—you'd be dead, too."

Fear rattled Annie's bones and shook her internal organs, causing an acidic nausea to overcome her. "Then what?" she wavered.

"Then what?" Shelly returned the question. "You, damn well know what. I'll give you the days hiding in your room trying to forget the whole horrible mess. But, never going back to school? Chasing after a bunch of low-life's to fulfill some fantasy of being loved by all—and getting screwed over in the process? That, I don't give you; that was bull-shit."

From out of some deep mental recess a searing rage burst through Annie. She jerked her hands away from Shelly, stepped back and spat, "Screw you! *Screw you!* What was I supposed to do? Huh? Ever see someone you love taken from you, ever had those last images flash in your head, reliving it over and over and over again? Ever wonder when you'd be next, when some piece of shit was gonna grab you up and kill you? Well, have you? No, you haven't; and guess what? You never will, because you're stinkin' dead, bitch!"

Shelly reached out and slapped her hand soundly across Annie's reddening face. The two girls stared at each other—stunned by the assault.

"Damn, girl," Shelly started giggling, "I'm sorry. Are you okay?"

Annie shook off the strike and started to laugh, "Yeah, I'm okay. You hit like a ho."

Shelly let her giggle subside. "Seriously, Annie, don't you know why I'm so pissed?"

"No, Shelly, I don't," Annie responded. "I wish if people had something to say, they would say it. I'm tired of these guessing games. Okay, I'm stupid; I can't figure things out, so what—kiss my ass."

"All right, then," Shelly said, straightening herself out on the stone. "I told you to run so you would live. I gave you a gift, the gift to keep on living. And what have you done with that gift? You've been pissing it away."

Annie had no response. She stood silently taking in Shelly's words and replaying her actions since Shelly's death. It was true; she had been pissing it all away. She had in fact courted death, and gambled her whole future for one moment of ultimate universal acceptance that never came and, as she fully realized, never would.

"It's not right, Shelly." Annie shook her head slowly, her jaw taunt as she repetitively clenched and unclenched her fists. "Why? Why me? I should have been the one who died. I'm nothing; and you were so full of life. I should have stayed and given you a chance to get away."

"Don't say that," Shelly chided. "I did what I did because I love you."

"I didn't deserve it—I still don't." Annie looked down at her feet.

Shelly lifted Annie's chin and looked her in the eyes. "No one deserves life; it's a gift or a lucky accident—however you want to think of it. You have as much right to it as anyone else; the question is: what are you going to do with it?"

Her words pervaded Annie's mind, coming into conflict with her habitual self-loathing. Was that it? Was that the reason she began falling headlong into a spiral of self-destruction? All because she didn't feel she deserved life; that Shelly had wasted herself with her sacrifice? And there it was: the truth. The pain of being loved by someone so much that they were willing to die for her had been too much to bear. She had courted death in a misguided attempt to balance the books and never feel that feeling again.

"You're right," Annie admitted. "You gave me a second chance, and I shit all over it. I'm sorry, Shelly, I didn't know what I was doing, and I never wanted to betray you."

Shelly's voice softened. "I know, sweetie. You'll do better, I'm sure of it."

Annie stepped forward and wrapped her arms around Shelly. "I love you, Shelly, my sister, my friend."

Their embrace lingered; Annie could feel the key around her neck begin to warm, and she knew it was glowing. A blinding light exploded from between them, enveloping the girls in a radiant shell. Annie felt a roaring wind suck the air out of her lungs, while all her nerve endings tingled in a chorus of sensation. Her abdominal muscles started to spasm, and her awareness spun into dizzy disorientation. The howling of the wind grew to a crescendo until, like a switch had been flicked, the light and wind were gone.

Annie stepped back to catch her breath; her knees wobbled. She looked up and saw Shelly as she once was. Gone was the decaying flesh, gone the poorly stitched wounds, gone the dead eyes and the bloodied scalp. Shelly sat on the stone in her favorite pants and t-shirt, grinning from ear to ear.

"Shelly! You're all better. You're healed."

"Thanks to you, Annie."

Annie touched the key and nodded, "Right, the dragon's gift is supposed to perform a great healing. This must be it; I've completed the task. Now what?"

Raising her hands for Annie to slow down, Shelly said, "Hold on there, girlie, it ain't over yet. You've taken a step by facing your pain, but you still have some work to do."

Annie nodded in acknowledgment. "I promise I won't waste the life you've given me. I'm gonna do better."

Touching her gently on the cheek, Shelly said, "I know, but I have to go—he's coming. Are you ready?"

Annie looked around trying to take in information from her physical senses and from the extra sense the key often provided. "Yeah," she said, drawing out the word as she continued to scan. "I feel him. He's been sent to kill me. He's not here yet; still down the road a bit."

Annie looked back toward Shelly, but she was gone. Alone in the woods, she started to falter. From inside old voices called out to run, to turn back, to back down: to stay in her place. But Annie knew the only way to finish this journey was to move forward and get through it. A smile spread on her face as a familiar yowl sounded from behind.

"Hey, Shiva, where've you been?" she greeted the white wolf. Bending down, Annie hugged Shiva and giggled as the animal licked her face. "You missed the action, but I think there is more to come. This time we'll do it on our terms."

Annie stood up and, with new resolve, headed down the path. "Come on, girl, let's go make some noise."

Chapter Twenty-Four

Rex's first sensations were a stiff neck and shoulders along with a pasty-cotton feeling in his mouth; no doubt the effects of dehydration the drug had left behind like a calling card. The aroma of fresh baked biscuits hovered just ahead of the crackling campfire's smoky scent. He groaned his way into a sitting position, his heart pounding not from exertion, but from the caress of a familiar perfume that told him, long before the blur in his eyes cleared, that Esmeralda was there.

"I see you still snore. I was afraid you'd attract some wild beast in heat with your rumbling," said Esmeralda, her voice rich and clear.

Rex rubbed the fogginess out of his eyes and beheld her sitting across the fire from him. She was as fresh as the evening he first met her. Dressed in her green manifestation, she wore a billowing forest green shirt with matching brush suede pants and boots. Her jade and emerald jewelry worshipped her olive complexioned skin; skin he longed to touch again. Sea green eyes accentuated her smile with each languid blink of her lids. Every cell in his body recalled distant memories of young manhood; he became painfully aware that he had aged and felt awkward in the face of her timeless beauty.

Rex stretched his arms and rolled the soreness from his neck. Clearing his throat he said, "I see you're still beautiful, my love." He waited for Esmeralda to rebuke him for the term of endearment but, as she didn't, he continued, "I take it you and Annie have had a talk; I can think of no other reason for you to have me drugged."

Pouring Rex a cup of tea, Esmeralda said, "You were always so bright and clever, Rex dear. We did have a talk, and now she is on her way."

Rex got up stiffly and hobbled over to take the cup from her. "Without me," he said in disappointment. He sipped his tea and gazed down at her green highlighted black hair that splashed like a wave past her shoulders.

Esmeralda dripped warm honey on some biscuits. "I had to bake a new batch; the others were hard as stones." In response to Rex's silence she added, "You're angry with me."

"Angry with you?" Rex perked up, spilling hot tea on his hands from his sudden animation. "Why would I be angry with you? You refuse to see me or speak to me for years, and then, when I'm nearby, you drug me and abscond with my traveling companion. Angry? Stars, no, you've been such a peach."

The smile and look of loving pride never left Esmeralda's face. She continued to hold out a flat stone of biscuits until Rex took them and sat down beside her.

"I know it's been difficult for you, darling," she said sadly, "but it's the way things had to be."

Rex thought better of his tone in the light of her countenance and removed the bite from his words. "I know I did wrong by you. I shouldn't have left you like that, and it has tortured my heart ever since. I've tried for years to tell you I was sorry, but you hid from me."

After brushing random crumbs from the bristly whiskers on his chin, Esmeralda touched Rex on his cheek. "I was never angry with you."

"Really?" Rex said in surprise. "Because I nearly drowned in that storm you conjured."

Esmeralda laughed, "Oh, yes, that was a good one. I had to do that to keep you from returning, but I wasn't angry with you."

Rex gave her an incredulous look.

"Well, I was angry," she admitted. "But I was angry at the fates, not at you. Do you understand?"

"No," he said honestly. Many times, he had employed this same twisting approach to answering a question or addressing an issue, and now he recalled just how irritating it was to be on the receiving end.

A gloom washed over her face, and she struggled to speak. "I didn't want you to go, but I knew you had to. It had to happen, and you had to stay away otherwise all this wouldn't have come to be; the stage wouldn't have been set."

"Esmeralda, please," he beseeched. "Stop dancing about. What wouldn't have happened? What are you talking about?"

"Holdfast, Gororm, Dezair, the princesses, all required your exile in order to be ready for Annie."

Rex blinked, and then blinked again. "What?"

She rubbed his shoulder with her hand and looked deep into his eyes. "Don't you get what's going on?"

As if imprisoned in a spell cast by her gaze, Rex responded in a monotone, "No."

Esmeralda leaned over and whispered in his ear. She withdrew nodding her head to underscore the truth of the secret.

Like a *Möbius* strip, his life looped around, twisting and turning in on itself. Rex's face slackened and he barely managed to say, "For the love of Triduana's eyes, it can't be."

"It's true," she confirmed with a sigh. "And there's more, so much more."

Annie strode down the winding path, watching Shiva dart into bushes after unseen things, only to reappear from a thicket further on down the road, crunching leaves under her paws. After one of the wolf's forays into a bramble path, Annie crested a hill. The path dipped and, waiting beside the trail at the bottom, there a man stood beside a horse.

There you are. I must be getting closer. Annie put one protesting foot in front of the other, pushing herself to walk on through the familiar apprehension mounting inside. *I have to go through with this; it may be my only chance to save myself.*

As she neared, the man held his ground with a smile and a wave of his large hand.

"Hallo, young traveler!" he called out. He walked away from his mount and approached Annie.

"Hello," Annie said in return, stopping in the middle of the path.

The man came near, but kept a polite distance. As he spoke, he slowly circled Annie. "You don't look like you're from around here. My name is Damek. If you're lost, I can assist you."

"Thanks, Damek. My name is Annie." She noted the protective leather strapped to the man's lean muscular body, and the hilt of a sword on which his fingers drummed. She did not turn around to keep pace with his circling, suspecting that he wanted to make her dizzy and put her off balance. Instead she stood still and let her eyes follow him as best they could until he disappeared behind her, and then picked him up again when he came around the other side.

"Are you alone, Annie?" he queried. "No wizards or monks to guide you through these difficult woods?"

Annie looked around and shrugged, "Doesn't appear to be."

"I can help you find your way," he said with an uneven smile.

Still holding her ground, Annie said, "I don't remember saying I was lost or needed help. Although, I am curious about how you plan to do it."

"Easy enough, I know these lands like my own living quarters. I can take you anywhere you want to go." Damek's fingers wrapped around his sword handle.

"No, I don't mean how do you plan to guide me, I mean, how do you plan to kill me?"

With that statement, Damek stopped in his tracks. "Whatever do you mean?"

The horse reared up with a gut-wrenching neigh and galloped away. Damek quarter drew his sword and glanced quickly about. His scan ended as he focused on some bushes, from which a low snarl emitted.

"Don't move," he cautioned, standing very still himself.

"Why?" Annie asked as she stepped around to the left of him.

The snarl persisted, full of teeth, throaty and promising ill intent. Shiva emerged from the growth, crouching, her tail held stiffly straight behind her. With eyes wide open, the wolf slowly walked stiff-legged toward them, her stare never wavering from Damek.

"If we're still and lower our eyes, it will not attack," he informed her as he averted his eyes downward. He tried to slowly look around as Annie had gone behind him and was now coming up on his right side. "What are you doing? Stay still."

"Not for my sake. Just so she doesn't get *you*. I mean," Annie chuckled, "she is looking right at you."

Shiva halted her advance, but continued to glare at Damek with a wet snarl punctuated by an occasional snapping bark. Damek glanced up at Annie as she passed in front of him.

"Do you know this animal?" he asked.

"Time to make a stand, Damek. Time to put your convictions to the test."

"What is this all about?" he demanded as he split his glances between the threatening wolf and the circling girl.

A loud laugh escaped Annie. "I'm sorry, I didn't mean to laugh like that. It's just that look on your face is so priceless. Oh, man, it was like I could see the moment you realized you were the one hunted. That was so cool."

"Is that right?" Damek's face turned stern. "I could take you both out, no problem. I may suffer some injuries from the beast but, in the end, I alone will walk out of these woods alive."

"Perhaps," Annie agreed, his threat finding no footing in her. "Is this what it's come to for you? Killing little girls? You don't look like a murderer; you look like a soldier. Aren't you supposed to protect the innocent?"

"Innocent, are you?" Damek snorted. "You may be ignorant of the trouble you'll cause if I let you live, but that doesn't make you innocent."

Annie laughed again as she continued to circle him. "Trouble? Me? I'm just trying to free a girl trapped in a crystal. What trouble can there be in that?"

Damek had ceased to look at Annie; he remained poised to draw his sword and stared at the ground between himself and Shiva. "Your med-dling will get her killed."

Annie stopped in front of the warrior and touched his sword arm, the gesture prompted Shiva to cease her aggressive posture and lay down to lick her paws. Cautiously, Damek released his hold on the weapon and stood less crouched, more relaxed.

Maintaining contact with him, she slid her hand down his forearm and wrapped her fingers around his. A warmth spread across her chest as the key began to glow beneath her shirt. "You're in love with a woman who's in a lot of pain. You love her so much, you'd even kill me and suffer a lifetime of guilt just for her."

Damek withdrew his hand from her and rubbed the fingers she had touched. "Are you an enchantress? Are you using some spell to get into my head?"

"An enchantress?" Annie giggled. "No, afraid not. The look on your face tells me everything. I've seen that look before; the look of a man who knows what the right thing is, but fails to do it for whatever reason. It's eating away at you, isn't it?"

Damek stood dumbfounded as Annie spoke, his eyes shutting tight as if to shield him from the truth of her words.

She reached out and retook his fingers, encountering no resistance she continued, "Deep inside, in the thoughts you keep to yourself, you know the truth. You know your lover needs you to say 'no' to her fears and stand up to do the right thing. Her fear blinds her from the truth; the truth that you can clearly see. And you know, Damek, what the truth is: the girl must be freed."

To Annie's surprise, the burly soldier surrendered the last of his de-fensive posture. He nodded in sad agreement.

"You must be an enchantress or soothsayer," he said. "How else could you read my deepest thoughts?" Withdrawing his hand again from Annie, he placed it on her shoulder. "I knew Zoila had lost herself to obsession ever since Arias was found trapped in the crystal. And come to find out, it was Zoila who imprisoned her own sister! After that she became so unstable, you know what I mean?"

"People in pain are confusing, because they're so confused inside," Annie offered. "That's why you have to see past the pain, see past the confusion, and do what she is too afraid to do."

"Free Arias," he said, removing his hand from her and stroking his chin.

"Help me, Damek. You know it's the right thing to do."

Rex contemplated the implications of Esmeralda's revelation as he stirred the dying embers with a stick. He did not doubt her; she would not deceive nor would she be mistaken about something so enormous. His whole life twisted and turned around this new framework and, surprisingly, events over the years began to make more sense. Should he be angry, insulted, or honored? He knew the perception of the situation he chose to hold would determine what reaction he would experience. But it was too difficult to discern; the shock of the revelation had not yet lifted, and she had promised more troubling information to come. Dare he hear it?

Sitting next to him, Esmeralda finished the ditty she sang while braiding her hair and binding it up behind her so it cleared her face.

> *"Did you know in Carthage,*
> *She didn't want him to go,*
> *So a tale of love ended in woe?"*

"There," she announced, patting her hair and checking its shape with her fingertips. "What's done is done."

Rex looked up and managed a weak smile, the corner of his mouth lifting against the weight of his sullen face. "It looks pretty. I like your hair that way."

Looking confused for a moment, Esmeralda responded, "Oh, my hair. Thank you, but I was talking about Annie."

The mention of the girl's name roused Rex, his attention zeroed in fully on Esmeralda. He didn't want to miss one tidbit of information about this strange girl whom he'd plucked from the ground, and whose presence changed the whole meaning of his existence. "What about Annie? Is she all right?"

"So far so good," she assured. Standing up, Esmeralda smoothed out her clothes. "It's almost over; she's headed for the end. That means it is time for you to go. I've stalled you long enough."

"Stalled me?" Rex sprang to his feet. "What do you mean stalled me? Whatever game you're playing, I can tell you, I'm tired of it! Who are you anyway? Green Goddess? Red Queen? You wax and wane like the moon, manifesting as child, mother or crone whenever you please. Is it asking too much for you to cork the bottle and be done with it?"

Esmeralda kissed Rex tenderly on the forehead. "I'm so proud of you Rex. Watching you grow and discover the world has been one of the great pleasures of my life."

A look of fear replaced anger and confusion on Rex's face. A hollowness grew inside him, a hollowness that rang in his ears, trying to drown out anymore sound. "Who are you?"

"You have to go, Rex, she needs you; Annie needs you," Esmeralda said looking pale.

"Is she in danger? I must save her." Rex looked about frantically, grabbed his pack, and threw his things into it.

"Rex!" Esmeralda called out in a commanding voice.

Rex stopped his rummaging. Feeling the breaking of tears over the rim of his eyes, he stood lost in the moment.

"Rex, dear," she continued in a soothing voice, "you can't save her and, in fact, she doesn't need saving; not by you or anyone. She has to save herself or there is really no point in the matter."

"There has to be a point no matter what happens," he insisted, "or there is no point in me. You as much as said so yourself."

"You do have a purpose in this, but it isn't to save her. You have to go to her; go quickly; she has a morning's head start on you and continues to travel." Esmeralda combed her fingers through Rex's hair and straightened his robe. "She needs you to be a witness."

"A witness? Witness to what?"

"To whatever she ends up doing. She just needs someone who cares about her to be there for her; to witness her life."

Rex took Esmeralda's calm hands in his trembling ones. The pain of helplessness and uncertainty crushed him, causing him to labor for air. "Come with me, we can go and witness together."

"I cannot," came her firm reply.

"Then conjure me away to where she is."

"I cannot." Again, she stood her ground, her eyes pleading that he ask no more of her.

Rex let loose her hands and went back to packing, his frustration showing with every item he roughly thrust into his bag. "Would you leave me so distraught, so desperate? Is this punishment for what I did to you? You say you're not angry about it, but this cruel treatment proves otherwise."

The calm Esmeralda had projected began to show signs of strain. Her face continued to pale as a deep sorrow set into it. She rubbed her belly slowly as if to ease an ache, as she struggled to keep her voice steady. "I can't explain it all; I'm only doing what needs to be done. Annie doesn't stand a chance if you show up early, you'll just interfere, and she won't survive. You can't help it; you'll feel compelled to save her from her pain, and that's the last thing she needs."

"I see," said Rex tersely. With his bag packed, he grabbed his staff and faced Esmeralda. "And cutting me out of your life over one mistake, was that something that needed to be done?"

"Yes, but, as I said, you needed to go; it wasn't a mistake. You don't understand."

Rex waved his staff furiously in the air. "I don't understand, because you won't explain anything to me. You tell me plenty of things I don't want to hear, but then leave all the details to the imagination."

Esmeralda doubled over in pain and spewed out a frothy sea-green liquid. "Ooo," she moaned, "that hurts. Got my hair back just in time."

Rex rushed to her side and gently rubbed her back. "Are you all right? What's wrong? What's going on?"

"Fine, I'm fine," she said slowly straightening up. "I do wish you'd hurry on, I don't know how long I can hold out."

"How can I leave you like this?"

"You have to go to Annie before it's too late, or I'll get worse." She wiped traces of the fishy smelling liquid from her chin.

"You can't just vomit and expect me to go," he said feeling her forehead with his hand.

She pushed his hand from her, and with irritation in her voice said, "Well, I'm sorry, but you have to go before it's too late."

Rex did a frenzied four-step dance of frustration. "What are you talking about? Explain to me why I must go!"

Esmeralda's body heaved again, retching out another stream of translucent green now filled with strands of seaweed. "The goddess be damned!" she cursed. "Would you please go? Hurry!"

"Tell me what's going on first," Rex demanded.

She straightened up and grabbed Rex's shirt, pulling his face close to hers. With a livid desperation burning in her eyes, she shrieked, "Hurry, you old fool, before we all go under and die!"

Rex stood speechless, unable to move.

"Oh, for the love of mother earth!" Esmeralda pushed Rex back, threw her hands up in frustration and commanded, "Take him."

Vines reached out, wrapped around Rex and pulled him sharply into the foliage. After a tumultuous journey, the vines deposited him carelessly on a path in the woods and then retreated into the background. The monk quickly got to his feet, his head spinning as he tried to find his physical and mental balance.

"Better hurry," said a girl's voice.

Rex looked over to see a healed Shelly standing on the trail.

"Better hurry," she said again. "You're going to have to run if you want to make it on time."

"Who in the blazes are you?" he asked, having had it up to his neck with all the surprises.

"Who are any of us?" she replied.

For a moment, the question hit him hard, breaking through his attempts to block the issue from awareness. Esmeralda had whispered the answer, but he didn't want to believe it, didn't even want to consider it. So, he did the only thing he could think to do. He ran.

Chapter Twenty-Five

It was late afternoon by the time Annie and Damek broke from the woods and crossed a field, heading toward the castle on the hilltop. Somewhere between leaving the forest and trekking the path that wound its way through the red-orange dying field, Shiva had left, as she was well known to do. Annie did not give the wolf's wanderings much thought; she felt certain when the moment was right, Shiva would reappear.

Damek had spent the day telling her about the king and queen and the two sisters the monarchs had captured under the guise of a charitable adoption. He seemed eager to take advantage of an opportunity to converse freely. Even over a modest lunch of dried rabbit's meat, stale flatbread, and spring water to wash it down, Damek mused aloud about the difficulties of his relationship with Zoila. Annie had never heard a man talk so much or for so long. Rex had certainly been able to hold up a conversation, but could also pass the time in silence. She felt a pang of loneliness and wished he were with her now.

She welcomed the distraction; however, she found her own thoughts beginning to muddle and the energy in her body start to drain away. She didn't know if it was the meal of soldier rations that caused a queasiness to develop inside of something else, but the closer they got to the castle, the more ill she felt.

"I always had a special feeling for Arias," Damek said with a grin. "Of course, I never told Zoila. Not wise to tell a woman you have stirrings for her sister. At first I thought Arias was just a spoiled brat, but when she started going into the villages, helping the people, inciting them to stand up for themselves and reclaim their lands—well, officially I could not support her, but, inside, I admired her."

Annie vomited on the trail. Once the liquid had cleared her throat and mouth, she sucked in air through her nostrils. Her flaying hand grabbed onto Damek's arm to steady herself until the dizziness passed. "Yuck, that's nasty," she announced smacking her mouth and spitting, the sting of the briny aftertaste prompting a look of disgust on her face.

"Are you all right, Annie?" Damek asked. "You look pale and

unsteady."

"I'll be okay," she assured and released Damek's arm, showing him she could stand on her own. "That's been happening to me over the past few days. It'll pass."

Annie didn't believe the words even before she said them, and now hearing them spoken, believed them even less. She doubted Damek believed her either, since no doubt she looked as sickly as she felt inside. It would not pass she knew, but would instead worsen. She was sure of it.

Damek looked toward the sun and rubbed his chin. "Perhaps you should rest. We can visit the king in the morning and take care of business then. This whole mess has been going on for so long, what's another night?"

"No!" she said with more urgency then she meant. Adjusting her tone she said, "I'm sorry, but no. We can't wait; by morning I will be dead along with Zoila and Arias."

Annie screamed out in pain, clutching her head and squatting straight down on her haunches. "Damn it!" Her head and lungs burned and, for a moment, the pain blinded her. She struggled to breathe; even though the fall air was cool and crisp, she felt as if she'd taken in humid air—more water than oxygen.

Damek started to hold her steady, but Annie just pushed him away. As her panting subsided, she wobbled back up and wiped the spittle from her mouth and chin.

"You can't go on," he insisted.

Grabbing Damek's shoulders, Annie growled, "We will go on. We will finish this." She pushed off him and staggered back. Turning around, a glint of sunlight off something metallic caught her eye. "There they are," she told Damek.

He peered out in the direction Annie had motioned toward. "The king's coach," he confirmed. "And headed this way."

"Well, Damek," she smiled slyly, "lucky you. You won't have to carry me."

They waited on the trail watching the white carriage with gold trim lumber up the dirt road. Two white horses pulled the enclosed coach; the creaking of its solid wood wheels could be heard even from where they stood. Above them, storm clouds gathered, creeping up from behind Annie and Damek and spreading throughout the late afternoon sky.

"Remember what I told you," Damek reminded as the carriage neared, "they will not appear as they really are."

Annie steadied herself with a firm jaw and a resolve not to let the turmoil inside flood out and betray her in the face of the approaching enemy. "Don't worry about me; I won't be fooled by their looks or their lies. You just remember what I told you: trust me if you want the princesses to live."

The coachman pulled the reins bringing the hitched animals to a halt. The small carriage rocked, adjusting to the absence of momentum and, once stilled, its door opened. Out stepped a kindly, white bearded old man in royal robes. He smiled at Annie and then turned to help his stately robed queen from the compartment.

Annie returned the smile and waited patiently. She noted a slight blur about the two as well as an artificial manner of movement, a sure sign of pretense.

"Damek," the king greeted. "Bless the stars, have you found her? Tell this weary elder it is true."

Damek bowed his head dutifully and said, "My lord, it is true. May I present Annie, the bearer of Holdfast's gift. Annie, this is the King and Queen of Gororm."

With a curtsey, Annie greeted, "Pleased to meet you, your highnesses."

"Oh, husband," the queen cried as she dabbed a tear from her face with a silk handkerchief, "does this mean our dreams have come true? Will poor Arias be saved?"

Time was running out, and Annie knew it. She did not want to waste one moment playing games, but instead decided to sell herself out quickly and get to the endpoint.

"Yes, my queen," Annie announced before Gororm could respond. She reached into the top of her shirt, removed the key and held it out. "Damek has told me the tragic tale of your imprisoned daughter. Here is the gift of Holdfast; a key that will no doubt free her and destroy your enemies."

Annie worried that the confused looks on the monarchs' faces meant she had given in too soon and aroused suspicion. She also sensed Damek stealthily putting hand to hilt in case she had betrayed him. The air was heavy as she imagined everyone running a multitude of calculations and probabilities through their minds. Annie looked at Damek; a slight cock of her head and widening of her eyes seemed to put him at ease. His body relaxed as he folded his arms around his chest.

"Splendid, my dear," the king said to Annie. "Damek, you have done your duty well. Not only have you brought our salvation to us, but she has already been told our tale of woe and is willing to assist."

The queen clasped her hands fervidly over her head, "This is truly a blessed miracle!"

Keeping her disgust at the deceptive display of compassion under control, Annie, now assured her own ruse had worked, stated, "We must hurry, your majesty. The dragon's gift is temporary, and I'm afraid, if we do not get to your daughter quickly, it will vanish."

"Quite right, my dear," the king nodded in agreement; doing so made a shimmer flicker over his face and gave Annie a millisecond glance of the hideousness underneath the guise. "Damek, you and Annie will ride on the back of the carriage. We will go straight away to the bottom of Arias's hill. When we arrive, you will take Annie to the top to release the princess; for, as you know, the cursed spell will not allow the queen and me to draw near."

"As you wish, my lord," Damek said. He looked at Annie with a lingering hint of doubt in his eyes, but said nothing further. He merely assisted the king and queen into the small coach and then helped Annie onto the back.

"I hope you are certain about this," he said taking a seat next to her on the wooden ledge at the rear of the coach.

"Dead certain," she responded, clutching her stomach and fighting back the nausea as the sky darkened.

Rex's breathing had become more labored with each step of the last two kilometers, and now he wheezed and gulped at the air like a fish stranded on the beach. He could smell the rain well before the drops blasted through the autumn foliage of the woods.

Body's not what it used to be. Have to keep moving, keep fighting through the pain, he coached himself as thighs, knees and calves protested this sudden demand for prolonged performance. *When I was younger training at the Brotherhood, this would have been no problem. Even two years ago while at the mountain sanctuary of...* He stopped his ponderings, coughed and tried to shake the stream of memories from his thoughts.

If it even happened at all, if I ever happened at all. Am I really running through the woods? If what Esmeralda whispered is true, then why do I bother running? It's a hard truth to swallow that you are not the central character in your life's story, but only exist to support another. I think Brother Joseph tried to tell me that once. That to truly live, you must die to your own need, your own self.

Rex stopped suddenly and bent over with hands on knees, bracing himself and gasping for air. Standing up again, he crossed his arms over his head and, with some effort, slowed his breathing down as he walked around in a loose circle. Once he had his breath back under control, he turned his face to the rainy sky above, shouting through the tree branches, "If he ever told me anything at all! If Brother Joseph or the

Brotherhood ever even existed!"

Noticing a field through the thinning tree line reenergized Rex to continue. "Thank the stars; I thought I'd never get out of the forest."

He pushed himself to continue. Once he broke free of the woods, he jogged into the open countryside and unimpeded rain. On the trail ahead stood Shiva.

"What are you doing here? Where have you been? Where's, Annie?" he fired off.

Shiva cocked her head and yowled at him.

"Well, pardon me," he said and scratched behind the wolf's ears. "I'm just worried. We have to find Annie, and quickly. You know where she is, don't you?"

Shiva shook her rain soaked pelt, sending water spraying out around her. She pranced around in a circle three times, loped ahead 10 meters, turned to look at Rex, then continued down the trail that cut through the fields.

"Thought so," Rex muttered. He wiped rain from his face and followed the wolf.

The fire that Rex had built in the morning spat and hissed in protest as the raindrops' relentless assault fizzled it out. Esmeralda watched the flame's losing battle as she sat with her back against a tree, wondering if the fate of one person stood a chance against the onslaught of nature.

I have to believe there are moments that will take our lives in a different direction. If only we can recognize them and seize those moments. If only Annie will seize the moment.

A makeshift canopy of tightly woven branches made by her fairies spared Esmeralda from the rain. It comforted her and eased her suffering to have companions that fawned over her in this dark hour. Her comfort was made bittersweet, though, since the memory of Rex still lingered at the campsite.

"Rest easy, my lady," Lai cooed as she brushed Esmeralda's hair.

Isabel massaged Esmeralda's feet while Kizze and Babes massaged their queen's hands.

"I am tired before my time," she told her followers.

"You're burdened, my queen," Kizze said. "You can't carry this weight any longer. Let it go, there's nothing else you can do. You've given all your love and guidance. She'll rise or fall on her own accord now."

"Yes," Babes agreed, "What good is it to agonize about things out of your hands?"

"It pains us to see you suffer so," Isabel added.

Esmeralda sat up, and the fairies buzzed around her, then settled at her feet. "My darlings, you're too good to me. But you know as well as I do that when love binds you to others, there is no end to worry." She rose up as the last of the coals went cold under the downpour. "However, we must manage this and hold on to the wonder love brings. So, on that thought, it is time."

The four fairies clapped their hands with glee.

"Time to do our part?" Isabel asked.

Babes flew up, hopefully. "Who will it be?"

"This time it's to be Kizze," Esmeralda answered, reaching out to the delighted ebony fairy. "I need a funeral carriage, my dear. Can you manage?"

"Of course, my lady." Kizze bowed graciously and, as the other fairies swirled around, circling further and further from her, she started to shake. Kizze vibrated until she became points of light and color separated by space. The living dots expanded out, rearranged themselves, and then joined back together. A black coach with red trim stood where Kizze had once been. On the back of it, secured by iron brackets, a plain wooden coffin waited to be filled.

"Here I go," Babes called and flew in front of the hearse.

Isabel joined her with an excited, "Me, too!"

Both fairies broke down their molecules like Kizze had. They reconstituted as gray spotted mares, hitched to the carriage with red plumes adorning their heads.

Lai spun around until she became a whirlwind of color. When she stopped, she was a full-grown woman in coachman's clothing. Her red garb made her black hair and dark eyes stand out. She tipped the brim of her red top hat to Esmeralda, opened the carriage door and offered her hand to her queen.

"Thank you, Lai," Esmeralda said accepting her hand and stepping into the coach's compartment. "Make haste, and don't mind the bumps in the road."

Zoila sat with back against the crystal soaking up the warmth it emitted. Fatigue weighted her eyelids, and she struggled in and out of wakefulness. The world became a dreamy place, voices and images within played readily with external stimuli. She felt the sprinkling drops that heralded an oncoming storm, but inside her mind flashed images of her first meeting with Rex, long ago on a stormy night when he had somehow seen her in the shadows of the forest. He had shown her a way out of her pain, a way not to become the monster her adoptive parents were.

Perhaps her birth parents had been monsters too, how could she know? She couldn't, but something had put the rage and confusion in her blood. It had always been there, and the king and queen had merely animated it from its hibernation. But, Rex had told her of the other qualities that hibernated inside her; things like loyalty, perseverance and justice. Things that, if cultivated, would give her life meaning and help her crawl out of her personal hell.

"It's all come down to tragedy, old man, there's no escape for me," she muttered not knowing if the words stayed in her head or if she'd uttered them aloud.

The warrior princess stretched her legs out in front of her and then pulled her knees up close to her chest. She hoped to ease the soreness of a night's battle; the motion elicited thoughts of Damek. Perhaps it was a trick of the mind responding to the rain, but she felt her connection to him drift away along with any hope of a life with him. *Oh, wretched existence,* she thought as drops from the sky blended with tears.

A rhythmic lullaby eased her despondency and wrapped around her like a friendly presence. *Soft drums, soft drums, bring rest. Where have I heard this before?*

"Heye nene ya àa
One is thinking about it, one is thinking about it, holaghei.
Its main beam, Earth is to be made the main beam,
One is thinking about it,
Now Sa'ah naaghei, Bik'eh hozhoo *are to be made the main beam,*
One is thinking about it."

Zoila's breathing slipped into the easy automatic regularity that sleep brings. The distant song spoke to her, called to her to reinforce her resolve. Her ability to search mentally for its origin weakened as the dream seduced her.

"Its main beam, Wood Woman is to be made the main beam,
One is thinking about it,
Its main beam, Mountain Woman is to be made the main beam,
One is thinking about it,
Its main beam, Water Woman is to be made the main beam,
One is thinking about it."

Her eyes fluttered open with a start, and her body jerked awake. She looked around as she scrambled to her feet. The sight that greeted her caught her in mid-breath and wouldn't let her go.

Diné circled his ground painting with careful, deliberate dance steps. Accompanying his native chant with a rattle, he sang:

> *"Its main beam, Corn Plant Woman is to be made the main beam,*
> *One is thinking about it,*
> *Now* Sa'ah naaghei, Bik'eh hozhoo *are to be made the main beam,*
> *One is thinking about it,*
> *One is thinking about it, one is thinking about it,* holaghei.*"*

Arias pounded desperately on the crystal with frightened eyes. Zoila stumbled back as she saw her sister's capsule fill with water; it was knee high and rising.

"Do something!" Zoila shouted to Diné.

The Navajo stopped his dance, his kind eyes smiled sadly. "I cannot. I can only show the way. You must do something. *Hágoónee,* Zoila."

Flabbergasted, Zoila stood frozen as Diné picked up his bag and left the plateau. Finally, finding her voice, she cried out through the intensifying rain, "You can't leave us like this!"

Annie struggled alongside Damek to climb the rain-drenched hillside. Grass gave way from underneath their feet and shrubs easily uprooted when they needed to grab a hold for balance. It was like running in the surf, every gallantly fought for step meeting with the pull of the tide back into the deep. Their resolve, undampened by the apparent hopelessness of the task, and their shared determination spurred them on, and they made steady progress up the hill toward Arias despite the rain.

Glancing over her shoulder, Annie peered through the downpour. She assumed the king and queen's coach had driven onward, as she could no longer see it. Neither could she see where they had dropped them off at the tree line earlier, as Damek and she traveled further up the hill. Annie knew the spell imprisoning Arias in the crystal also prevented the king and queen from approaching Arias; the monarchs needed to take a longer route on a winding path, arriving only after the spell had been broken.

Annie wished she had a crystal of her own to keep the wretched of the world away from her. All she possessed was a rose quartz that was in her backpack in a land far away at Davey's house. She had spent hours gazing into it, losing herself in the stone's inner glow to escape, for a time, the pain of her existence. *But, I don't need it now. I'm not going to hide away in a fantasy; I'm going to live my life for Shelly—for me.*

The cry of a bird cut through the sound of the storm. Annie looked up and saw a red-tailed hawk fly from the top of the hill and swoop over Damek and her. At that moment, the hawk spoke to her in Diné's voice, his words a whisper echoing in her mind. Then the hawk vanished into the sky over the woods below.

"We have to hurry," Annie called out. She slipped and slid back, feeling like the earth was pulling her under.

Damek caught hold of her arm and steadied her. "I know; we are almost there," Damek replied against a howling wind that had shown up to batter them. "Dig in!"

"I'm trying," Annie declared, the words echoing the strain her body felt. Her thighs and calves burned along with her belly muscles as she fought to gain footing and pull herself up the slick, mucky hillside. Sandals did little to help dig her feet in as toenails cracked and bled with each hard won jab into the earth.

Inside Annie, the old familiar voices called out to her like dead fingers from the grave yearning to pull her back into death's sleep.

Give it up, it's not worth it, it's too much for you. What do you think you're doing? You know you're a loser, and nobody wants you. Your daddy left you, and your mommy has to stay high just to stand the sight of you. Not to mention leaving Shelly to die. You should have died. Shelly would have done something with her life instead of just take up space.

"Screw you!" Annie shouted as exhaustion choked tears out of her. "I'm not gonna quit, so shut up. I'm alive, and I'm not gonna quit!"

Annie looked over at Damek, who still held her arm, but now with a wide-eyed stare of bewilderment on his face. Then sadness overcame him as he lowered his eyes, staring into the mud. With a nod that showed an understanding of Annie's outburst, he refreshed his grip on her as she grabbed his forearm. Together, they forged upward.

Chapter Twenty-Six

As the ground flattened out onto the plateau, Annie could hear a woman yelling, "You can't leave us like this!" and then the woman cursed the fates, the storm and anything else that caught her wrath. Her fiery words soon turned to pleas for help to save her sister.

Damek looked urgently at Annie. "Zoila! Something's wrong, Arias must be in trouble. Come on, one last push, and we're there!"

Fighting against wind, rain, mud and fatigue, Annie and Damek reached the flat top of the hill as thunder rumbled and lightning flashed. Annie collapsed next to a panting Damek. Meters in front of her, she saw Zoila, who had worked her sword tip into a crack in the crystal and was now straining to pry the rock open. The chest high water bubbled, gushed and swirled in the crystal from an unknown source. Inside the crystal, the frightened Arias pounded on the translucent walls, stopping only long enough to give Annie a hope-filled glance.

"Zoila!" Damek called out. "What's going on?"

Zoila twisted toward them. The desperation in her face turned to seething anger when her eyes fell on Annie. Annie felt an icy shiver run down her already cold back as Zoila removed the sword from the crystal and strode straight toward them.

"You brought her *here*?" Zoila bellowed against the storm. "Damn you, Damek, did I not say that the only part of her I wanted to see was her head?" Zoila raised her sword over her shoulder. "Do I have to do everything myself?"

Annie found a reservoir of strength to scramble up and circle away from Zoila.

Damek positioned himself between the two and shouted, "No, Zoila, you don't understand. She can help."

Zoila shook her head, "You idiot! She will destroy us."

"She has the key, Zoila, she can help," Damek, arms outstretched to protect Annie, crouched—ready to leap. Trying to cut through the din of the storm and Zoila's rage, he pointed to Arias, who struggled to keep her nose above the water, and shouted, "There's no time to argue; Arias is drowning!"

A blast of wind brought the storm to a crashing crescendo with exploding thunder, burning flashes of light, and a rain that pounded down hard. The storm's intensity was maddening, and Annie feared she would not be able to bear it a moment longer. *I've got to see this through. I won't be broken again, never again.*

Zoila's frantic glance shot from Arias to Damek to Annie. The seething anger in her face remained evident as she lowered her sword. She turned to Annie and said, "You'd better pray to the gods this works, or I'll send you to meet them. Now, hurry. NOW!"

Annie boldly approached Zoila, grabbing the princess by her wrist. "You have to come with me. We have to do this together."

With an instinctual jerk of her arm, Zoila tried to pull out of Annie's grip. The grip held, however, and the two women glared at each other.

"You understand, don't you?" Annie said sternly to Zoila. "Our fates are tied together; apart we die, joined we live."

Zoila looked over at Arias struggling as the water covered her head, immersing her fully. The defensive wall of Zoila's hard features broke down, and she uttered a heartfelt, "Yes, by the goddess, I see it."

"For the love of the fates unlock the crystal," Damek implored, frantically gesturing toward Arias and stepping aside.

Hand in hand, Annie and Zoila approached the crystal as if moving in a dream.

Inside Arias ceased struggling when Annie's eyes locked onto hers. Air bubbles rolled up Arias's face from her mouth as she reached out and placed her hands against the crystal. Floating in the water filled cell that had become her tomb, the princess fought to keep her last breath from escaping.

With her free hand, Annie grasped the key and tore the thin leather band from her neck. She placed the key between her and Zoila's hand. Once they both held the key, Zoila dropped her blade, and the women placed their free hands on the crystal opposite Arias's hands. Annie experienced a tingle buzz through her muscles. Looking at Zoila and then Arias, she felt a growing sense of unity as a golden aura enveloped them. Then together Annie and Zoila inserted the key into the keyhole and turned.

In a blinding and sudden flash, lightning struck the crystal with an earsplitting crack and reverberating report, showering the area in evanescent sparks. Damek crouched instinctively into a defensive posture, shielding his eyes from the intense explosion of light.

The three women held steadfast until the crystal's door turned to light and vanished, releasing a flood of water that knocked the feet out from under Annie and Zoila, and sent them face down to the ground as

Arias spilled out on top of them. Arias quickly grabbed Annie and Zoila's hands; the three women lay on the muddy earth clasping each other's hands and coughing from the gushing water and acidic smoke. Their sprawled bodies radiated out from the circle formed by their embracing hands.

The storm suddenly died down to a wet breeze that accentuated the panting of the three women and the hiss of random raindrops hitting the superheated crystal. The women slowly sat up, wiping mud from their shivering bodies and looking nervously at each other.

Arias cleared her throat, and with a raspy start said, "So, you must be Annie."

"Yeah," Annie coughed, "that's me. How'd you...?"

"Diné," was all Arias had to say for Annie to understand.

Zoila shook off the disorienting effects of the explosion. "Is everyone all right? That was a powerful spell reversal; I haven't felt anything like that since—well never mind. My thoughts are clouded."

Arias giggled first, then Annie started to laugh, and soon Zoila started to chuckle with relief.

Damek stumbled forward, mouth moving to form words. "I never noticed...can it be?"

"What are you gawking at, Damek?" Zoila asked still caught up in the mirth of the moment.

Damek blinked and said, "The resemblance between you three—like you were all three sisters."

"Maybe the mystery goes deeper than that," Arias tittered.

"And maybe," Annie said, the laughter leaving her voice as she looked beyond Damek, "we have a bigger problem."

From the far end of the hilltop, King Gororm and Queen Dezair made their way onto the plateau. Gone were the magical disguises that had not fooled Annie, but their true exposed hideousness astounded her and turned her stomach. Fanning out from behind the monarchs, 30 armed, hooded ghouls formed a semi-circle on the perimeter and awaited a command. The three women stood up as the army took its position.

"Our daughters together again at last," the king sniggered to the queen. "Isn't it heartwarming?"

The queen cleared phlegm from her throat and licked her black lips. With a jagged toothed grin she added, "Makes me want to shite. I'm glad to see your dog has obeyed your order and delivered them all to us."

Damek's expression soured and he backed away, drawing closer to the women.

"Pity," Gororm shrugged. "Looks like I'll have to find a new Captain of the Guard."

"Zoila, go for your sword and join me," Damek instructed. "Arias and Annie stay behind us, and when you have a chance make haste for the slope. We will hold them as long as we can."

The queen cackled, choking momentarily on her own spittle. "None of you are leaving this hill alive; you can be certain of that."

"It won't be so easy, you pathetic creatures!" a voice called out from behind Damek. It was Rex. He wheezed slightly as he strode onto the flat terrain from the steep route Annie and Damek had taken. Twirling his double spear-tipped staff, he found solid footing on which to stand his ground.

Zoila turned to retrieve the sword she had dropped beside the crystal, but Annie seized her hand.

"No," Annie told Zoila, reaching out and grabbing Arias' hand also. "We have to stay together. It's going to happen soon."

"What's going to happen?" Arias asked.

"Your death if you don't let us fight," Damek insisted. "Zoila, get your weapon!"

Zoila moved closer to Annie and Arias, "No, Damek, she's right. I can feel it." Although her voice remained steady, tears were streaming down the warrior princess's face. "It's going to happen. It's going to end soon."

"That's so true, Zoila," the king added. He held up his stubby arm and with one wart infested finger, prepared to give the attack signal.

"Annie, get out of there!" Rex entreated.

"Zoila, pick up your sword!" Damek demanded.

"Get this over with," Dezair said with a yawn.

Gororm took a breath to issue the final order, when it got caught in his throat.

The earth began to rumble and shake, unbalancing everyone who stood on it. All but the three women, who turned toward each other, put their arms around one another's shoulders and touched foreheads.

Annie turned her head from her band of sisters and said directly to Gororm and Dezair, "You can't have us ever again."

The land continued to buckle with a deep growl, spewing sulfur infused steam. From the circle of the three arose chanting. Diné had earlier whispered the words to Annie and now through their new connection, Zoila and Arias also spoke the words of the Red Hawk Navajo women of Diné's homeland:

"Happily may I walk,

Holdfast rose above the plateau casting a shadow over the hilltop, sending ghouls, monarchs, monk and soldier diving to the ground for cover. She screeched terrifyingly at the beings scurrying below her.

"Run!" Rex and Damek called out simultaneously to the three women who stood unmoved by the dragon's arrival.

Holdfast hovered above Annie, Zoila and Arias. Her massive wings flapping back and down to maintain position. From the center of the circle of the three, Annie held up the key to the dragon, and the women completed the chant:

And with that, Holdfast reared her head back and lunged it forward, issuing out a torrent of fire.

The glow of the flames danced wickedly on Rex and Damek's faces as they looked on in horror from their prone positions. They could only watch helplessly as the inferno engulfed the women without so much as a scream from any of them. As the river of fire poured forth, Holdfast's head burst into flames and her body began to burn. The fire that consumed the dragon rained down on the huddled women.

Gororm and Dezair struggled to their feet in slow amazement at the roaring pyre.

"Serves you right, you traitorous whores!" Dezair shouted, spitefully.

Rex broke his ghastly fixation on the burning bodies and turned all the rage boiling inside him toward the king and queen. With a warrior cry from deep inside, Rex hurled his staff like a spear. The tip chunked into Dezair's throat and tore through the back of her fatty neck. The queen grabbed the staff below her chin; gasping and gurgling, she was dead before she hit the ground.

Damek sprung to his feet as the dragon disappeared into and became part of the burning mass on the ground where once stood Zoila, Arias and Annie. Swinging around with sword at the ready, the soldier prepared to be overrun by the ghoul army.

Gororm drew his blade, hissing grotesquely, and rushed headlong toward the now unarmed Rex. Rex set himself to meet the attack. He dodged the first slash coming straight down. But, Gororm reversed direction and sliced at an angle, catching the monk from ribs to the bottom of his chin—a blow that sent Rex tumbling backward down the hill.

"I'll take you all on to the death," Damek called out to the horde.

"Stand down," a voice firmly ordered from behind Damek.

Damek turned around and gasped.

Annie arose alone out of the burning heap of Holdfast's last breath. Stepping unsteadily out of the blaze, she faltered briefly, then walked powerfully toward Damek.

His sword dropped to the ground from his trembling hands as he looked upon this new creation. It was Annie, but not exactly Annie. Dressed in Zoila's warrior garb, she held Zoila's sword with confidence; yet her face radiated the sweetness of Arias. But, the eyes that peered at him reminded Damek of a determined girl he had met in the woods earlier that day.

"Annie?" he asked hoarsely.

"Yes, Damek, it's me." Annie cut the air in a figure eight with the sword. Stretching her neck muscles and causing several popping sounds, she said with a smile, "It's me, but I'm more than I was."

Damek moved toward her and put out his hand, stopping shy of touching Annie. "What about Zoila and Arias?"

"Attack!" the king commanded, interrupting Damek's questioning.

Furrowing her brow, Annie focused her piercing stare at the 30 ghouls swarming down toward them and said, "This is my fight, Damek, please step aside."

Annie effortlessly waded through the ghouls, hacking and stabbing her way through the assault. With a singular purpose, she strode straight to Gororm. The king's eyes bulged and darted about looking for escape routes as he shuffled back from Annie's unwavering approached.

"Kill her!" Gororm shouted, but his army fell into pieces and ended up in bloody piles in Annie's wake.

Without breaking her stride, Annie was upon the king. He raised his sword and commanded, "Stop or I'll..."

Annie's blade cut across Gororm's throat sending a spray of putrid blood pumping from the wound. Circling her arm around and down, she came back up and disemboweled the king from pubic bone to rib cage. A rush of foul air left the king as he toppled to the ground in a lump of his own steaming entrails.

Annie looked around with her sword leveled in front of her. What few living yet critically wounded ghouls remained quickly ran from the area. She fixed her gaze on Damek and found him still dumbstruck, standing frozen in the same spot.

"Who are you?" he quivered.

"I told you, it's me—Annie," she said warmly.

Damek stumbled a few steps forward. "I do not understand. Where's Arias? Where's Zoila?"

"I'm not sure I understand it all myself. But I feel them; we are one."

Sorrow cut deep on Damek's brow and his voice trembled, "No, this can't be; I can't lose her. I love Zoila, I must have her back."

Annie walked up to Damek and caressed his face with a steady hand. "I know you love her and, in fact, you loved us all," she soothed. "But you can't have her, not now, not here. I'm sorry." Annie kissed him on the cheek.

"Don't leave me without my love," Damek beseeched.

Annie looked at him, and her heart panged for his loss. "I'm sorry," she repeated; it was all she could honestly say. She wanted to stay and console Damek, but an urge inside her beckoned her to leave. She didn't understand why; she just had to get back down the hill alone.

Still searching for an answer with his reddened eyes, Damek asked, "What am I to do?"

"Go, and be king. Give aid to the weak and temper the powerful. Honor my spirit. If you can't do it for yourself or your people, then do it for Zoila and what she meant to you."

Annie turned and walked away, heading down the hillside the way she had arrived. Damek lowered himself to the ground exhausted and lost.

At the bottom of the slope, Annie came upon Rex lying on the ground. His body lay contorted unnaturally, indicating several broken limbs. The wheezing and periodic coughing up of blood told Annie that he was not long for the world.

"Who's there? Who comes?" Rex called out, unable to lift his head.

"Just me, old man," Annie greeted as she sat beside him and leaned over, peering into his face.

Rex looked at her with confusion at first, but as their eyes searched each other out, a sly smile crossed his bloodied lips. "Hey, you," he sighed.

"Hey," she smiled.

"Watch that first step coming off the hill; it's a big one," Rex chuckled then coughed painfully and expelled crimson specks that peppered his beard.

Annie stroked his hair and said, "I did. I'm here."

"Yes," Rex said with shallow breath, "and look at you; you're healed."

"Just like you said, the dragon's gift was for a healing."

"A great healing," he added. "A healing I thought I was destined to perform."

She kissed him gently on the forehead and whispered, "I couldn't have done it without you, Rex."

"Now you see me as I am—a broken man," Rex coughed, painfully.

"Don't," Annie started and then began to cry softly.

The monk cleared his throat and regained a steady voice. "It's true, what a fool I've been. A life spent chasing the elusive, while I lost the only real thing I ever had."

The air turned chilly, soft white flakes of snow floated down from the bleak sky. A wayward wind whistled by, offering the moment a hollow and sad refrain.

Rex's eyelashes fluttered as the flakes landed on his face. With a smile he said, "Is that snow? I love the winter; it makes me think of her. Why did I ever leave that cabin? Why did I ever walk away from her?"

"I don't' know," Annie answered honestly. "Life seems full of blunders and mistake; not all of them of our own making."

"There's no doubt about that," he agreed. "But this mistake *was* of my making." Rex paused to close his eyes and take in several shallow breathes through his nostrils. Reopening his weakening eyes he said, "She's coming. She'll be here soon. I really wish she wouldn't see me like this, but I suppose it serves me right."

"No," Annie said shaking her head. She brushed snowflakes from Rex's face. "You're a good man."

The monk wheezed his words now, while his eyelids closed unable to take the strain. "I tried to be, and maybe I could have been again. But, I just turned and walked away from my love. What kind of man does that?"

"But you saved me." Speaking the words sent a shudder through Annie, and a moan escaped her quivering lips.

Rex took Annie's hand and gave it a weak squeeze. "Hush, child; you know the truth as well as I do. Esmeralda told me everything in a single whisper."

"What did she say?"

"It's about you, Annie. All this was about you, and I'm honored to have been a part of it. You have done very well, my child, very well."

Sniffing back tears, Annie kissed him again and said, "That doesn't make me feel any better about losing you."

"I suppose not," Rex said distantly and then breathed his last.

Annie sat on the ground cradling Rex's head and rocking gently to and fro. From a distance, she heard the clinking sound of tackle, hooves and carriage wheels. The sound drew near as the snow continued its silent descent to the ground.

A black carriage pulled by two gray spotted mares and driven by a slender oriental woman in a coachman's outfit came to a halt beside the grieving Annie. Lai stepped down from the coach, opened the cabin door, and ushered the passenger out.

The woman wore white. White hair billowed in the winter breeze, wrapping and spidering across a face aged splendidly by time. Esmeralda was not the crone Annie had first met on the beach, but she was older than when Annie had last seen her in the forest, and she seemed more at peace. In a white woolen cloak with rings of pearl, white sapphire and white quartz adorning her hands, she went to Annie and stood beside her.

"He's dead," Annie said, sadly.

"I know, Annie." Esmeralda motioned to Lai who had gone to the rear of the carriage to open the coffin.

Annie looked up at Esmeralda. "He loved you, you know. I think he wanted you to know that."

"I know," the elder woman repeated, but this time her words harbored a deeper sorrow.

Lai came over, squatted down carefully and scooped her arms under Rex. Annie swept the fallen snow off his limp body with her hand; she couldn't bear to see him lying helpless like that. Then she helped roll him into the woman's crooked arms and to her surprise, Lai effortlessly stood up. Rex's body seemed weightless as the willowy woman carried him and then laid Rex in the casket. The back of the carriage sunk with a slight squeak and the driver replaced the coffin lid.

Esmeralda crouched down to look into Annie's face. Brushing a strand of hair from Annie's eyes, she said, "You're going to be all right, Annie. Keep your eyes open and your wits about you, and you'll be all right."

"Is it over?" Annie asked, her eyes pleading for it to be done with.

"Almost, dear, be patient. Just a moment longer." Esmeralda kissed Annie on top of her head and, standing back up, walked over to her coach.

Annie called out to the departing enchantress, "Where will you take him?"

Esmeralda turned briefly and smiled, saying, "To my cabin; or do you think I should return him to the monastery?"

Shaking her head with a content smile, Annie answered, "No, to your cabin. It's where he'd want to be."

Lai assisted Esmeralda into the compartment and then climbed onto the carriage. With a snap of a whip and a sharp whistle, the team pulled the carriage onto the now snow-laden trail and disappeared into the darkening woods.

Alone in the snow, Annie felt the cold closing in on her. She balled her knees up close, tucked her head down, and shivered. *Now what happens to me?*

In response to her thoughts, the warm breath of Shiva moistened her shoulder. Annie looked up and wrapped her arms around the wolf.

"There you are," Annie greeted. "I knew you'd come."

Annie rubbed her face past Shiva's wet outer fur and into the warm thick coat underneath. After a time, the wolf backed away with head hung low. Annie looked around and found herself once again in the center of a ring of black wolves. This time, however, there was no saliva-drenched, vicious snarling. Only a few whimpers sounded in the quiet winter evening as snow blanketed the world around her.

Shiva approached again, and this time Annie leaned her head back, exposing her neck.

"Hurry, girl," Annie whispered, "before I start drowning again."

The wolf gently took Annie's neck into her mouth and closed her powerful jaws. After a horrid crack, the last thing Annie saw were black wolves converging on her from all directions.

PART THREE

Chapter Twenty-Seven

The wet compacted sand grounded into Annie's palms and knees as she crawled from the dark ocean waters, coughing and spewing saltwater while flinging pieces of seaweed off her head. A nocturnal offshore breeze buffeted her naked body, causing teeth to clatter a backbeat for her shivering body. Drained from struggling against the waves, Annie reached the dry sand above the tide-line and collapsed. As her breathing settled, the exhaustion-induced tunnel vision began to diminish, and the environment piecemealed itself together in her awareness.

Sirens screamed and bellowed from somewhere beyond her. Looking up with a sand-caked face, she shook grains from her hair and spat. As her eyes worked to focus, it seemed to her the whole world was on fire. A flame engulfed, boardwalk hotel cast an orange-yellow glow on her, but offered no warmth from the chilly night.

Annie struggled to move past the image of wolves converging in on her—she needed to figure out what was happening right here and right now. She quickly took stock of the immediate area. She was back on the beach, the same beach, as far as she could tell, and a hotel burned a few blocks away. Her body had returned to its adolescent state, gone was the adult power and tone of Zoila. Her hair, however, remained as short as when Esmeralda had cut it.

I'm frozen to the bone, she thought, her mind still sluggish and her body shaking hard enough to impair coordination. Annie attributed her own crying and moaning to exhaustion and low body temperature; with no reason to dwell on her groans, she set about rubbing herself and working out muscle cramps.

Annie didn't doubt the tide had taken her clothes away, after all, she had stripped down in the water; still she looked around hoping to catch a break. There were no clothes to be found, however, not even an abandoned beach towel.

Great, no clothes, no warm tent, no Esmeralda. Maybe, if I can get myself moving, I'll find something. That's what Zoila would do. Annie slowed her body rubbing as the memory of Rex lying dead on the cold ground

239

transfixed her. Grief and loss weighed down painfully, yet she wasn't going to run away from the feelings like before. She would face them, let them wash over her; accept the discomfort of living.

The concussive sound waves of an explosion blasted from the direction of the burning hotel and stole Annie's breath; she scrambled further inland on all fours, nestling up against the seawall. A distorted ringing vibrated in her head for several minutes before the roaring sounds of the surf, the burning buildings, and the screeching of sirens and human chaos came rushing back. The rocks in the seawall had retained some of the day's heat, so she curled next to them and brought her limbs in tight to the core of her body.

What's going on? Her heart rattled in her ribs, still startled by the explosion. Annie tried to calm herself by taking in slow nasal breaths. *Keep it together, Annie; clear your head and see what's happening. Don't run around like some scared animal.*

Although chilled, she crawled backward in order to peer over and look past the seawall. Flames billowed from gaping holes where parts of two neighboring hotels had been blown away. She scrunched her nose and winced at the acidic smell of incinerated material irritating the lining of her nostrils.

What's happening? Is the city under attack? This is terrible! The thought of innocent people lying in pieces dead or crying out for their lives against the merciless flames chilled Annie more than the night air on her wet body. The image of Shelly's abduction flooded Annie's thoughts, along with twisted flashes of what her friend's last moments must have been like as that maniac sliced her up.

"Shelly!" Annie managed to blurt out, louder than expected. It surprised her that she could still speak, although she couldn't understand why she thought that. "I haven't forgotten you; I haven't forgotten what you did for me."

Can a dream or vision seem so real? Annie wondered. She grew aware of her body which, although cold to the bone, felt lighter, felt liberated, felt... *forgiven. Yes, this must be what being forgiven is like. No wonder so many people search for it. You haunted me didn't you, Shelly? And, this thing that happened to me; well, it was like some sort of exorcism.*

Shouting came from just past the seawall. First, a gruff male voice said, "That's too far. Come back; no one would've gotten that far."

Then a younger, smoother male voice responded, "I heard a voice, Captain, I really did." The voice called out, "Hello! Anyone there? Do you need help?"

Annie took a deep breath and called out, "Over here!"

She heard the young voice proclaim in excitement, "See, Captain, did you hear that?"

"Yeah," the elder voice responded. "Yeah, I did. Go check it out."

Annie sat waiting with knees held to chest, while calling out an occasional, "Here!" as the voice's owner found his way toward her.

The firefighter leapt the short distance from the top of the seawall to the sandy beach. He was dressed in sooty, tan turnout pants and coat, and wore a black helmet. When he saw Annie, his flashing blue eyes went from exhilaration at finding her to uncertainty at finding her naked.

"Are you all right, ma'am?" he asked as if falling back on a well-practiced script. The "ma'am" didn't really fit the situation as he looked early 20s and she looked young for 16.

Finding his response sweet and enduring, Annie smiled and said, "I'm okay, just very cold."

"Of course, sorry," he replied, gallantly removing his coat and draping it on Annie. "Here, this will cover you until we can get you to an aid station."

"Thank you," Annie said.

The older firefighter came off the seawall in his tan protective clothing and red helmet. "Everything okay?" he asked, his gravel like voice showing the strain of dedicated service in hazardous environments.

"She's ambulatory, Captain," the younger man reported.

The fire captain looked kindly into Annie's eyes and asked, "Were you in the hotel when it blew?"

Seeing an opportunity to explain away her naked condition on the beach in the middle of the night, Annie blurted, "Yes, I was getting out of the shower. What happened?"

"A couple of bombs as far as we can tell, probably terrorist of some sort," the older man said. "How in the world did you get all the way out here?"

Annie shrugged and answered, "It's all a blur; I just ran."

The captain's downturned mouth and nodding head told Annie he had taken her answer at face value. He turned to the younger firefighter, "Take her to the aid tent, have her observed for shock, and see who might be looking for her."

After walking a short distance, the firefighters and Annie found a set of stairs and, having climbed them, the fire chief headed back toward the fire. Annie and the younger man walked over to a parking lot full of activity. Having no shoes, she stepped carefully onto an area of gravel that announced the end of nature and the beginning of civilization.

"Do you want me to carry you?" the firefighter asked.

"No, I'm okay. Thanks, though." Her legs still felt weak from the cold and the struggle against the tide, so Annie took hold of his wrist and said, "But you can keep me steady."

He smiled and nodded, lifting his arm and tightening it to create a more solid support for Annie. Clearing his throat, he asked, "So, what's your name?"

"Annie. How about you?"

"Steve."

She smiled up at him as she made her unsteady way across the gravel. "Steve, huh? Steve the fire-guy. Thanks for finding me."

Steve chuckled, his professional demeanor giving way to a warm smile. "I don't know how I heard you with all the noise, but hey, that's what we're here for. 'Ready to serve 24/7' that's our motto."

"I bet you say that to all the naked girls you find on the beach," she joked.

"No, you're my first. Of course, I'm new on the job, so you're also my first rescue."

"Good, then you won't forget about me," she added with a wink.

The gravel turned to concrete, but Annie still held on to her escort, and Steve made no attempt to break contact. Her flirtation struck her as strange given the circumstances, however innocent their exchange had been. Still, she was naked under his coat and it was embarrassing, but she didn't want him to know that.

Just let the awkwardness pass and move on. It'll be okay, Annie repeated to herself until she felt less uncomfortable.

The aid station was a hastily constructed tent with a red cross on top, and set up in the parking lot of a hotel safely down the street from the disaster. The first explosion must have happened sometime earlier, because the city had already mobilized to provide comfort and safety. Trucks were arriving with supplies for victims and emergency workers alike. Hotel guests filtered in and out, some crying, some silent and dazed as volunteers worked to ease anxiety, help reconnect families and bring some order to the havoc.

Inside the tent, Steve introduced Annie to Jean, a woman in her late 50s with an easing smile and a seemingly endless supply of energy.

"Jean, this is Annie. She was in the building when it exploded, and she is looking for her parents."

"You're safe now, Annie," Jean said and laid a comforting hand on Annie's shoulders. "We'll help you get things sorted out, but first it looks like we need to get you some clothes."

Annie nodded in agreement and followed Jean over to a box of donated clothes that the aid workers had on hand. Annie found some oversized jeans, a man's white button up work shirt of which she'd have to roll up the sleeves, and some old black canvas high-top sneakers.

"You can get dressed over there," Jean said indicating a hospital privacy screen in the corner.

After dressing, Annie emerged from behind the portable curtain and looked around. Jean moved about helping other victims who came for assistance, and Steve stood talking to another firefighter. Steve glanced over, and Annie gave him a wave that she immediately thought was dorky.

"All set then?" he asked as Annie handed him back his coat.

"Well, I'm not naked anymore, that's a start."

"Of course," he said, and then with assurance he told her, "I hope your folks show up safe and sound. We're going to do everything we can to make that happen."

"Thank you, Steve," she said. Annie gave in to a sudden urge to hug him, which the firefighter returned.

"You'll be all right, Annie," he said smiling as their embrace ended. With a tip of his helmet and a wink, he left the safety of the tent and returned to the pandemonium outside.

Annie watched him leave and marveled at him. She did not often meet people who put the welfare of others first. Too many individuals she had crossed paths with were into taking, into sucking others dry. Shelly hadn't been that way; she had made the ultimate sacrifice for Annie, and Annie had run away from the gift.

I'm going to do better, Shelly; I swear it.

There had also been Rex and Esmeralda who had reached out to help her, and in the end, Zoila and Arias had given her a strength she still felt coursing through her. Annie thought of Damek and Diné and the role they had played in her life—and of course the four fairies. Then just on the edge of her thoughts, lurking silently in the background, was the memory of Shiva, the white wolf. Annie smiled, taking comfort in the idea of her animal spirit watching over her. Yet were any of them real?

When did reality change? Before I entered Esmeralda's tent? Did I ever leave the ocean or did I black out and somehow save myself from drowning? Did I imagine days going by that were really just minutes? Doesn't matter, she concluded. *Either way, I remembered. I remembered Shelly and what she did—that, I know, was real. I won't waste her sacrifice.*

Annie suddenly decided she should do something, anything; besides, it would distract her racing mind for at least a moment or two. She sought out Jean, and with a tug on the woman's sleeve, she offered to help.

"Well, bless your heart," Jean said. She put Annie to work making beverages, handing out blankets, and running messages for her.

Annie worked until three in the morning, but when a new shift of re-lief workers showed up Jean had insisted Annie sit down.

Now resting and sipping on hot chocolate from a Styrofoam cup, she had time to reflect again on the events of the evening. She couldn't get over how so many people had come together to help each other.

So much good will, she pondered. *Where has it all been hiding? Does it only come out after a tragedy? Or, maybe I'm the one who's been hiding, hiding away in my own miserable world while other people lead a normal life, while they connected with each other.*

Shuffling her feet underneath the metal folding chair, Annie looked at the new faces coming in and out of the aid station. The bustle and flames were dying down outside, and she wanted to go home, back to Davey and Martha's house. It was at their house that she felt wanted, and it dawned on her they might be worried about her. That thought felt strange to her, probably not strange to a normal person, but strange to her considering the emotional deprivation she had suffered in life.

What had Esmeralda said? That I wasn't normal, and that my life wasn't normal? I will have to fight just to keep myself together. I want the fight, though; I don't want to go back to falling apart. That might be romantic in songs and movies, but it is a bitch in real life.

She shifted her weight on the hard chair and listened to the small radio tuned into a local station with up-to-date news. The broadcast an-nounced that a radical group had already taken responsibility for the bombing. It was for their point of view that so much destruction and bloodshed occurred. They promised more until every knee bent and every head bowed to their will.

Annie gritted her teeth and felt heartsick. Even in *this* world Hold-fast was untethered and striking out in pain; a corruption of nature, a beautiful creation perverted. Annie realized that this rage, the engine driving murder, rape and oppression was ancient; older than anyone could know, it came from broken places within human complexity. Every violent act left a mark on the violator and the violated, forming a twisting chain of retribution and pain longing for relief. But, the relief never comes, like an unbearable itch you scratch until you bleed, inflam-ing more flesh along the way.

Where's the love? She wondered. Love. It flickered like a dying ember deep inside her. She could extinguish it and avoid the pain it caused when unrequited or betrayed. She could do that like so many had; she could do it and become part of the rage. It would feel good in a sense—better to hurt than be hurt. She could untether her own Holdfast, watch it turn black and scream, and then rampage against all that had tried to crush her: the people, the society, the world.

Taking another sip of the now cooling drink, she looked around her at the volunteers who worked gladly, and the responders who took to action without question, without knowing there was some other way to be.

The ember glowed within. Had any of these people been hurt before? Like her? Some probably had, some probably not. It didn't seem to matter. They seemed to refuse to succumb, refused to get sucked into their own wounds or become overwhelmed at the enormity of the task. The task of doing good in a mad, mad world.

She would not let the sickness that infected her grow, would not allow it to extinguish the ember. If she did, she would blacken, and it, whatever it was, would win.

And, she was damned if she was going to let that happen.

Walking in the predawn city, now quieter with the disaster scene a few miles behind her, Annie wondered if Jean felt distressed or betrayed when she discovered her missing, and when a search of the area did not produce a girl in baggy jeans and a white shirt.

I miss, Rex. It's weird; how can I miss someone who maybe wasn't really there? Well, I miss my father, and he wasn't really there; more of a ghost in my head. I wonder if my dad's thinking of me. I wonder if he's sorry he left; if every day he wishes he had stayed.

The night was crossing into day; the time when the world looks like a movie special effect: clean, fresh and a little too real. The air smelled filtered, recycled and ready for yet another day of use. Coming out of her thoughts, Annie noticed she was in her old neighborhood as she headed to Davey's place, and felt a pressing urge to go to her mom's apartment.

As she turned a corner onto her street, the vibrating flashes of police and ambulance lights caught her eye. *What now?* Annie felt uneasy as she neared her mom's building and saw that the commotion centered in front of it. She stopped and blended into the shadows of a nearby doorway to avoid detection.

The few neighbors who had been awakened by the clamor stood around like a loose gauntlet, as EMT's unceremoniously rolled a stretcher carrying a sheet-covered body down the front stairs, across the sidewalk, and then lifted it into the back of the ambulance.

Heavy hearted, Annie looked at the squad car. Her mom's boyfriend, Daryl, stood tearful and shivering. Shirtless, he huddled by the police car with his hands cuffed behind his back. Looking at his frightened face, she could see him mouth "not my fault," and if she could look closer, she would see the infected tracks on his arms; if she could look through objects, she knew she would see her mom under that sheet. Her face and body would be unnatural colors, colored from the palate reserved for those deceased from overdose.

It didn't matter that her mom had not stayed strong after Annie's father split; and it didn't matter that for years she failed to protect Annie or to think outside her own pain and invest in her daughter. All the anger Annie felt toward her mom faded into the background, leaving only the raw fact that her mom was dead.

Annie slumped down in the doorway and wept. She wanted badly to go to her mom, to look at her again, to touch her once more, but she didn't want to risk any entanglement with the police. Best to let that chapter close then get dragged down by its pitiful ending. Even in death, her mother had managed to cheat her out of any normal experience; Annie would not be able to grieve by her mother's side.

A police officer guided Daryl into the back of the squad car, shaking his head sadly at Daryl's ramblings and bawling. The ambulance pulled away, followed by the squad car; the people dispersed. The street was quiet again in the dawning of the day, setting the scene for the hustle and bustle that would follow in a few short hours.

Annie collected herself and walked away. She didn't know what the future held for her, but she was certain a good place to start was with Davey and Martha. Then there was a matter of some unfinished business. *He owes me for what he did to me, for stealing my song. Ogre owes me.*

Chapter Twenty-Eight

Standing at the front door of the small house, which was sandwiched between other houses like it in a low-income area of the city, Annie knocked and then rang the doorbell. She perused with a touch of bewilderment the paint-peeling red door, the faded lime-green siding, and the browning grass. Her attention returned to the door, as locks clicked and unbolted.

"It's her!" she heard Davey say from inside the house.

The door opened, and Annie was glad to see Davey's smile; the desperate hug that followed took her by surprise. Through the doorway, she could see Martha beaming, as the woman pulled her grey-touched brown hair into a ponytail.

"Hey, Davey, can I come in?" she giggled as he lifted her in his bear hug and pulled her inside.

Davey put her down and closed the door. Before Annie could form a thought, she found herself in Martha's arms.

Wrapped in the embrace, Annie felt cared for as the woman cried, standing accidentally on Annie's feet with her big fluffy, pink bunny-slippers. Annie hadn't known Martha that long, and the woman had always been kind to her, but Annie never thought much about it. She never allowed Martha's feelings to touch her, instead opting a wait-and-see approach. How many other genuine people had she shied away from in fear of being hurt?

After releasing Annie, Martha looked her in the eyes and said, "I'm so glad you're all right, honey. We were so worried when you took off, and we couldn't find you. We were up half the night waiting for you to come home."

The phrase sounded funny to Annie. Come home? She had only slept over there a handful of nights. But, that's the sort of people Davey and Martha were.

"It's okay," Annie announced. "I'm okay, really."

"We were so scared," Davey said, repeating Martha's sentiment. "Hey, honey, can you put on some tea?"

"For sure, come on, Annie."

Martha led Annie by the hand through the beads that hung in the doorway between the living room and the kitchen. Although she hadn't stayed with them long, Annie was very fond of their kitchen. Besides the fact it was always stocked with food, it also felt happily lived in. Martha and Davey shared time as a couple cooking together, and the warmth of their moments seemed embedded in the room.

Annie sat down at the kitchen table as the couple busied themselves. Martha, who wore well the extra pounds living life gave her, hummed an old rock song, providing no clue that she had just woken a few minutes ago. The soft winkles on her face were unapologetically free of makeup, which Martha had given up years ago. The upbeat woman went to the stove, turned on the gas and set match to burner. Davey, who had not aged as gracefully as Martha—his wife, his old lady—but who still retained an optimistic sparkle in his eyes, half opened the window blinds to let a glimmer of the morning sun in, and then lit an orange incense cone before joining Annie at the table.

"How'd the rest of the set go?" Annie asked to stir some conversation.

"Forget the set, what happened to you?" Davey questioned with concern.

"Oh, I just took a walk on the beach," Annie said, casually, then her eyes widened, and she added, "Hey, two hotels on the boardwalk were bombed last night."

"I know," said Martha with a breath. She sat three mugs with peppermint herbal tea bags in them on the table. Sliding one down to Annie, she said, "We were watching it on the news before we turned in. Awful, just awful. Were you down at that part of the beach?"

"Yeah, I helped out at the aid station."

Taken aback, Davey said, "Really? You mean to say while we were worried you were dead in a ditch, you were actually out helping disaster victims?"

"Disaster survivors, Davey, they are disaster survivors," she said with a smile, recalling a bit of protocol Jean had shared with her. "And, yes, that's what I was doing."

"Well, I'll be damned," Davey laughed.

Martha reached out and gave Annie's head a caress. "That's our Annie; such a good person."

Annie blushed. She suddenly became very self-conscious of an urge to hide from the compliment. *No, I won't run and hide. There's nothing to hide from. This is good stuff, not bad stuff; I gotta do a better job telling the difference.*

Still touching Annie's hair, Martha took hold of some strands on the back of Annie's neck. "Hey, you cut your hair. I like it; it's cute."

"Yeah," she replied, reaching back to feel the length. "A friend of mine cut it for me." Wanting the attention off her exploits for now, Annie asked, "Still playing tonight?"

"Remember what you found out?" Martha said gently, but firmly to Davey.

"Yeah, it's just so... I feel so bad. Annie, I'm so sorry. I didn't know, but I should have known, or I just didn't want to know. I..." Davey stopped stammering and just sat with pain twisting through his face.

Annie remained silent and looked at Martha who shook her head and pinched her mouth with one hand. A tear made its way down Martha's rosy-soft cheeks, and the woman gave Annie's shoulder a squeeze. The kettle started to hiss and form the beginning of a whistle, signifying that, either more time had passed then Annie had thought, or there had been little water in it. The sound animated Martha; she retrieved the kettle from the stove and poured hot water into the mugs.

"Davey," Martha said to spark him back into dialogue.

"I quit the band last night. I'm not going back," Davey revealed.

"Why?" Annie asked.

Davey took pause as if to steel himself against the words to come. "During the break between sets I tried to find you. I went to the backroom and heard Ogre bragging to one of the bouncers about," he swallowed hard. "About what he did to you."

Martha joined them again at the table.

"So he admitted to stealing my song," Annie said with a huff.

Davey looked at her confused and Martha rubbed Annie's back.

"No," Davey said with anguish. "What he *did* to you."

A wave of shame overcame Annie. She wanted to shrink away as past pains twitched inside her and the memory of whiskey-stink burned in her nostrils.

"Oh," was all she could manage to respond with as an all-to-familiar habit began to immobilize her.

"That ugly bastard," Martha blurted out, swiping at her tears.

"It's my fault," Davey confessed. "I knew Ogre was a shady character, and I should have tried harder to protect you." Davey slunk down in his chair and hung his head.

Annie bobbed her tea bag in and out of the hot water. She didn't know how she felt about this. She had never told him about the assaults, but now he admitted to suspecting danger and not warning her. On one hand, she was angry he had failed to help her, and yet there was more to her feelings then that, something just out of reach.

Davey looked up, but upon seeing the hurt and confusion on Annie's face, cast his eyes downward again. "Well, I confronted Ogre about it, and he told me to mind my own business. So, I told him to go screw himself and left; just walked out, left all my stuff and didn't even get paid. I don't know what they did to finish the show, and I don't care."

After taking a deep breath to calm herself, Martha said, "Are you okay, sweetie, I mean, I know it's not easy—but right now with us—are you okay?"

Annie's body wanted to lock up and send her mind somewhere else to avoid the pain of the moment and escape the topic of conversation. *Stay here*, she commanded herself. *Stay here in this moment and face it.* Forcing the words out, she said, "Yeah, I'm as okay as I can be, I guess."

As if sensing Annie's discomfort, Martha stopped rubbing her back and withdrew her hand, laying it uneasily on the table. "When Davey told me what had happened and how he could have stopped it, I was so pissed at him." She turned to Davey, "A little too much go-with-the-flow, and not enough against-the-grain in your philosophy, Davey."

Davey nodded silently in agreement, and then said, "I tried to keep you busy, send you on errands and stuff, you know? But, you just kept going to him. I just wish I had been less... less passive in my efforts, I guess."

Martha granted him a sad smile. She said to Annie, "When I was 13 a neighbor molested me, and I kept it a secret for years; I know what shame can do to a person, what it does to them inside." She turned back toward Davey. "You see what turning a blind eye did to this poor child?"

A glow in the center of Annie's chest, like the illuminated center of a rose quartz, started to warm her and spread throughout her body. Annie slowly, but surely, reached her unsteady hand out and placed it on Martha's. "He didn't do anything," Annie said softly.

"That's my point," Martha responded while still glaring at Davey. "He didn't do anything, or at least not enough."

"There's nothing else he could have done, believe me."

Davey broke his silence and said, "No, Annie, I could have warned you about him; I could have done something. I just didn't want to believe he would actually do what he did to you."

Annie looked at Davey unconvinced. "Could you have? I wonder. You don't know how willing I was to go into the darkness, to let it possess me. I don't think you could have stopped me no matter what you said."

"Oh, honey, don't say that," Martha said, placing her hand on top of Annie's. "You make it sound like it was your fault, but it wasn't. Ogre had no right to do what he did."

"You're right, Martha, he is responsible for what he did," Annie
agreed. "Some people are attacked, but I jumped smack in the middle of
the shark tank. It was a stupid and dangerous thing to do—I'm not excusing him—but I can't excuse myself either."

"Still," Davey said, "even if you wouldn't have listened to me, it was
my responsibility, as your friend, to do everything I could, and I didn't;
and I'm sorry."

"What a mess, what a mess, what a mess." Martha mumbled the
words like they were a mantra. "It wears me out that people just can't
respect each other. Live and let live."

"I just wish," Davey strained to speak in a steady voice, "I wish I
could take it all back. I know I can't, and I know there's no way I can
make it up to you. I'm sorry, Annie, really sorry, you gotta believe me."

And there it was, the something inside her that had been just out of
reach of her awareness, but was waiting patiently to reveal a truth.
Davey's passivity was like her silence about Shelly. If she had reported
the abduction instead of hiding in her room trying to forget the whole
terribleness, then Shelly might still be alive. The chances of that were
slim, Annie knew, he probably would have killed her before the police
found him—if they could have found him. But that was no excuse, she
should have tried, she should have done something besides hide in fear.
She shared with Davey a common negligence and, by the look on his
grief stricken face, she knew they also shared the conviction to never
make the same mistake again.

Annie stood up and motioned Davey over to her. "Come here."

He went to her, and she hugged him, saying, "I believe you, Davey;
and I forgive you." In that moment, a power surged through Annie, and
she felt whole, like a healer who had done her job. She started to cry, not
a cry of despair, but a cleansing cry that rejuvenated her being.

Davey began to blubber in Annie's arms, as Martha, exclaimed, "Oh,
my loves; oh my babies!" She got up, threw her arms around them both,
and shared their tears.

Annie didn't know how much time passed as they all held each
other; she only knew she felt loved and wanted. When the embrace
came to an end, the three returned to their seats, laughing sporadically at
the sudden emotional outpouring that had left them feeling a little
heady.

"That was good," Martha announced. "We needed that; that's what
keeps us strong."

"Yeah," Davey agreed, "that is the good stuff. Thank you, Annie,
thank you for your forgiveness."

"Well, thank you both," Annie said. "Thanks for caring about me."

"Oh, that's easy," Martha smiled. "You're such a beautiful person."

Annie blushed again, but didn't mind it so much this time. She cleared her throat and addressed Davey, "There is something you can do for me."

"Name it."

The faded brown van made its way through the city streets as dawn continued to wake the day. Inside, Annie and Davey rode in silence. The heaviness of the approaching task weighed down on them both.

Clearing his throat, Davey asked, "What do you plan on doing, exactly?"

Annie shrugged. "Don't know, exactly."

"You sure you wanna do this now?" Davey asked, tugging at his scraggly beard. "Maybe we should wait and give him a chance to wake up and be in a better mood."

Annie gave Davey an inquisitive look. "Don't you ever get tired of running, Davey? I'm tired of it; tired of being afraid and hiding in corners like some mouse."

"It's not so bad to keep a low profile," he smiled, weakly. "Sometimes you have to, to survive."

Annie rubbed his arm and gave it a squeeze, maintaining an easy grip, maintaining contact. "Davey," she stated, her manner gentle but firm, "do you really believe that bullshit?"

The smile faded, and Davey shook his head. "No, I guess not, not really. I don't know what got into me over the years. I did jail time for protesting against state logging policies, for chrimminy sake. And now, I just want to hold on to what I got, don't want to make waves."

She could tell him a thing or two about waves, about how they will pull you under and turn you around until you didn't know which way was up. She could tell him the only way out was to fight your way to the beach. Passivity was fine in smooth water, when you can float and conserve energy. But, life was replete with rough water, and you had to fight against the riptide. She could tell him these things, but Annie didn't feel the need. He knew the truth; he had just grown tired. Instead, she let another squeeze of his arm do her talking.

"He raped me," Annie said. "He took something from me I can never get back, and nothing I do will ever change that. But, what he can't have is me, not this me. Last night something happened, Davey, something I can't explain. All I know is that I'm not that scared little girl in the corner anymore. I'm a princess, a warrior, a traveler on a strange road. I'm going to front him out about what he did. Come on, Papa Bear, are you with me, or not?"

Davey took a deep breath and nodded his head as Annie released his arm.

Annie joined him in a round of head nodding, like two bobblehead dolls. "I need to make a call."

Davey patted down his chest and pockets, and, coming up empty, shrugged. "Oops."

Annie frowned, and then pointed. "Pull over to that market."

An hour later, they pulled into the alleyway that separated the club from Ogre's place. Annie hopped out of the passenger side of the van and let the door slam behind her. Davey came around the front and, together, they looked silently at the cold metal stairs leading up to Ogre's apartment.

Returning to the scene of the crime.

She remembered the sensations she had last time, returning to his apartment after he raped her. But, this time was different. This time she no longer had delusions of stardom that created plausible excuses to allow for Ogre's behavior. In the illuminating light of morning, Annie saw things clearly—as they really were. He had penetrated her the first time without consent, and that was the bottom line. The second time was under false pretext and resulted in broken promises. That was her fault for trusting a known monster, for gambling her dignity on the illusion of pursuing instant fame.

Fool me once...

"Hold on a sec," Davey said and went to the back of the van.

Annie heard some tinkering and clanking, and then Davey returned with a crowbar.

"Just in case," he nodded.

Together they walked up the still dew-dampened stairs. At the door, Annie pounded with one fist and called out, "Ogre! Ogre, it's Annie and Davey! Come on, we need to talk; get your ass out of bed, and open the door!"

The two visitors shrugged at each other. Annie had just raised her fist to repeat the pounding when the door flew open, revealing a freshly awakened Ogre heaving in anger.

"What the hell is this all about?" he growled.

"We gotta talk," Annie insisted as she pushed her way into the apartment.

Ogre shook off his sleep, "Oh, by all means, just come right in. What kinda bullshit is this?"

Davey sheepishly followed Annie into the room.

Ogre snarled at him, "Where'd you get lost to last night, asshole?" Ogre slammed the door and turned to face the unwanted visitors. He spied the crowbar in Davey's hand. "And what the Christ do you plan to do with that?"

Davey shook the crowbar at Ogre and ranted, "Had about enough of you, you sick bastard. Now you do the right thing or so help me and all the stars..!"

Ogre's eyes narrowed. "Put that crowbar down before I shove it up your ass, old man."

The two men began to shout at each other. Surrounded by all the clamor and braying and frothing words of malice and menace, Annie felt herself shrinking small and helpless. Setting lip between teeth to bite and bleed, this once mindless act of relief came full bloom into her awareness and she saw, she observed, she beheld the inclination. And she stopped.

A breath, fresh from the stench of the room and clean of the crushing weight of violence, led her awareness into nostrils, now easing their flare; into throat, relinquishing its dryness; and into lungs whose bellows slowed in the pumping. And she experienced the moment. Experienced it clear and full as if kissed on the forehead by Esmeralda, as if disciplined by the focused narrowing of Zoila's brows, as if touched on the heart by Arias' healing presence, as if given fresh resolve from the comfort of Rex's hand in hers. And she spoke.

"In my life," she announced calm and clear, allowing the proclamation to hang in the air until it had fully hooked Ogre and Davey's attention.

Davey blinked and Ogre scowled at Annie's short circuiting statement. The silence that followed rang like a Tibetan singing bowl calling for prayers.

"In my life," she repeated and then continued, "I will have many fathers and many brothers. I am daughter and sister to you all."

A flutter of doubt beat its fairy wings inside her belly. She acknowledged it as a welcomed guest and set her mind to the task. She said, "But I'm not anybody's possession. I belong to the First Mother and the unbroken chain that connects me to her."

Davey and Ogre shifted weight and glanced at each other.

Ogre smirked, "Look, girlie..."

"You hurt me," Annie retorted. She held his gaze that now turned to a glare on his meaty face.

"You're the one that danced too close to the fire," Ogre growled low.

Annie circled around Ogre like a wolf seizing up its opponent, drawing Ogre's attention along with her and away from Davey, who stood as silent witness. "That's right," she admitted. "I did dance, I did thirst for kindness, and, yes, I did drink from dark waters, it's true."

Annie stopped her prowl, standing her ground as she raised an emphatic finger toward Ogre. "But *you*. You did not provide light and warmth. You burned me instead. And the flame you burned me with will consume you until the day you ask for my forgiveness."

Ogre snorted, "Don't hold your breath, little Annie."

Annie lowered her accusing finger and, with a smile, added, "I won't. I'm already done with you. But you owe me money, and I've come to collect."

"Yeah, Ogre, you owe her for the work she did," Davey piped in, suddenly animated by Annie's demand.

As if cued by some cosmic director, Ogre's door popped open and his band members shuffled in, led by Tye. Davey looked at Annie with a questioning gaze.

Annie mouthed to Davey, "My phone call."

Ogre grinned wide, "Nice timing boys. Davey here is fired. Help him and this child out of here and onto the street."

"I don't think so, Ogre," Tye uttered, he seemed uncertain of what lost courage now spoke through him.

"What? Don't be an asshole. Get these losers out of my sight," Ogre commanded again.

"You *owe* her," Tye insisted. "You owe us all. Pay up, and then we'll all be gone."

"What's that supposed to mean?" Ogre asked, the confidence draining from his face. A violent cough shook his body, and he spewed thick, bloody mucus onto the floor. "What's going on?"

"It's over, Ogre," Tye said. "We quit. Find another band."

Ogre snarled, "I don't need you pricks. People come to see *me*. Understand? A band is just background noise." He fished in his pocket for a key and threw it on the table where the cash box sat. "Open it yourself and then get out of my sight. I quit you all."

Davey approached the table as Ogre dumped his wheezing body on his bed to fight off another coughing fit. Catching his breath, he looked over at Annie.

Annie stood and watched Ogre's sickness grow and strangle him as Davey and the band members divided the spoils of their labor. When Annie's eyes met Ogre's, she saw the look that Holdfast had given the moment the dragon turned from magnificent to vile. *What hell turned a baby so full of promise into a beast full of hate and discontent?* she wondered.

She felt the conflict inside her between disgust at facing her violator and deep sorrow at the lost promise of someone's son. And she knew she would have to live tolerating the pull of these and many other opposites in her life.

"Let's go, Annie," Davey said. "It's done."

The band members filed out through the doorway in front of Davey, who paused and beckoned again to Annie. "Come on. It's over."

Annie and Ogre's connection remained, however, unbroken.

"Say you're sorry?" Annie offered without demand.

The fire was dying in Ogre's eyes as something far away and chained down came through. "I can't," he muttered. Then defiance replaced the momentary message from deep inside and he spit, "I won't. I'm in your head now, little Annie. I'm the unwelcomed guest sitting at your table."

Annie considered this and, before turning to leave the room filled with pain and crime, she offered, "Maybe so. Sit if you must, but I'll no longer feed you."

With that she left, slamming the door behind her like a judge's gavel pronouncing a life sentence on an unrelenting offender.

Chapter Twenty-Nine

"That asshole Jared hit me," Shelly said with a huff as she stormed toward Annie one spring afternoon after school.

Annie had been waiting for her friend at their meeting spot behind the gym. She noted the abrasion on Shelly's cheekbone and said, "That asshole. Why'd he do that? I thought he liked you."

Shelly gave a, "Hurmph," and spat, "He just wanted to screw me and move on. He doesn't give a shit about me."

"Well," Annie said, measuring out her words, "we did do the panty spell so you two could be together."

"Are you trying to cheer me up?" Shelly asked with a frown, and then gave Annie a sad-felt command, "Don't."

"Sorry," Annie shrugged.

Tears pooled in Shelly's defiant eyes; her voice harbored a defeat Annie had never heard from her friend. "I just wanted him to like me, you know. Just feel something for me, and I would've given him any-thing. I told him how I felt, and we snuck into the auditorium to talk. That was a mistake; I'm so stupid."

Annie felt the weight of Shelly's sorrow. She reached out to her friend, pulled her close, and held her as Shelly cried into Annie's shoul-der.

"It's okay," Annie consoled.

"He kept trying to kiss me and shove his hand down my pants. I pushed him off and kicked him; that's when he hit me, and then do you know what he said?"

Annie stroked the back of Shelly's head. "What?"

"He said I was a stupid cock tease, and he was gonna tell everyone what a slut I was."

"That asshole."

Shelly broke the embrace, wiped a renegade tear from her cheek, and cleared her throat. "Yeah, well, I gotta go. I'll see you later, okay?"

"Wait," Annie said. "Where are you going?"

Shelly shrugged, "Just home, don't worry about it. I'll see you tomorrow."

Annie reached out and grabbed Shelly's arm, halting the girl's departure. "You're not going to go home and..."

"And what?" Shelly asked with a raised brow, eyeing Annie's hand on her arm.

Annie released her grip and stepped back. "Last week when I was waiting for you to change, your door was kinda open."

"You peepin' on me, perv?" Shelly snorted with a smile.

Annie screwed up her courage and blurted, "Shelly, I saw the cuts on your leg."

Shelly's demeanor sobered. "You know what? Mind your own business."

"But, Shelly..."

"Look, Annie, it's not like I'm going out getting wasted or whoring around, okay. I just need to feel better sometimes before my head explodes."

Annie dared to hold eye contact with Shelly. "I knew this girl who cut and, after a while, she couldn't stop. Now she's all screwed up."

Shaking her head slowly, Shelly said, "You don't understand."

"*I* don't understand? What, do you think I'm some poser chick? Cause, yeah, my world's all shiny and new. Look how Barbie I am!" Annie punctuated her sarcasm by twisting a finger into her dimple.

"Don't make me laugh," Shelly demanded, laughing.

"Come on, don't go," Annie pleaded with exaggerated sad eyes.

"Like you have room to talk; you're not exactly the Queen of Coping yourself. You just hide away and try to disappear—let everyone shit on you."

"I'll try to do better if you will." Annie gave Shelly's shoulder a little shove. "Come on, there's gotta be something better to do then hurt yourself over some loser."

Shelly rolled her eyes and struck a thoughtful pose. "Well, I know which way he walks home, and I got a bat."

"See, now you're thinking like the Shelly I know and love. Feel better?"

Shelly mussed Annie's hair and said, "You're crazy, do you know that?"

Annie nodded in agreement.

"But you're also a good friend."

"Oh, I don't know..."

"No, really," Shelly insisted. "You're different; it's like this place hasn't ruined you yet."

Annie felt suddenly empty and said, "It doesn't feel that way. I feel like I'm ruined."

Shelly gave Annie's arm a rub. "No, you could actually make it out of here, have a decent life. I don't know, just something about you. And you know what?"

"What?"

"I'm gonna watch over you and get you through this."

Annie laughed and, crossing her hands over her heart, said, "Oh, my guardian angel."

"Got that right," Shelly grinned.

It had been two weeks since her strange odyssey, as Annie stood shin deep in the ocean on a Saturday morning remembering her past conversation with Shelly. Annie held a single pink carnation, which Martha had told her symbolized the sentiment: I'll never forget you.

The salty air smelled fresh as it rode an offshore breeze that chilled her. Annie dropped the flower into the surf. Nodding at the memory of Shelly's promise to look after her, Annie smiled and said to her absent friend, "You sure know how to keep a promise. And you know what? I'm gonna keep mine, too."

Annie turned toward the beach and walked to where her shoes waited for her. Brushing off the sand from her feet, she put on socks, shoes, and rolled her jean pant legs back down before strolling to the boardwalk. Crews still worked at the site of the bombed-out hotels, carefully going through the rubble; debris lay scattered throughout the area like tombstones in a poorly planned cemetery. The closer she got to the site, the more a stench she couldn't describe assaulted her nostrils.

Her expression soured, and she thought, *How screwed up is this world? I'll never understand what people get out of hurting others who never did nothin' to them. It's sick.*

She came upon a discarded arcade machine broken and tilted against what looked like a stove. The machine was a Madame Tarra fortuneteller that used to give out fortune cards for two quarters a turn. With the glass booth broken and the pretty mannequin's face scorched and half melted, its fortune days were over. Annie looked from Madame Tarra's disfigured face to the crystal ball in front of the replica. As she reached out and touched the crystal ball, a shiver rocked her spine, and a hand latched onto her shoulder.

Annie's body froze up, but on the inside her heart pounded, and her mind raced. *Uh-uh, you ain't gonna hurt me without a fight.* She clutched the crystal ball, preparing to jerk it free.

"Don't turn around, Annie."

The voice was soft; Annie's fear and anger dissipated as she recognized it.

"Esmeralda," Annie said and tried to turn around, but the hand would not allow it. "You trying to scare me to death?"

"Sorry, sweetie, I just had something to tell you."

Annie let loose the ball and said, "Why can't I look at you?"

"It's just better this way, besides I'm fading out."

"You won't fade from me," Annie assured. "I'll never forget you."

"I hope you don't forget any of us, but we won't be around—not directly."

"So that's it, huh? Ghosts are all I have left?" Annie tried to reach up and touch the hand on her shoulder, but her arms felt like lead and too heavy to lift.

"Not all you have left."

"Oh, no?" she challenged. Annie felt a familiar frustration smolder inside. She said, "I'm haunted by my deadbeat dad, my dead mom, Shelly, and now you and Rex are going to join in the fun?"

"That's what I came to tell you. Tell you the same thing I whispered to Rex before I sent him to find you."

"I know what you told him. You said it was all about me, everything that happened in *that* world was about me."

"Something like that, but we're in this world now, and you have to know..."

Annie braced herself for Esmeralda's words, hoping whatever was said or whatever happened, she would not be taken away from this reality.

Esmeralda spoke, her words fading away as her grip on Annie's shoulder weakened. "*This* world isn't about you or your misfortune, I'm sorry to say. You have to find a way to be part of life." And, as the woman's voice blended into the sea breeze, Annie heard her say, "You have to run fast just to stand still... if you want to get anywhere, you have to run faster..."

The hand left Annie's shoulder, and the girl spun around. A ray of sunlight glinted off a random piece of metal, temporarily blinding Annie. She shielded her eyes and, after the flash, she saw no one behind her or around her.

Annie raked her fingers through her hair, pulling the short strands back. "Why do I even try to fight the weirdness anymore?"

Wiping her hands off on her shirt, she left the machine, the beach and the devastation. Crossing a street, Annie made her way to the filling station where Davey stood in front of his brown van, contemplating the end of the oil dipstick. Martha emerged from the gas station's store with some bottles of water and a large bag of sunflower seeds.

"Hey, Annie," Martha said, waving at her with the bag of seeds. "You ready?"

I guess I'm not just left with ghosts. I may not be able to get rid of the past, but I don't have to live in it.

"I'm ready," Annie replied. She met up with Martha at the rented trailer hitched to the van.

"Well, let's go then," Martha smiled.

They climbed into the van as Davey slammed the van hood shut.

He got himself comfortable behind the steering wheel and asked, "Did you get to say goodbye all right?"

"Yeah," Annie nodded, "yeah, I did."

Martha handed Annie a water. "So how cool is this? Heading up to the Blues Festival."

"Yeah, great," said Davey, with a tone of reluctance clearly in his voice. "It'll be nice to hook up with my brother and see the family again."

Martha opened the bag of seeds and offered some to Annie. "Does he sound excited?" she asked.

"Not really," Annie said reaching into the bag for a handful.

"It's just weird, you know, quitting our jobs and moving out of the house like that," Davey brooded.

"You worry too much," Martha said. "I think you and Joe working together again is the best thing for you."

Annie settled back into her seat as Davey started up the engine. She felt drained from her encounter on the boardwalk and needed to rest.

"Yeah, I know. Okay, well, off we go."

"Woo-hoo," Martha whooped and gave Annie a wink.

The time spent traveling north on Highway 101 felt like salvation. From the gritty heat of the city, to the scenic coastal drive, and now into the foothills of northern California, Annie had never felt so free. It was late afternoon, and the sun flickered through the trees, as the rumble of the road lulled Annie in and out of sleep. In her drowsy state, she listened to Davey and Martha's banter.

"Are you sure we went the right way after that construction detour?" Martha asked.

"Yeah," said Davey. "Have I ever steered you wrong?"

"Okay, I didn't want to bring it up again, but yesterday we went two hours out of our way when you got turned around after we stopped in town."

"One time, one time," he reminded her. "It's cool now; I know what I'm doing."

Martha gave his shoulder a squeeze and said, "Oh, honey, I do think you know what you're doing. I'm just wondering if we're going in the right direction."

Davey laughed, "Woman, you drive me crazy. Good thing I love-"

"LOOK OUT!" Martha screamed.

Annie heard and felt the sick screeching of brakes locking up tires and causing rubber to grind into asphalt. She propelled forward as the van decelerated faster than physics allowed her body to. The seatbelt caught her and, as the van fishtailed to a halt whipping the trailer behind it, a secondary force threw her back into her seat.

"Holy shit, did you see that?" Davey called out.

Martha looked back at Annie and asked, "Are you okay, Annie?"

"Yeah," she responded. Given there was no sudden impact or the sound of twisting metal, and that they were upright, she knew they hadn't been in a wreck. But, the sudden stop still begged the question, "What happened?"

"Look at that. Magnificent," was the only reply Davey gave.

"Come look," Martha invited with a flurry of her hand.

Annie unbuckled and made her way to the front of the van. She peered out the window, scanning the empty road until she saw it standing on the unpaved shoulder.

"It just darted across the road," Davey explained.

On the side of the road, staring at the van, staring directly at Annie, stood a large white wolf.

"I didn't think wolves came this far down," Martha said.

"Well," Davey replied, "they have been spreading from Oregon to the mountains of northern California, but this one is far from where it should be."

Martha gave him a credulous look. "How do you know that?"

"I saw a documentary on it," he shrugged.

Annie looked into the wolf's eyes and smiled. This wasn't a migration phenomenon; this was for her. The wolf's panting looked like a smile or even a chuckle. It bobbed its head and then disappeared into the woods that lined the highway.

"Martha," Annie announced, giving the woman's head a rub. "I think we are right on track."

While Davey and Martha rehashed the experience between them, Annie settled back into her seat and watched the scenery whisk by outside the van window.

Annie hadn't told anyone about her experience at the beach, her transportation to an ancient land, or her adventures there. That was for her and her alone—besides who would believe it was anything but a dream triggered by a near-death experience? She hadn't been sure herself whether it really happened or not, but the encounter with Esmeralda on the boardwalk eased her doubts. Something had happened, and it didn't matter to her what that something had been. Whether it was mystical or temporary insanity, it felt real, and it had impacted her life.

I never thought I'd be saved, never thought I'd escape from the darkness. I mean, it's still there, and I think it always will be; but it's not pulling me under anymore.

It was late afternoon when they pulled into a diner. The place was not a modern Superplex, where you could gas up, eat, shop, shower, rent videos, and watch some TV. It was an older, locally owned and run eatery with a neon sign beginning to buzz on as the sky started to dim. The "R" in diner was broken, and so the sign read "DINE." Annie nodded to herself, feeling a confirmation of her thoughts. On top of the "E" perched like an accent was a red-tailed hawk. It screeched once and then flew off as the sign came to full light.

Martha pointed to a beat up recreational vehicle parked on the side of the diner. "Hey, isn't that your brother's?"

"Yeah, imagine that. I thought Joe would've already been camped out up the road."

"Probably got turned around," Martha joked. "It's a family trait."

"Woman," Davey responded with a headshake as he pulled into a parking spot.

The three travelers piled out of the van and stretched their road weary bodies.

"Well, Annie," Davey said. "Are you ready for this? Knowing Joe, he's packed his RV full of family and friends for this festival."

"That's for sure," Martha confirmed. "Some of these other cars are probably part of what he calls his gypsy caravan. Get ready to be overwhelmed by musicians."

Annie gave a thumbs up and a salute. "Bring 'em on," she said, holding her nervousness about meeting new people at bay. *Get over yourself, Annie. Live the life.*

The diner was full of chatter, clatter, and bursts of laughter. A tired waitress in a faded blue uniform stopped to address them, balancing a tray of drinks on one hand. "Just find a spot somewhere, and I'll be with you. We got invaded," she smiled.

"Not to worry," Davey said. He pointed to a group of people.

"We're with that sorry lot over there."

"Lordy," the woman chuckled. "Well, squeeze on in."

Davey led Annie and Martha over to the back corner of the diner and bellowed, "We have arrived!"

The clamor in the diner swelled as greetings from the group of men, women and children flooded forth and surrounded the newly arrived trio. Annie followed behind as Davey and Martha waded into the warm reception.

An older version of Davey came up and gave him a hug. "Oh man, oh man. It's good to see you, Davey. You've been gone too long."

"I know, Joe, I know; it's good to see you, too."

Joe released Davey and turned to Martha, embracing her. "Damn, Martha, you look great. If you ever want to trade up, I'm still a bachelor."

Martha laughed. They ended their hug, and she said, "Thanks, but it took me long enough to break this one in. Think I'll keep him for awhile."

"And who do we have here," Joe asked, smiling at Annie.

Davey put a proud arm around Annie and said, "This is Annie. Think of her as one of the family."

"Well, then, Annie," Joe said hugging her, "Welcome to one kooky clan. Call me Uncle Joe, if you'd like."

Annie returned the hug, "Thanks, Uncle Joe."

Joe turned and gestured toward four tables full of family. "Come on and meet everyone."

The warm embrace of the gathering gave Annie mixed feelings. There was still a part of her that distrusted signs of affection and good-natured interactions; always fearing it was a mask for an underlying malevolence.

This is the good stuff, she reminded herself. *Just get past the discomfort and enjoy it while it's here.*

Annie met Davey's three other brothers and their wives and kids, before settling into a booth next to Martha. Martha put a comforting arm around Annie, and gave her a squeeze and a smile.

"You doing okay, sweetie?" Martha whispered.

"Yeah, I'll be okay."

"Don't worry, it grows on you."

Annie fiddled with a fork. "What grows on you?"

"Family," she stated.

Annie took in the din of multiple conversations swirling around her as folks told stories and caught up on one another's lives. One little boy came up to her while she ate and offered her a french fry. She took it with a "thank you" and he returned to his seat only to retrieve another french fry. It wasn't long before she had a collection of soggy fries beside her plate.

The air felt stuffy, and Annie's head throbbed. The company was pleasant, but Annie felt she had had her fill and needed a break. After all, she was still new to this type of environment, and it would take some getting used to.

Excusing herself from the table, she went outside for a taste of fresh rural air. The starry sky still made her feel insignificant, but the feeling no longer bothered or perplexed her. She was here, she was alive, and that was all that mattered. She would do her best with what she had to create a life worth living.

Annie heard guitar strings ringing out a ghostly tune, and she went to investigate. Behind the diner stood a doublewide trailer that she presumed was the restaurant owner's home. And, off to the side was a wooden swing set, where a teenaged boy sat on a swing, playing a guitar. His dark curly hair framed a friendly face, and a ring pierced his lip. He wore heavy black boots, black jeans, and a black t-shirt whose short sleeves revealed a tribal tattoo on his upper right arm.

He's kinda yummy, she caught herself thinking.

The boy stopped strumming when he saw Annie.

"What's up?" he said more as a greeting then a question.

"I like what you were playing," Annie said. "It was haunting."

"Thanks, just something I've been working on."

The conversation lay dormant, until Annie felt a pressure to take her turn and speak next. "So, you live here?"

The boy looked at the trailer and then shook his head. "Naw, I'm just here with a bunch of my family. We're on the way up to the Blues Festival."

"Oh, you're with them. I don't think I met you in there. My name's Annie." Annie walked over and sat on the swing alongside him.

"Yeah, I've been out here; too much jabbering going on in there. I'm Denny, by the way. Who are you with?"

"I came up with Davey and Martha."

"Oh, Uncle Davey and Aunt Martha are here? Sweet. I'm glad they made it this year. Haven't seen them in a while, but it hasn't been long enough for them to get a daughter."

Annie laughed, "Oh no, I'm not their daughter, they just kinda took me under their wing."

Denny looked to be piecing the information together in his mind. "So, we aren't related?"

"No. Nope. No relation."

"Whew, that's good," came his relieved reply.

Annie's heart sank a beat, confused as to why he wouldn't want to be related to her. "Why is that a good thing? Something wrong with me?"

"Oh no," Denny said. "Nothing at all. Do you know how frustrating it is to have a pretty cousin?" he winked.

Annie tried to suppress a grin and said, "Oh, I see you're a dog."

"Naw, just a wandering minstrel who likes a nice smile."

Annie covered her mouth, rolled her eyes, and then let her hand drop. "Does that line of bullshit ever work for you?"

Denny swiveled on his swing. "I don't know; you're the first one I've tried it on."

"Well, ditch it as fast as you can," she advised. "It's not very good."

Denny's blue eyes sparkled as he gave Annie's arm a small push. "Okay, I'll work on it. So you're living with my uncle and aunt now?"

"Yeah, we're moving up by his brother, well, after the festival."

"Which one?" Denny asked.

"You know, the Blues Festival."

"No, I mean which brother."

"Oh," she said feeling like a ditz. "Joe."

"Uncle Joe, cool. We'll be neighbors, well, in the same general area."

"Yeah? Huh. Cool."

The conversation hit another lull, as they twisted in the swings, letting their feet shuffle on the dirt. Annie broke the silence.

"So, you're really good on the guitar. Maybe you can teach me some."

"Ever play?" he asked.

"Davey taught me a little, but I got a lot to learn."

Denny strummed the strings. "No problem, I'll show ya some stuff. I'm supposed to play with Uncle Joe and his band at the festival. I'd like to play the tune you heard, put I don't have lyrics with it, and it's not exactly a blues tune. I guess it doesn't really matter, but it would be nice, you know. Not good at lyrics."

Annie let the statement hang in the air for a moment, and then said, "I write songs."

"Really? Sweet, maybe we can team up," Denny said as he played the poignant melody Annie had first heard when walking out of the diner.

Annie watched as Denny closed his eyes and put a deep feeling into his playing. He hummed along to the music, lost in the forlorn sound. She *was* home. She thought about others who had suffered as she had, or even worse; wondered if they would ever get a chance at salvation. Maybe they would, but would never see the opportunity, or maybe they would become too lost to ever find their way through the nightmare. All she knew was she had claimed her chance, and she wouldn't give it up easily.

From his mesmerized state, Denny asked, "Got anything to go along with this?"

She swayed in the swing and said, "Yeah, I think so."

"Well, okay then. Jump on in."

And she did.

"Black-winged angel; sword in hand,
Watch over me whenever you can.
I didn't sin to get here;
I only fell once or twice.
But when you're down and broken,
You're not wanted in paradise.

Ooooooooh, Ooooooooh, Ooooooooh

So I'm running out of Eden;
To find my way.
Running out of Eden;
Too fallen to stay.
And I can't beg for love,
And I can't walk that road.
So I'm running out of Eden;
'Cause I can't do as I'm told.

Ooooooooh, Ooooooooh, Ooooooooh

Tasting knowledge; I've lost belief,
Darkness offers such sweet relief.
I see the way you see me;
I hear the things you say.
But if you dared to know me,
Would you still want to walk away?

Ooooooooh, Ooooooooh, Ooooooooh

So I'm running out of Eden now,
Just to find my way.
Running out of Eden,
Too fallen to stay.

And I can't beg for love,
And I can't walk that road.
So I'm running out of Eden now,
'Cause I can't do as I'm told.

Oooooooh, Oooooooh, Oooooooh

Hmmmmmmmm, Hmmmmmmmm, Hmmmmmmmm"
Running out of Eden now.
Oooooooh, Oooooooh, Oooooooh
Hmmmmmmmm, Hmmmmmmmm, Hmmmmmmmm"

The End